The Stone Maiden

"With grace and affinity like few others, Susan King evokes the people and land of Scotland."
—*Romantic Times*

Praise for the lush, sensual novels of Susan King

The Heather Moon

"A wonderful tale filled with adventure, noble characters, and heartwarming emotion."
—Amazon.com

"If you like spellbinding romances with intrigue, passion, and unforgettable characters, here's a book for you! . . . A brilliantly woven tale of history and romance, as lush as a tapestry. Susan King is a gifted storyteller, with an emotionally intense, visually evocative style." —*Romance Fiction Forum*

"Passion, adventure . . . striking and plausible . . . an excellent escape." —*Affaire de Coeur*

Laird of the Wind

"King spins a complex, mesmerizing story of betrayal, retribution, and healing. . . . A lyrical, compelling love story. . . . King's exquisitely vivid descriptions are beautiful bonuses."—*Library Journal*

"Susan King sweeps readers away into this lavishly crafted love story that brilliantly combines history and romance. Mysticism, passion, beauty, treachery, intrigue and unforgettable characters . . . spellbinding." —*Romantic Times* (4½ stars)

Continued on next page . . .

Lady Miracle

"Strong sense of time and place, masterful plotting, compelling love story—and more. . . .
Extraordinary . . . mythically lovely . . . King's brilliant storytelling and painstaking historical research elevate this tale."
—*Publishers Weekly* (starred review)

"The latest treasure from a writer whose star is in ascendance. . . . Riveting . . . superb . . . marvelous. . . . Truly a treat, like savoring fine Belgian chocolate, reading her work is almost sinfully delicious." —Paintedrock.com

The Raven's Moon

"A marvelous Scottish tale. Absolutely wonderful characters, breakneck pacing, and a great setting. I couldn't put it down." —Patricia Potter

"A wonderfully dark and delectable read. Susan King evokes the Lowlands as few writers have— with all the passion, intrigue, mystery, and beauty of the land—and tells a unique, well-crafted romance." —*Romantic Times*

The Angel Knight

"Magnificent . . . richly textured with passion, and a touch of magic." —Mary Jo Putney

"Ms. King, a visual writer extraordinaire, has blended a mystical and historical tale so precise that the reader will be drawn in and won't ever want to leave." —*Romantic Times*

"A romance of tremendous beauty and heart. Readers will not be able to put this one down. . . . Her books will stand the test of time."
—*Affaire de Coeur*

The Raven's Wish

"Powerful, magical, and delightful . . . a memorable romance that will keep readers on the edge of their seats." —*Romantic Times*

"Destined to be a major voice in the genre."
—*Affaire de Coeur*

"Historical romance at its best." —Rexanne Becnel

The Black Thorne's Rose

"A glorious romance from an exciting new talent of the genre." —*Romantic Times*

"Magnificent . . . Susan King's talent is a gift from the gods." —Virginia Henley

"Excellent . . . filled with mythical legends that add mystery and mayhem . . . extremely powerful . . . four stars for quality and imagination." —*Rendezvous*

ALSO BY SUSAN KING

The Stone Maiden

Susan King

A SIGNET BOOK

SIGNET
Published by New American Library, a division of
Penguin Putnam Inc., 375 Hudson Street,
New York, New York 10014, U.S.A.
Penguin Books Ltd, 27 Wrights Lane,
London W8 5TZ, England
Penguin Books Australia Ltd, Ringwood,
Victoria, Australia
Penguin Books Canada Ltd, 10 Alcorn Avenue,
Toronto, Ontario, Canada M4V 3B2
Penguin Books (N.Z.) Ltd, 182–190 Wairau Road,
Auckland 10, New Zealand

Penguin Books Ltd, Registered Offices:
Harmondsworth, Middlesex, England

First published by Signet, an imprint of New American Library,
a division of Penguin Putnam Inc.

 REGISTERED TRADEMARK—MARCA REGISTRADA

Printed in the United States of America

ISBN 0-7394-0935-2

Dedicated in loving memory to my sister
Barbara Jean Longhi

Her ways are ways of pleasantness
and all her paths are peace.
—Proverbs 3:17

Thanks are due to Walter S. Arnold, sculptor, for sharing his knowledge of stone carving techniques; to my agent, Karen Solem, and my editor, Audrey LaFehr, for much patience and support; and especially to Mary Jo Putney, Jacci Reding, Jo-Ann Power, Jean Brashear, Eileen Charbonneau, and Julie Booth for seeing me safely through this one.

Is beadarrach an ni an onair.
Honor is a tender thing.
   —*Scottish Gaelic proverb*

The Stone
Maiden

Prologue

Seven riders crested the snow-covered hill like warriors out of legend, sweeping away the sun's glow,
bringing twilight in their wake. The setting sun bur-
nished armor to silver and shields to bronze as the
riders streamed forward.

Alainna stood on the hill and waited as they approached. Cold wind stirred her russet hair and filled
the plaid draped over her gown, but she remained
motionless. Another few moments and she would be
trampled unless they slowed, unless she leaped aside.
Yet she felt no danger.

Sunlight surrendered as the riders came closer.
Alainna felt the subtle pause in the breath of the world
said to happen in the time-between-times. Her great-
uncle, the clan bard, had said that at moments of fleeting change—dawn, sunset, mist—the earthly and the
mystical realms could interweave. She was sure that
happened now, while she watched, entranced.

In the glen below, she heard her kinsmen shout, involved in a hunt. They had not seen her standing on
the crest of the hill. She did not glance toward them,
but kept her booted feet firm in the snow. Her hair
blew back like flames, restless and vivid on the wind.

The first of the riders neared her and pulled back on
the reins. His tall, creamy stallion rounded, danced on
slender legs. The other warriors drew to a halt and
waited as their leader walked his horse toward Alainna.

"Who are you?" she asked.

He watched her, helmeted and silent. The shield suspended on his saddle carried the painted design of a

single diagonal arrow, white on a blue field. That symbol of his identity held no meaning for her.

The warrior lifted away his helmet and tucked it under his arm, then pushed his chain mail hood from his head. The last of the stolen sunlight glinted in the dark gold of his hair. The stars and the night seemed part of his cloak, midnight blue edged with silver. His eyes were clouds, gray and deep.

"Alainna MacLaren." He knew her name, but she did not know his. "You are the daughter of the chief of Clan Laren. Now that he is gone, you are clan leader in his place."

"I am," she answered. "Who are you? A prince of the *daoine sìth*, the faery people? Or do you lead the warriors of the Fianna, the warband of Fionn MacCumhail, come out of the mists of time?"

"We are not they," he said.

"Aenghus the Ever-Young, god of the sun, with your host of men. That is who you are," she said. The stories of the golden, handsome hero-god Aenghus mac Og were among her favorites of those told by her great-uncle of an evening. Somehow, she was not surprised to see a warrior god appearing at sunset, in the magical moment between light and darkness.

His smile was subtle. "Do we look of that realm?"

"You do. Why else would you ride over our lands at the changing of the light?"

"Why else," he said, "but for you."

"For me?" She stared at him.

"You sent for us. Sent for me," he added quietly.

Her heart bounded, her breath caught. Hope, swift and bright, soared within her. She and her clan desperately needed help. Yet she, as their leader, had sent for no one. How had this warrior heard her plea, whispered only in her prayers, and held as a silent yearning in her heart? How else, but by magic?

"Who are you?" Her voice was a breath.

He watched her steadily. "I will help you if you want to save your clan," he murmured. "But you will have to give up what is most dear to you."

"I would give up anything to save them," she said fiercely, returning his intent gaze. "I swear it."

He extended his hand toward her. "Then so be it."

She looked into his handsome face, gazed into his eyes, like steel, like silver. He was not of this earth, she was sure. He must be a prince, even a king, in the faery world, capable of magic, capable of helping her people.

"What do you want of me?" she asked.

"Come with me," he answered.

She drew a breath. "If I do, all will be well for them?"

"It will." He watched her, his hand outstretched.

A feeling rose within her like a torrent—not fear, but a sudden wrench of longing. She wanted to go with him. As the desire grew stronger, she closed her eyes against its power.

"Alainna," he said, his voice mellow as the lowest chord of a harp. "Come with me."

She glanced down the long hill, where her kinsmen hunted. She loved her clan and her kin deeply, and she could not bear the thought of leaving them. Yet she must do whatever she could for the clan, no matter the cost to her. She had made that promise to her dying father.

If she could find the courage to ride into the Otherworld never to return, her clan would flourish and be safe. Their proud and ancient heritage would last forever.

She drew in a long breath and looked up at the shining, silent warrior. "I must have your promise that my clan will continue," she said.

"You have it." She knew, somehow, that she could trust him.

She lifted her arm in acceptance. He stepped his horse closer, holding out his hand and leaning toward her. His fingers were warm over hers, and her heart leaped within her breast like a bird new to the wing.

Alainna awoke, sitting upright in the dark, heart pounding. *A dream,* she told herself. *Just a dream.* She caught back a sob and sank her head into the support of her hands. If only the dream had been real. Her clan needed just such a bold warrior, some miracle of intervention, to help them. Try as she might, Alainna could not save her diminished and threatened clan alone. She could ensure that her kin were sheltered and fed, and she could do her best to preserve their proud and ancient heritage. But she could not fight their enemies in battle, and that help was most desperately needed.

Clan Laren now consisted of a handful of elderly men and women with only Alainna to lead them. The rival clan that had feuded with them for generations would triumph soon, unless they could be stopped. Once spring arrived, the ancient spell that had aided her clan for so long would end, and their enemy's power over them would increase.

Her kinfolk urged her to find and marry a Highland warrior, a champion with comrades at his back willing to fight. Clan Laren needed such a man, but no one would take on the risk of a failing clan and a strong enemy.

If only the dream had been real, she thought again, and sighed deeply. The golden warrior did not exist, and time grew short.

Steel sparkled in the dawn as Sebastien wheeled and sank the tip of his sword with masterful control. The edge whistled in a fast, low arc and surged upward again. Muscles taut, gripping the leather-wrapped hilt with his right hand, he spun on bare feet. The balanced blade sliced and soared through the cool morning air.

Frost rimed the battlements around him, and a brisk wind sifted the dark golden strands of his hair. His back was sweat-coated and cool beneath his loose linen shirt, but his exertion created heat within.

He focused on footing, timing, balance, strength. Each step and thrust was fierce, edged with desperation, punctuated with fury, but he felt powerless. His blade cut nothing but air. He had no enemy to fight, no way to protect what was most precious to him.

The wind was high and fast on the rooftop of the royal tower. He paused, breathing hard, while the breeze whipped at him. His gaze swept the forest treetops, the glinting towers of the abbey, the vast blue mountains far in the distance. Scotland was a beautiful land, full of promise for Norman knights seeking favor and property. He had come here for that purpose.

Now he must leave as soon as he could. He clenched his jaw in frustration. He had spent three years in this cold northern place. If he stayed longer, he could reap the reward the king would undoubtedly offer him—but he had no more time to wait.

He turned to wield the sword with banked power. Lunge, strike, pull back, spin. His weapon practices provided action and solitude, both of which he craved. Whenever the king stayed at his royal tower in Dunfermline, the rooftop guards were used to the training habits of this particular Breton honor guard. They often left Sebastien alone on the battlements while they fetched an extra serving of breakfast.

Before dawn, he had left the garrison quarters and had gone up to the roof. He liked this time of day for its mystical promise, liked the soaring view from the roof, and secretly cherished the lift he felt within his soul.

Another thrust of the sword grazed steel on stone and raised blue sparks. Even that strike gave him some satisfaction, although he knew the edge would require extra care later. He wanted conflict, hungered for encounter. Frustration roiled within him, demanding release.

A letter had arrived for him yesterday, carried by a Breton messenger whose ship had been greatly delayed. The news Sebastien had received, several months late, had stunned him to the quick.

His small son, housed in a Breton monastery, had been in danger six months ago, and Sebastien had not been there to protect him. He was not even certain where the boy was now.

Half a world away, half a year late in learning the news. He cursed the strong ambition that had taken him to Scotland when he might have stayed in Brittany with his five-year-old son. Instead, he had put Conan in the care of monks and had accepted another term of knight service.

The letter had been sent by the abbot of the monastery where he had left Conan, and where Sebastien himself had been raised as a boy. A fire had ruined the Benedictine complex, injuring many, killing some, among them monks Sebastien had known well. His son, along with the other boys, was unhurt, but all of them were in dire need of a home.

The monks desperately sought a benefactor to provide housing and goods until the monastery could be rebuilt. Without that support, they must disperse among different religious houses. Their young charges were to be sent elsewhere too, some turned out in the streets.

The abbot had inquired of Sebastien where Conan should be sent. He had hinted that the knight, a favorite of the duke of Brittany and the king of Scotland, could help all of them if he would lend the use of one of his Breton properties.

Months had elapsed since the abbot had sent out his plea. Sebastien, unaware of their dilemma, had not replied.

He growled in despair and swiped at the buffeting wind. Then he lowered the sword and faced the rising sun, hair and shirt billowing, body and spirit still and strong.

He had allowed his hunger for land wealth and chivalric renown to rule him, and his son was no longer safe as a result. Since the death of his noble French wife, he had continued to pursue his ambitions on behalf of the child whom he adored.

Conan would someday own his mother's dowry property, still in the possession of her family, who had only disdain for her widowed husband. Sebastien had earned the love of his late, sweet wife, but her family thought him unworthy.

What worth he possessed had been conjured from nothing. Sebastien le Bret, famed for prowess and valor on the jousting field and in battle, knight in service to dukes and to kings, lacked ancestry, inheritance, and an old, proud surname.

Left as a foundling at the monastery of Saint-Sebastien in Brittany, he had only the name the monks had given him. The rest he had gained for himself. He was weary of striving, but he would continue for his son's sake.

Now he must set aside his dreams and goals and return to Brittany as soon as possible. He lifted the sword over his head and slashed it downward in a final blow, sweeping it into another arc, spinning with the turn. He stopped and stood in the wind.

The sun crested the mountains like a glowing wafer. Morning brought duties that required his presence as an honor guard to the king of Scots. Sebastien turned, snatched up his tunic and belt, and headed for the stairs.

Chapter One

In the hushed, shadowed time before dawn, Alainna set a small sack of oats and a handful of wildflowers at the base of the stone pillar. She murmured a blessing and stood back. Beyond the tall stone, the loch swept rhythmically to shore, and a pale glow edged the sky.

She twisted her hands anxiously, then stilled herself, realizing that impatience would not hurry the beneficent spirit of the Maiden.

The pillar called the Stone Maiden rose twelve feet in height, a column of gray granite shaped like a gowned woman. Ancient carvings on the front and back were worn smooth in places. Mist wreathed the stone, cool and damp.

"Maiden," she said, "I am Alainna, daughter of Laren of Kinlochan, son of Laren, son of Donal, son of Aodh—" She did not continue, although she knew the names of her ancestors back to the Stone Maiden herself—with whom she shared a name, from *àlainn,* beautiful—and to Labhrainn, the Irish prince who had founded the clan centuries ago.

Legend said that the stone housed the spirit of a maiden who had been captured there, long ago, by a faery spell. The Stone Maiden, tradition claimed, acted as a guardian for Clan Laren. Generations of the clan had left offerings and had spoken charms to appeal for the Maiden's protection. As clan leader since her father's death a few months earlier, Alainna hoped for a reassuring omen to report to her kin.

Now she murmured her heartfelt wish to see her clan safe and flourishing, and waited.

Wind whispered over her head, loosening strands of her braided, red-gold hair. She heard birdsong, the shush of the loch, her deerhound's bark as he fretted a field mouse nearby. The rising sun glinted on the wooden fortress of Kinlochan across the narrow stretch of water. She stood patiently beside the stone, but no clear sign appeared.

She sighed. Somehow she must save Clan Laren from vanishing into Highland memory. The solution she needed would not come from offerings and chants. Only swift action would solve their dilemma.

The deerhound ran toward her to circle her anxiously, barking. He faced the hill that sloped away from the lochside. Peering through the mist, Alainna saw a red deer there, nosing through old heather.

"*Ach,* Finan, do you long to chase the deer, then?" she asked, touching his head, which reached above her waist. The dog's fierce growl raised chills along Alainna's spine. "Finan, what is it?"

A man walked over the top of the hill and came down the hillside. Alainna knew him by his height and heavy build, by his wild black hair and the red and brown hues of his plaid.

Cormac, the young chief of Clan Nechtan, her enemy, came toward her. Had she known that he was out here, that he watched her when she was alone but for the dog, she would not have lingered.

"Hold, Finan!" she commanded. She curled her hand in the dog's leather collar. His long body quivered, growls rumbled in his chest, and his wiry blue-gray coat lifted. But he stayed, as she knew he would.

"Alainna of Kinlochan!" Cormac halted a few feet away, spreading his feet in a wide stance. His deep, thick voice sundered the peaceful atmosphere. "I saw you while I was hunting with my kinsmen. I want a word with you in private."

"Cormac MacNechtan," she said. "We have nothing to say."

"We do. Are your kinsmen about?" He glanced around.

"They will be here soon," she said, knowing they would

search for her when her absence was discovered, or when-ever someone inside Kinlochan glanced across the loch toward the stone.

She knew Cormac by sight, but had rarely spoken to him since childhood, when their paths had crossed too often as she wandered the hills with her two younger brothers and their foster brother. Cormac had proven himself mean-spir-ited both as child and as man, and she wanted nothing to do with him.

But she and Cormac were the leaders of their feuding clans, and she could not shun him if he was willing to talk with her. The beginning of peace between them might be but words away.

She stood proud and straight, like a small twin to the great pillar stone, and held the growling dog's collar firmly to show Cormac that she was protected by the dog as well as by the stone and its legend.

"Quiet that great blue hound of yours, or I will do it for you." Cormac touched the dirk sheathed at his belt.

"Finan *Mór*," she said. "Big Finan. Hold, you." The deerhound stayed still, his growls low.

"A great hound like that is a man's dog, and no hound for a woman," Cormac observed.

"Finan has been mine from his birth."

"Then he has been spoiled by a woman's hand."

She watched Cormac evenly. "Try him, and see if it is so."

"You are safe," he said. "For now. The legend of the Stone Maiden ensures that no man of Clan Nechtan can harm a woman of Clan Laren, or he will suffer the consequences."

"It is a shame no legend prevents the men of Clan Nech-tan from warring on the men of Clan Laren," she snapped.

"We bear an ancient grudge toward you that gives us the right to war upon you."

She glared at him. "Your hatred of us is ancient, but ours is just as old! You would destroy us all if you could."

"Not you, Alainna. You, I want for my own."

"Do not say that to me in the Maiden's presence!"

"She cannot protect you much longer. The faery spell ends in the spring—we all know that." He scowled at her.

He was not unhandsome, even with a thrusting, wide jaw, but the anger in his dark eyes spoiled his countenance more than any flaw. "Some say that the Maiden's power to help her people wanes even now."

"Our bard says the Maiden's power will increase when the faery spell ends," she said. In truth, no one was sure what would happen when the stone's magic ended the next spring.

"Old Lorne MacLaren would say so, rather than say your clan is lost!" Cormac flipped his fingers in dismissal. "The Stone Maiden will no longer keep you safe, if ever she could. The Maiden and her clan will both crumble."

"We may be diminished by feud, and illness, and poor luck," she said hotly. "We may have few left of our name. We may be threatened by a cruel enemy"—she glared at him—"but our pride, our legacy endures. You cannot destroy that with your raids and your hatred!"

He shrugged. "If you will listen, I have good tidings for your clan."

"Glad news for Clan Nechtan cannot be glad news for Clan Laren," she said. She glanced across the narrow loch toward Kinlochan. Tendrils of smoke rose from the hearth fires; soon her kinsmen would come looking for her. If they saw Cormac here with her, there would be another skirmish.

"I have petitioned King William for the hand of the Maiden of Kinlochan. The living maiden, not the stone one." He snickered at his poor jest.

She gasped. "I would never wed you!"

"You are an heiress now, and must wed soon. Your father is gone and cannot arrange your marriage."

"Gone by your hand!"

"Not mine, Alainna girl." He shook his head. "Not mine."

"Yours or another's, a MacNechtan blade killed him, and took my brothers too. I would never marry you or any of your blood!"

"You and your elder kinsmen want to end this feud, I know. And my own kinsmen urge me to wed you. It is time I married."

"You can wed the handfasted wife you cast aside," she said.

"Not her. You." He swelled his chest. "We can gain no honor fighting the old men of Clan Laren. You cannot oversee this vast property alone. So you must become my bride. I know your father wanted this."

"Never," she said through her teeth. Finan growled low, and shifted forward. She touched the dog's head with trembling fingers. "You would take our land and our very name from us!"

His scowl was dark and deep. "The king has the right to decide your marriage, since you are sole heiress, holding title and land. We will leave this up to him. I have sent a message to King William to offer for you. Such an easy end to this feud will please him."

"The king himself cannot force me to do what I will not."

"A stubborn woman is a foolish woman," he muttered. "I heard that you are a willful girl, but I hoped you had sense." He gestured impatiently. "The men of Clan Laren are too old to wield swords. Your foster brother, Giric MacGregor, is young, but he is one man, and we are many." He stepped forward, but moved back when the dog barked sharply. "Wed me, and the blood of Clan Laren will live on in our sons."

"I want no sons with the name of MacNechtan!"

He chuckled. "Lovely but troublesome. I hear you are strong, too. They say you are trained as a stonemason, like some others in your clan, and use a hammer and chisel like a man." He skimmed her body with a gleaming gaze. "I have a hammer and tools you can handle whenever you like." His smile grew wicked.

"Go away," she snapped. "My arm is strong, but it tires from holding back this great hound."

Cormac narrowed his brown eyes. Cold anger flickered there. "Maiden of stone," he hissed. "Heed me well. Spring will come, and your safety ends with it. Who will protect your clan then? Not a girl with a mallet. Not a few old men."

"My clan will kill you someday, Cormac," she murmured.

He smiled, flat and hard. "I could take you now if I

wanted, at the foot of that stone. Neither hound nor faeries could stop me. Or I can bide my time until spring. I have a choice. You have none."

"I do." Alainna lifted her chin. "I will not wed you. And neither king nor Highlandman can force me."

"I will be generous, and grant you until Saint Brighid's day, when the faery spell ends, to agree. By then the king will have sent word of his approval. Wed me, or watch your clan die." He shrugged. "Either way will end the feud."

He whirled before she could reply, and strode up the misted hill to disappear over the top. Alainna watched, her heart pounding. The dog barked, but stayed beside her, his growl relentless, his body taut.

She flattened her palm on cool granite and closed her eyes, wishing fervently for a solution, a savior. A miracle. She bowed her head to pray, and whispered an old Gaelic blessing to please both her Christian and her ancient heritage.

Then she turned to walk toward Kinlochan. Finan ran ahead of her through long brown grasses as she rounded the end of the loch, where the water shushed peacefully over pebbles and stones.

The morning sun had burned off the mist, and the wooden tower of Kinlochan, inside its surrounding timber palisade, glowed earthy red in the dawn light. Beyond it, dark mountains soared into the distance, their rugged crests ringed by clouds. The long, narrow loch spread like a pool of silver at their base.

The fortress gate swung wide and three men ran out, plaids flapping over bare legs. They waved and skirted the loch along the path she had taken earlier.

She waved back and walked ahead, then nearly tripped when her toe struck a stick in the ground. Bending, she picked up a discarded arrow that lay deep in the heather. The arrow was weathered and shabby, although the iron point was still sharp.

She wondered if this was the omen she sought. If so, it was a poor one, for it must mean more war.

She began to toss it away, then stopped, remembering her recent dream of a golden warrior whose shield bore the design of a single arrow. He had offered to save her distressed people. Entranced, she had been willing to go with him, even to the Otherworld.

She sighed, thinking of that strong, beautiful warrior. But dreams were of no use to her now.

Finan barked and ran toward her kinsmen. She followed thoughtfully, the arrow clasped in her hand.

"Alainna!" Her foster brother, Giric, called and ran toward her through the long grasses, alongside her elderly cousin Niall and Lulach, one of her two great-uncles. The dog bounded toward them. Giric touched a hand to Finan's head in passing and received an adoring look in return.

They came toward her, Giric moving with agile grace despite his tall, large build. His brown hair blew loose around his handsome head, and a belted plaid fluttered over muscular legs.

"We saw you with Cormac," he said. "Are you harmed?"

"Can we slay the man? Where did he go?" Niall asked. His cheeks were sunken and whiskered, his thin lips tight with anger. A breeze fluttered his silvery hair over his face. He pushed it back with the scarred stump of his left wrist.

"Are you hurt, girl?" Lulach stepped forward, his hair iron and silver, his blue eyes angry. "I would have killed Black Cormac myself if I had seen him sooner."

"Your old legs could not catch him," Niall said.

"I will worry what my old legs can do," Lulach snapped.

"I am fine," Alainna assured them quickly. "I was under the protection of the Maiden. Cormac would never harm me there."

"True, he would be a fool to forget the spell," Niall said.

"He *is* a fool," Lulach pointed out.

"You need the protection of a stout blade, not a standing stone," Giric said. He was normally relaxed in manner, but his face was taut and his hands fisted. "Do not trust any man of Clan Nechtan."

"Cormac does not dare to harm me," she reassured them. But she shivered inwardly, recalling Cormac's threat to take her at the foot of the stone, spell or none.

"She has no blade, but she does have an arrow," Niall said. He peered at the shaft in her hand. "Where did you get that?"

"I found it in the grass."

"Elf-arrow," he muttered. "Put it down, it may have been lost by the faeries."

"It is human-made," Lulach said. "Needs new feathering, but the point is still good."

"I found it after I made an offering to the Maiden. It may be an omen for us," she said.

"A sign that there will be one less MacNechtan," Niall said. "It is good to make an offering on such a fine day, but you should not have come out here alone."

"You will not have the Maiden's protection for long," Lulach said. "Soon we will mark the end of seven hundred years of the faery spell."

"It is months until Saint Brighid's day," Alainna said.

"So what did Black Cormac want?" Niall asked.

"To take your other hand," Lulach drawled.

"Baothan," Niall grumbled, "blockhead."

Giric stifled a laugh. "Peace, now, I beg you," he said. "Alainna has asked all of her kinfolk to bide the winter at Kinlochan. We must have peace among ourselves. Alainna has enough to worry her."

"True," Niall said. "Alainna, we came down from the hills late last night after seeing Esa. She refuses to come to Kinlochan. We even offered to carry her great loom, but she wants to stay by her own hearth."

"I wish we could convince her to join us," Alainna said.

"Convince slate to turn to marble," Lulach said. "She has made up her mind to stay there for the winter."

"She mourns her Ruari *Mór* still, though it has been over a year since we had word of his death." Alainna sighed. "Such an enduring, strong love is hard to lose."

"We will go and talk to her again," Giric said. "Tell us what Cormac wanted, Alainna."

"It is obvious what Cormac wants, and we should take his head off for it," Lulach said, fisting his hands on his hips.

"He spoke of marriage," Alainna said.

Lulach snorted in disdain. Niall blinked as if horrified.

"What did he say?" Giric asked sharply.

"I will explain all over some hot salted porridge. I am

hungry." She stepped forward and whistled to Finan, who had strayed to the loch's edge.

"Cormac MacNechtan thinks to wed our *toiseach,* our leader, our own youngest one?" Niall asked, as the men walked beside her. "That can never happen!"

"Never," Lulach said. "Our clans need peace, and she needs a husband, but not that husband."

"We have discussed it often since Laren MacLaren's death," Giric said. "It is time you married, Alainna."

"It is not easy to find a warrior willing to join a feud, yet one who will please this clan," she replied.

"Marriage to the chief of Clan Laren offers fine rewards," Niall said. "Forests filled with deer, a loch thick with fish, grass for cattle, a beautiful girl of proud blood—"

"And a blood feud generations old," Alainna added bitterly.

"You are our youngest one, the last of our blood," Lulach said. "A carefully chosen marriage can make our clan safe for generations to come."

Safe. She wanted them all safe, so much. Her throat tightened. "But whatever man I wed will give his name to our children. What then for Clan Laren?"

Her kinsmen were silent as they walked beside her.

"The man she marries could take our name," Niall suggested.

"It is sometimes done, I have heard." Lulach said.

Alainna frowned. "Where would we find a man to accept the name of our clan, as well as our troubles?"

"If only you could marry our Giric," Niall said. "He is not your blood kin, and he loves all of us well."

"But he is her foster brother," Lulach pointed out.

"It is up to the king to decide whom she will wed," Giric said. "He has the right to choose a husband for an unmarried heiress. Alainna, you must pay homage for your inheritance soon. Ask King William for help in the matter."

She nodded, realizing that she could appeal to the king before Cormac's petition was considered and approved. "I will, but it must be soon."

"Giric can ride with you to the royal court," Niall said.

"The king winters in Dunfermline, two days' journey

from here. He will surely know of some Highland warrior hungry for land, and hungry for a feud."

"What if he suggests a foreign knight?" Lulach asked.

Niall shook his head. "We will tell him what we want. We are loyal, and he does not want to see an ancient clan disappear. He will support us and find us the Celtic champion that we need."

"Alainna," Giric said quietly, watching her. "This is what you desire in a husband, is it not?"

"What pleases my kin pleases me," she said, but her voice trembled suddenly.

Her secret desire would be impossible to fulfill, she knew. The golden warrior she had seen once in a dream did not exist.

She turned away, still gripping the old arrow in her hand, and walked toward the rocky slope that led to Kinlochan's wooden gate.

Chapter Two

The king's chamberlain called the next petitioner forward. Sebastien stood tall and disinterested on the royal dais, scarcely listening. As a woman parted from the crowd, he glimpsed only the bronze sheen of her braided hair until she glided closer.

His attention was wholly captured then. He remained silent and still, an honor guard for the king of Scots, and narrowed his eyes, alert. She was like a lush blossom among winter weeds in the crowded chamber, and he could not keep from watching her.

The two knights standing with him breathed out low whistles. Sounds of admiration rippled through the throng: a gathering of knights, ladies, merchants, peasants, even barbarians from the hills, all of whom waited in the great hall to seek justice from King William. The morning had been tedious, and the girl's appearance broke the monotony.

Sebastien felt more than relief from boredom. He felt briefly stunned, as if something more remarkable had happened than a girl stepping out of a crowd. He frowned, keeping his head high, shoulders straight, a hand on his sword hilt. He could hold that motionless stance for an extended time, ignoring distractions while keeping his attention honed.

This distraction he could not ignore. Sunlight streamed through the high windows and transformed her into a vision. She sank to her knees with fluid grace, dressed in a midnight blue gown and a plaid mantle woven in brown and purple.

The chamberlain asked her to state her name. *"Àlainne nighean Labhrainn mac Labhrainn an Ceann Lochan,"* she murmured in Gaelic, although the chamberlain had spoken in English. Sebastien heard the pride in her low, entrancing voice.

"Who is the Highland lady?" the knight beside him asked.

"She is called Alainna MacLaren of Kinlochan," Sebastien answered quietly, pronouncing the name *ALL-inna* as the girl had done. Hugo and Robert, the two knights who stood flanking Sebastien, both nodded.

Seated in his chair, William of Scotland leaned toward her, his cropped hair a darker red than hers, and greeted her in Gaelic. Sebastien's position gave him a clear view, and he could easily hear most of what was said as the girl explained her business with the king.

"Bastien, you have had enough lessons in the native tongue to translate for us." Robert de Kerec, the knight standing to his left, spoke again using English, a habit between them no matter where they were—France, Brittany, England, or Scotland. Robert was his oldest friend, and though both were of Breton origin, they had trained together in England as squires and knights.

"He has had plenty of instruction." Hugo de Valognes, standing beside Robert, grinned. "The pretty girl who teaches him shares more than Gaelic, though I will wager Bastien is more teacher than pupil in some things, eh?"

"We do still meet for lessons," Sebastien answered smoothly, staring straight ahead. Hugo chortled and elbowed Robert.

Most Norman knights at the Scottish court spoke English and French, and most knew little of the native language. Sebastien had mastered French, English, and Latin as a youth, in addition to his native Breton, and Gaelic had proved easy for him. With a three-year tenure of service to the king of Scotland to fulfill, he had welcomed the challenge.

The knight's daughter had offered to teach him, and as it turned out, she had been eager to enjoy more intimate interests too. He had a natural affinity for both pursuits. Bartering one gentle skill for another was fair, he and the girl had agreed. His teacher liked his quick wit and his flawed handsomeness, and admired his strength and valor, yet she asked no more than the friendship and comfort they gave each other.

"What else does she say?" Robert asked.

"Alainna of Kinlochan is the leader of a Highland clan, here to pay homage for her inheritance following her father's death," Sebastien replied.

His two Breton comrades nodded again. Dressed similarly in chain mail and deep green surcoats trimmed in silver, the three tall knights stood nearest the king as members of an elite honor guard prized for valor, military skills, discipline, and golden looks.

Robert was slim and pale haired, while Hugo was broad and coarse, with hair like brass. Sebastien knew that his own unmatched skills and dark golden hair had gained him a privileged place among the knights sent by the Duke of Brittany to serve King William.

"A Highland heiress? Interesting," Hugo remarked. "She does not look the savage."

Sebastien silently agreed as he studied the girl. Her pale creamy skin, was now blushed pink, and long, thick braids of a coppery tint fell over the front of her supple body. Her eyes appeared to be the same dark blue as her elegantly cut gown. She looked like any Norman or English lady, he thought, but for the plaid mantle draped over her shoulders and pinned at her throat with a large silver circlet. Belted at her waist, it spilled in gentle gathers over her hips.

Nicely shaped hips, Sebastien noted, along with a slip of a waist, long legs and arms, square shoulders, full breasts. Her form and her flame-colored hair had an earthly allure in contrast to her serene oval face.

"Ah, what a sweet morsel," Hugo whispered. "If she is here to seek a husband, then I am her man."

"Perhaps that one is her man," Robert remarked.

Sebastien saw a Highlander step toward the dais. Alainna MacLaren rose to her feet. She was not a small woman, but this man towered beside her. He wore a plaid length of brown and green, draped full and skirt-like over a pale shirt. He was broad as well as tall, his bare legs hewn, his head large and handsome, long auburn hair tamed by braids. He addressed the king in the fluid language of the Gaels.

"Barbarian," Hugo murmured. "He does not wait for the king's permission to speak, but plows ahead like an ox. And the king allows it! Such a lack of manners would not happen in France."

"Hush," Robert murmured. "You have been here long enough to know that Scots behave as if no man has greater rank, even their king. Their pride in their equality has its charm, and does not offend the king. If he does not mind, why should you?"

"No wonder they have such problems here," Hugo muttered.

Sebastien watched the dais. At the same time, he kept his hand on his sword hilt and stayed alert for any rumble of discontent or sudden movement that might indicate a threat to the king.

He was a keen and cautious observer. He could perceive a great deal quickly about people and situations, and had come to trust those abilities. In the lift of this girl's chin and the set of her head on a long, graceful neck, he saw pride and strength. But the blue depths of her eyes held a subtle, haunting sadness. A fragile lioness, he thought, frowning.

At the king's murmured request, the girl addressed him next in English. Educated as well as lovely, Sebastien thought. Hardly a savage. She changed languages with ease, her speech accented but precise, her voice low and lovely.

Beautiful and intelligent women were not a rarity in his experience, but he recalled no woman of his acquaintance who radiated such grace and strength, or glowed with pride as this one did. Brilliance filled her like a light in a horn lantern. He watched her with increasing fascination.

"Sire," she said to the king, "my kinsman, Giric Mac-Gregor, and I have traveled to court so that I can pay homage for my inheritance. My father, Laren MacLaren, chief of our clan, was killed in a battle with Clan Nechtan last September. My two brothers were killed in earlier skirmishes with Clan Nechtan, leaving me chief of Clan Laren and sole heiress to Kinlochan." The warm timbre of her voice slid through Sebastien like a caress.

"We extend sympathies to you, Lady Alainna," the king said.

"My lord." She bowed her head sadly and raised it again. "I am here to pay a relief fee for my inheritance."

"One or two knights in service to the crown is the customary payment."

"Sire, I can offer no knights in service just now. My clan is reduced by tragedy. We have wealth in land and ancestry, but few goods left to us, and fewer men. We have been nearly ruined by this blood feud. Please allow me to offer another token to fix my claim on Kinlochan."

The king nodded. Alainna of Kinlochan turned to her Highland kinsman, who withdrew a cloth-wrapped object from the folds of his plaid and handed it to the king.

William opened the gift to reveal a rectangular stone a hand-span in size, its surface carved in relief with a design of a cross and circle in the interlaced style of the Celts. Even across the dais, Sebastien could see that it was beautifully crafted.

"A fine piece," the king said. "Is it the work of an artisan local to Kinlochan?"

"It is," Alainna answered.

"We will accept this token, my lady. One carved stone will be required of Kinlochan in fee each year. The writ will be drawn up for you."

The girl smiled. "My thanks, sire. If you will, I wish to address another matter, that of my marriage."

"That we must ponder further."

"Sire, 'tis your right to choose a husband for me, I know. The elders of my clan have asked me to present some conditions regarding my marriage, if you will permit it."

"Conditions?" the king asked.

"My kinsmen wish me to wed a Celtic warrior who can defeat our enemies, sire, one whose lineage is equal to ours. He must speak the Gaelic, and be a man of compassion and courage. And he must be able to travel to Kinlochan from his own lands within a day's time."

"Your kinsmen have decided upon a riddle to be solved by some champion, with the prize your hand?" The king sat back in his chair. He sounded amused.

"Sire." Her cheeks flamed pink. "We pose no coy riddle."

"We have exemplary Norman knights at court with honorable legacies and military prowess. One of my honor guard may do well for you."

Hugo and Robert straightened like peacocks. Sebastien remained expressionless.

"I do not wish to wed a Norman, sire. My kinsmen wish me to wed a Celtic champion." She drew a breath. "Sire, there is one further condition. We ask that my husband give up his surname and take the name of our clan for his own."

Sebastien stared at her. She had pride, temper, beauty—and a good bit of conceit, with which he had not credited her.

"Huh!" Hugo muttered. "Now she asks too much."

"That is a great deal to require of any man, Norman or Gael," the king said, "though 'tis sometimes done when the property is valuable. Even if such a selfless warrior existed, 'twould be unwise to involve another Celtic clan in this feud."

She lifted her chin, an elegant, stubborn figure. "Nevertheless, that man will I wed, and no other."

She glowed like a candle, Sebastien thought, her strength luminous and passionate. He frowned, listening.

"Your property is good land, Lady Alainna," the king said. "One of our Norman knights will do well for a husband for you."

"Sire, please." Her voice faltered. "Consider my request."

In the quiet, Hugo shifted his weight, and his chain mail hauberk chimed. The girl glanced toward the sound.

The clarity of her eyes touched Sebastien like a spark. Her gaze was like a penetration of spirit, a tug deep within, as if she had pulled on his heartstrings.

He had no heartstrings left to pull, he told himself. Each strand, he imagined, had been torn off, leaving remnants that no one could grip.

Before she looked away, he glimpsed desperation in her troubled blue eyes. Unexpected sympathy coursed through him. He stood impassive as stone, but his heart beat faster. He had known need and fear, had buttressed them with pride and will, as he suspected she did.

"The king will deny her request," Robert murmured.

"That area needs the stable military might of Normans, not another Celtic warlord."

"I want land and a wife, and I have come to Scotland to gain them," Hugo muttered, "but I will not give up my surname for them." He nodded to Sebastien. "You could adopt her name without a second thought, where we cannot."

"Enough," Sebastien said in sharp warning.

"I meant no harm," Hugo said. "You lack—"

"Enough," Sebastien hissed. He trained his eyes ahead, his back straight as iron. Hugo grunted as Robert reprimanded him with an elbow jab. Hugo often spoke without thought, Sebastien knew. The man had saved his life in battle, and was a good fighting comrade, but he had the courtesy of a boar.

No matter the worth of the land or the worth of the woman, Sebastien could never accept a woman's surname for his own. He had struggled long and hard to bring value to the name of Sebastien le Bret.

To give that up was inconceivable.

The king murmured to the girl, and she looked at her Highland companion, her cheeks rosy with dismay or temper. The Gael smiled at her.

Ah, Sebastien thought. Alainna MacLaren displayed her strength to others, and revealed weakness only to this man. They contrasted in savagery and grace, but their bond, whatever its nature, was strong. The Gaels of Scotland held kinship and loyalty in highest esteem. He saw that shining in these two.

A pang of envy seized him. He frowned and let it slide from him like an unwanted cloak.

Sebastien hoped the girl would find the proud Celtic warrior she sought, a man who could meet her impossible standards and match her fine spirit.

He, for one, was not her man.

Chapter Three

"Lady Alainna, the matter of your marriage will be carefully considered," King William said. "Word will be sent to you when a decision is reached. Farewell to you both."

Alainna glanced anxiously at Giric. She and her foster brother had traveled so far to reap so little. The king seemed determined to choose her husband according to his conditions rather than her own. "Sire—" she began.

The king ignored her, and looked toward the three knights who stood on the dais, matched in green surcoats and chain mail, matched in blond handsomeness and brawn. "Sir Sebastien, escort Lady Alainna and her kinsman. See that they receive provisions for their journey."

"Sire." The tallest of the three men came forward. Alainna had noticed him earlier. He had watched her throughout, his gaze steady, but guarded.

The Norman stood before her and inclined his head politely. "My lady, come with me," he said in Gaelic. She felt the warm press of his fingers through her sleeve. Startled by his warm touch as much as by the use of her language, she looked up at him.

"I will not," she replied in Gaelic. "I have something more to say to my king."

His brow lifted. "As you wish," he said mildly. He stood beside her, solid and strong, his mailed sleeve brushing her shoulder.

She stared at him, distracted for a moment by his hard beauty, which was flawed slightly by a scar that seamed his left eyebrow. His hair was dark gold, his eyes gray and cool, his face lean and strong-boned, angled at the jaw.

Calm control emanated from him in appearance and demeanor.

She pulled her gaze from his and looked at the king. "Please, sire, about the issue of my marriage—"

"My lady, you have made your plea," the king replied.

"Sire, my clan's enemy, Cormac MacNechtan, means to petition you for my hand. He wants only to possess Kinlochan and subdue our clan by marrying me, their chief."

"It is true, sire," Giric offered. "This feud is based on old anger, inherited through generations."

William frowned. "Marriage between enemies can solve such a dispute."

"I cannot marry Cormac!" Alainna burst out. "I beg you to understand. We need warriors to fight on our behalf."

"You need a man who can raise a castle on that site, install a host of men, and bring peace and protection to that region of the Highlands."

She sighed in relief. "A Highland warrior."

"A Norman knight," he corrected. "One will be chosen from among the worthy men in my court. Farewell, my lady."

Alarm rocked through her and nearly buckled her knees. "Sire—"

The Norman knight took her arm. "Quiet, lady," he murmured. "If you want your way in this, submit a petition. He is done with you now."

She jerked out of his grip. "I cannot write," she snapped. "But I can speak, here and now."

"At the peril of your cause."

She scowled at him, but kept silent.

"A handsome couple," the king said. "Handsome indeed. Sebastien, as I recall, you are widowed. . . . How long have you been in my service?"

Alainna glanced at the king, stunned by his implication. The knight paused. "Nearly three years, sire."

"And not yet granted a suitable reward. You are not wed, as I recall."

Alainna's heart pounded. She glanced wildly from one man to the other.

The knight nodded. "The privilege of serving as honor guard to the Scottish king has all my devotion, sire." His answer was smooth and courteous, but his fingers tensed like steel on Alainna's arm.

She turned her alarmed glance to Giric, who frowned warily.

"We must see what can be done for you," the king said. "My lady, Sir Sebastien le Bret may be just the warrior you need." He smiled.

"Sire—" Alainna protested.

"I am not the champion for this lady," the knight said, quietly and firmly.

"Modest sir. You are a paragon among knights, renowned as a fighter of strength and spirit," the king said. "Exactly what Lady Alainna has requested. And you speak Gaelic." He continued to smile. "That should please the lady."

"I doubt it, sire," Sebastien murmured. Alainna felt tension thicken between the two men.

"Nevertheless, your presence at Kinlochan, with a garrison of men, will please me greatly."

Alainna gasped. "My clan will never accept Norman knights at Kinlochan!"

The king looked at her. The resoluteness in his eyes made her hesitate. She knew that King William was not a cruel ruler, but he could be swift and decisive. To refuse could be treasonous.

"We shall speak later, Sebastien. Lady Alainna." The king motioned for the chamberlain to call the next petitioner.

Sir Sebastien circled his strong grip around her arm and guided her away. She twisted to look back. "Sire—" she began.

"Be silent," Sebastien hissed.

"He means to give you my lands!"

"He can give me naught that I will not accept," he said sharply. "Come this way. Sir," he said to Giric, "I will send a page to fetch your horses."

"The horses are in a stable in the town," Giric said. "I will fetch them myself. Alainna?"

"I . . . I will wait in the abbey," she told her foster brother in Gaelic. "I want to see the stonework before we leave. Giric, I cannot wed a Norman!" she added frantically.

"Be calm. Go now, and I will meet you at the abbey."

"Allow me to escort you to the abbey, my lady," the knight said. "The stonework is beautiful. The sight of it will surely calm you. This way." His Gaelic was cool and polite.

He guided them through the crowd. Alainna lifted her head proudly, but her heart beat a pattern of panic as she followed in his wake.

Anger fueled her tread, tightened her mouth, and clouded her eyes with tears. She blinked hard as she and the knight walked up the sloping path that led away from the tower. Dunfermline Abbey crowned the top of the hill, golden stone and twin towers gleaming in the sun.

She walked so fast that she tripped on the embroidered hem of her dark blue skirt, and had to stop. Autumn leaves cluttered the gown's long train. Grabbing a fistful of the soft woolen fabric, she shook it with more temper than grace.

"Easy, my lady." The knight bent to brush at the leaves. "You will ruin your gown."

She sighed and smoothed her skirt more gently. Although she rarely wore the gown of midnight blue wool, with its embroidered hem of gold and red threads, it was the most exquisitely made garment she had ever owned. "My kinfolk said wearing this would help my plea in court," she grumbled. " 'Twas useless to me."

"A pretty plea, nonetheless," he said, "and a pretty gown."

She sent him a sour look. His smile was fleeting but genuine. Its warmth sank into her. She looked away and adjusted her plaid *arisaid* draped over her shoulders and belted at the waist.

"That patterned cloth is a fine weave," he said.

" 'Twas made by a kinswoman," she said. "She weaves good woolen plaids, warm and lightweight and much sought after. We are accustomed to simple clothing in the Highlands, but we are not the savages you think, sirrah. My father had this gown made for me in Glasgow. He thought to see me wed in it. Instead, I wore it to pay homage for his lands," she added sadly.

"Your father would have been proud of you this day," he murmured in Gaelic. His quick use of that language felt comforting, like a caress. For a moment she softened toward him. Then she turned abruptly to resume walking.

"Not many Normans speak Gaelic," she said.

"I took the time to learn it. When I act on behalf of the crown, it is useful. Your English is well spoken."

"My father insisted that my brothers and I learn it, so our priest taught us. Father Padruig says most foreigners think Gaelic is harsh and barbaric. But it is the tongue of bards and poets. It is like music."

"When some speak it," he murmured, "it is indeed."

She felt the heat of a blush. "I have never conversed with a privileged knight before, in English or in Gaelic."

"Not so privileged as you might think, my lady."

She frowned, puzzled. His armor and weapon were costly, and his dark green surcoat was trimmed in silver thread. He radiated confidence, authority, intelligence, and controlled power. Norman privilege was in his very blood. "My foster brother and I heard that the king's foreign honor guard is highly regarded at court and favored by the king."

"We were assigned to the Scottish court by our liege lord, Duke Conan of Brittany. 'Tis an honor to serve King William."

"Is that chivalric humility, sirrah? I have heard of the vows of virtue that foreign knights take."

"We try to honor our knightly vows. Though few would call me humble, my lady," he said wryly.

She tipped her head to look at him with curiosity. "When the king spoke of sending you to Kinlochan, you showed courtesy, but you grew tense, as if you were much displeased. Or was it merely your eagerness to obtain Scottish land that made you grip my arm so quick and hard?"

He narrowed his eyes, the scarred brow tugging down. His irises were gray and cool, but she saw a hot spark there. "The king made no true offer to me. You fret over naught."

"I do not fret," she snapped. Her frustrations and fears,

stoked by her audience with the king, kept her temper close
to the surface. "But I will have much to fret about if he
sends you—or any of your comrades—there!"

"There is no king's writ on this yet. Be calm."

"I have been calm, and for naught. Now I must wait
while the king chooses me a Norman husband. My kinfolk
expect a Celtic hero to save our clan! Now I must tell them
that I failed!"

"You tried your best. If the king sends men there, he
does it to ensure peace."

"Peace! There will be more war if he sends Normans!"

"You did ask for the king's assistance," he reminded her.

"In what my clan wants, not in what he wants!"

"He thinks of Scotland. You think of Clan Laren."

"What else should I think of?" she demanded, glaring
at him.

"You are wondrous full of argument," he commented.
" 'Tis good we go to church. Prayer might cool that Highland ardor."

She sent him a fuming look and walked on. He strode
beside her. After a while, she glanced sidelong at him. Despite her resentment, she wanted to know more about him,
especially if the king thought him suited to her and to
Kinlochan.

"You must be heir to some great lord to earn such favor
from a king," she said. "Is your family French or English
Norman?"

A fierce glint flickered in his eyes. "Not all men succeed
through birth. Some achieve through merit and prowess.
And determination." His tone was curt. "I was raised in
Brittany and spent years in England, if you will know. I am
Breton, rather than Norman from Normandy, or Norman
English." He paused. "And I am no one's heir."

"A younger son come to Scotland to acquire land and
status and wealth, then. I suppose you think the Scots to
be simple barbarians."

"Not all Scots," he drawled, glancing at her.

Lifting the hem of her gown, she walked faster. The
knight strode beside her steadily despite chain mail and
broadsword, as easily as if he could climb Highland hills in
twice the armor.

"You have the look of the Norse, tall and fair, as do your comrades," she said. "Are you related, you three? Are your kin descended from Vikings, like some Highland families?"

"So many questions," he said. "We are not related. The knights of the Breton honor guard are matched for size and fair coloring. And there may be Norse blood in me. I do not know for certain."

She blinked in surprise. Every Highlander she knew could recount his or her heritage. "I suppose Normans do not keep so careful a memory of their family lineage as do the Gaels."

"Bretons and Normans are proud of their lines of descent," he said. "And proud of the worth of their surnames."

She glanced at him, startled. He smiled politely, but a fleeting spark in his eyes belied that coolness.

He was like a wild cat sunning on a rock, she thought suddenly—calm on the surface, taut power beneath. He would be ferocious if provoked. Yet she saw kindness in his gaze, and in the gentle curve of his upper lip.

They reached the grassy courtyard that fronted the west entrance of the church. Twin towers soared above oak doors framed by stone arches and slender pillars. Alainna did not see Giric. The abbey grounds were deserted but for a few black-robed Benedictines who walked there.

She mounted the steps to look at the carvings on the column capitals. The knight joined her. "A beautiful abbey," he said.

"Yet it must seem humble compared to cathedrals in France and England. I hear they are like miracles of stone and glass."

"This place has strength and simplicity. I prefer that to showy grandeur."

" 'Tis similar in design to Durham Cathedral in England. Some of the stonecarvers who worked at Durham came here too."

"You know the abbey history well for one who is not local."

"My father's cousin made carvings here twenty years ago. He was a stonemason," she explained. "I have long wanted to see his work here." She touched a column. "He told me that Dunfermline has become a pilgrimage shrine because our beloved Queen Margaret is buried here. She was so good a soul that many Scots believe she should be declared a saint."

"I have said a few prayers to her myself. She has become a patron for the poor and the lost." He reached out to touch the stone too, his hand large and strong, dusted with golden hairs.

"You are here in Scotland to gain land from Scots." She turned away. "I doubt our Queen Margaret would consider you poor and lost."

"You share your temper with me easily enough. Will you not share your saintly queen as well?"

"I meant—"

"I know what you meant. You think little of Normans."

" 'Tis not that," she said, "exactly."

"Ah," he said. "And what exactly is it?" He rested his hand on the stone, his gaze winter cool, the small scar pale where it slashed through his left eyebrow.

A blush heated her cheeks, and she looked away. "I know that the Normans have helped Scotland and our kings in the past, and the Scottish crown values Normans for their military strength. But they bring too much change to Scotland."

"And you do not want to wed with one."

"I do not," she agreed.

"Your clan might benefit from such a union."

"Never."

"You are a stubborn girl, I think," he mused.

"I am. I have to be so, for the sake of my people. I cannot watch my clan be disbanded and destroyed."

"And you fear that a Norman husband would do that. Why?"

"I know he would." She drew her fingers over the grainy texture of the sandstone. "Normans would destroy our legacy, our history, our very name, and make it their own."

"This Highland enemy of yours is more likely to do that than a Norman."

"And I will not wed either one."

A wry smile played at his mouth. "You make that clear

enough," he said. "Lady, I am not a Scottish subject. I am not obligated to accept a grant from King William if he offers one to me."

She blinked. "You would refuse Kinlochan?"

"I have other plans," he said quietly.

She felt relief, but also a surprising disappointment. Of course she wanted him to refuse, she told herself. Yet she felt curious about him, drawn to his strength, to his wit, and his keen, kind gaze.

She caught her breath as she realized that he resembled the faery warrior in her dream. How ironic that a Norman would match that perfect warrior—ironic, disturbing, and unthinkable.

Handsome blond warriors were common, she told herself.

"The king will offer you Kinlochan," she said sharply. "No Norman would refuse such a gift. You are an ambitious sort, eager to foster your fortunes on Scottish soil."

He leaned toward her. "My ambitions do not include marrying a hot-tempered Highland girl and settling on some remote mountain to fight her war. I will leave that to your Celtic paragon, wherever he may be."

She blinked, stunned. He stared at her, nearly nose to nose, his arm buttressing the stone jamb, his hand just above hers. She would not tilt back, refusing to yield even that much. They breathed in tandem and watched one another.

She had rarely seen eyes of so clear a gray, or sparking so with anger. Her eyes surely matched his for flash and fire just then. She lowered her brows in a scowl to make certain of it.

"You must not accept the grant if it is offered you."

"Is that a warning?" he asked softly.

"It is." Her heart thudded. She could not take her gaze from his. She sensed his powerful will, as strong—even stronger—than her own. The feeling was odd and exciting.

"I do not do well with warnings," he said in a low voice. "I have a habit of going against them."

"Celtic clans do not want Normans among them," she said. "The barbarians of the Highlands attack anyone who attempts to take their land. It is why the Highlands have so few Norman settlers, while the Lowlands are filling with them. Rein in your greed and your ambition."

"Are you a leader of rebels, to speak so hot?"

"We would certainly rebel if someone tried to take our land," she replied. "But we do not rebel against our king."

"I rode beside your king while he defeated a host of Celtic rebels last year. After what I saw there, be sure that my ambitions do not include sharing land with savages."

"Good," she snapped. "Tell the king that Kinlochan goes only to a Celtic warrior."

"God help that Celt." He turned to pull open the great arched door. "My lady, you wanted to see the abbey."

Heart pounding, Alainna hesitated. Then she remembered that the entrance porch of a church, where she stood with the knight, was the traditional site for marriage ceremonies. The thought was so distressing that she stepped past him quickly.

"I did want to see the stonework," she admitted.

"Here is your chance." He held the door open.

Alainna stepped into the heart of peace and silence. The light was lucent and golden, and incense lingered in the air. She walked to the altar and knelt to pray. Sebastien knelt too, then rose with her. Their glances touched, slid free. She looked up.

Massive columns soared toward whitewashed walls. Above them was a clerestory pierced with windows of milky glass, the whole crowned by a curving ribbed vault. Alainna walked into a shadowed side aisle, her steps a soft echo.

She saw the knight standing in the nave, silent and patient, her own honor guard. Light glossed his hair to gold and flashed in his steel mesh hauberk. In chain mail, he seemed fiercely beautiful, hard and perfect.

She looked away, striving to focus her attention on the stone carvings. Familiar with her cousin's artistic hand, she saw its quiet assurance in several of the carved capitals, and she immersed herself in that pleasure, like finding a lost friend. Wandering the church, she searched for his mason's mark, a cut signature.

As she strolled through the church, she thought of her own carved reliefs in her small workshop at Kinlochan, and sighed. Even if she used more finesse with her chisels, she would never achieve the mastery of what she saw here.

Standing beneath a wreath of carved acanthus leaves on a capital, she took out a piece of linen and a stick of burnt willow from the leather pouch that hung suspended from her belt. Carefully she began to draw the leaf pattern on the cloth. Cousin Malcolm had always insisted that good carving depended upon good drawing, and she often made sketches to record ideas or to copy images and learn from them.

She looked at the knight, who glanced away as her gaze touched his. In the church setting, he reminded her of a warrior saint. Dynamic in his static pose, he fascinated her. Despite his fiery words, he made her feel safe. Closing her eyes, she felt her constant burden of worry and fear lift a little. Too soon, she would return to a world of uncertainty. For now, she wanted to savor the serenity and the reassurance she felt in this place, and in the knight's presence.

After a moment, she strolled onward. As she looked up, she gasped. High overhead, Malcolm's carved signature mark gleamed in the stone of one column. She hurried forward.

He scanned the shadows out of habit, though he knew no danger existed here. The abbey seemed to glow, he thought, glancing around its familiar interior. Perhaps its luminosity came from the afternoon light—or perhaps the girl created it, like a flame inside a lantern.

She was indeed a flame, for she had stirred him to fire when he preferred coolness and control. In scarcely an hour's time, she had ignited in him fascination, lust, envy, anger, and frustration. Now she roused something else in him, an urge to keep the world away from her and allow her peace. He wanted to give her that.

When she disappeared among the columns for a long while, he crossed the nave out of curiosity. Rounding a wide column, he stopped in astonishment.

Alainna stood on the narrow edge of a column base, toes balanced, chest and torso pressed against the pillar. One arm hugged the column, and the other hand stretched toward the groove of a carved chevron as if to seek a hold.

"Do you mean to climb all the way up, my lady?" he asked.

She gasped and shifted. Her foot caught in the train of her gown, and she tilted, arms flailing. He lunged forward so that she tipped neatly into the cradle of his arms.

"Ach," she said breathlessly, looping an arm around his neck. She was long-limbed but not heavy, her body firm through layered fabrics. She was strong, too, for she squirmed so that he nearly dropped her.

"Let me go, sirrah!" she insisted.

"I will," he promised. "First tell me what happened. Did you turn your ankle? Were you startled by a mouse?" He turned, holding her. "Shall I vanquish the creature for you?"

"Spare me your chivalry," she said, "and your poor jest. You surprised me, and I fell. Set me down!"

"So be it." He lowered her gently. "Tell me, why did you try to scale that column like a squirrel in a tree?"

She was not amused, he saw, although he could barely hide his own smile. A blush spread beneath her translucent skin, her sapphire eyes darkened, her brows lowered. Sebastien felt as if he watched a gathering storm. He rather liked storms.

"If you wish," he drawled, "I could fetch a ladder."

She opened her mouth to reply, then laughed reluctantly. The sound echoed like small bells. He chuckled, though it felt strangely dry and rusty. He did not laugh often, he realized.

"I wanted to see my cousin's mark, up there." She pointed.

He looked up. "His mark?"

"His mason's mark," she said. "A symbol engraved in the stone. When a mason dresses a block or makes a carving, he cuts his mark. They are paid according to the work they sign. That one is my cousin's mark."

The vision in his left eye was not as sharp as it once had been, but he saw a distinct symbol cut into the stone. He nodded.

"I just wanted to see it. Touch it," Alainna said.

Sebastien frowned, thinking. He picked up the cloth and charcoal she had set down on the floor. Reaching the mason's mark presented no challenge when he boosted a foot onto the plinth and stretched his arm up. He smoothed the cloth over the carving, and rubbed it with the charcoal to obtain an impression. Then he stepped down and handed her the cloth.

"A remembrance of your cousin," he said.

Her gaze was wide and earnest. "My thanks. You must be devoted to your own kin to know why this means so much to me."

"I . . . value family," he said vaguely. He glanced at the cloth. "I see that you are an *imagier*."

"I had some training from my cousin. Come, I will show you his work." She strolled with him, pointing out acanthus carvings and panels of interlaced vines. "See those flowers there? Malcolm always curled and fluted his leaves like that, to make the edges thin and delicate."

He nodded, listening, admiring the fine work she showed him, although he glanced at her more often than at the carvings. Her voice was low and soothing, and the sight of her was like a balm. As they neared the arched doors, she turned to him.

"My foster brother will be waiting, I think."

Sebastien felt an odd dismay, but nodded and held the door open for her.

Outside he saw Giric MacGregor riding toward them, leading a second horse by the reins. Both mounts were the sturdy garrons common to the Highlands, smaller and shaggier than Norman horses.

Sebastien turned. "Farewell, *Àlainne an Ceann Lochan.* We will not meet again. I plan to leave Scotland soon."

Her cheeks colored pink. "Oh . . . oh. A thousand blessings on you, then, and may God make smooth the path before you," she said in Gaelic. "May the faeries protect you."

He smiled, having heard similar Gaelic greetings, and farewells. "May you be safe from every harm," he murmured. "May the angels bless you."

She nodded, then whirled and ran toward her foster brother, who assisted her into the saddle. She took the reins and glanced back.

Sebastien raised his hand in salute. When they left the

abbey grounds, he took the path leading to the king's tower. But he could not resist the powerful urge to look back.

Alainna swiveled to look toward him just as he glanced toward her. Both turned quickly away. He walked down the sloped path, surrounded by trees and birdsong, and found himself straining to hear distant hoofbeats, like a thread linking him to her for a while longer.

Sebastien approached the stone tower lost in thought. He felt as if something remarkable had happened, but he could not define it. The Highland girl had entered his day like sunlight falling over shadows. In her absence, the world seemed somehow duller, colder.

A twinge of jealousy at the thought of her marrying some warrior, Celtic or Norman, rippled through him. Frowning, unsure why he should care at all, he walked on.

Chapter Four

"There will be snow tonight," Una said. "Lorne's aching bones tell me so." She peered out of the window of Alainna's workshop. The dim light silvered her hair, covered in part by a white linen kerchief, folded and tucked over her head. She was a small woman, and she rose on her toes, balancing a thin hand on the window frame as she looked out.

"My bones do not ache, woman," Lorne said. He picked up a small carved stone in the shape of a cross and turned it gently in his long-fingered hands.

"*Ach,* they do so—you asked me to put a dose of willow into your ale today," Una said impatiently. "Snow for certain, between what your long bones and those gray clouds out there tell me. The sky is the same color as some of your stones, Alainna."

"I see," Alainna answered without looking up. Her great-aunt and great-uncle had entered her workshop a few moments earlier, but she had scarcely glanced at them. "Let me clear a little more of this section, Una, and I will look."

Alainna circled the bench, critically studying the partially carved slab of gray limestone propped there. Then she angled her claw-toothed chisel blade against the stone and tapped the handle with the wooden mallet held in her right hand.

"This is a good piece," Lorne said, setting the little cross on the table. "Finer even than the one you brought to the king. I have not seen it before."

"I carved it this week," Alainna said, blowing away the stone dust she had created. "I promised one of those to Esa."

"When you bring it to her, try again to convince her to come and stay here at Kinlochan," Lorne said. "She is stubborn, but the winter will be fierce this year. All the omens point to it." His deep, smooth voice, whose magic Alainna had loved since childhood, held a distinct weariness.

She glanced up, and saw him pause by the long trestle table that held several stone slabs, each as long as a man's forearm. He bent to study them, his shoulders bowed, his long white hair swinging down to hide his handsome, hawk-like profile.

"This place is freezing." Una closed the wooden shutter with a decisive bang and latched it shut. "You will catch a chill in your lungs, keeping the window open all day."

"I need the light," Alainna said, tapping again. She paused to blow at the powder that collected at the chisel's edge.

"It is dark as night in here," Una complained. "I can hardly see at all." She stepped forward.

"You just closed the window," Lorne reminded her. "None of us can see now."

"There are candles on the shelf," Alainna answered. "The brazier gives out a little light, too."

"Not much light," Una said. "And not much heat. So you might as well stop working for a little. You have not stopped all this week, I think. Oh, move, you greedy hound, taking up all the room in here. Alainna, I know you like this dog, but he is not much of a guard, or much company, lying about all day."

Alainna glanced at the large deerhound who slept contentedly by the brazier "Finan is a fine guard when he needs to be. And I like his sort of company. He leaves me alone."

Lorne chuckled as he found a candle and lit it with a dry stick touched to the brazier's red coals.

"Alainna, we came here to ask you to share supper with us this evening," Una said.

"And we came to see how you are progressing in your work," Lorne added. "It is good indeed. The story stone you have just finished is even finer than the others."

Alainna smiled. "Thank you. And I am not hungry,

Una." She set down her chisel to choose a pointed iron tool, and used the mallet to drive the sharp end into the slab to clear away a small chunk of stone. "Morag brought me food earlier."

"Morag has brought your meals in here for two days. She told me that you came late to your bed last night, and rose early to work again. You will exhaust yourself and become ill."

"I have much to do," Alainna said as she blew away pale dust from the stone's face. "This is the seventh stone. The scenes I plan to do will need twenty stones, maybe more."

"You have set yourself quite a task, child," Lorne said. "But you need to rest. No one can finish a lifetime's work in months."

"I must." Alainna smacked the point with the mallet.

"Come into the hall, eat with us, and get warm," Una insisted. "The old ones will all be pleased to have you among them."

"I have much to do," Alainna repeated, clearing another chunk of stone.

"It grows dark," Una said. "A candle does not give enough you light. You have hardly set foot in the hall for two days. I have a hot venison stew in the kettle, and after we eat, Lorne will tell a fine tale. Morag has seen that all is in order in the household, the floors swept and clean rushes laid down, the linens and plaids aired, the beds and pallets readied for the night." She glanced at her husband, then back at Alainna. "All is in order at Kinlochan, except that the chief of the clan shuts herself in a tiny workroom with unswept floors and no food in her belly while she works like a laborer."

Alainna flexed her aching shoulders. "Cousin Morag manages our household well. She loves the work she does for Kinlochan, and she never rests until she is satisfied that her tasks are done to perfection. And I love the work that I do, even if it is messy. I want to continue, too, until I am satisfied that it is done."

Una sighed impatiently. "What you do here is not done in a day, girl, like most household tasks. You must eat, you must rest! And your kin need their chief among them. Lorne, speak to her."

"Niall wants me to begin the cycle of the Fionn stories tonight," Lorne said. "But Una and Morag want to hear the tale of Deirdre and the sons of Uisneach again. Which shall it be? Niall says he is tired of love tales, and wants to hear one of war and men, with a long passage about a battle in it."

"I like the tale of Deirdre of the Sorrows," Alainna said. "I never grow tired of that story. When Deirdre sees Naoise and his brothers for the first time . . ." She sighed. "Ah, it is beautiful, that."

"Then Deirdre it will be, if you join us this evening. Leave your work. There is time."

As her uncle spoke, Alainna tipped her head to assess the scene that she carved. Three men in a ship, holding upright lances, had been lightly sketched on the surface of the stone. Only the excess limestone had been cut away, with clawed chisel marks over much of the rest, to form a high relief.

She sighed and glanced at Lorne, whose blue eyes gleamed with affection. Beside him, Una, not even as tall as her husband's shoulder, watched her with a frown of concern. Alainna sighed again and set down her mallet.

"You are right. I am tired."

"Good. Your kinfolk miss you," Una said.

Alainna wiped her tools with a soft cloth and set them aside. Then she covered the stone with another cloth and straightened, stretching her arms. "I must sweep this," she said, glancing at the floor, which was covered in stone chips and dust.

"Tomorrow we sweep," Una said. "Tonight we rest. Come, girl. You work yourself too hard. You fret too much."

"I do not fret," Alainna said stiffly. She removed the kerchief that protected her hair from stone dust, and shook her braids free. "I never fret."

"Of course you do not," Lorne said. "Tonight you must eat well, listen to a story, and think about only what is most pleasant."

"Especially do not think about those Norman knights that the king may send here," Una said.

"Una," Lorne said, "I think your stew needs stirring."

"Morag will see to it," Una said. The deerhound rose from his place by the brazier and yawned, stretching his long legs. He padded toward Una and nuzzled at her, his head just below her shoulder. She patted his nose, and was licked for her effort.

"Come, Finan *Mór,* you lazy thing," Una said. "I will give you a piece of meat." She went to the door with the dog.

Lorne waited while Alainna blew out the candle and took off the old tunic that she wore over her gown for an apron.

"You worry about what the king will do, my girl," he said. "I have seen it in your eyes these two weeks since your return. That is why you work so hard on your stones."

"Carving does help ease my mind. It is hard, this waiting for word from the king."

"Difficult for all of us. Come ease your mind with good food and good company. Perhaps the tale of Deirdre is not right for you tonight. You need something to make you chuckle, like the tale of the simpleton at the wedding, and how he tried to bring the pond indoors to serve fresh fish to the guests."

Alainna smiled. "Niall likes that one, too. We want him to be happy, since he must wait to hear stories of the Fianna."

"He will not be unhappy if our chief is safely in the hall, well fed and laughing, with her worries forgotten."

"Never forgotten, Uncle," she murmured, and sighed.

"And the sound of her sigh was as the whisper of grass in the autumn," Lorne said softly, watching her. "Or as dry leaves beneath the wind, shifting to their winter sleep."

She smiled sadly. "How could I refuse a chance to listen to such a poet? We had better hurry. Una will be tapping her foot because we are not yet seated at the table, and the food ready."

"She will be too busy keeping Finan's snout out of her stew to think about that," Lorne said.

"Sire, I am not the champion for the task." Sebastien stared into the flaming hearth in the king's private chamber as he spoke. "The lady wants a Celtic warrior in plaid and braids."

"She has no choice," the king replied. "She will have you."

Silently, his jaw clenched, Sebastien walked to a table and lifted a bronze jug to pour hot spiced wine into wooden goblets banded with silver. The steamy fragrance wafted up as he handed one to the king, and then placed a bowl of apples near his chair. He returned to the hearthside and remained standing as he sipped from his own goblet.

"Lady Alainna asked for an exemplary warrior, and I will send her one," the king said. He peeled an apple with a small knife. "You witnessed her audience. You know that her clan is in need of a protector."

"Aye, my lord, I remember." Alainna MacLaren's graceful dignity and the haunting need in her blue eyes were not easily forgotten. The girl had even appeared in his dreams, disquieting sequences of lust and heartbreak that left him with a sense of longing. He felt an undeniable urge to help her and her clan, yet he wondered at the origin of that desire.

"My lord," he resumed after a moment, "I am honored by such favor, but I plan to reside in Brittany and marry there."

"A widower with a son needs a wife. I am giving you a Scottish heiress with vast property. As my champion in the north, you will add immeasurably to your status in Scotland, England, and France. Live where you choose with your family after you ensure that Kinlochan is in a state of peace."

"The lady will protest the grant and the marriage. No doubt her clan will protest it too."

"As do you, I think," the king said. "Why do you hesitate?"

"I prefer my land and my women tamed, sire," Sebastien said in a wry tone. William chuckled.

In truth, Sebastien wanted to accept this choice parcel of land, but he did not want to marry to keep it. He hoped to find a noble French or Breton bride to replace the wife he had lost. His son did indeed need a mother, but Conan had a claim to a French inheritance through his deceased mother, and needed to be brought up in France or Brittany, not in cold, distant Scotland.

Still, the thought of marrying Alainna MacLaren sent a deep and subtle tremor through the core of his being. He frowned, thinking, staring into the vivid flames.

Wild, remote Highland slopes inhabited by barbarians— even those led by a beautiful damsel—would not help him establish the legacy of land and heritage that would secure his son's future. He sighed heavily.

"Surely Lady Alainna pleases you," the king said.

"She is . . . lovely. But Scotland is a long way from Brittany, sire. And this girl expects her husband to take her family name." He paused. "I cannot do that."

"Then refuse to take the name." The king shrugged. "If you want the rights to this land, and the title and privilege of owning such a grant in Scotland, you will have to marry the lady. She paid a relief fee. Kinlochan cannot be granted to anyone else for a year, except through marriage. When you send a copy of the nuptial contract between you and Lady Alainna to my chamberlain, the new grant will be drawn up in your name."

"And not before," Sebastien commented flatly. He felt a muscle thumping in his jaw, felt a trap closing about him.

"And not before," the king repeated easily. He sliced off a wedge of apple. "Tell me, Bastien, what land do you own now?"

"A small castle and manor house in Brittany, of fifty and a hundred acres each, held of Duke Conan," Sebastien answered. "In York, a fortified house and a thousand acres held of King Henry for services to him years ago. He promised a title with the grant, but he seems to have overlooked that since I came to Scotland," he added dryly. "I have never resided at my properties, but rent them to tenants."

"Are there lands owned of your late wife?"

"Not personally, sire. My son is heir to a castle and lands in France, but his mother's family resides there still."

William nodded pensively. "Your original fealty is owed to Duke Conan, of course. But he assigned you and your comrades to me for so long as I require knight service from you. The pledge you signed is not yet expired. And it can be renewed."

"I am honored, my lord." He spoke slowly, warily. "But as you are aware, an urgent matter requires my presence in Brittany as quickly as possible."

He had explained his son's dilemma, and that of the monks of Saint-Sebastien, to the king days ago. The privilege of a royal messenger had been extended to him, so that he could send his answer to the abbot. In his letter, he had loaned them the use of his Breton properties, and had promised to return as soon as he could buy passage on a ship bound for France.

"Certes, you must go back, but not yet. To ease your mind, I will dispatch a messenger with a letter for Duke Conan and his duchess, my sister. I will recommend that they look into the welfare of this group of monks."

"I am in your debt." Sebastien bowed stiffly, clenching his fist. He was no fool. He realized how deep that debt had just become.

"It is my charitable duty. The debt can be repaid in continued service. Your signed pledge to me stands for several months more. For now, your skills are needed at Kinlochan."

Sebastien watched the king with narrowed eyes. He felt a surge of anger, but knew that outright refusal of the grant could destroy not only his chances for land in Scotland, but any help the king would extend to Conan and the monks.

"My lord is generous," he said curtly. "But I remind the king that I am not the warrior that I once was."

He started, then, catching the apple that William flipped toward him. He had not seen it coming from his left side until almost too late due to his impaired vision. But he cupped the fruit in his left hand with rapid agility. Had it been the edge of a blade, he would have deflected it with shield or weapon out of sheer instinct.

"I think, Bastien," the king said softly, "you are every bit the warrior you once were, though your abilities be little used of late. Go to Kinlochan and see to this matter for me."

"Sire," Sebastien said.

"And see that a stone castle is raised there."

"A castle?" He felt as if the quagmire that sucked him down had just gotten thicker, deeper.

"Kinlochan sits like a gateway to the mountains of the western Highlands. Norman military presence there is essential to ensure our authority and discourage Celtic rebellion."

Sebastien stared at him in dismay. "Such a project could take years." He very much wanted an opportunity to supervise the building of his own castle, but not this way. Not in Scotland.

"You will have the time as baron there. You have some experience in the building of castles, do you not?"

"I have taken some interest in their design. The English baron who sponsored me as a squire and young knight built three stone castles in England while I was in his household and later in his service. He allowed me some responsibilities in overseeing the hiring of stonemasons and approving the design. I am not unfamiliar with the process."

"You will need that experience when you hire stonemasons and initiate the work. With help from royal funds, of course, although Kinlochan's own revenues will go toward it too."

"Let us hope Kinlochan has some revenues, sire. From what Lady Alainna indicated, it is a poor holding."

"No doubt you will discover that soon enough. Take twenty men for now, and ride out. Leave me enough Bretons to keep an honor guard. Send for more men when you determine what is needed there." King William sipped his wine, relaxed and confident in his orders.

"What of this MacNechtan, who submitted a petition?"

"He claims his loyalty, but if he proves a threat to the lady's clan or to the crown, he must be quelled."

"And if he is not a threat?"

"I am not so foolish as to give him that holding." The king set down his cup. "There is another reason that I want you garrisoned up there. The MacWilliams are still adamant that they have a claim to this throne through their descendence from King Duncan. They may have found support in that part of the Highlands."

Sebastien frowned. "We routed a group of those Celtic rebels over a year ago. Those who did not die on the field, and escaped capture and execution, sailed for Ireland and exile. They would be fools to return."

" 'Tis said at least one of them has sailed out of Ireland to raise support in the Highlands for their cause—Ruari MacWilliam."

"I remember the name. A fierce Celt, and a force to be reckoned with," Sebastien said. "I thought he was dead."

"We all did. My source has been in Ireland and the western isles recently, and says this man left Ireland not long ago, and headed for the area around Kinlochan."

"Why? He can find no useful support from a failing clan."

"The MacNechtans may provide that support. Find out if they side with the rebels. They might be harboring this Ruari MacWilliam. If so, they must be dealt with, and harshly."

"Loyal or not, MacNechtan may rebel when he learns that Kinlochan has been granted to a foreigner. Highland blood fires easily, and does not cool well."

"That hot blood is precisely why Kinlochan cannot remain in Celtic hands alone. A knight of calm temperament and military experience is needed there. I will rely on you."

Sebastien bowed stiffly and walked away without a word. When he reached for the door latch, his hand was so tightly fisted that his knuckles were white.

Chapter Five

Alainna thought she heard the thunder of horses, and turned, lowering the bow she held. She saw only hills and bare trees silhouetted against a vivid sunset sky. Just the wind pummelling the trees, she told herself, and turned back.

In the narrow glen below the slope on which she stood sentry, her kinsmen and their dogs pursued a small herd of red deer. Alainna had climbed higher to keep guard while the men and dogs drove the deer into the bottle-shaped glen. The dogs barked at the deers' heels as they ran along a rapid burn and deeper into the trap. Giric, Lorne, and Lulach veered off to stretch a net across the entrance to the glen, which was enclosed by snow-frosted hills.

Now Clan Laren would not go hungry, Alainna thought with relief. The deer herd was large enough that a few stags and hinds could be cut out of it, allowing the hunters to spare the majority, along with mothers and fawns. Mac-Nechtan raids had left her clan few cattle and sheep to slaughter for winter meat. Venison carcasses, salted and stored, would help to feed her people through the winter months.

Holding the bow, with a few arrows tucked into her belt, she watched for escaping deer as well as approaching enemies. With so few men left in the clan, she often provided an extra set of hands and eyes during hunts. While the hounds took down the deer with their powerful jaws, and her kinsmen followed up the kill, Alainna stood guard.

A thin crust of snow crunched beneath her boots, and the wind swept over the slope. She was glad that she had worn male clothing that day; the versatile wrapped and belted plaid, layered shirts, and the woolen trews beneath

were warm and snug against the bitter cold. She loosened
the long pin that held the plaid on her left shoulder, and
pulled the gathering over her head as a shield from the
wind.

The thunderous noise rumbled behind her, louder this
time. She glanced toward the hilltop. The setting sun threw
pink streaks across the sky, and she lifted a hand to shade
her eyes against the brilliance. Then she gasped in
astonishment.

A group of horsemen appeared on the hill crest like a
host of bright angels, their cloaks winging out, their shields
shining in the late sun. As they skimmed the hilltop, their
leader paused to wave at the others, and they drew to a
halt.

Even at this distance, she saw that they rode tall, fine-
blooded horses, carried good weapons and elongated
shields, and wore quality armor and fur-lined cloaks. Few
Lowland knights and fewer Highland men could afford such
horses or armor.

Normans. Her heart thudded heavily. She had been
dreading their arrival for weeks. Normans rarely traveled
into the Highlands except on royal business, and although
many of them had Lowland properties, none so far held
land in the north.

She climbed toward the hilltop. The king must have sent
them to Kinlochan, she thought. If the king had made his
decision, her land, her future, and the welfare of her clan
now hung in the balance.

Two knights split away from the rest and rode toward
her, both hooded and cloaked over their chain mail, one
on a dappled gray horse, the other riding a beautiful horse
the color of rich cream. She wondered if the Breton, Sir
Sebastien, was one of them, but she could not see their
faces.

The dogs' furious barking drew her attention back to the
glen. The deer, sensitive to new sound and movement, had
scattered, some of them leaping over the net. Alainna cried
out in dismay to see the deer, pursued for hours, lost so
easily. She realized that her kinsmen, trying to corner the
deer once again, had not yet noticed the knights on the hill.

Temper sparking, she strode toward the knights, hardly

caring who they were. Those deer had been essential to the welfare of her clan. She stood before the riders, fisting a hand on her hip, the other hand gripping her upright bow.

"Be gone from here!" she shouted. "You ruin our hunt!" She spoke in Gaelic without thinking, then realized that the knights would speak English or French. If Sebastien le Bret was among them, let him translate, she thought sourly.

"Ho, lad! Good day to you!" The knight on the dappled horse waved and pushed back his cloak hood. He was a large man with blunt, pleasant features, a face reddened with cold, and hair the color of brass. "Tell us the way to Kinlochan!" As she expected, he spoke English.

Her heart slammed hard. "Be gone!" she shouted again in Gaelic, waving her arm. She had seen him weeks ago, guarding the king beside Sebastien le Bret. She looked at the other knight.

She knew him then, even hooded, knew the wide set of his shoulders, the length and power of his mail-encased legs. A delicate shiver went through her, neither cold nor fear, stirred by the memory of steady gray eyes, and a pair of strong arms that had lifted her in a church.

Sebastien le Bret dropped back the hood of his fur-lined blue cloak, worn over the dark green surcoat she recognized from the first time she had seen him. Chain mail framed a face whose striking planes and steel gray eyes were familiar. His brows drew together as he looked at her.

"Have we met before?" he asked in Gaelic.

She gave him a frown to equal his, her heart still pounding. "Leave, you," she said, pointing in the direction they had come.

"He speaks only the native tongue, Bastien," the other knight said. "And he seems annoyed with us."

"We have disturbed their hunt. Look down in the glen."

"Ah. They were trapping the deer. I have heard that the Highlanders practice that barbaric method of hunting."

"When men are hungry, they are practical," Sebastien said, watching Alainna.

Her gaze locked in the grip of his. She suspected that he recognized her—but if both men assumed she was a boy, she would take advantage of that anonymity.

"Ask him to tell us where the castle is," the other urged.

"Hugo, we must ride farther northwest. I was told 'tis situated by a narrow loch at the foot of a mountain. We will find it soon. Disturbing their hunt was not necessary." He lifted the reins. "Our apologies, lad."

"This damned wind is cold," Hugo complained. "The hills are more vast than I thought. We must find shelter soon or sleep in a cow byre tonight. What is the word for castle? *Dùn*," he said clumsily to Alainna. "Kinlochan."

"There is no castle near here," she told Sebastien. "Kinlochan fortress is three leagues northwest. What is your business there?"

"King's business," he answered. "What of Turroch, which belongs to Clan Nechtan? Where is that holding?"

"Turroch! Why do you want to know?"

"King's business again. Which direction is it?"

She glared at him. "The fortress of Cormac MacNechtan," she said in precise, clipped English, "is five leagues west from here. If you are welcome there, you are surely not welcome at Kinlochan. Ride on."

"Your English is surpassing good for a Highland savage," he drawled. The steady glint in his eyes told Alainna that he knew her now. She reached up to draw back the plaid that obscured her hair, and stared up at him openly.

"So I thought," he said. "Greetings, Lady Alainna."

"The Highland lady, by God!" Hugo crowed.

"I wondered if she had a brother with the same eyes, but 'tis the demoiselle herself." Sebastien inclined his head.

"It is," she answered. Hearing a shout, she glanced back at the glen. Her kinsmen climbed the long hill, spears in hand.

"Those savages are in a mood to attack," Hugo said. "Iron-tipped spears and bare-legged barbarians are no match for mounted and armed men. Shall I summon the others, Bastien?"

"A few barbarian spears can bring down armed knights," Sebastien said. "Ride back and tell the others to hold. We want no trouble here." Hugo wheeled and rode toward the others.

"Go with him," Alainna told Sebastien. He did not move, watching her, his hands relaxed on the pommel. After a moment, she held up her hand to signal to her kinsmen to wait. They stopped cautiously, standing on the hill, spears ready.

"I am not leaving," Sebastien said. "I have ridden a long way to talk to you."

"Last we spoke, you were planning to depart Scotland."

"I will do that soon enough. For now, I am here in the king's name."

"What is your mission?" she asked, heart pounding.

"The king sends you a champion, and a husband," he said.

She frowned up at him warily, unsure if he referred to himself or one of the other knights. Her gaze flickered there, returned to him. "Which of you is this champion? And why do you have orders to go to Turroch?" She fervently hoped the king had not chosen Cormac MacNechtan after all.

"My comrades and I would be happy to discuss it out of the cold. I believe there is a Highland custom of hospitality."

"Find your welcome at Turroch," she snapped. "We have another Highland custom—my enemy's friend is my enemy."

"Then your friend's friend is your own, I think."

"We have no shared friends between us."

"The king is your friend, lady, and mine. He sent me here to offer you a solution, as you requested of him."

"I did not request interference from Normans."

His eyes, winter gray, swept her from head to foot. She raised her chin under his silent scrutiny. Cold wind skimmed her cheeks and strands of hair fluttered across her eyes. She would not look away for pride.

"Cool your ardor, my lady, we mean no harm," he said. "This wind may not bother you, but I am not overfond of it, nor are my men. We have been riding since dawn. Will you offer welcome to us or not?"

She sighed. "We will." By tradition, hospitality was never refused, even to an enemy. Nor could she refuse a messenger sent by the king. "Wait with your companions. I will speak to my kinsmen, and we will lead you to Kinlochan. Now that the deer are gone," she added, "we have no reason to stay out here longer."

She glanced past him and counted at least twenty knights. Without venison, she was not sure how Kinlochan's hospitality would feed such a large host of knights. She doubted that Normans liked porridge any better than they liked cold weather.

"We will await the lady," Sebastien said courteously, but his eyes sparked like steel. He gathered the reins. As the horse turned, Alainna saw the blue painted shield that hung at the side of his saddle, until now partly obscured from her view.

The shield bore a simple design of a single white arrow on a blue field. She had seen that design before, in a dream, carried by a mysterious golden warrior. *Dear God,* she thought. Just as in her dream, she now stood alone on a snow-coated hill to greet warriors, while her kinsmen hunted in the glen below. The golden warrior in the dark blue cloak, with his shield of a single arrow was here too; all he lacked was the magic of the faery realm.

Her breath caught in her throat.

"Wait!" she called, running a step or two after him.

He drew rein and turned. "What is it?"

"Your . . . your shield shows an arrow on a plain field. What does it mean?"

" 'Tis for Saint Sebastien," he answered. "An arrow is his symbol, and serves well for mine."

Why would she dream of Sebastien le Bret before she had met him, and why would she have found an arrow in the grass, as if it were an omen? She did not understand what any of it meant. He was not the warrior her clan needed.

"Sebastien," she repeated. "Why your baptismal name? What of your surname, Le Bret? The crests that Norman knights carry on their shields and banners refer to their family names."

"There are many knights," he said, "from Brittany." He circled the horse and cantered away.

Alainna stared after him. The wind whipped at her plaid, stirred her hair. The sunset glowed over snowy grasses, and sparked bronze in the armor of the warriors and the leader who waited for her. Her dream had come to life.

Her heart pounded hard. The golden warrior did exist after all. But he brought destruction, not salvation.

In the glen below, her kinsmen shouted as a stag bounded across their path. They began to chase it, following the dogs. Alainna stood on the hill and watched them, caught in the maze of her thoughts.

Although she did not look at him, she was intensely aware of the Breton knight who waited with his men.

By the time her kinsmen returned after losing the deer, the setting sun cast blue shadows over the hills. Alainna began to walk down the hill toward the men. A white hare scurried across her path to disappear beneath a gorse bush.

She sighed. Clan Laren did not even have a hare to put in their kettle, with so many mouths to feed this evening. A fortunate day had turned unlucky indeed.

Another hare scuttled after the first. Alainna stopped, wondering what stirred them from their hiding places to cross her path. She turned then, and froze all movement.

A few yards from where she stood, a boar emerged from a stand of trees. The small, high-set eyes gleamed, the long snout lifted to reveal yellowed tusks and a black mouth. Mottled brown, huge, and ugly, it appeared agitated, head swinging up and down as if it meant to attack.

The horses on the hill and the hunting dogs in the glen must have disturbed the boar while it foraged among the trees. Alainna knew the animals had uncertain tempers. She stepped cautiously down the slope.

The boar snorted, wagged its long head, and trotted toward her. She began to run, stumbling a little on the steep hill. Crashing noises behind her told her that the boar followed.

They were fast, dangerous, and temperamental animals, she knew, with poor vision but for what lay directly in their path. If she ran a crazed path and got out of its sight, and if she could find a tree to climb, she would be safe until her kinsmen could reach her.

If the beast came near her now, it would swipe its powerful tusks at her ankles, following an instinct to cut prey down at the feet, rendering it helpless to escape.

That horrifying thought gave her renewed strength. She turned and ran past a cluster of gorse bushes, ignoring the stinging needles that pierced her skin through her woolen trews. She began to zigzag in an effort to confuse the boar.

She glanced back, stumbling again, nearly falling, dropping her bow in her haste to get up. The boar swung stubbornly after her, crashing through the gorse. Alainna pushed onward, running through dry bracken toward another group of trees.

Behind her, she heard shouts, barking dogs, and the thunder of hooves, but could spare no more backward glances. The boar's relentless snorting was loud and insistent.

She saw a wide alder tree ahead and ran toward it, reaching for a lower branch. Leaping into the tree's sanctuary, she steadied herself on a thick limb, and glanced down. Without her bow, she had no defense, and clung desperately to the tree.

Seconds later, the beast rammed the trunk, jarring her perch. Her foot slipped with the impact. The boar swiped at her dangling boot. She jerked her leg out of the way and scrambled higher, shaking in terror. The beast slammed into the tree again and again, bellowing its fury.

A movement nearby caught her attention. She glanced up, startled, as a pale horse approached, carrying a rider in steel and indigo. A blue shield with a single arrow gleamed on the saddle. Sebastien le Bret, lance couched under his arm, guided his horse quickly toward the alder where Alainna clung.

Quickly, efficiently, he wheeled sidelong, lifted the lance, and hurled it at the boar. The point sank into the target, and the boar grunted and fell heavily at the base of the tree. The wooden shaft quivered in its flesh.

Alainna stared, stunned, at Sebastien. Her breath burned in her throat and her heart slammed. She could not seem to move her limbs, could not seem to think, her mind emptied by panic. Nor could she shift her gaze from the knight's.

He reined in his sidestepping horse. Men gathered behind him, Highlanders and Normans both. Alainna saw only the knight who rode close to the tree. He turned his mount so that he could lean toward her, and extended an arm, his gaze steady on hers.

Clinging to the branch, she clung to his gaze as well. She felt as if she were drowning and he held the only rope. All else but his eyes, his outstretched hand, faded around her.

"Alainna," he said gently. He moved his fingers, beckoning. "The beast is killed. Come out of the tree."

She nodded stiffly, her panic clearing. She felt foolish. Refusing his hand, she edged along the branch, and paused uncertainly when she saw the dead boar.

"Alainna," Sebastien said firmly, "come with me."

Come with me. His words brought back the memory of her dream, where the golden warrior had held out his hand to her—although she had not been up a tree, shaking like a terrified child—and had said the same words. In the dream, she had known that her life would change—might even end—once she took his hand.

She hesitated. Sebastien reached out and grabbed her arm, tugging her toward him. She swung into place behind him, looping her arms around his waist for balance. He urged the horse forward, and her kinsmen ran toward her.

"Alainna girl, are you harmed?" Lorne asked. He looked so old, she thought, his long face gone gray with worry, his white hair straggling, his shoulders bowed. But his keen, sky-blue eyes were sharp with concern.

"I am fine," she said. Lorne grasped her hand, and nodded thanks to Sebastien. Then he walked past them to kneel beside the fallen boar.

Giric came near them and murmured thanks in Gaelic to Sebastien. While he spoke, he held Alainna's hand, and she smiled down at him. She saw Sebastien cast them a small frown. Lorne returned, holding the javelin that he had pulled free. He wiped it clean on his plaid and handed it back to Sebastien, who dropped it into a saddle loop.

"Clan Laren thanks you, sir knight," Lorne said in English. "You killed a boar as fierce as the one who took down the mighty champion Diarmuid in ages past. You have saved our beloved girl. We are forever in your debt."

Alainna stared in amazement. She was not surprised to hear formal words of thanks from Lorne, but she was startled by his use of English. Lorne rarely used the southern tongue, regarding it as inferior to Gaelic. That demonstration of respect went far beyond his words of gratitude.

" 'Twas an honor to help the demoiselle," Sebastien said.

"My thanks as well, sirrah," she said, although she would not declare herself indebted forever, as Lorne had done. She swung her leg free to scramble down from the horse.

Sebastien grabbed her arm to help her down, and held her wrist once she stood beside the horse. Even through the thick leather of his glove, she felt the comforting strength of his grip. She pulled away.

"I hope some fresh boar meat will help to make up for the loss of the deer," he said.

"It will," she answered, then stepped back.

"Good meat, and a fine champion to thank for it," Lorne said, smiling. "You and your men are welcome to share our meal at Kinlochan, of course. It was your kill, after all."

"We are grateful for your generosity," Sebastien said. "Some of my men will help you tie up the boar. My lady, I am glad you are safe." He nodded briefly to her, and guided his horse toward his men.

Safe. The word echoed in her mind as she watched him ride over to speak to his comrades. *Safe.* He could not know how essential safety was to her. No champion, even if he slayed a monster at her feet, could vanquish the fear that haunted her daily—that her clan would disappear forever.

She sighed and passed her hand wearily over her head. Lorne circled an arm around her, and she leaned gratefully into his sinewy embrace. As they walked away, she wondered how truly safe any of them were now that the king had sent Normans to Kinlochan.

Chapter Six

"We would like one of our guests to tell the evening story now that our supper is done," Lorne said from his chair beside the central open hearth. "Sebastien le Bret, tell us a tale from your own country, if you will."

Sebastien took another sip from his cup of ale to cover his surprise. The men and women of the clan, most of whom seemed as elderly as Lorne, looked at Sebastien from their seats around the hearth. His own men, seated on benches alongside two trestle tables, stared at him also.

His impulse was to refuse. He paused. The fire in the circular stone hearth cast a reddish glow that reflected on the waiting faces, and a hot crackle filled the silence.

He glanced around the room, a large chamber that showed solid construction and simple comfort. Kinlochan's main hall was a long, raftered room made of stout timbers, with wooden piers dividing side aisles into bays that flanked the central area. A thick layer of clean dry grasses and flower petals on the floor added a clean fragrance. The planked walls were hung with lengths of wool woven in colorful patterns, and various weapons and targe shields studded in bronze were suspended around the upper walls.

Seated on benches and stools were a host of Highlanders, Norman knights, and the squires who had accompanied the king's men. All of them looked expectantly at Sebastien. He cleared his throat, and sipped from his cup once again. He had sometimes told stories to his little son while the child drifted to sleep, but he was no bard, and had no desire to display that lack of ability.

"The gifts of the Scottish storytellers are well known," he finally said. "I would rather hear an authentic Scottish tale told by a true bard."

"It is Highland custom for a guest to tell a tale the first night of his visit," Alainna said in English. She stood beside her great-uncle's chair. "We would like to hear something that is told at hearth-sides in your country."

Sebastien watched her as she spoke, half distracted. Firelight slid over her body, enhancing its supple curves and sheening her long braids to rippling bronze. He had been aware, ever since he had recognized her out on the snowy hill, that she was to become his wife by order of the king. No matter what conflicts he had concerning the marriage, she was a rich prize for a man's bed. His body reacted to the sight of her, and to the sultry sound of her voice.

Soon he would have to tell her why he had come to Kinlochan. He did not relish the moment. None of the Highlanders, he was sure, wanted this marriage.

Nor did he relish explaining that he would leave Kinlochan as soon as possible. Knights with different lords to serve and various holdings to oversee often left their wives and families for months and years at a time. He knew that too well, yet had no choice now but to repeat that again.

He glanced around at a rainbow of smiles, small and large, bright and dim, toothless and full. His own men plainly grinned as if to dare him to accept Lorne's request, while the Highlanders looked eagerly toward him. Clearly he had no choice but to oblige.

"Come to the hearth." Alainna stepped before him, the hem of her simple gray tunic swinging around her ankles. Over it she wore a plaid mantle of brown and blue, belted at her waist, its upper drape fallen back in folds behind her. Her braids were bright and glossy. He wanted to slide his fingers over that fascinating silkenness.

"Tell one of the stories you heard in Brittany as a child," she said.

"I did not hear many tales as a lad. Outside of scripture, that is." He paused. "But I can recite one of the Breton tales that troubadours tell in the court of the duke of Brittany."

"That will do." She held out her hand as if touch was natural and common between them. Her fingers closed over his, smooth, graceful, and pale. Warmth sprang between them, and something fine and hot leaped within him from groin to heart. She tugged on his hand, and he rose to his feet.

He felt awkward, preferring to be on the outskirts of a group where he could observe and learn. He liked his back to the wall, his thoughts to himself, and the advantage his.

Alainna looked up at him with a quick, sparkling smile. His heart seemed to turn within him. The chatter and the faces and the firelight faded, and only her smile, meant for him alone, existed.

Beside the hearth, Lorne gestured toward an empty stool. "Please," he said, "sit by our fire."

Sebastien let go of Alainna's hand and sat. The central fire gave off much heat, and he was glad that he wore only a tunic of brown serge, hose, and boots. He had shed his heavy armor, padding, surcoat, and fur-lined winter cloak, as had his fellow knights. They had left their belongings in a corner of the raftered hall, where sleeping pallets had been stacked for their use later.

Someone handed him a cup filled to the brim with ale, foaming and slightly flowery in taste and scent. He sipped and looked into the fire. The room grew quiet around him. Alainna settled on the floor at his feet, her back close to his knee.

"Long ago," he began in English for the benefit of the Normans, "there was a knight of Brittany named Sir Lanval, who visited the court of the great King Arthur. Sir Lanval rode out in the forest and came upon some beautiful ladies dressed in green, bedecked with flowers, dancing. They were the handmaidens of the Queen of Faery, who stepped forward, the most beautiful woman the knight had ever seen. She beckoned him into the Otherworld with her. . . ."

Alainna sat at his feet, echoing his words in Gaelic, her shoulder brushing his knee. As he spoke, he watched the firelight gleam in the bright strands of her hair.

"After he wed the faery queen and returned to his own world, Sir Lanval unwittingly insulted Queen Guinevere by saying that he loved a woman who was more beautiful than any earthly queen. She was deeply offended and called for the knight to be put on trial. The court gathered before King Arthur."

He went on, while Alainna spoke in a lilting tone. He wanted to continue just to hear her soft voice interweave with his own.

"And so he waited for the king's judgment when the faery woman whom he loved, and thought he had lost forever, appeared in the midst of the court, gowned in dazzling green, to speak on his behalf, for she loved him as well as he loved her."

When he finished and Alainna had translated the ending, she glanced at him. All he saw was her smile, despite the pleased expressions that surrounded him.

"You are a storyteller as well as a champion," Lorne said. "And you are welcome at Kinlochan for both talents, of course."

"If you have more tales like that one, you must stay long enough to tell them all!" An old man with one hand, the other ending in a scarred stump, grinned at him.

"The knight and his men will not be here that long," Alainna said. She straightened where she sat, the line of her back proud. "He bears a message, although we have not yet heard it from him."

"You have not yet asked me," he murmured, low enough that only she could hear him.

. Her eyes smoldered blue. "I did not yet ask because I will not disturb the pleasant mood with poor news from the king."

"The king's message must be revealed to you privately, by his order. I do not intend to present it to your clan. That is for you to do. Whenever you want to read the king's message, I am ready to oblige."

"Later," she answered, looking away.

"We thank you for that story, Sebastien le Bret," said the old woman seated beside Lorne. Sebastien recalled that she was Una, Lorne's wife. She had helped to serve the food earlier, although he had noticed that she had eaten little herself in her efforts to make certain the others were satisfied. "Food and storytelling first, Alainna," Una went on. "It is Highland custom to extend hospitality before discussing matters of business."

Another woman, large-boned and handsome, her dark hair threaded with silver although she seemed of middle years rather than elderly, walked toward him. She handed him a small cup. "I am Morag MacLaren," she said, smiling. "And that was a fine story. This is *uisge beatha,* the water of life," she said. "A fitting drink for a bard and a warrior."

Sebastien took the cup with murmured thanks, and sipped, blinking his astonishment. The stuff was potent. He had tasted a similar Danish drink called *aqua vitae,* and had seen it take down men more accustomed to watered wine and ale. He sipped again, slowly, letting the burn of it ease down his throat.

He rose and bowed to Lorne. "My thanks for the privilege of a seat by your hearth. I look forward to a tale from a master." He walked back to his seat, but the bench where Hugo and Robert sat was crowded. He stepped into a side bay and sat on an empty bench in the shadows.

Una handed Lorne a small harp, and the bard began to play a melody that filled the room with exquisite sound. Sebastien sat in his darkened corner and sipped the *uisge beatha* again. He liked its earthy flavor, its slight sweetness, and its mellowing magic.

Alainna rose from the fireside and crossed the room toward Sebastien. She sat beside him in the shadows while they listened to the music. While Lorne played, Alainna looked up at Sebastien. "You told a fine tale, and did a fine thing."

He leaned toward her. "What was it I did?"

"You left your seat when you were done, and gave Lorne the warm hearth-side for his own again. It was a courteous gesture, and I thank you for it."

"Ah," he said lightly. "I am a courteous man."

"A virtuous knight," she agreed wryly.

Sebastien chuckled. "Your great-uncle Lorne told us the names of your kin when my men and I first came into the hall," he said, "but I confess I did not hear them all. Giric is your foster brother, I know, and Lorne and his wife, Una, are your great-uncle and great-aunt. Who are the rest? Is the woman who brought me this drink, Morag MacLaren, your mother?"

"My mother died when I was young," she said. "Morag is Lorne and Una's daughter-in-law, widowed since their son died in a battle against Clan Nechtan. She lives with us and helps Una manage our household. The two of them are adept at anything to do with hearth, pantry, chamber, and garden. I am not quite so competent as they, so I keep out of their way." She smiled. "I have other tasks to busy me, and Una and Morag leave me free to attend to them."

Then, with the careless grace that he had noticed before in her gestures, she indicated Lorne the bard. His voice was reverberant, even though he spoke quietly to Giric. "Lorne MacLaren is my great-uncle—my father's uncle. He is a trained storyteller, a *fili* taught in a Highland school. He was bard to my father and to my grandfather, his own brother. Una is his wife. Her people are Clan Donald of the Isles. You may have heard of them. Morag's husband was their only son."

"And the others?" he asked.

She leaned toward him to speak quietly and be heard above the din of voices. Sebastien, relaxing under the spell of the drink, the company, and the girl, enjoyed the closeness.

"The old man seated beside Lorne is Niall of the One Hand, a cousin," she said. "He lost his left hand in a battle with Clan Nechtan many years ago. The man with the iron-dark hair is Lulach, Lorne's brother. Their father was my grandfather, and chief of our clan before my father and myself. Lorne, Lulach, and I are descended from the first Laren of Kinlochan, an Irish prince who settled here long ago."

Sebastien nodded. He saw the resemblance in their tall, lean, strong-boned bodies, in their straight features and stubborn chins. He saw a more subtle resemblance as well, and found its traces in nearly every Highlander there. A vein of pride ran through each, hinted at by posture, gaze, and speech.

"That wide woman there," Alainna continued, "is Beitris, Lulach's wife. She and Lulach have come here to stay the winter with us, as have some of the others. The other women are Niall's wife, Mairi—who has grown far too quiet since she lost her sons last year—and those three are Isabel, Margaret, and Giorsal, all widows of men we have lost."

Sebastien nodded in grim sympathy. "And Giric Mac-Gregor?" he asked, looking at the handsome, dark-braided Highlander who laughed with Niall over some jest. "How is he related to you?"

"He is not related by blood," she said. "His father and mine were friends, and he fostered with us as a boy." She smiled as she watched him, and Sebastien felt a quick pang of jealousy. Compared to their elderly Highland kin, Alainna and Giric seemed striking in their youth and beauty, like the lord and lady of spring in the midst of winter.

"And the others?" He nodded toward several men and women, all as elderly as the girl's immediate kinfolk. "They are members of Clan Laren too?"

She nodded. "They are tenants of Kinlochan, and most are distant cousins. They came here because Giric and Niall carried the news of the Normans' arrival, and told them that a great boar would be roasted on our spit, and that all were welcome."

"Normans too?" he asked, tipping a brow.

She laughed. He liked its bright ring. "For now," she agreed. "For the boar you provided, and the story you told."

"Who are the two men leaning against the wall?" he asked. One was short and thick, the other tall and burly, with a shock of white hair. Both wore wrapped plaids over loosely shaped shirts like the other Highland men. Sebastien thought the garments looked exceptionally comfortable, although he wondered about their practicality when walking in the wind and cold.

"Cousins. Donal, the white-haired man, is supposed to keep watch on the walls tonight, but he has come in for the meal. The other is Aenghus *Manndach*, Aenghus the Stammerer. He does not say much. He herds our cattle—or did, when we had some."

"You have lost your livestock?"

She scowled. "Clan Nechtan's thievery left us but two milk cows, and three others that we slaughtered at Martinmas to store the meat for winter. We may not have as many mouths to feed in Clan Laren, but we want them well fed. I care about each and every one of my kin, as you surely do about your own."

"Understandable loyalty," he murmured.

"We have another kinswoman, Esa, who is not here," Alainna said. "She lives in the hills and refuses to come to Kinlochan for the winter, although the other elderly ones came when I invited them. We often go to see that she is well, and invite her each time, but she is stubborn, and she is sad, and clings to her loneliness. Her husband is dead, and their son as well, you see. Her husband was called Ruari *Mór*." She paused.

Sebastien glanced at her sharply. "Ruari?"

"Ruari MacWilliam," she said. "He was a brave man, a great warrior, and a tall, large man, so he was called *Mór*."

He narrowed his eyes. "When did he die?"

"Over a year ago." She glanced at him. "Have you heard of him? His reputation as a warrior was widespread, but I did not think tales of him reached the king's court."

"In a way. Part of the reason the king sent us here is to hunt a man called Ruari MacWilliam, a rebel and outlaw."

"Outlaw!" she said.

"It is said he went into exile in Ireland following the defeat of his rebel clan, but rumors report that he has returned to the Highlands to gather support for the MacWilliam cause. They claim a right to the crown—"

"I know their claim," she said. "Their bloodline goes back to the Pictish kings of Scotland. And Ruari *Mór* was a good man, and no outlaw!"

"Among his kin, that may be true. But he is a rogue who will serve as an example if he sets foot in Scotland and is caught. The rebels will be imprisoned and tried, mayhap hanged as traitors if they venture back from Ireland."

"Ruari is dead, so there is one king's order you do not have to follow," she said sourly.

"Was there proof of Ruari's death?"

"Is not a woman's broken heart proof enough? His bloodied plaid and broken sword were brought back to his widow. His son died too, that day. Esa mourns them both still. It is part of the reason she will not come out of the hills. *Ach Dhia*, you have never seen such sorrow, and there is your proof! I believe she hopes every day to join her husband and their son in death."

"I will send that word to the king, then," he said, frowning. He wondered how the king could have been misinformed about the Celtic rebel. Sebastien was glad of the news, though; without a rebel to hunt down, he could leave Kinlochan, and Scotland, that much sooner.

"Can you recall the names of my kin?" Alainna asked.

"Giric MacGregor, your foster brother," he said. "Lorne MacLaren, the bard, Una his wife. Lulach his brother, with his wife, Beitris. Morag, Isabel, Giorsal, and Margaret, the widows. Niall of the One Hand, Donal the guard, Aenghus the Stammerer, and one not here—Esa of the far hills, widow of a champion called Ruari *Mór*. And seven others, tenants and cousins whom you have not named to me."

Alainna nodded. "You learn quickly. You have a bard's memory, I think." Her eyes sparkled.

"And one more," he continued, "the *toiseach* and Maiden of Kinlochan, with hair the color of new bronze and eyes the color of the sea along the coast of Brittany." His heart gave a slow, bold bound as he spoke.

"Ach." A tiny smile touched her lips. "I am thinking a seat by the fireside has turned you into a poet after all, Sebastien le Bret."

"Or your *uisge beatha* has," he said, and sipped it.

"Now that may be." She laughed.

"How many more are there in Clan Laren?"

"The old ones," she said, "are all of my people."

He stared at her, sure he had misheard. "These few? Not a child or a young person among them?"

"Not a one. We have had years of war, of sickness and lack. Many have died, many have moved on to live in other parts of the Highlands, with other kin. The old ones and myself are all that are left of Clan Laren."

He frowned. "You have many men at your beck and call now, should you need them."

She glanced at him. "So says the king?"

"So say I," he answered.

She turned her graceful profile to him. "Now name your men to me. Robert de Kerec and Hugo de Valognes I know. They seem to be good friends to you."

"Near as close as brothers, if I had any," he said.

"Who are the others? Bretons all?"

"Some Norman English, some Norman French, some Lowland Scots. Etienne de Barre, Richard de Wicke, Walter of Coldstream, William FitzHugh. . . ." He said their names and told her a little about each man, some of them comrades to him, many still strangers.

He noticed as he spoke that the knights had been drawn into lively conversations with some of the Highlanders, while Giric and Lorne, who spoke both Gaelic and English, helped them to understand one another.

"If only these few remain, your clan has lost much to this feud," he remarked.

"Too many. Sons and brothers and fathers killed in battle, daughters lost to illness or childbirth, or who have left to remarry. Children dead from sickness, or taken away by mothers seeking better lives." She glanced down. "I lost my two brothers two years ago, and my father six months ago."

In the angle of her bowed head, Sebastien glimpsed the vulnerability she tried to hide. He felt an urge to touch her shoulder to offer comfort. "I am sorry," he murmured.

She stared toward the hearth. "I am the last of the chief's blood." He saw tears shine in her eyes. She blinked them away. "I am the youngest of the bloodline of the original father of Clan Laren, the father of the Stone Maiden."

"The Stone Maiden?"

"Tomorrow you will meet her. Tonight there have been enough sad stories." She smiled, a wistful curve. "I want to ask you to read the king's letter."

"Certes, but not here. We need a more private place."

"Lorne is about to begin a story. No one will notice if we leave." She stood, and Sebastien did too.

"I was going to ask you to read the letter tomorrow," she said, looking up at him in the shadows. "I wanted one more night of peace, one more night as the leader of my clan before our future is taken from us."

He watched her. "What changed your mind?"

"Your eyes," she said. "It was the kindness in your eyes. It made me feel as if I could bear hearing the king's message tonight, after all. And I will have to find the courage to face it sooner or later. Let us go outside and talk." She gave him a rueful smile and turned toward the doorway, picking up a pair of shoes from the floor as she left.

A large blue-gray deerhound rose from a spot near the fire and padded after her. Silhouetted in the doorway, she touched the tall dog's head and stepped outside.

Sebastien admired her exit, which had the grace and dignity of a queen out of legend. Then he fetched his cloak, and followed quietly through the shadows.

Chapter Seven

Cold night air frosted Alainna's breath as she crossed the yard with Finan beside her, drawing her plaid over her head and shoulders against the chill. Hearing the knight's steps behind her, she stole a glance at Sebastien le Bret.

He had picked up his dark blue cloak as they left the hall, and its folds swirled around his legs as he walked beside her. He matched the darkness somehow, his cloak like midnight, his hair gleaming in the starlight. That stirred the memory of her magical dream of the faery warrior, and she shivered, then rushed ahead.

She walked toward the timber palisade that surrounded the bailey. An earthen incline ringed the inner wall, forming a grass-covered wallwalk. She climbed the slope to its flat top to peer over the spiked ends of the palisade.

Finan stood beside her, a simple, devoted soul, a friend. She rested her hand on his tufted head and looked out over the wall. The loch gleamed dark and sparkling beneath the shadowed mountains. Overhead, the moon shone, a slim curve in a lavender sky.

" 'Tis not yet dark, though 'tis late." Sebastien joined her beside the palisade. Although she had to lift on her toes to see a wide view, he simply gazed out.

"The light will stay like this for hours, not fully dark, especially in the spring and summer months."

" 'Tis a peaceful sight."

"But it is not a peaceful land." She turned to him. "Have you come to help us regain peace? Or to bring more strife?"

"I am here as your champion, not as your conqueror."

"You are not the champion I wanted."

"I know," he said quietly. He reached into the leather pouch on his belt and removed a folded parchment, which he offered to her. "The king's letter."

"Be his voice as well as his sword arm. I cannot read."

"Then break the seal yourself, for the king ordered it delivered to you alone."

She took the parchment and slipped a finger between the two dangling strings fused by the seal. Opening the page, she saw neat writing, indecipherable to her. She handed it back to him.

"Can you understand Latin, when spoken?" he asked.

"I can," she said. "Read." Although she stared calmly at the loch and the sky, she clenched her hands in front of her. She guessed what he might say, and dreaded hearing it.

" 'William, by God's grace king of Scotland,' " he read in Latin, " 'to Lady Alainna of Kinlochan, greetings.' "

His Latin was that of a monk, she thought as he continued, fluid and precise, an art in itself. She closed her eyes and listened. He had the voice of a bard, clear and rich, soothing, although the words he spoke sundered.

" 'In the matter of the inheritance of Kinlochan and the welfare of its heiress and subtenants,' " he read, " 'be it known to all our subjects that we declare, as is our right, that the said property of Kinlochan, fortress and environs, be given into the care and service of Sir Sebastien le Bret as baron and—' "

Alainna sucked in a breath. "So it is you!"

"Listen to the rest," he said brusquely.

"Say it out plainly, then, instead of in clerkish Latin."

He held out the parchment to her. "Very well. You may want to study this later, or have someone do that for you."

"None of us can read but the priest. Go on."

He drew in a long breath. "Alainna of Kinlochan is to be given in marriage to Sir Sebastien le Bret. There is to be a nuptial contract between them, according to the king's wishes as stated in this writ." He paused and glanced at her.

"Marriage," she repeated softly.

"Aye," he answered. She heard gentleness in his voice. It did not matter if he were kind or cruel, she told herself. He was not the one her clan needed. He was a Norman. The king had not considered her clan's request.

She stared at the loch, her head balanced high on her neck. Her heart beat hard, her limbs shook, her thoughts whirled. The hope and promise of a Celtic warrior to defend her clan and continue their bloodline had been snatched away.

"You told me that you would not come to the Highlands," she said in a wooden tone. "You said that you had no interest in this land, or in a Scottish wife."

He watched her steadily. "Neither of us has a choice in this."

"You do."

"I am obligated by the pledge of my signed contract of knight service to the king. And I owe a debt of gratitude to William of Scotland. To repay that faith, I accepted the responsibility, and the grant."

"And the wife," she snapped.

"And you," he agreed.

She tipped her head downward. "Go on. Tell me what more is in the writ."

"I have been instructed to raise a stone castle here."

"A castle!" she burst out. Her hands trembled so much that she joined them into a fisted ball.

"We can discuss the details later, when you feel calmer."

"I am as calm as stone," she said curtly. "What else does the king declare?"

"Minor issues of land measurement, tenants, knight service as my relief fee for the land, and so on. And he directed me to meet with Cormac MacNechtan to judge the man's loyalty to the crown."

"Cormac is a thief and a liar and a murderer. Take that word to the king."

"I am to determine if he has leanings toward rebellion. The king is concerned about this feud between your clans. MacNechtan petitioned the king with a promise of support and a pledge of loyalty if he might have your hand and your property. King William is distrustful of it, as am I."

"At last, a matter we can agree on."

"If he is determined to be disloyal, he is to be stopped by force of arms. That should suit you, at least."

"It does," she said. Finan nosed under her hand, standing between her and the knight. "Tell me," she said. "How can the king give you this property when I paid the relief fee for it? Was the stone cross not enough? He accepted the token. It was all I had to give. I thought the inheritance was secure."

"He could have granted me the land without the marriage," Sebastien said. "He honors the payment of your token by providing you a husband and a protector, as you require."

"This is not what I require!"

"Your people need protection that you cannot provide," he said, a little sharply. "Is it so?"

She looked down and nodded. "It is so."

"The king is your guardian, since you are an unmarried heiress." He paused, and again she nodded, knowing that what he said was true. "The king owns Scottish land, not the people, no matter their rank. He portions it out as he sees fit. Holdings are traditionally passed down in families, but in this case, the king must decide who will best care for the demesne."

"In the crown's interest," she amended.

He inclined his head. "That may be. But all of this is properly done by law and by obligation. There is naught you can do—naught I can do—but comply."

She closed her eyes, overwhelmed by all that he had told her. She drew a deep breath, struggling to maintain her composure, to master her temper and her fears.

"I expect that you will settle the land with Norman knights, and toss Clan Laren out into the cold. I have heard that has been done by other Normans. Your reputation is not the best."

"My own reputation is impeccable, I believe," he said. "I have no plans to toss anyone out into the cold." Again that calm tone. If he had been sharp with her, if he had displayed his greed, she would have a reason to be angry with him. She wanted desperately to be furious with him, and with the king—and most of all with herself for appealing to the king for royal mercy.

She caught back a sob as despair struck her, swift and keen. Fighting tears, she stood still and silent. The knight watched her, leaning a shoulder against the rampart, his cloak billowing in the breeze.

"I trusted the king to aid a Celtic clan."

"He must see to the welfare of Scotland above all." Terse words, but not unkindly said. "Surely you realized that when you came to him for help."

She shook her head as she stared at the mountains. "I thought only of my people," she said. "I was a fool to think no further. I am no leader to them, to bring this upon them."

For a moment, she felt as if she could not breathe, as if her heart grew impossibly heavy within her. She stood motionless, her face and hands chilled from the wind. Strands of her hair slipped free from the confines of the plaid around her shoulders and looped out in the breeze.

Across the loch beneath the violet sky, the Stone Maiden stood pale and eternal, a monument to strength and tragedy. The Maiden had given hope and beneficence to her clan. Now all seemed finally, utterly lost.

Finan nuzzled at her hand. She lifted it away, not wanting to touch or be touched. Comfort could break her. She needed to stay strong. She felt dull and cold within, as if she too were formed of granite, the fire of her anger smothered by sadness.

"Lady Alainna," the knight said. He reached out a hand and cupped her shoulder. "I know this news is not welcome to you. There are other issues to discuss, but—"

She stepped away from his warm touch. "I cannot listen to any more from you just now," she said. If he spoke again in that low, mellifluous bard's voice, if he touched her—*dear God,* if he touched her, she would crack open like a flawed stone.

Stifling a cry, she ran past him and headed down the earthen slope with the dog behind her. She needed to go where she could be alone, where she could find solace. Reaching the gate, she waited impatiently while Donal, who had returned to his post, opened the gate after Alainna told him that she wanted to visit the Maiden for a special blessing, promising to return shortly.

Donal slid the heavy beam aside in its iron brackets. She stepped through the gateway with Finan beside her, and took the path that led around the loch toward the Stone Maiden.

*   *   *

Sebastien sighed, watching. The girl should not run about the hills at night unescorted, prey for wolves and MacNechtans. He strode forward, amazed that her elder kinsman let her go. He touched a hand to the hilt of the dagger sheathed in his belt, deciding it would have to be enough to ward off trouble if any were met. Then he walked quickly toward the gate, glancing around the starlit yard as he went.

The bailey was spacious, its wide circular shape defined by the timber palisade, its center dominated by a high wooden tower. Smaller buildings huddled against the inner walls: sheds, stables, kitchen and brewhouse, one or two other buildings whose function he could not identify. Only the kitchen, built of stone where the others were of timber or wattle and daub, glowed with a lighted hearth. A woman's shadow crossed the open doorway as she tended to some chores. Elsewhere, a cow lowed from a pen in the corner, along with quiet snorts from the horses in the stables.

The tower soared above all, three stories high on stout timber posts. A few narrow windows cut in the wooden walls blinked like sleepy golden eyes. Music and laughter floated out from the second story, where the long hall was located. Nearly everyone present at Kinlochan would be inside, either in the main hall above the storage chambers, or in the sleeping chambers on the third and uppermost floor.

"And your business, Norman?" the guard at the gate asked.

"To protect your clan chief," he answered bluntly. "Do you want to follow her yourself, or would you rather I do it?"

"Your legs are younger than mine. You go. I will shout a warning if any demons be about. But the Stone Maiden protects our own Maiden of Kinlochan."

Sebastien cast him a puzzled look at the odd remark, and stepped through the gate. The air outside was cool and unconfined and moist from the loch. Overhead, the night sky deepened to indigo.

He narrowed his eyes and scanned the countryside, seeking a flitting shadow or the bark of the deerhound. Then he glimpsed the girl and her dog running through the high grass, already on the opposite shore of the loch.

He headed cautiously down the rocky slope, through the shadows of the unfamiliar landscape. Once on level turf, he struck out with a long, sure stride.

Alainna ran toward the tall stone that jutted into the sky on a bank of the loch. She disappeared into its shadow.

Sebastien slowed his step. If she needed time to herself, he did not want to disturb her. But he would not leave her alone out here, hound or none.

He could not lag discreetly, for the dog barked and ran toward him, panting in a friendly manner, already familiar with him. He nosed at Sebastien and then shoved his huge head under the man's outstretched hand.

"Ho, you ugly brute," Sebastien murmured affectionately. "Ready to protect your mistress, eh? I am no threat to her, though she thinks I am. Good lad." He strode ahead, the dog loping beside him.

The stone loomed large as he came closer, a tall pillar of granite, like a serene giantess overlooking the loch. He glanced up as he walked. Even in the darkness he could see the graceful linear carvings that marked the front and back surfaces.

Alainna stepped out of the shadow of the stone like a wraith. The dog ran toward her, circled beside her, then ran back toward Sebastien, covering the lessening distance between them, back and forth.

"Finan," she said. "Here." The dog circled toward her and ran back to Sebastien. "Finan!"

Sebastien reached out to ruffle the dog's head. Finan licked his hand and ran back toward Alainna, accepted a pat from her, and ran back again, his tail floppy and eager.

Alainna walked toward them. "I do not understand it," she said. "He treats you as if you were one of my own kinsmen, though he hardly knows you. Finan, here!"

The dog turned toward her, tongue lolling, and turned back to Sebastien for another vigorous rub on his head. "He did growl quite a bit when my men and I first came to Kinlochan," Sebastien said. "He seems used to my presence now."

"He has seen Cormac MacNechtan many times, but he acts as if Cormac is the devil's spawn each time."

"Ah, your Finan is a good judge of men, then."

"Not always," she observed. "He would defend me to the death if I needed it, but most of the time he seems to have very little wit. Finan *Mór*! Here!"

Sebastien urged the dog back toward her. "He's confused," he said. "He wonders why we wander about in the dark when we could be inside"—he bent as the dog returned to him, and rubbed his head—"lying beside a great fire, sleeping while the humans listen to stories, eh, my lad. There you go, back to your lady."

Alainna patted the dog's head. Sebastien came close. "He is devoted to you, that hound," he said mildly. "See how he looks at you, so eager to please. He will do whatever you want of him. 'Tis a gift to inspire such devotion in a creature."

"*Ach,* there is nothing to it. A pat on the head makes him silly with delight." She stroked the dog's head and glanced at Sebastien. "You are among the few who know Finan's secret now."

He tilted his head. "Secret?"

"Finan *Mór* is more than a fierce hunting hound," she said. "He is a fool for cuddling."

"Ah." Sebastien laughed. Alainna smiled. His heart gave an odd lurch. "The fiercest creatures might be rendered gentle by the hand of such a lady," he murmured.

She turned away without answer and went to the pillar stone. Finan bounded beside her, then looped back toward Sebastien.

Sebastien glanced up at the stone, examining it in the shadows. It stood nearly twice as tall as he was and twice as wide, and was covered, front and back, with strangely beautiful incised designs.

"We have standing stones in Brittany," he said. "Out in fields like this, or beside streams. Thousands of them, old as the hills. Some are immense, and some have symbols carved on them, and some have stories connected to them of sacrifice, or magic, or miracles."

She said nothing, but he sensed that she listened closely.

"The stones were put there by ancient Bretons," he said.

"A Celtic people, they were. Our language is not unlike yours."

"Are you descended from a Celtic bloodline?" she asked.

He shrugged. "It could be. Tell me about this stone."

She flattened her palm against the granite. "This is our Stone Maiden, who has watched over Clan Laren for generations. The Maiden was a daughter of Clan Laren, long ago." She drew her hand over the stone as if she soothed a friend. "But her magic, some say, endures no more. It may be that she is . . . weary. She has been trapped inside this stone for a very long time."

Sebastien watched her, and idly scratched the dog's head. "I would like to hear her story."

"I may tell you someday. If you are still here."

"I will be here for a while, at least." He paused as a thin, eerie, nearly human cry rose out in the darkness somewhere and faded. The sound sent chills up his spine. "What was that?"

"A wildcat," she said. "They are about at night here, especially up in the hills. As are wolves. And boars, as we know quite well."

"In winter such animals are hungrier and even more fierce. Best that you are never out here alone, my lady."

"I am protected here beside the Maiden," she said simply, placing a hand on the stone. "I come here often by myself to make offerings on behalf of my clan. I have always been safe."

"I admire your faith in tradition, but a little caution on your part would ease my mind."

"Why should I bother to ease your mind?" she asked crisply.

"You are to be my wife," he pointed out. "Lady Alainna, I know that the news I brought you is not easy to bear. The king's orders were not welcome to me, either."

She said nothing, silhouetted in the dark beside the stone.

"I told you in Dunfermline that I have other plans. They still stand. I must return to Brittany to attend to . . . some important matters. Personal matters."

She nodded again, silent. He frowned. The passion that seemed so strong in her was diminished. He did not want to be responsible for any subduing of her spirit, but feared he was.

The dog nudged against her and sat on his haunches, watching her with pure devotion. She touched his head, bending, the rippled fall of her hair a shining cloak.

"What was it you wanted, if you did not want to marry a Scottish wife for a Scottish grant?" she asked.

"I have always intended to settle in Brittany when my knight service is done. I have . . . strong ties there. The longer I stay in Scotland, the more I risk to lose in Brittany."

"Then leave," she said simply.

"I gave my pledge to the king. This arrangement is for your benefit as well. You need our protection here."

"I need no one's protection."

"Your clan does," he reminded her. "And I think you would do anything for your clan."

She lifted her head. "I would."

"Even marry a Norman."

"I will not marry a Norman if it means harm to my clan, or the loss of our lands."

"I am not the Celtic champion you wanted, but there is no other available to you, by king's order."

She patted the dog and said nothing.

"My lady," he said, "we are both caught in this predicament. If we dispute it or refuse, the king will grant the land to someone else entirely. That man might be inclined to toss elders out into the cold and mistreat you, where I am not so inclined. We both have no choice but to accept, and to tolerate the situation."

"You are asking for peace between us."

"Peace, or a truce."

"Tell me this, Sebastien le Bret." He liked his name on her lips, like the susurration of wind over water. "Will you take my clan's name for your own?"

He paused. "I cannot do that." He would say only that. Kinship and home were natural rights in her world. How could she understand how much his simple, self-created name meant to him?

"Will you allow our children to bear the name of MacLaren, rather than Le Bret?"

He sighed, thinking of Conan, and hardly daring to think of other children in the shadowed future. "I cannot agree to that either, my lady."

"Then," she said, "we will have no peace between us. And I do not know how we can have a marriage." She stepped away, turning past the stone to disappear into its shadow. Finan followed her.

Chapter Eight

Sebastien walked around the stone, expecting to find Alainna fled into the darkness, obliging him to lope off in pursuit. But she stood so close in the stone's shadow that he nearly bumped into her.

"Listen to me," he said firmly. "I am not your enemy. I am not your conqueror. I do not wish to bring harm to your people. But these are now my lands by king's decree, and I honor my obligations, whatever they are."

"And I am one of them now," she murmured.

"You are," he agreed.

She was silent. A turn of her head revealed the sheen of tears in her eyes. He knew what the king's message, and the king's grant to him, had done to her. He felt responsible for her distress.

"I would rather go into a convent and give my inherited rights to the Church than give them to a Norman," she said after a moment. She stood as firm as her pillared sister.

"That can be arranged, if that is what you truly wish." He said it harshly, feeling his temper stoke, as if she had added kindling to the banked fire in him.

"Or," she said, "I can refuse to give up Kinlochan or myself to your . . . ownership."

"You could, but to go against royal orders is treason."

"There are Celtic rebels in the Highlands who care nothing for treason. They do not even acknowledge William as the rightful king of Scotland, for they claim he is not descended of the ancient royal line. I can go to them and plead for help."

"Do you know where to find these Celts?"

"I can find people who might know."

"Be careful what you say to me," he said abruptly. "I am here to hunt rebels, as much as to accomplish other things."

"If I found them, they would not fight MacNechtans for us, but they would fight on our behalf against the crown."

"Alainna," he said, "do not be foolish."

"I am never foolish!" she snapped. "You do not know me."

"Somehow," he said slowly, "I feel as if I do."

Her glance flickered away. "What do you mean?"

He turned to face her. "I know that you are proud and stubborn. I know you would do anything to save your clan and your heritage."

"Anyone knows that of me," she said. "I do not hide that."

"And I know," he said, leaning toward her, "that you will not flee to a convent and abandon your kin. Nor will you join rebels, for that would be unsafe for your clan. I know"—he leaned closer still, his voice dropping to a murmur—"that you are not only proud, but passionate and loyal." He gazed at her. "It shines in you like a light."

She kept her head high and remained silent. He could hear the soft sound of her breathing. He let his gaze travel the graceful length of her throat to where her breasts rose and fell beneath her gown.

By God she was beautiful. The pride and fierceness in her would challenge a man, heart, mind, and soul. He had always liked a challenge, a risk.

He leaned a shoulder against the stone, enveloped in shadows as he looked at her thoughtfully. "You are scared, deep within," he murmured. "I saw pride and fear in your eyes weeks ago, when you stood in the royal hall. I see that in you now."

"You do not." She slid him a quick, vulnerable glance.

"I do. 'Tis here, in this lifted chin." He touched her jaw gently. Her skin felt silken and delicate.

She drew in her breath as he glided his hand to her shoulder, as his fingers skimmed her spine, sank to her waist, lifted away. "And here, in these shoulders and this straight back," he went on. "Capable, proud girl, they tell me, one who cares deeply, works hard, and never complains." She was lean and strong, her firm curves so evident beneath the plain gown and gathered plaid that his own body surged, instinctually tempted.

She did not protest his touch, although her eyes closed briefly. He lowered his hand. She glanced at him, sidelong and wary. The dog cocked his head and watched them curiously.

Her profile was clean and pure, her silence eloquent. She would not rail at him in temper, he thought; that initial storm had passed. But he was certain she saw peace as yielding, and would not grant it to him.

"I will not be charmed into making peace with you, either to make your tasks here easier—or more pleasant," she said.

"You are very much like your Stone Maiden, I think." He touched the cool, smooth granite. "Strong and proud. But lonely and unprotected, even while you watch over your people."

She angled her head down as if to hide her thoughts. "What does it matter?"

"It matters," he said softly. He was not certain why, but he knew that it did, very much.

She shook her head. "You have what you came to Scotland for. Chartered land, a title, a bride—" She caught her breath.

"The lady asked for a champion." He shrugged. "I am here."

"So you came here only out of some virtuous chivalric duty."

"You do not know me," he countered. "You do not know what gives me purpose."

"I know you at least as well as you know me."

He looked down at her, lifted a brow skeptically, and waited.

She tilted her head to study him. "Pride," she said. "Strength. And secrets—indeed, many of those."

He straightened away from the stone. "Most men have pride, strength, and secrets. And many women too—yourself included."

"I do not keep nearly the secrets you do," she said. "I have scarcely any."

"More than you will admit," he murmured.

She frowned. "I know that you protect others. It is your task in life. But I think you protect yourself too, very carefully." She rested a hand on his arm, which he had folded, with the other, over his chest. "Here, you hide your heart," she said.

She reached up and touched his jaw, which he had set tight. "Here is the pride, and the effort to keep secrets," she said. Her fingers, feather light, traced up the left side of his face. "And here are the secrets themselves." She touched her fingertip to the scar that seamed the corner of his brow.

Her touch was melting gentle. He leaned away, though his body tightened, his heart pounded. She lowered her hand and the link was gone, like a bird flown.

"Pride, and loneliness, too," she said. "You are a solitary soul, the kind that seeks its home."

He narrowed his eyes in the darkness, and was silent.

She glanced at the pillar. "I am weary, and I a stranger," she murmured in Gaelic. "Lead me to the land of angels."

"What was that?" he asked, intrigued and puzzled.

"A charm, an invocation for aid. An ancient Gaelic prayer," she explained.

> *I am weary, and I a stranger,*
> *Lead me to the land of angels.*
> *Be my eyes in time of darkness,*
> *Be my shield against hosts of faery,*
> *Be my wings till I find my home.*

"That is beautiful," he said, stunned by her poignant words.

"We have many such charms and prayers. I often come here to say them to this stone and ask for protection from the soul who was the maiden. We revere her as a kind of local saint here."

He nodded. "There is a place in Brittany, near the monastery where I was raised, where seven stones are thought to house the spirits of seven brothers who all became saints."

She tilted her head. "You were raised in a monastery?"

"Until I was eleven, when I was taken to England and became a page, and eventually a knight. You sound surprised."

"I thought you became a knight as the son of some fine French lord. You must be the youngest, then. How is it that you are not a religious, if your parents gave you to the church?"

"I was a foundling," he said, more abruptly than he meant to do. "The monks took me in."

"You do not know your parents?"

He shrugged. "I learned something about them eventually. But I sought my own way early in the world."

"Ah, that is what I saw in your eyes," she said softly.

"What?" he asked warily.

"You have the look of a wandering soul," she said. "A soul seeking a home."

He watched her silently, too proud to turn his gaze from hers or to speak in his defense. To do either would be to admit that she was right, that his soul yearned desperately. But that part of him was core, and precious, and could not be shared. To admit that would be to show a weakness, a wound. No one had ever seen into him so deeply, so easily.

He inclined his head. "I think," he drawled, "that I have been reprimanded for my bold claim to know the lady."

"You were honest with me, and I with you. We may be alike in some ways, I think."

"In pride only. But if we understand that in each other, we can declare peace between us."

"We might understand each other better than most strangers," she said. "But we are still strangers."

"Not for long, by order of the king."

She opened her mouth to reply, then suddenly turned and walked toward the path that rounded the loch and led back to Kinlochan. The dog bounded along ahead of her.

Sebastien watched them go, while darkness deepened around him. He glanced up at the stone's silhouette, and traced his fingertips along the lines carved in the cold, smooth surface.

" 'I am weary, and I a stranger,' " he mused. " 'Lead me to the land of angels.' " The words haunted him as he turned and walked back to the fortress.

Kinlochan's gate stood open. Donal rumbled a greeting when Sebastien strode through and gave him a courteous nod. Ahead, Alainna and the dog crossed the bailey together, her stride purposeful.

He debated whether he should follow her once again.

She went toward one of the small wooden buildings that nestled against the inner protecting wall. After she entered and closed the door, Sebastien saw candlelight flare and outline the rim of the small, shuttered window.

"Let her go," a voice said. He turned, and looked down to see Alainna's great-aunt Una standing beside him. He had not heard her approach. "She needs to work out her sadness and confusion. She can do that in there."

"What place is that? A chapel?" He spoke in Gaelic, as she had.

"Her workshop," Una said.

Sebastien frowned uncertainly. No woman he knew had a workshop, unless it was a bakehouse or a brewhouse, or a place where cloth and garments were made.

"She will lose some of her anguish in her work," Una murmured. She glanced up at him. "Sebastien *Bàn*—I call you that for your fair hair," she added, "you are a golden hero to all of us for saving our girl from the boar, but you have a dark side too. You bear a message that has brought our girl sorrow."

"A message from the king," he said.

"Alainna looks as if a candle flame has been blown out in her heart. And yours was the breath that did it, I think."

Sebastien sighed. "I did not upset the lady by choice. The king's message was not to her liking."

"Did our king give you these lands, and Alainna to wed?"

"He did," he answered.

"Ah." She nodded over and over, and Sebastien realized that he watched a tremor in her small, white-haired head. Finally she looked up at him. "I hoped you were sent here as a champion, and I think you will answer our prayers. But I want you to make a promise to me."

"Whatever you wish, Dame Una," he said, smiling kindly.

"Do not break our girl's heart."

"Upon my honor, I will not," he murmured.

She watched him. "Honor is a tender thing, Sebastien *Bàn*," she said, and turned away.

Chapter Nine

The bailey was quiet in the silvered dawn as Sebastien crossed the yard. He glanced up, and saw Alainna leaning in the doorway of a long, thatched-roof building tucked against the palisade wall, Finan at her side. He saw that it was the same building she had entered on the previous night.

She was lovely in the dawn, her skin pale, her braids red-gold ropes, her tunic plain dove gray. He wondered why she was up and about before the day had even bloomed.

"God's goodness to you," she murmured in Gaelic.

"And his blessings to you," he replied politely as he came near. Finan wagged his tail and lifted his head until Sebastien leaned down to caress his tufted brow and bearded muzzle.

"It is early," Alainna said. "The others are still abed."

He shrugged. "I am often up early. I like this part of the day. I thought to walk out to look at your Stone Maiden again. It is peaceful there." He spoke in English, and she nodded.

"Peaceful it is, unless MacNechtans are about."

"I can protect myself."

"Surely you do not intend to go out on patrol so early, and alone."

"Not yet. I have long kept the habit of practicing sword skills early in the day. I think I may do that this morning. Later your foster brother has agreed to ride out with me and some of my men to look at the property." He ruffled the dog's head and shoulders. Finan rumbled his pleasure. Sebastien glanced at Alainna. "You are awake early, too," he remarked.

"I often begin my work before the others are about."

He looked at her curiously. "Your work?"

"My stonework."

He blinked in surprise. "Stone?" He thought she would answer baking or cooking, for her hands and clothing were dusted with a pale powder that he had assumed was milled grain.

"Stonecarving. This was my cousin Malcolm's workshop. 'Tis mine now."

Intrigued, he peered past her shoulder. "May I see?"

She stepped back. He ducked his head to clear the lintel post and entered. The room was long, low-ceilinged, and cluttered, crowded with benches and stones. A square window in the front wall provided some light, but was partly shuttered against the chill. An iron brazier at the center of the room created a circle of heat. Sebastien saw the cool vapor of his breath in the dimness as Alainna closed the door.

A thick layer of stone chips covered the floor, crunching beneath his boots as he stepped forward. Benches held stones of various sizes and colors, and wall shelves were filled with tools, candles, and other items. A long table against one wall supported several flat, carved stones. The air seemed permeated with the vaguely earthy smell of stone, and a sense of coolness.

He noticed that the whitewashed walls were covered with drawings, some on cloths tacked up with nails, some drawn directly on the walls. In a far corner, a large slab of pinkish stone rested like a thick tabletop on stout trestles.

Finan padded toward the brazier and lay down on a thick pallet there, resting his great head on his crossed paws. He watched the humans languidly before drifting back to sleep.

Sebastien turned. "All this is your work?" he asked.

"It is mine." Alainna walked toward a bench that held a stone propped at an angle. Tools tumbled alongside as if recently laid down. A small table supported an iron bracket holding two flaming candles.

"You never told me that you were a stonemason, even at the abbey when we looked at your cousin's work."

"You did not ask."

He half smiled and shrugged to admit her logic. "I knew

you were an *imagier*, but I never thought you might be a stonecarver. 'Tis not a usual occupation for a woman."

"My cousin traveled to many cities to do stonemasonry. He told me that women are often artisans and artists alongside their husbands and brothers, trained by them and working with them in painting, book crafting, and sculpture as well. Women are not limited by their delicate natures to embroidery, sirrah, as some knights-errant might think."

"I did not think that. And I have seen female artisans and merchants in cities. Did you learn the craft from your cousin?"

She nodded. "Malcolm spent several months each year at Kinlochan with his kinsmen, since masons do little work in the winter. He traveled a great deal, but when he stayed here, he did work for the local parish churches—crosses, corbels and tympana, tombstones. He set up this workshop, and tried to do carvings here as much as possible, except when he had to work *in situ*." She shrugged. "I had a quick eye and a quick hand, and he needed an assistant. So he taught me the basics of the craft. I am not a highly skilled carver, as he was."

Sebastien glanced at some of the stones. "I think you have skill enough for any stonecarver, male or female," he said. "These show a fine strong hand for design and technique."

"My thanks," she said.

He strolled around the room, looking at the carved and half-carved stones, at iron chisels, wooden mallets, measuring devices, and other tools he did not recognize. He lifted a tool that looked like a small iron poker, and hefted its weight.

"That is a point, or a punch" she said. "It is used to clear chunks of stone away, when driven with the mallet."

He put it down, and shook his head a little in bemusement. "I confess that I am still amazed that a woman does such work."

She came closer. " 'Tis not difficult. The tools require a careful hand more than brute strength, and the softer types of stone are no harder to carve than wood."

"I see." He glanced around. "How do you manage to move the stones? Some of these are very large blocks."

"I am not helpless," she said.

He tilted a brow at her. "I do not doubt that."

"A stone of any size can be moved with levers and rollers. If a stone is small enough to lift, I either do it myself, or find someone to help me. I am stronger than I look."

His gaze skimmed her body appreciatively. This time he took note of the straight, square set of her shoulders, the balanced grace of her slim body, her long, nimble hands, the firm shape of her arms beneath her gown. She undoubtedly had some strength, and he was sure she would excel at work requiring dexterity. He knew she had determination enough for any task.

He wandered around the room, looking at the stone carvings. Alainna watched in silence. He paused by the long table. The stones arranged there varied from the size of bread loaves to several much larger. All were carved in raised relief in designs that showed the same firm hand, skilled at fine detail.

"This is excellent work," he said. The smaller stones were shaped like crosses and carved with linear, complex relief designs in the Celtic manner. He touched one of the crosses. "You gave a piece like this to King William. That was your work, then, although you did not claim so at the time."

"It was. Those I am making for our parish church. Father Padruig wants a set to mark the stations of the cross."

He nodded. Nailed to the wall in front of him was the cloth that he recognized from the abbey church, which held a few sketches and the rubbed impression he had made of her cousin's mason's mark. He noticed, too, a small drawing of a standing knight in chain mail. The figure's sword looked very much like his own. He made no comment, nor did she, although he noticed a rising blush in her cheeks while he examined it.

Most of the large rectangular stones laid side by side on the long table were carefully finished. The stones were similar in their soft gray color, which had a delicate silvery sheen, and were alike in design and size, as long as a man's arm and half that across, each a handspan in depth, clearly meant to be a set.

"What kind of stone is this?" he asked, touching one of them. It felt cool beneath his fingers.

"Gray limestone," she answered. "It is quarried a little south of here. My father had these brought here a year ago, cut and dressed with the axe by the quarrymen, after I told him that I wanted to make a series of stone pictures. There are twenty blocks of the same size. I have finished seven. But I do not think twenty blocks will be enough for what I want to do."

"What is it you want to do?" He studied a finished stone, then another as he moved the length of the table.

"I mean to record the history of Clan Laren in pictures."

He glanced at her, stunned by her ambition. Then he looked more carefully at the stones. Each completed slab featured carved border designs of interwoven vines and knots framing various interior images. He had seen similar plaited and interlaced designs in manuscripts, and in the carvings in Scottish churches. The interwoven designs Alainna had made were carefully done, rhythmic and graceful.

The overall style had a simplicity of form and design that suited the gray stone. The images portrayed human figures, animals, birds, boats, and weapons. He saw scenes of men in boats, men hunting, a woman fighting a wolf, several figures on horseback, and a scene of a mermaid on a rock.

"These are beautiful," he commented.

Alainna walked over to stand near him. "Each one tells a story from my clan. This one shows the first Labhrainn who left Ireland with his brothers and came to Scotland. He fell in love with a mermaid who lived in a loch." She pointed to the image of the mermaid seated on a rock, holding a mirror in one hand and a comb in the other.

He nodded. "And this?" He pointed to the scene of the woman facing the wolf. She clutched a knife in one hand, and in her other arm carried a swaddled child.

"Mairead the Brave, wife of Niall, son of Conall, who killed a wolf to protect her child."

"Ah. The women of your clan have courage all."

"We do what we must to protect our own."

Sebastien glanced at her. A pink blush stained her creamy cheeks. She stood so close, looking at the stones with him, that her shoulder brushed his arm. He angled toward her.

"I think," he murmured, "that Alainna, daughter of Laren, has inherited the courage of Mairead the Brave, wife of Niall. You defend your clan with all the fierceness of a warrior . . . or a mother." He reached out on impulse to lift away the shining strands of hair that had fallen over her brow. "God help any who threaten your clan."

She looked directly into his eyes. "Then God help you."

Sebastien sighed. "Tell me about the other stones," he said. She clearly did not want a truce with him. He would have to discover moments of peace with her along the way, or find himself striking head to head with her each time they were together.

She complied, explaining the next picture, and the next. He was entranced by the images and stories, and by the low-pitched murmur of her voice. His hand grazed hers as they touched a stone together, his large and well-knuckled, hers smooth, the fingers long and tapered.

She folded her fingers quickly, but not before he saw calluses and small healing cuts. The gesture revealed a tender vulnerability beneath her outward show of prideful strength.

"The stones tell my clan's history through generations, or they will when I finish them."

"You are fortunate to have such a rich heritage."

"Everyone has a heritage."

"Not everyone," he murmured, brushing his fingers over stone.

She did not ask, nor did he offer. "I fear our tales will be lost forever." She lifted her chin. "I mean to save our heritage by carving it in these tablets."

He was astonished by the will and determination she possessed. He had seen pride in many guises, but never entwined so exquisitely with honorable intent.

"You are a storyteller, like Lorne."

She shook her head. "I am . . . a guardian. A preserver. Lorne keeps hundreds of tales that go back a thousand years, into the mists of time. He is a strand in the long rope of storytelling that binds the generations to their Celtic culture, and he can spin that magic over and over. I save the stories of our clan. When they are set in stone, my task will be done."

"Others might record their heritage in a chronicle, or on a tree of genealogy."

"Parchment and ink are easily lost or ruined. And I can neither read nor write."

He leaned a hip against the table and folded his arms over his chest, facing her. "This is a lifetime's work."

"Then so be it. I will set down the tales in stone if it takes my entire life to do it. Someday we of this blood and this name may well be gone. I do not want our heritage lost to memory, and I do not want it put on parchment."

"Stone will last forever."

"It will. When there is no one of our bloodline to tell the tales of Clan Laren, these stones will hold our legacy."

"Alainna," he said, "your clan will not die."

"You have come here to destroy what has existed for generations. I am the last of my name, so my children must carry that name."

He exhaled impatiently, and circled his hand around her arm. "I did not come here to destroy anything. And I will not carry the burden of blame for your anger and sorrow."

She pulled back against his grip. "Whatever your intent, the end of this clan may well be the result."

"Listen to me," he said, keeping his hold firm. "Stay here," he said, drawing her closer with his hands on her arms when she tried to yank away. "I have listened to you. Now allow me the same courtesy." He held her as he might hold a recalcitrant child.

"Speak, then." She stilled in his grip, her brow knotted.

"I am here because you asked for a champion—"

"I did not ask for you! I asked for—"

"I know, a Celtic warrior. But I am here to do what I can to save your clan. You must accept that, for the good of all."

"Save my clan? A Norman knight who cares only for how much land he can acquire, how much wealth, how much fame? Give me none of your Norman salvation. Saving my people satisfies Norman needs—your own needs—not theirs!"

He narrowed his eyes, and drew her close until her

breasts, beneath gray wool, crushed against his chest and her thighs warmed his. "If I thought only to satisfy my needs," he growled, "you would be the first to know it."

She stared up at him without flinching, her breaths rapid against his chest, her body supple and warm. His own body pulsed at that sweet pressure, and his blood surged, filled with sudden fire. But he gave no clue to what he felt, keeping gaze and grip constant.

He waited for her to react, waited for her to understand, finally and utterly, that he would not harm her or her clan.

The cadence of her breath calmed, but he could feel the deepening thud of her heart against his chest. She seemed to grow even warmer in his hands.

If she continued to burn like a candle flame before him, he thought suddenly, if her natural fire ignited his passion any further, he would find it immensely difficult to honor his intent to leave her be.

She angled her head toward his, looking up at him with a deep spark in her blue eyes. Her soft, rosy lips were but a breath from his. He lowered his face until her skin radiated warmth near his. She closed her eyes slowly. He fought his urges and struggled against something he had underestimated when he had drawn her toward him.

"You see," he finally murmured, "I can resist your lure, though I hold you as close as a lover. No matter that I feel a strong urge to satisfy my needs . . . and yours," he added, watching her lids lower and lift in an instant of truth. "So believe that I have enough honor to see that your kin, and your land, remain safe and unharmed."

"Let me go," she whispered.

He opened his hands slowly. She stepped back. As soon as their bodies parted, Sebastien felt something intangible within him tug and protest. He folded his arms over his chest.

Alainna stared at him, her chest heaving deep and slow. He reached out and supported her chin with his fingers. "I was sent here to be the champion you requested. But you must trust me."

She closed her eyes briefly. "I cannot," she whispered.

He stroked his thumb over the clean line of her jaw. "We both have temper and pride, and those are not easily

forsaken for peace. But I must do what the king bids me
to do. I will leave you in peace as soon as I can. You
will find life more secure for your clan when all is said
and done."

"You mean to leave?" she asked.

"I must return to Brittany," he said. "Though I am baron
of Kinlochan, though I will soon be wed to you, I have
matters to attend to there, other properties, other . . . other
ties. It is not unusual for knights to travel a great deal and
leave their homes and wives for long periods of time."

"I see." She closed her eyes, this time over a glistening
of tears. Sebastien felt that odd tug in his chest and gut
again. He slipped his fingers along her cheek, surprised as
much as compelled by feelings far deeper than lust but
somehow inexplicable.

A tear slid free from her closed lids. She tipped her head
out of the cup of his hand and turned away. "If I see that
you bring some benefit to my people," she said in a husky
voice, "I will make some peace with you. Not until then.
It is all I can offer you."

She walked toward the long, low bench that held a partially carved slab of gray limestone. She pushed her long
braids behind her shoulders, then picked up an iron chisel
and a wooden mallet, and bent to her task.

She angled the chisel blade against the roughened surface
of the stone. With the rounded, battered mallet, she beat
a rhythm of strokes against the tip of the chisel's wooden
handle.

Sebastien knew that the resuming of her work was meant
as a dismissal. He decided to be obtuse about the hint, for
there was much he wanted to learn about this intriguing
girl and her curious work. He came closer and looked over
her shoulder.

"Which story is this one?" he asked. The surface was
still flat and smooth in places, covered with light sketches.
Alainna manuevered a toothed chisel blade over areas
where her tools had already bitten into stone. The cleared
stone cast the flat, original level of the surface into raised
relief that would be enhanced by detail and finishing
touches as the work continued.

"This," she said after a few moments, "is the story of the Stone Maiden, who died beside the loch."

"I am eager to learn that particular story."

"I will tell you," she answered, "someday." Her mallet thumped and the chisel faintly clinked against the stone.

Sebastien watched her edge the blade around a sketched border of interlacing vines, similar to those he had seen on the other stones. The center scene showed two figures beside what must be the loch. The design was rough and unclear as yet.

She was silent while she focused on her work, After a few moments Sebastien straightened. "My lady, I thank you for showing me your work. 'Tis remarkable. I will leave you in peace for now. I want to seek out my men and some of your kinsmen to ride the boundaries of Kinlochan's lands."

"Please tell them I will come to the hall soon myself," she said without looking up from her work. "I want to speak to my kinfolk about the contents of the king's writ, and I must tell them about the . . . marriage we are ordered to make between us."

"Would you like me to be there?" he asked quietly.

She did not answer for a moment as she tapped the chisel over a small area of stone, and bent to blow the dust away.

"I would rather talk to them alone," she said finally.

He murmured assent and farewell. She did not reply and did not look up.

As he walked across the bailey, the steady pounding of her mallet sounded like a fast, passionate heartbeat.

Chapter Ten

"We must talk to Father Padruig soon," Una said. Beside her, Morag and Beitris nodded earnestly.

"We will all go see the priest on the Sabbath in a few days," Lorne announced, looking at his kinfolk from his seat beside Alainna. "No doubt the knights will want to see our parish church of Saint Brighid, where Alainna and Malcolm did so many fine stonecarvings."

Niall and several others nodded agreement. "We will ask Father Padruig to arrange the marriage," he said.

Alainna sighed. To her dismay, none of her kin had protested the king's decision. They had listened and had asked careful questions, but no one had shown the anger and fear she felt herself, and half expected from them. Even Niall and Lulach had nodded in somber agreement.

"But the knight is not the Highland warrior that you wanted me to wed," she protested. "He is Norman."

"*Ach,*" Lulach said. "We need warriors to fight for us, and with us. These are strong young men with fine weapons, sent by the king on our behalf."

"This knight and his men are willing to defeat the Mac-Nechtans. We are fools to refuse that," Donal added.

"No one said they were going to defeat the MacNechtans—" Alainna began, but Niall leaned forward eagerly.

"We will live in peace once the Normans slay the Mac-Nechtans," he said. "With our help, of course. Normans cannot defeat Highlanders alone."

"Their weapons and armor, and their horses, will hinder them," Lulach said. "They will need us with them." He looked pleased. "We will have a strong warband once again with these Normans to march behind us. I wonder how many the Breton knight can summon from the king's forces."

"He brought twenty men," Donal said. "We should ask for two hundred more."

"Two hundred!" Alainna burst out. "And just how are we to feed two hundred knights and their horses?"

"You say he will build a castle here and establish a garrison in it," Lulach said. "Clan Laren will be strong again."

"I thought some of you would be angry at their coming here," she said. "But you want to support them."

"We knew what the coming of the Normans meant without hearing what the king's writ says," Lorne said. "We all agreed it is a necessary thing."

"We cannot ignore a king's order," Niall said. "He has the right to take the land away entirely. But now Clan Laren can keep rights to the land through your marriage and your children."

"Are we so foolish as to try to hold Kinlochan ourselves, the few of us, with one stubborn girl to lead us?" Lulach asked. "We have no choice but this. It is clear to all of us."

"All of us but Alainna," Niall said. "Think, girl."

"Where is the pride of this clan when Normans come in and take over Kinlochan?" she demanded.

"We are proud, but we are practical," Donal said. "Hot pride is better suited to hot youth. We are old, we, and cooler in heart and mind than we used to be."

Lorne leaned toward her. "Small kettles boil over, while larger kettles simmer and keep. We have seen tragedy, and we have watched our clan diminish until only a handful of us are left. We are old enough and wise enough now to know when a thing is to be resisted—and when it is not."

"MacNechtans are to be resisted," Donal said. "King's will is not, when it benefits us."

"Our name will be gone forever with this marriage!" Alainna said. "Kinlochan will belong to le Bret and not MacLaren! How will that benefit us?"

"Ach!" Una wagged her hand in dismissal. "You can convince that one to take our name for his own. It will be simple to do."

"I cannot convince him! He is determined to keep his name."

"You will change his mind," Lorne said firmly.

"Ask him to allow your children to carry our name," Morag said. "He can keep his own, if it matters so much to him. Scottish women do not take their husband's names for their own, so it is only the names of your children that must be MacLaren."

She frowned. "He will not agree to that."

Lorne folded his arms over his chest and smiled at her. "There is time. Somehow there is a way. I feel this in my bones. Do not fret."

"His bones are accurate about many things," Una said. "When he feels a thing, it is so."

Alainna sighed, feeling as if an additional weight had been laid upon her shoulders. Her kinfolk were utterly convinced that the knight would give up his own name for theirs. But they had not spoken to him about the matter; they had not seen his rocklike stubbornness. The task of convincing him seemed like the greatest challenge she had ever faced.

"I do not think I should marry this man," she ventured. A gasp went around the room. "It is not the best thing for us."

"You will marry this one," Una said. "It is the wise thing to do for the clan. And for you," she added.

"He is a fierce warrior," Niall said. "He slayed a boar as great as the one that killed the hero Diarmuid in the old tales!"

"He tells a good tale," Aenghus said. "A m-man who tells a good tale has a g-good heart."

"He has men at his back willing to fight," Lulach said. "What more can we want than that?"

"And he is a golden man, like Aenghus mac Og in the old tales," Beitris said. "A man to make hearts flutter."

Niall and Donal grumbled, and Lulach frowned at his rotund wife, who had gone red-cheeked at her own boldness. Una and Morag smiled and cast glances at Alainna, who scowled at all of them.

"We must fetch the priest and get this done," Una said.

Alainna felt as if a strong wave swept her along against her will. "But the banns must be posted for three Sundays," she protested.

"Banns, bah," Lulach said disdainfully. "What do banns matter when none of us can read?"

"No banns!" Niall said. "We cannot let Cormac learn of this before the marriage!"

"Cormac cannot read either, you idiot," Lulach barked.

"We must get the marriage done before he gets word of it!" Niall insisted. "He will be furious. He cannot be made furious until we have all the king's men here."

"True," Lorne said. "When Cormac finds out, he may attack."

"Sebastien le Bret plans to speak to Cormac," Alainna said.

"Hah!" Lulach burst out. "Speaking is a waste of time! Fighting, now, that will accomplish something."

"Giric will fetch Father Padruig," Una said, looking around. "Where is he?"

"He is in the stables with the knights, preparing to take them out to show them the boundaries of Kinlochan," Alainna said.

"We must have a feast," Beitris said to Una and Morag. The three women began to chatter about the plans.

"Padruig loves a feast," Niall said. "He will be glad to come here with the promise of meat and drink and stories."

"We have nothing to celebrate," Alainna said.

"You are to be wed," Una replied calmly. "We are all glad about it. You should be too. Soon we will have young ones here once again. You will birth children to carry on our name and brighten our hearts. Beautiful children, from such beautiful parents," she added, leaning toward Morag, who nodded with her.

"Indeed, we will have a feast," Lorne said. "First we will take the Normans out on a hunt, so we will have enough meat for all. Then we will see the priest at the church, and after that we will have a feast, and a wedding. We have much to celebrate. Clan Laren has hope again."

Alainna rubbed her fingertips over her brow as if she could wipe away her dismay. Her kinfolk leaned forward to chatter in excitement as they began to make more plans. Their trust and their hope settled over her like a heavy cloak.

"I am eager for Father Padruig to hear our glad news,

but we can wait a few days," Una said. "We must plan the wedding."

"How can you call this glad news? We have lost Kinlochan," Alainna said, just short of a dismayed moan.

"Sweet girl," Lorne said, leaning forward to take her hand in his. "We have not lost Kinlochan. You and your husband will hold it, and your children will hold it after that. All you have to do is convince this man to take our proud name."

"He will do that," Niall asked. "Our ancient heritage, from Irish kings, is one to envy."

"We have not lost anything, Alainna," Una said. "We have won our future, which was lost to us."

Her kinfolk murmured to each other, planning the hunt, the wedding, and her future. Alainna hung her head and took her hand from Lorne's grip. She wondered if they knew that they had just rested all their hopes and dreams upon her shoulders.

Somehow, she told herself fiercely, the Breton knight would have to agree to bear their clan name. But she knew that she had met, in Sebastien le Bret, a will as strong as her own. He had flatly refused to change his name or allow his children to bear her clan's name. The future at Kinlochan would belong to the descendants of Le Bret rather than Clan Laren.

That would hurt her kinfolk deeply, and they had endured enough sorrow and loss. No matter what the Breton knight wanted, she could not allow the last bit of hope to be taken from them.

If that meant she had to look elsewhere for a husband, then so be it, she thought, frowning while the excited chatter continued around her. There was one more chance remaining to her to avoid this Norman marriage, and she meant to grasp it before the day was out.

"Giric!" Alainna called as she saw her foster brother cross the bailey, leading a saddled garron toward the gate. "I would speak with you." She clenched the skirt of her tunic in her fingers as a frisson of uncertainty went through her.

She was determined to speak her thoughts, although she

could guess Giric's reaction to her impulsive, even implausible, plan. But if he would agree, it could solve her dilemma.

Giric waved at her. Beyond him, she saw several Norman knights and Highlanders inside the long, low stable. The Breton knight stood near the doorway. She saw the glint of his golden hair in the shadows as he spoke with a young squire, one of the three boys who had accompanied the knights, and who now helped the men ready their horses to ride out.

Giric left his horse standing in the care of Aenghus at the gate, and came toward her, his gait easy and long-limbed. "What is it, then?" he asked her. "We are nearly ready to ride out."

"I know. A few words, please, before you go."

He frowned. "Alainna, I know you are unhappy about the Normans. I will speak with you about it later, if that is what you need of me."

"I did not call you over here to complain. Walk with me. We can wait outside for the knights." She tugged on his arm. Giric took hold of the garron's bridle and led the animal alongside.

They climbed down the rocky slope toward the loch, where calm waves flowed. Alainna walked toward the water and held up the hem of her gray skirt when the froth seeped near her leather shoes. She waited while Giric left the garron to graze in the meadow.

"Alainna, what is it?"

She heard the concern in his voice. "What would I do without you, Giric MacGregor?" she asked, turning to smile. "You have been a good friend and a brother to me since you first came to foster with my father as a lad."

"I was not so good a friend when I first came here as a seven-year-old," he drawled. "I did my share of teasing you and tripping you, and running from you, as I recall, even though you were three years older and bigger than me."

She smiled ruefully. "You did treat me ill sometimes, you and my brothers. But I thank you for it now. All that teasing from three boys made me stronger, I think."

"You rarely cried, and often got us back, I remember. And you are most welcome for the toughening." He winked at her.

"Ah, Giric," she said, gazing around, folding her arms against a sudden chill. "I miss them. I miss them all . . . so much." She bit back a sob. "I wonder what they would think to know we have lost Kinlochan to a Norman." She fisted a hand to her mouth and listened to the wind moan over the loch. *"Ach,"* she said. "Do you hear their sorrow in the wind, as I do?"

Giric put an arm around her shoulders and drew her against his side. "Your brothers and your father may be gone, and most of the men of your clan too," he said. "But I am here, and the old ones. You are not alone." He rubbed her arm.

"I know. You are so loyal to all of us. We are grateful. I know you must leave to return to Clan Gregor, but I . . . I hoped you might want to stay with us."

"Now that the king has sent help to Kinlochan, I will soon be free to return home. I would like to do that." He looked at her. "What is it you need, girl? Only ask, and it is done."

She gazed at the mountains overlooking the fortress, and shivered in the shelter of his arm. "Tell me what you think of the king's decision, Giric."

"I think it is a necessary thing," he answered grimly. "You can no longer fight the troubles of this clan alone. You need the help of a husband, a warrior with men at his back. I think the Breton is well suited to the task."

"He is not suited to me, nor I to him."

"With such a man for a husband—a champion in many courts, his knights have told me—your clan will prosper at last."

"He will not have our name. And he is not a Gael. My father would not have approved him."

"Your father would have been glad of this," Giric said. She looked at him, stunned. "I am sure of that. He would agree that the clan, such as it is now, needs the protection of Normans."

"What we need are men to vanquish our enemy, and the Normans do not promise that."

"True, the old ones would rather have vengeance against Clan Nechtan. Is that what you want?"

"Vengeance is a man's word. I want peace, an end to

this feud. But marrying Sebastien does not guarantee it, and will invite more trouble! Cormac will be furious, you know that." She stepped away. "This will bring more battles upon us, and could destroy us all. Normans do not have the skills to fight Highlanders. How can you say my father would agree? How can you agree? I do not understand! None of you side with me. Not even you!"

"Peace." Giric raised his palm. "I am not your enemy."

She sighed and nodded. Her foster brother could often calm her. She loved him as her dearest friend, but he often only placated her, offering her no argument, no challenge.

"I am the last of them," she said, gazing over the loch.

"They are glad that you will be well married, and that their blood will continue that way."

"Well married—that is the problem."

"The Breton knight is the right choice for you, I think."

She stood as straight as the pillar that overlooked the loch, while the wind beat her skirt about her, tugged at her braids. "Giric," she said. "There may be a solution to this."

"What is that?"

"Marry me. Take our name." The words hung in the air.

"Alainna." Giric walked over to stand behind her. "I would do anything for you. But this I cannot do."

"You can. We could marry, according to the Roman church. We are not of shared blood."

"But our priest follows the Celtic church. According to Celtic law, fostering makes us as close as brother and sister. Closer, some say. Father Padruig would refuse to witness our marriage. Alainna—"

"There must be some way," she said. "If we wed now, if we handfasted ourselves today, without the blessing of the priest, I would not have to wed the foreign knight." She began to pace over the pebbled beach.

"Why are you so intent on this? It is not what you want."

She ignored his calm logic. She wanted action, a passion to protect her clan that matched her own. "He refuses to take our name," she said. "That will tear the heart from my kinfolk!"

"Alainna," he said quietly. "Even if we could wed, I

cannot take your name either. My father is a chieftain among the *Gregorach*, and I answer to the *toiseach* of Clan Gregor. He would be furious if I were to do such a thing, and so would my clan." He touched her shoulder, kneaded it. "I wish the *Gregorach* would send help to Clan Laren, but our chief has refused to enter into a dispute with the MacNechtans."

"I know you have asked them to help us," she said. "Giric, what else can I do about this? You are the only man who can understand why my husband must take my name."

"I do understand. But I cannot do this."

She looked down at the stones around her feet. "I did not think you would agree. But I had to ask."

He placed a hand on her shoulder. "You do not want me for a husband. We are foster siblings, and we are friends, but we are not suited otherwise. You with your temper and your iron mallet, and me with my great fear of you, since I was a lad not as tall as your shoulder." His tone was teasing.

She blinked tears away. "And now I am the one not as tall as your shoulder, and I need your help."

He gathered her under his arm. "*Ach*, you know how I love you," he murmured. "You know I want you to be happy. I do not want to see your tears. And when I take a wife, I want her to be exactly like you."

She sniffled. "Stubborn and solemn, as you always call me?"

"Fine as rain and bright as stars." He held her away from him to look down at her. "I thank you for the honor. But listen to your heart, not your fears. You need a man with fire to match your own."

"You have enough fire for me," she said petulantly.

"You have too much of it for me. That hair, that temper. You singe me, and I but a coward, and a quiet man."

"I like quiet men."

"The Breton knight is not a loud or a boastful man," Giric said, smiling a little.

She dashed more tears away. "You and all the rest of my kin think I should wed him. Not one of you argued against the king's orders."

"Not only because the king orders it," Giric said, "but

because this Norman is a true warrior, which all your clan needs, and he has the strength and spirit you need in a husband. Marry this warrior."

"That is what the rest of my kin say. They want to talk to Father Padruig and have the marriage made quickly. The knight wants the marriage done soon, too. He will not get the king's signature on the charter unless he produces a marriage contract," she added, scowling. "Am I the only one who sees the danger in this?"

"I, too, urge you to do this." He looked thoughtfully at her. "You spark like fire when you are near him, did you know?"

"That is not a good thing," she muttered.

"Sometimes not, but that sort of spark between two people can make a good strong fire."

"What would you know? You sound like an old woman." She slanted a glance at him.

He chuckled and put his arm around her again, then turned with her toward the meadow. "Look there, the riders come down from the fortress," he said. "It took them long enough to ready themselves. So many trappings for the horses, and for the knights as well. I prefer Highland simplicity."

"So do I," Alainna said. She watched the knights guide their horses down the slope and pick up speed on the flat meadow. Even over the rushing rhythm of the loch, she heard the thud of horses' hooves and the jangle of mail and weaponry.

"Shiny as new coins, each of them, and riding fine horses from Spain and Arabia," Giric remarked. "I suppose we should tell them that those slender-legged horses will falter and be injured on our rocky Highland slopes."

"We should tell them, true," she agreed. "They do look fine, all gleam and sparkle, like a host of faery."

"Ah, caught by the glitter of chivalry? Next I will hear you do want a knight for a husband instead of a Celt."

She did not answer. As she watched the knight riding in the lead, her heart leaped within her like a salmon upriver.

Giric hugged her close, and she leaned against his comfortable strength. Her foster brother was right in guessing what she needed. She craved more than warmth and complacency. Fire to match her own would make a marriage challenging and strong rather than dull.

The Breton knight contained a banked power that felt almost tangible to her. She felt odd, exciting rushes of desire whenever he was near her that startled and confused her.

Yet if she wed him, she feared that her clan would fail, that the loss of their name to a Norman would eventually mean the loss of their entire heritage. She stepped away from Giric as the riders came closer.

"Go now, they are nearly here," she said. "I thank you for listening to me. Please do not think me a fool for what I said."

"Not a fool. A desperate girl who loves her kin. There is no shame in that. I wish that I could do what you want." He smiled sadly at her, watching her for a long moment. Then he turned to walk toward his grazing garron.

Alainna stood on the beach while the water whispered at her heels, and watched Giric mount up and ride to join the company of knights. Sebastien le Bret reined in his ivory stallion and looked over at her, his gaze an intense flash of awareness across the meadow.

Wanting to look away, she could not. The sky grew gray and overcast, the edge in the wind grew sharper, and she felt a few drops of chilly rain. She watched him ride past her, and hugged her arms about herself, feeling the cold.

A storm was about to roll through her life as well, bringing powerful forces that could destroy as easily as they might renew.

Chapter Eleven

Cold dawn air invigorated Sebastien as he ran past the loch that mirrored the wide pewter sky. Frost iced blades of grass and formed delicate patterns on the rocks and pebbles on the narrow beach. He ran to the rushing sound of the water, steadying his sheathed sword with one hand, his breath misting.

Ahead, the pillar stone thrust into the gray sky, and he followed the path through the meadow toward it. Waking before dawn was a longstanding habit that had proved true every day that he had been at Kinlochan.

Near the pillar, the ground was flat. He dropped his cloak on the grass and unsheathed his well-balanced sword to begin the thrusts, spins, and lunges that filled his practices. He flexed his grip on the leather-wrapped hilt, hand wedged between the straight guard and the disc-shaped pommel of shining brass. He circled the stone, his footsteps sure and his swing strong.

He did not think about his skills, nor did he strive, as he often did, to challenge the periphery of his sight. Instead, he thought about the striking beauty of this place, and its people, and he thought about the lovely girl at the center of all of it, like the brightest flame in a hearth.

He brought no glad news to Clan Laren, but these people—with the exception of their fiery-tempered chief—had accepted him, and the news of the king's decision, with generosity, warmth and even enthusiasm. They praised him still for his prowess with the boar on the first day of his arrival, and they had showed him only their approval, although he brought the tide of change into their lives.

He recalled the previous night, when he had sat late in the great hall with the rest of the clan and with his own knights to listen to another story told by Lorne. Alainna had not been there, and Una had told him that she worked late at her carvings, as she often did. In her absence, he and Giric had translated for the knights. The Gaelic was clear enough to follow, and Lorne's phrases were simple but poetic. While forming his own translations, Sebastien had felt his soul stir in response to the courage and beauty the bard described in the tale.

Perhaps, he told himself now, as the sword whistled and sliced through the air, he had felt the effects of the *uisge beatha* and not the rousing of any part of his soul.

Alainna had called his soul a wanderer in search of a home. He spun in the cold air, remembering. Although he would not have admitted it to her or to anyone, he knew she was accurate. This girl who scarcely knew him had seen the truth in him when no one else ever had, this girl whose eyes were as blue as a deep sea, whose hair was sunset bright—

There, he thought, stopping, breathing hard, sword lowered. Their poetry had already seeped into his soul, as their heady drink had seeped into his blood.

He frowned and shifted his shoulders, swiped the sword blade to the left, keeping the pillar stone at the edge of his vision.

Alainna had thrown him off balance with her direct gaze and her rose-lush cheeks and lips, and with her quick grasp of his secrets. He preferred the mystery that silence and privacy had always given him. That aura had taken him far, from an orphan squire with no name to a knight of property and some renown.

Yet she saw past his shield of silence. He found that disconcerting and exciting.

The blade cut crisp and clean through nothing. He sank its tip into the earth, where the hilt swayed and stilled.

He stood, breath heaving, and looked at the long, mirrored loch, the white-ringed mountains, the brightening sky. Poetry and savagery mingled in the land, in the very air here, he thought. No wonder Scotland produced bards as well as warriors.

He passed his arm over his damp brow and walked down toward the edge of the loch to sit on a large boulder near the stony beach. He scanned the mountains and the narrow loch, noting for the first time the long, low island that jutted up from the glassy surface a good distance away.

He opened the pouch looped at his belt, taking from it a wax tablet in a leather case, larger than his palm, and a thin, sharp bone stylus. A small drawing of a castle filled the center of the tablet. With quick, deft lines, he drew an island beneath the building, then scraped it away and redrew the base, replacing it with a rocky promontory jutting out of a high mountain.

If he had grown to manhood in such a place, if he had been part of a caring family, part of a legacy—he added a square tower and made the surrounding wall higher—he would never give it up on a king's whim. He would fight to the death for it. If Clan Laren had had the strength to resist the grant of their lands to a Norman, he did not doubt they would have done so.

Across the water, the wooden fortress sat solid and peaceful on its mound, a home to those who shared a name, a heritage. He, a man who lacked what these people had in abundance, would forever alter their lives and their future.

He would ring the changes, and he would leave. He could not remain here. Once he left Scotland for Brittany, he was not sure when he would see Kinlochan or its beautiful chatelaine again.

She would be his wife, and he knew well that he should not leave her. He had learned that bitter lesson long ago, at a high price. The ironic choice he was forced to make between the wife he had not asked for and the child he loved so much cut hard and deep into him. The dilemma seemed insurmountable. Alainna MacLaren would not take his name and leave Kinlochan for Brittany, and he could not take her name and stay at Kinlochan.

He shook his head in utter dismay, unable to understand why the king would have demanded this of both of them. By rules of heart and honor, he should not marry her. He should not hold Kinlochan. By rules of law and king's writ, he had no choice, bound by his pledge.

Honor was indeed a tender thing, as Una had said.

He put the wax tablet back into his pouch and left his

perch. Pulling his sword free from the ground, he sheathed it in his sword belt and picked up his cloak.

Remembered words, spoken in a soft, lovely voice, haunted him like a litany as he walked away.

I am weary, and I a stranger. . . .

"Did you not set aside hay to winter the animals?" Heavy footsteps sounded across the wooden floorboards of the great hall, and the Breton knight's voice, sharp with impatience, echoed in the nearly deserted chamber.

Alainna glanced up as he came toward the hearth, where she sat with Una and Morag. She lowered the distaff and spindle she held and looked up at him calmly, though her heart pounded.

"Set hay aside? What do you mean?" she asked.

He shoved his chain mail hood from his head and stripped off his leather gloves. He looked tired, Alainna thought, and angry, his eyes shadowed, his brown-whiskered jaw taut.

"We have just returned after being out all day, and I now learn that there is no supply of fodder for the horses, nor for cattle," he told her. "Just sacks of oats, Niall says. Did your people not cut grass from the fields and meadows to feed the animals in the winter months?"

Alainna glanced at Una and Morag, who blinked in silent reply and bent to their tasks of pulling tufts of dyed wool into strands and winding them around handheld spindles.

"We have never done that," Alainna answered.

"Why not?" he demanded. He slapped his gloves down on the table. "How do you expect to feed animals in the cold months, when they cannot graze due to the weather?"

"It is not a Highland custom to harvest hay."

"Not a custom? Then it should be." He gave an exasperated sigh and shoved his fingers through his hair, a sheen of dark gold in the dim light. "What are we to feed twenty horses?" he asked, half to himself.

"Oats and barley, as we feed ours," she said. She glanced at the other women and translated what had been said into Gaelic. "Is there enough for the Norman horses?" she asked them.

Una shrugged, and Morag shook her head. "I doubt it,"

she answered, as she drew a length of blue yarn through her fingers.

Alainna looked up at Sebastien. "If we had known you were coming," she snapped, "we would have grown more oats."

"We have a problem, lady. Give me none of your temper."

"Then give me none of yours! I will not be reprimanded for what was not my doing. I am sorry if Highland customs do not match Norman standards, but so be it."

He tossed his cloak over a bench, and sat, dangling his hands from his knees. "Something must be done about it if we are to stay here."

"Then do not stay," she retorted. She saw his mouth tense, saw a muscle jump in his jaw, watched his eyes narrow. Expecting a sharp reply, she looked away and concentrated on wrapping more strands of red wool around her distaff and spindle.

He blew out a long breath. "Your kinsman said there is neither hay nor fodder kept anywhere, here or on the small tenant farms," he said more calmly. "What exactly is the custom in the Highlands for feeding livestock in the winter?"

"We have but a few horses, and those we feed on oats and barley. We do not keep much cattle or sheep over the winter, but for a milk cow or two, a bull, a few sheep. The rest we either slaughter in November to smoke the meat, or we let them go."

"You let them go? To fend for themselves like deer?"

"Of course. What are we to feed them?"

"Hay," he snapped. "When spring comes, you have no herds?"

"Those that survive the winter we gather into herds again," Alainna said. "We take them to grassy pastures to feed until they are healthy. Though some of them are so weak they need to be carried," she admitted.

"Carried?" Sebastien asked incredulously. "Cows?"

"It is the way it is done."

"Then it must change in the future."

"It does not have to change. Nothing has to change but one thing—take your twenty horses and go south again."

He stared at her. "We will find a way to feed the horses

if I have to go out into the meadows and cut brown grasses myself."

"You could," she said blithely. "Or you could go home."

Sebastien looked away, huffing out a long breath in clear exasperation. He pounded his fist softly into his palm as if he wanted to master his temper. "What of the other animals?" he asked. "Aenghus said there are but three cattle and four sheep in the pens out there."

"That is true," she said. "The MacNechtans took the rest. We lacked men and women to herd and protect our cattle and sheep, and so we lost them to raids, or to wolves."

He watched her for a moment. "And you do not want things to change here," he commented wryly.

She wound the wool, shifting the distaff and adjusting the weight of the spindle. "Some things should stay the same," she said.

"What of food stores for your people, and mine?"

"We have stores of oats and barley, baskets of apples, carrots, onions—" She turned to Una and Morag and translated his request into Gaelic.

"We have food," Una said. "And barely enough for the king's champions through the winter, too, if that is what he wants to know. The king did not send fodder for his knights or his horses." She grinned at her jest. "But they can hunt and fish for additional food while they are out hunting MacNechtans."

Sebastien sighed. "She is right, of course. We will help provide food so long as we are here."

"And how long will that be?" Alainna asked.

"Until my tasks are met."

"Too long," she murmured. Her fingers fumbled, and she dropped the spindle. It rolled across the floor, spinning out a trail of red yarn. Sebastien stopped it with his booted foot. She went near him to fetch it back, bending down.

He leaned over to pick it up as she did. Her head knocked into his with an audible *thunk*. Wincing, she reached out to touch his head, sure she had hurt him worse than he had hurt her.

At the same instant, he rested his palm on her brow. "Are you hurt?" he asked, still leaning over her. The warmth of his hand was amazingly effective, and dispelled the pain almost immediately. She caressed his high, smooth brow, his hair thick and surprisingly silken to the touch.

"I am not. I thought you were," she said.

"Not I." He withdrew his hand, and she lowered her own a moment later. "Your head is hard," he admitted, rubbing his temple.

"As is yours," she said, and reached for the spindle.

"That must be the sign of a stubborn girl," he murmured.

"Did you need a sign to tell you that?"

He chuckled. "Not at all." He began to wind the spilled yarn into place while she held the distaff upright. "One way or another," he murmured as he worked, so low that only she could hear him, "you will have to ease some of that stubbornness, and accept that your life is going to change, Lady Alainna."

She was silent, for she had no answer for truth. She watched his long, agile fingers handle the wool gently and deftly. A chill went through her, for she suddenly felt as if he held the thread of her very soul in his strong, capable hands.

She snatched the tail of the yarn from him and went back to the hearth.

"All the hounds and warriors of the Fianna saw that fearsome boar," Lorne said as the Highlanders and knights gathered later that evening to hear a tale. The timber hall was warm and slightly smoky, and the blazing hearth cast a golden glow over the faces of the listeners. Outside, sleet pelted the outer walls, and a cold draft leaked through the door.

Sebastien felt the chill, for he sat nearer the door than the hearth. He leaned his back against the wall and listened to the tale that Lorne told in a deep, rich voice. He had come to prefer this solitary bench in a shadowed side aisle for its privacy in the midst of the crowded hall.

"The sight of him could frighten a man to his death," Lorne said. "Blue-black as a thunderstorm, bristles sharp as iron, eyes red as the flames of hell. His teeth were long and yellow in his ugly black lips, and his bellow could shake a man's bones.

"They came toward him, hounds and men, and the beast lunged, ready to slaughter and tear any who came near. As they drew closer, some of the men shrank back, and the dogs began to yelp, and more of the men hesitated, and warned the others to beware.

"But of them all, Diarmuid, the beloved friend and nephew of Fionn MacCumhaill, Diarmuid, who betrayed his friend for love, he alone was not afraid. And he alone went forward."

Alainna sat on a bench flanked by Robert and Hugo, with other knights seated at her feet. She translated Lorne's story into English in a quiet voice, her words interweaving with his like a velvet shadow. Sebastien watched her idly, tipping his head back against the wall, turning his wooden cup in his hands.

". . . When his friend Diarmuid lay wounded and dying," Lorne went on, as Alainna echoed him softly, "Fionn had a choice to make. He could save his soul-friend, or he could seek the vengeance he deserved for the wrong done to him by Diarmuid and Fionn's own wife, who had betrayed him with their love, so strong that it overstepped the honor of marriage and friendship. . . ."

Sebastien listened to the artful blending of the male and female voices in two languages. He studied Alainna's swan-throated profile as she spoke, noticing how the hearth's glow deepened the blue in her eyes and brought out the red-gold luster of her braids. His gaze glided over her body, traveling its lush curves and long, firm lines. Without effort, he imagined the warm, luscious skin beneath the draped woolen clothing, and he was aware that his own body stirred in response.

He sipped the *uisge beatha* in his cup. The drink flowed into him like fire and cream, and he swallowed again. Gazing at Alainna, lost in the mellifluent sound of her voice and the allure of her finely shaped body, he felt a spark ignite deep within him, subtle and powerful.

Later, when those around him smiled and applauded and asked for more from Lorne, Sebastien realized that he had been so entranced by what he saw, so caught in his own thoughts, that he had missed the end of the story.

Chapter Twelve

A lainna walked out of the morning mist like a wraith, startling Sebastien so much that he jerked backward to avoid hitting her with his extended sword as he spun around. His left elbow knocked into the pillar behind him with an audible crack.

Breath heaving, he glared at her as he tossed the sword to the ground and rubbed his aching elbow. "Why the devil would you walk up on a man like that?"

"Pray your pardon," Alainna said. "I thought you would see me. I came out to talk to you. Why are you out here with the Maiden? I have seen you out here before, around dawn."

He cradled his elbow. "I prefer to practice my swording early, and alone. I might have killed you, for love of God— you came up on my left side." He paused. "My vision is not as clear on the left."

She set a bundle on the ground and came close to him. Her hand settled easily on his arm and she kneaded his elbow with strong, capable fingers. The pain dissolved quickly.

"Your vision is not clear because of the scar?" she asked. "How did it happen?"

"A few years ago, when I rode escort for the duchess of Brittany," he answered. "As we traveled through a forest, we were attacked by a host of brigands. I defended the van that the ladies were in, and several rogues took me at once. I fought them off, but—" He shrugged, unwilling to describe the bloody fray that had followed. "I was fortunate to take away only this wound. Many others died that day."

"*Ach Dhia,*" she murmured. She reached up toward his face. Sebastien leaned away out of instinct, but her gentle fingertips found the scar and traced its length, sending shivers along his spine. "How fortunate you were not blinded."

"For a while I could see naught with this eye," he admitted. Her fingers were cool and pleasant, and she stood as close as a lover. He could smell the subtle floral fragrance in her hair. She always seemed clean and freshly scented with lavender or heather, and he found it distracting and enchanting.

"The duke's physician was certain that I would remain half blind," he went on, bringing himself back to his tale. "It healed, but my vision is not as wide out of the left. And so," he added in a lighter tone, "you were able to surprise me, slipping like a sylph out of the mist."

"I am glad you are not blind," she said, lowering her hand.

"As am I." He smiled in rueful agreement. "The duke and duchess rewarded me with property in Brittany. When I recovered, Duke Conan gave me a coveted post in Scotland as an honor guard for King William, who is brother to the duchess of Brittany. And that is my tale, lady." He inclined his head politely before turning to retrieve his sword.

"Not all of your tale, is it," she remarked.

"Not quite all." He sheathed the sword and picked up his fur-lined cloak.

She tilted her head. "You have not found much to challenge you in Scotland, I would think."

"Only hot tempered, fiery-haired clan chiefs," he drawled. Alainna's cheeks turned rosy, and he smiled. "True, there is little excitement. We did chase after a host of rebels last year, and routed them soundly."

"They fled to Ireland," she said. "I know. But a warrior of your caliber must be dissatisfied to stand behind a king most of the time, with little else to occupy his time and his talents." She tilted her head. "Is that why you want to return to Brittany?"

"There are many reasons for that." He lifted a brow. "Did you seek me out for some other purpose this morning other than to startle me out of my wits?"

"I came to tell you that Giric and the knights are readying the horses to ride out with you again. I will ride with you this time, if you do not mind."

"I do not mind at all," he said. "It is a privilege to tour the holding with the chief of the clan."

She slid him a wry glance. "I also came out here to bring an offering to the Stone Maiden." She indicated the bundle that she had placed on the ground.

"Where is your great blue hound? He is usually with you."

"He took a thorn in his paw yesterday. Morag tended to it, but he is limping, and prefers the comfort of the hearth-side."

"On such a bitter day, any sensible creature would prefer the fireside."

"You can go back to the hearth if you like," she said blithely. He chuckled. She picked up her bundle and walked to the pillar stone to lay it at the foot. Sebastien saw her set out a little sack of oats, a round cheese, and a bowl of cream on the grass.

"Offerings for good fortune?" he asked.

"And a show of gratitude to the Maiden for her protection," she answered. She walked around the stone three times, and then paused to trace her fingers along the carvings. She began to murmur in lilting, musical Gaelic.

Woman of the faery realm, guardian of our hearths,
Shield us and keep us safe
This day and this night and forever.

"A lovely charm," he said. "Why do you circle the stone?"

"It brings good fortune to go around *deiseil,* in the direction of the sun."

He nodded, intrigued. "Do you often come out here to speak chants to your Stone Maiden?"

"It is wise to do that before undertaking journeys, and on special days, and at times of need or change."

"Which is this?"

"Need," she said. "Change."

"Ah." He understood. "I wonder if she will protect you from the Norman invaders who have come to Kinlochan."

"She will do her best," she answered.

He stepped closer to the stone and glanced up the towering height. Reaching out, he touched one of the carvings. "This pillar has been here a very long time."

"Seven hundred years, so they say," she replied. "I remember visiting the stone when I was a small girl. I would hold my father's hand tightly as we walked here, for I was frightened of the great stone. My father never knew that," she said, smiling a little. "He used to boast that his little daughter had inherited his courage as well as his red hair and his stubbornness." She gave a sad shrug. "I miss him."

"He would be proud of you," he murmured. She stood very still. "And I suspect," he added, "that you put your courage and stubbornness into the wielding of mallet and chisel."

She laughed ruefully. "I suppose I do." She approached the stone and touched it like a friend.

"You promised to tell me the story of the Stone Maiden," he reminded her.

"I did." She glanced up the heighth of the pillar. "She was the great-granddaughter of the first Labhrainn. One day she went out to gather nuts and berries for her father's supper. As she returned to the fortress and walked past the loch, she thought of the faeries that live in the hills who were her friends, for she was a kind girl. She left some food for them and went on.

"A man called Nechtan, from a neighboring clan, approached her and greeted her. He offered to carry her basket and she waited for him. But he accosted her instead. She fought desperately, but he had a sharp knife, and wounded her."

Alainna turned toward the loch, and Sebastien turned with her. Brown grasses and reeds edged the stony beach, and waves lapped slowly into shore. Mist drifted on the water like wisps of silk.

"As she lay dying on the bank of the loch," Alainna went on, "with her life's blood pouring out of her, the faeries came out of the hill at the sound of her cries. They chased Nechtan and caused him to fall upon his own knife. Then they surrounded the maiden and tried to help her.

Faeries are very good at magic, but they are not much good at healing," she said.

"They could not save her life, but they used their magic to turn her into a stone on the bank of the loch, so that her soul would be preserved near her beloved home. Then the faeries cast the spell that has affected our clan and Clan Nechtan ever since. Two charms they made that day, one for good and one for revenge."

"The spell of protection?" Sebastien asked. Alainna shivered and clutched her plaid at her throat, nodding.

"The girl became a maiden of stone, to remain so for seven hundred years. Another spell was laid upon her murderer's clan." She paused. "If ever again a man of Clan Nechtan harms a woman of Clan Laren, the MacNechtan bloodline will die out in one generation."

Sebastien stared at her. "So that began the feud."

"They have tried, over generations, to wipe out our bloodline. They will not harm our women, but they have always fought our men, and one day they may destroy us."

"Cormac seems intent on bringing this to an end."

"A bitter end. He speaks of peace and plots ill. He bides his time, you see. The seven hundred years," she said, "will end on the first day of spring."

Sebastien exhaled sharply. "What happens then?"

"I want to show you something," she said, and turned to walk toward the stone again. She knelt down and pushed back some of the long grasses that fringed the foot of the pillar.

"What are those marks?" Sebastien dropped to one knee beside her. He ran his fingers along the rows of vertical strokes that wreathed the stone like the embroidered hem of a woman's gown.

"Six hundred and ninety-nine lines are incised there," Alainna said. "Each year, on the first day of spring, the chief of Clan Laren adds another mark. On Saint Brighid's day next, which we regard as the first day of spring, I will make the seven hundredth mark in the stone."

"And so the spell will end," Sebastien said soberly.

"And after that, we do not know what will happen. The curse on Clan Nechtan will be lifted, and the Stone Maiden's soul will be set free. Some say she will come back to life," she said softly. She traced her fingers over the cold granite. "Some say she is gone already, and her protection is no more."

"And the feud?"

"That may end, or it may grow worse. There will be no faery spell to deter our enemies."

She stood, and he straightened. "There will be knights to deter them. All will be well." he said.

"Will it?" She looked at him.

He frowned in silence. The story of the Stone Maiden echoed in his mind. He had scarcely heard a more haunting tale, he thought. Perhaps he was enthralled with the story-teller as much as with the story.

"What was her name, the Maiden of Kinlochan?" he asked.

"Alainna," she said. "It means 'beautiful one.'"

He held her gaze. "You are well named," he murmured.

She blushed. "She is very special to me. Like a sister, in a way." She smiled and stepped around to the other side of the stone, and he went with her.

"Tell me about these markings," he said, brushing his hand over the carved lines, simple curvilinear renderings of animals and objects. "Some of them are clear to me . . . a fish here, that one a boar. What are the others?"

"These are very old markings," she said. "There is a salmon for wisdom, and this round shape is a mirror, that one a comb. That triple spiral design is sacred to Saint Brighid. Not even Lorne knows what all the designs mean, but some say that they signify that the Maiden is within the stone."

"This is beautiful work. I see similarities to your own carvings."

"I have learned much from studying this stone, and from looking at other old Celtic carvings."

"The designs look as if they would be quite difficult to cut," he said, looking at a complex band filled with knotwork.

"Not really. They are designed on patterns of squares and circles. Any repeating pattern must be carefully drawn, but the actual cutting is not hard. A slow, steady hand is necessary. A gentle hand is best."

"You have both, I am sure," he murmured. She blushed again and looked away. "I have seen similar decorations in churches in Scotland, and in manuscripts as well."

With a lifted finger, she followed an undulating path along one of the interlaces. "These patterns are more than decoration. They have meaning as well. This one is a series of endless knots, see," she said. "The knots are like the mystical strands of life that bind the soul to the world. They cannot be undone."

"Ah. And here? These spirals?" he asked, touching a circle filled with three fanning spirals.

"Those represent the endless flow of life. And this long braiding, just here, is like the loom of life, the constant weaving of lives and events into one another." She glanced at him. "We have a riddle: Who exists, who has never been born, and never will be?"

Sebastien reached out to sweep his fingers over a section of plaitwork, moving in tandem with her hand, their fingers grazing. "The soul. These designs map the path of the soul."

"They do," she said, and smiled. "Every soul has strands that bind it to God, and bind it to the world. Souls can blossom and soar in their lives, or they can be lost, or broken, or stolen. We believe that wounded souls and wandering souls can be retrieved by the same strands that bind them."

He glanced at her. "Drawn back into the pattern of life?"

"Drawn back into the weave by caring. By love. It is a theme in many of our stories."

He nodded, touching the designs.

"The patterns are meant to remind us how fine our souls are," she went on, "and how we are each on a path in life. They celebrate the endless miracle of the soul and life. They sing the soul, in their way." Her fingers danced along the curves and swirls.

Sebastien stilled his hand. He no longer looked at the carvings. He watched her, and realized in that moment that the torn strands of his soul were not lost. They had simply fallen out of the weave of his life. That knowledge brought him a sense, unexpectedly, of hope.

She looked up at him, her eyes limpid blue. He reached

out to touch one of her bronze-colored braids. It felt like cool, glossy silk. "Plaited," he murmured teasingly, "like an ancient design." She smiled, and he tugged gently on the braid, so that she swayed toward him a little.

With his palm flattened on the stone above her head, he leaned toward her, the braid still gently captured. He felt drawn by some subtle, irresistible power. Whether it emanated from her beautiful, haunting eyes, or from the mysterious stone that they both touched, he did not know.

Barely a breath separated them now, and he saw her eyelids drift closed, saw her chin tip upward, a hesitant, shy movement that made his breath catch. Heart thundering, body surging with a hot, sudden flare of desire, he touched his lips to hers.

Her mouth was warm and pliant beneath his, sweeter and softer than he ever could have imagined. He let go of the braid and slipped his fingers along her cheek, tilting her head, deepening the kiss. Her hand lifted to rest upon his shoulder, and with the other she touched his jaw in a butterfly caress that somehow penetrated like fire into his marrow. He groaned low and caught her to him, kissing her again, taking his hand from the stone to cradle the back of her head.

He felt her arms wrap around him, slim and strong, and although he stood on solid ground, embracing her, kissing her, he thought for a moment that he whirled, thought he sailed.

The cold wind slipped between them like a reprimand, and Alainna gasped beneath his mouth, pushing away slightly. He drew back, his arms still around her.

She looked up at him, eyes wide, mouth lush and rosy, and covered her lips with pale, slender, shaking fingers.

He released her completely and stepped back. "Dear God," he said breathlessly. "Dear God." Whether he uttered an apology or his own astonishment, he did not know.

She stretched out trembling fingers to touch the granite surface of the pillar. "The Maiden," she said. "It could have been the Maiden. . . . Some say a powerful force surrounds her. A good force," she added hastily.

He nodded, and shoved his fingers through his hair. "It is a natural urge, this," he said gruffly, not certain if she had even been aware, up until this moment, that such a force existed between men and women. He had much experience, but he had never felt that sort of power in a kiss before, like a blend of lust and prayer. His heart still slammed in his chest.

"A natural urge," he repeated. "We are to be married, after all."

"I know," she said, picking up the hem of her gown and turning away. "I know." She half ran from him, skirting the edge of the loch to return to the fortress, her braids lifting out behind her.

He watched her go, then glanced up at the Stone Maiden and its knotted, entwined carvings. Suddenly he felt as if a few precious threads had found their way back into the design of his own life.

"Aye, 'twas the maiden," he muttered to himself, as he walked away. "But not the stone one."

"At the south end of the loch," Alainna said, pointing from where she sat on horseback, "Kinlochan has broad, rolling hills, with fine grazing pastures, and some arable land. Toward the north"—she swiveled in her saddle to point again—"the land is wilder, harsher, with high, rugged mountain slopes and crags. There is grazing land there, but little land for raising crops."

Sebastien nodded, mounted beside her on his creamy Arabian, whose mane shimmered like silk in the cold, clear air.

"Kinlochan sits on the edge of the Highlands like a gateway," he observed. "The loch itself is just on the border of the alteration in the land. That mountain face above the loch looks like it was torn from sheer rock by the hand of God."

"A dramatic and beautiful place," Robert said. Sebastien turned to glance at him. "I can see why it is a desirable holding."

Giric steadied his garron beside Alainna. "Clan Laren has fought for generations to defend this land."

"And so easily given away, out of their care," Robert said. Sebastien saw the concern on his friend's face, and realized that Robert, too, did not approve of taking land from those who had held it for generations.

"How many tenant farms are on the holding altogether?" Sebastien asked. "We saw but a few."

"Fifteen," Alainna answered. "Most of those are no longer inhabited."

"The farmers have either died, or they and their families have deserted Clan Laren and gone elsewhere to seek a safer life," Giric explained. "Herding cattle with the Mac-Nechtans stealing so much of our livestock is not so rewarding."

"I can imagine," Sebastien said grimly. They rode northeast toward a broad meadow fringed with trees. A thin layer of snow had turned the meadow to an expanse of white, and the bare trees created dark, elaborate patterns against the gray sky.

"We are out later than I expected," Alainna said. "It is nearly dusk, and well past time to return to Kinlochan."

"Una and the women will have supper ready," Giric agreed.

"And many of the knights have become accustomed to the bard's stories of a night," Robert commented. "Some of the others rode out on patrol while we were gone, but they are very likely back by now, and waiting for us."

Sebastien nodded and urged his horse to a quicker pace. He had ridden the Arabian out that day, but found that he had to select carefully which routes to take along the rugged hills. While Araby had a faster, longer stride than the shorter, heavy-framed garrons that Alainna and Giric rode, their mounts were far more suited to the terrain than his own. Robert, too, had borrowed a garron and seemed pleased with his choice, although his long legs sometimes caused his feet to drag over the taller grasses; Robert's easy manner had made this a subject of mirth rather than an indignity, as it might be for many Norman knights.

Sebastien slowed enough for Alainna to catch up to him. Her behavior seemed slightly cool, more formal than before, but he could hardly blame her after that astonishing kiss.

He pointed toward the loch in the distance. "There are

several islands in the loch. Are there structures on any of them?"

"Only on the largest one, there in the middle," she said. "An ancient tower ruin is there. Giric and I, and my brothers, used to go there when we were children. The fishing is good there. Sometimes I go there to gather stones for carving. The ones that are smoothed by the water take incising well, so I sometimes cut patterned crosses in them."

"You gave one to the king," he said. She nodded. "Does your loch have a name?" he asked then.

"Loch Eiteag," she said. "It means 'smooth white pebble,' though the word can also mean 'fair maiden.'" She smiled. "It is called so for the Stone Maiden, but we just call it the loch."

He lifted a hand to shield his eyes as he looked at the loch. "I wonder if that isle would be a good site for a castle."

She shrugged. "A beautiful setting, but is it practical? You would need a boat to access it unless you built a causeway."

"That can be done. The loch is narrow, and it would provide excellent protection."

"True," she said. "And some ancient clan did build on that island. The ruin is very old, and only houses birds now."

Sebastien nodded as he looked at the island, and planned to investigate it later when a chance arose. He would also sketch out his ideas, for the thought of a castle on an island had great appeal.

As they rode forward, he heard a growling sound, violent and alarming, echo across the meadow. He glanced back at Robert and Giric, both of whom frowned as they turned in their saddles.

"That sounds like a wolf," Giric said.

"More than one," Robert said. "It comes from there— in the woodland across the meadow." A scream, high and shrill, followed the harsh growling. Then a shout, and more growls.

Sebastien glanced at Alainna, who had turned pale as she pivoted to look toward the forest. "Stay here!" he ordered her. He touched his knees to the Arabian, who launched forward in response to skim across the meadow.

Behind him, he heard Robert and Giric thunder in pursuit. A quick glance showed him that Alainna rode behind them. He swore under his breath, but he had not expected her to listen to him.

As he neared the edge of the forest, he could hear the growling sounds and the shouts clearly, even above the pounding of hooves on the snowy meadow. He reined in his mount and entered the thick woven canopy of the bare-limbed trees cautiously, ducking his head beneath a branch. He grasped the hilt of his sword, wishing that he had brought his javelin.

Just ahead, he saw, through the mesh of branches, figures struggling in the blue shadows. The screams and horrible growls continued without abate. He tore off his cloak and dismounted.

Running forward, he cast one quick glance backward to see Robert and Giric close behind him. Alainna, he saw, was still on her garron. He only hoped she had the sense to remain there.

As he ran closer, he saw a man locked in a struggle with a wolf, while a second wolf leaped at him. The man, a Highlander to judge by his belted plaid and bare knees, lashed out with a foot and with a single kick knocked the second wolf senseless. The animal yelped and fell to the ground to lie still.

The first wolf kept a vicious grip on the man's arm. They wrestled together, turning in a horrible dance, the man standing and the gray wolf on its hind legs. Sebastien saw a woman scramble into a tree, boosting a small child above her onto a sturdy branch.

Sebastien spun toward Giric and Robert, several yards behind him. "Your bow!" he shouted, waving a hand in agitation. "Your hunting bow! Give it to me!"

Giric, who was carrying the weapon, ran forward and thrust it toward Sebastien, grabbing arrows from his belt and handing those to him too. Sebastien snatched them and whirled back.

The Highlander still fought with the attacking wolf, and now the second one lurched to its feet. The woman screamed.

Sebastien nocked and balanced the arrow and pulled the string taut in one fluid motion, releasing the bolt to shoot the advancing wolf. It fell to the ground. Sebastien ran forward, Giric and Robert on his heels. He could spare no moment to look toward Alainna.

He realized, coming closer, that he could not shoot the other wolf so easily. The constant twisting and turning of the man and the wolf as they struggled made the shot so treacherous that he feared he would kill the man instead of the wolf.

He stood, legs wide, and aimed, again and again without releasing, dropping the angle of the arrow each time, never seeing a clear shot. The growls and the vicious struggle he watched made him desperate with the need to help. The Highlander had clearly put himself in danger to save the woman and the child, who clung together up in the tree.

Only seconds passed while he stood there, but time was far too precious to attempt to wait. He handed the bow to Giric and drew his sword, running forward. From the corner of his eye, he saw Giric pull the bow taut and train it, and saw Robert draw a short dagger to follow, ready to guard.

Drawing his sword free, Sebastien ran closer and then stood, balancing lightly from one foot to the other, his sword raised. As the man and wolf turned again, Sebastien waved the long blade in the air, prepared to strike as the man and wolf circled.

As soon as he saw the wolf's long muscular back turn toward him, he sliced sideways with vicious power and speed, taking the animal down within the instant. The wolf slumped to the ground, losing its grip on the man's arm.

For a moment, Sebastien and the Highlander stared at each other. The man was coated in blood. The torn, light-colored plaid wrapped around his arm as a flimsy protection was saturated with red. He stood, breathing heavily, his face rugged and handsome though aging, his eyes striking blue beneath dark brows, his dark hair streaked with silver. He locked his gaze with Sebastien's. Then he glanced beyond him toward the others.

With a quick nod of gratitude to Sebastien, he turned and ran into the dusky shadows of the forest.

Chapter Thirteen

Alainna cried out and ran forward, hiking her skirt high enough to clear her booted stride as she crashed through the undergrowth and shoved slender branches out of her way.

Ahead of her, the struggle between the man and the wolf had ended. From a distance, she had seen Sebastien strike and kill one wolf, and she had watched in terror as he had run even closer, as if he had no fear for his own life, to strike the other down at close range with his sword.

She halted and watched as the Highlander faced Sebastien over the body of the dead wolf. Her heart, slamming in her chest, nearly stopped in that moment.

Ruari MacWilliam looked at Sebastien, then glanced over at her. Their gazes touched directly, knowingly.

Then he turned and ran.

Alainna gasped and clapped her hands over her mouth, hands shaking. Giric and Robert ran past her in pursuit, their footsteps crunching over snow and bracken.

She was sure the man she had seen was her kinsman Ruari *Mór*. But Ruari was dead, she reminded herself, killed by the king's men on a battlefield in the south of Scotland, a year past.

Yet she was certain. She would know him anywhere, under any amount of blood and beard. And he had known her. She had seen the awareness of it in his eyes.

Legs quivering, she moved forward. Sebastien wiped his blade clean in the snow and sheathed it, and stepped beneath the tree to assist the woman and child hiding there.

Alainna ran to help. As the woman climbed down to the ground, Alainna recognized her as a friend. Both women cried out and wrapped in an embrace.

"Lileas," Alainna gasped. "Oh, Lileas! You are safe now!" She looked up. "Is it Eoghan in the tree? *Ach,* lad, come down! The knight will catch you! Come down, now!"

"Eoghan," Sebastien repeated, stretching up to grasp the boy by the waist. "Come down to me. There you are," he said pleasantly as he took the child's slight weight into his arms.

He turned with the dark-haired child balanced easily in his arms and looked at Lileas, smiling. Eoghan, who Alainna knew was three years old, watched the knight and his mother with wide brown eyes, remarkably calm.

"Thank you," Lileas said in Gaelic. She looked at Alainna uncertainly. "Alainna? Did this knight come with you?"

"This is Sir Sebastien le Bret, who has come to Kinlochan with the king's men," she answered. "Sebastien, this is Lileas, daughter of Father Padruig, our parish priest. And her son, Eoghan."

He covered his surprise admirably well, Alainna saw, certain he had not often met the daughter and grandson of a priest. He blinked once and smiled immediately, inclining his head to Lileas in a courteous greeting.

"We are so grateful to you," Lileas said. She held out her arms for her son, who shook his head and clasped his arms around the knight's neck. Sebastien seemed at ease holding the child. Conversing with him quietly, he distracted him from the sight of the slain wolves and bloody snow as he carried him toward the outer edge of the forest, where the horses waited.

Alainna followed, her arm around Lileas, who pushed a trembling hand over her dark red hair. She shivered with cold, and Alainna stopped to take off her plaid *arisaid* and wrap it over Lileas's thin shoulders, seeing that the young woman wore no woolen plaid over her brown tunic.

"Eoghan and I were walking home from my father's house, back to our little cottage," Lileas told Alainna breathlessly. Sebastien turned to listen. "I did not mean to be out so late. The wolves appeared and followed us, so silent and menacing. . . ." She shivered again, this time with horror.

"Who was the man with you?" Sebastien asked.

"He was not with us. He came out of the forest to help us. He was suddenly there, thank God. I have never seen him before. He lifted Eoghan into the tree and pushed me up there too, and then faced those wolves as if they were nothing to fear." She looked behind them. "I hope they find him. I do not know why he ran. He is sore wounded, I am sure, though I gave him my *arisaid* to wrap over his arm as he approached the wolves."

"That likely saved his arm," Sebastien said. He glanced at Alainna, frowning. "Did you know the man?"

She swallowed. "I . . . I did not see him closely," she said carefully. "The sight of an armored knight is rare here. He may have been frightened and ran for that reason."

Sebastien laughed, curt and quick. "A man who takes on two wolves does not frighten easily." He glanced back. "Ah, Giric and Robert are on their way back."

Alainna turned. "Without the Highlander."

Her foster brother and the knight dashed toward them. "He is gone," Robert said breathlessly. "Vanished. For a man so wounded, it is amazing. Not even a trail of blood to follow."

Sebastien nodded. "A mighty warrior, this man," he said thoughtfully. He looked at Alainna, his gaze clear and keen.

She lifted her chin and returned his gaze, her heart thumping heavily.

"Did you know him?" Sebastien asked Giric.

"I did not see the man well," Giric said. He slid a somber, rapid glance at Alainna. She realized that her foster brother had also recognized the warrior.

"If he was a MacNechtan," Robert said, "that would explain why he ran."

"Now that could be." Sebastien did not sound convinced.

"Lileas, girl, are you hurt?" Giric asked.

"I am fine," she said. "And my son is safe too, thanks to this knight, and to the man who fled."

"Let me take you home," Giric said. He looked at Sebastien. "Robert and I will load the wolves onto one of the horses, and Robert can bring them back to Kinlochan. Then I will escort Lileas and Eoghan to their home. It is not far from here, but it is not on Kinlochan land. Alainna should not come along."

Sebastien nodded agreement. "I will take her back to Kinlochan." While Giric went to fetch his garron and Robert went back to the tree, he turned, the child still in his arms, and walked toward the horses. Alainna and Lileas followed.

Eoghan pointed to Sebastien's horse, quietly grazing on the sparse grasses protruding from the snow. "Is that your horse?"

"It is," Sebastien replied. "Come, I will introduce you. His name is Araby. His mother came from a land where it is hot and sunny. He does not like the cold much," he added.

"I like the cold," Eoghan said. "I like horses. White horses." He grinned.

Sebastien lifted Eoghan up so that the child could touch the horse's long, cream-colored mane and pat the great head while the horse stood passively. Then he vaulted Eoghan into the saddle.

"I will have a horse and a sword," Eoghan announced. "I will be a warrior like my father."

"I am sure he is a fine warrior, and you will be, too," Sebastien said. He walked the horse in a circle while Eoghan beamed, holding on to the reins.

"Come now, your mother is waiting," Sebastien said then. "If you visit Kinlochan, you may sit on Araby's back and ride him around again. Would you like that?"

Eoghan nodded earnestly, and Sebastien handed him into his mother's arms. He bid them farewell, graciously accepting Lileas's thanks. Lileas hugged Alainna and carried Eoghan to join Giric and Robert, who were walking out of the woods.

"You are cold," Sebastien told Alainna sternly, lifting his fur-lined cloak from his saddle and draping its weight over her shoulders. "Take this."

She shivered and nodded her thanks. Sebastien helped her mount her garron, and as he turned to mount his own horse, she glanced furtively toward the forest as if expecting Ruari MacWilliam to appear.

Ruari was far from there by now, she was certain. She

hoped he would go to the safety of his wife's house in the hills. Stifling a little gasp, she wondered if he had already been there, and if that was why Esa refused to come out of the hills to stay at Kinlochan.

Sebastien circled his horse to walk in tandem with hers. She smiled at him despite her racing, anxious thoughts.

"You were courageous back there," she said. He shrugged and murmured a dismissal. "That was a mighty deed," she insisted. "Giric will report it to my kinfolk, and Lorne will be delighted. He is already composing a poem about you and the boar. Now he will need to add more verses. And I am so grateful to you for acting so quickly and saving Father Padruig's daughter and his grandson. You will hear many thanks for this."

She babbled a little, she knew, but she wanted to keep her thoughts, and her glance, from skipping back toward the forest.

"I reached them first, that is all," he said. "Giric would have done the same, or Robert, or anyone else with the skill and the weapons. The brave man was that mysterious Gael who ran off before we could thank him."

She kept her profile to him. "I hope he is not badly hurt."

"Let us hope he has kin nearby who can tend to his wounds," he murmured, sliding a glance at her. She merely nodded and kept silent. "Eoghan is a fine boy," he commented after a moment.

"He likes horses and warriors, as small boys will do," she said. "You were patient with him."

"A pleasure. His grandfather is the priest?"

"Father Padruig and his wife have three daughters. Highland priests who are part of the Celtic Church, rather than the Church of Rome, often marry and raise families."

"I have heard that. I know Rome condemns the practice, but Highlanders do not seem bothered by that." He glanced at her. "Is Eoghan's father alive, or was he one of those lost fighting for Clan Laren?"

She hesitated. "His father is Cormac MacNechtan."

"Cormac!" Sebastien stared at her. "I thought he was not wed—he petitioned for your hand."

"A few years ago he and Lileas were handfasted," she said.

"Handfasted?" he said. "Like marriage?"

She nodded. "A step between betrothal and marriage, with the vows of the one and the privileges of the other. The couple are allowed to dissolve the union after a year and a day if they are not happy. Most go on to take vows before a priest."

"Lileas and Cormac did not have their vows witnessed?"

"She lived with Cormac at Turroch, but their handfasting did not last the year. She gave birth to Eoghan a few months after she returned to her father's house. Now she and the boy live in a house of their own, which Cormac provided for them. He acknowledges the child, as he should."

"Then he has some honor to him," Sebastien drawled.

She shrugged. "You were kind to the child. I hope knowing the name of his father will not change your mind."

"I would not visit the sins of the father upon the child," he replied. The wind caught the thickness of his hair as he looked up at the mountains. "He reminds me of someone."

"Eoghan does resemble his father."

"He reminds me of my own son," he said.

She gaped at him. "Your son?" The day had enough shocks in it already, she thought in a daze; first the wolves, then Ruari, now this. She continued to stare. "Your son?"

He gave her a slow smile, and she saw pride and pleasure in it. "He is a little older than Eoghan. I am widowed."

"You never told me," she said.

"You never asked." He echoed her earlier words. "This marriage came quickly upon us both. There are details we do not know about each other." He paused. "If you have anything to tell me, now may be the time to do it."

"I have no husband," she glowered. "Nor children."

"That is good to know," he said mildly.

"When were you married?" she asked, breathless suddenly, her heart thumping at the thought of him with an earlier wife—no doubt one he had wed from choice. Unbidden, the memory of their shared kiss made her cheeks burn.

"About six years ago. Over three years have passed since

she died." He fisted a white-knuckled hand on his thigh as he rode. The silent poignancy tugged at her heart.

"And the child? Where is he now?"

"In Brittany. He is just five. Conan is his name, after my leige lord, the duke of Brittany."

She watched him, astonished and curious. A deep well of feeling and experience existed within him, she realized. He had shared only the surface of that with her, but the glimpses beneath were tantalizing. He was a father, had been a husband, had grown up an orphan child in a monastery for foundlings. No wonder he had shown such patience and kindness to Eoghan.

"Will you tell me about him?"

Sebastien paused. "He is clever and strong, blond-headed like me, with his mother's brown eyes. He is . . . like sunshine." The subtle glow in his smile pulled at Alainna's heart to watch. "I placed him with friends, monks, in a monastery in Brittany, the place where I lived as a small child. I thought it best."

"He is safe and well-kept, I am sure, while you are away."

He frowned. "Conan is no longer there. A fire destroyed much of the complex, and they were all forced to leave. I learned about it just before I was sent here." He tensed his jaw. "I do not know where he is now."

"Oh, Sebastien," she whispered. She reached out to touch his steel mesh sleeve. "That is why you are so determined to go back."

"In part. I sent a letter as soon as I found out, offering the use of my own Breton holding, but I do not know if the letter will reach them."

"You must go back and find him," she said decisively. "And bring him back to Scotland with you."

Sebastien raised his brows. "Here?"

She nodded. "He has a home and a family here."

He slowed his horse and stared at her. Then he resumed riding in silence, looking at the hills as if he had forgotten that she rode beside him.

"Sebastien?" she asked.

"I . . . had not planned to bring him here," he said. "I have always planned for Conan to grow to manhood in

Brittany. He will become count of his mother's lands in France, which his grandfather now holds."

"Ah." Cold hurt crept through her. "I understand. You do not want your son raised as a barbarian in a savage land."

"It is not that," he said abruptly.

"I am not a fool." She would not look at him.

He sighed as if reluctant to speak. "I . . . I have had many dreams, much ambition in my life," he finally said. "I did not expect any of it to lead me here, but somehow it has."

"And you are sorry for it," she said. The wind picked up the hem of the cloak she wore, tugged at her hair. "That is understandable for a knight of your caliber and upbringing."

"You know little of my upbringing."

"Then tell me, so I will know."

"I have scarcely told anyone."

She waited, but he said no more. "You guard your past carefully."

"I am simply not one to talk about it. My past is . . . my own."

She frowned at him. "Someday you will take down that shield you hold over your heart, Sebastien *Bàn*." The name Una used for him came naturally to her lips.

"Someday I may," he replied.

Robert hailed them from behind with a shout. Alainna and Sebastien turned and halted while the other knight caught up to them, leading a garron carrying the two wolves.

Alainna walked out in a thick morning mist, carrying an offering of oats to leave the stone pillar. She noticed that the cream, oats, and cheese she had left before were gone, bowl, sack, and all. Usually her offerings were eaten by animals, she knew—but animals did not take bowls with them.

"Finan!" she called, as her deerhound wandered off to sniff the grass. Likely he scented whoever had most recently been near the pillar stone. He faced the crescent of forestland that stretched beyond the Stone Maiden and barked.

"Finan, hush," Alainna said. "We are not chasing deer today. Come back!" The dog ran toward her and circled away, following the same path, barking again. Alainna glanced around, but could barely see past the stone and the near edge of the loch, where the fog drifted in ghostly streams.

A fine, cold rain began, and she pulled her *arisaid* snug against the drizzle. She murmured a chant, circled the stone sunwise, and turned to walk back to the fortress.

"Finan!" she called. *"Ach,"* she muttered in irritation, for he had disappeared. When she heard him barking near the trees, which were blanketed in mist, she walked toward the forest, glancing cautiously around.

The dog's bark was the excited, pleased sound Finan used for her kinsmen and for Sebastien le Bret. But the men were still inside the fortress. They usually rode out every day to patrol the property and to visit the tenant farms one by one. Sebastien had also begun to estimate the acres in the holding by measuring the distances between the boundary stones. That task alone would take the Breton knight a long time to complete. But nothing could be done in such thick fog, so the knights had stayed inside Kinlochan today to repair and clean their armor and weapons and the horses' gear.

"Finan! Here, lad! Here to me!"

"Alainna!" A man's voice, hushed and urgent, came from the direction of the trees. The voice was familiar, though distorted by fog.

"Niall?" she asked. "Lorne?"

"Alainna, here. Help me."

A chill ran along her backbone then. She stepped toward the dog and grasped his collar. "Take me to Ruari," she urged.

Finan led her into the cover of the trees, into the thick fog. Alainna plunged ahead, and heard her kinsman call again.

A man loomed ahead of her. "Alainna," he said. She had not heard that familiar, welcome voice in a long time.

He leaned one broad shoulder against a birch tree and smiled.

She halted. "Ruari! Oh, Ruari, it is you!"

"Alainna *milis,* sweet one," he said. Finan ran toward him, and Ruari patted the hound's head and grinned at her again. His hair was whiter than she remembered, his beard whiter too, both still streaked with black. His eyes were the same keen blue she remembered beneath dark arched brows. And his smile, ever crooked, ever charming, had not changed at all.

He opened an arm to welcome her, and she ran forward. "Are you a ghost?" She half laughed as she threw her arms around him.

"I am no ghost," he said, with a little grunt. "Flesh and blood, and come back home, hoping for a welcome."

Alainna kissed his leathery cheek, then stood back, dashing away tears, remembering that he was wounded. One arm was wrapped in a ragged, bloodied cloth and held close to his chest.

"How is it you are here? We heard you were dead! Have you seen Esa? Does she know? Oh, Ruari, I could hardly believe my eyes the other day when I saw you there in the forest, fighting off those wolves! Are you sore hurt?"

He chuckled a little at her barrage of questions. "Esa does not yet know," he said. "I was on my way there when I discovered the wolves. I am not so hurt that I am dead, though."

"How is it you are here at all? We heard you were killed in a battle with the king's men!"

"I was sore wounded there. A few of my kinsmen escaped the field and took me with them. When I recovered my wits, I learned we were in Ireland, in exile. I had no chance to come back until recently, and that in secret."

"And you sent no word to us in all this time? Nor to Esa? How could you not? Ruari *Mór,* that was a terrible time for us all, the knowledge of your death, and you alive all the while!"

He looked sheepish. "I could not send word. But you have the right to be angry."

"I do, for Esa's sake! She has suffered so for you,

mourned you—and your son—she will not even leave her home in the hills."

"Is she well?" he asked urgently.

"Well in body, but failing in spirit. Will you go there now? Even in this fog, you will know the way by heart."

"I would, but I cannot. Alainna, I need your help." He stood away from the tree, which he had been leaning against. She realized then how weak he was, how pale his cheeks. In addition to his crudely bandaged left arm, his left calf was also covered in bloodied bandages.

"I need a safe place to rest. I found a cave, and kept a fire going to keep beasts away. Last night was the first I had the strength to walk out. The oats and cream you left for the Maiden were delicious." He smiled.

Alainna gave a moan of sympathy. "Stay here with Finan. I will fetch my kinsmen—"

"Do not," he said quickly. "There are knights at Kinlochan. One of them saved my life when he killed those wolves. Why are they there? Who are they?"

"The king sent them. He granted Kinlochan to a Norman, a Breton knight, the one who fought for you. We are . . . to be wed."

"You, wed to a Norman? Kinlochan is his?" Ruari frowned. "When did this happen?"

"Recently. I am not glad about it, but this will help protect my people from MacNechtans."

"*Ach,*" he said. "Alas. Your father is dead, then."

She bit at her lip, realizing that Ruari did not know. "By the hand of a MacNechtan, a few months ago," she said somberly.

Ruari nodded grimly. "Bless his soul. I am not surprised Kinlochan is lost to the crown now that Laren is gone."

"I must get help for you," she said urgently, seeing fresh blood on his arm. "Stay here, Ruari, please. I will be back."

"Alainna, wait. You may be safe with king's men, but I am not. I am a broken man, hunted and outlawed. If they learn that I am alive and here in Scotland, I will be hanged by my feet without mercy."

"The king's knights look for the rebels, but I told them you were dead. There is no reason to tell them who you are if you come to Kinlochan."

"I cannot take that risk for you, or myself, or my own kin. If they discover me, they will kill me, and bring harm to any who are close to me."

"Ruari, what is it? What are you doing here so secretly?"

He shook his head. "I am a MacWilliam, and that is enough. We claim the throne through a closer blood tie to King Duncan and the ancient Pictish kings of Scotland than King William boasts. We believe that my young cousin Guthred is in direct line for the throne. He is in Ireland now, but will never give up his quest for the crown. I came here to help him. I cannot reveal myself, or my kinsmen's cause, to Normans. But I need your help, girl. I must have food, and a place to hide until I heal."

Alainna nodded and turned anxiously, wondering what to do. "Ah! The island out on the loch! There is an old stone ruin where you can hide, and evergreen trees to keep you sheltered. I will take you there in the boat, and bring you food. You can have a good hearthfire there. My kinsmen will help, too, once they learn—"

"No one must know. Your kinsmen do not favor my cause."

"They do not, and never have. But they favor you for a great warrior. And Esa is their kinswoman. They will not betray her husband, no matter what he has done."

"No one must know," he repeated sternly.

"Giric MacGregor knows. He saw you in the forest too. Let me tell him. He will help." She saw Ruari sigh and relent. "And I must tell Esa. Her heart is breaking for love of you."

"Tell them," he said, his voice gruff. "No one else."

"I will bring Esa to you."

He looked away, nodded. "I do want to see her."

Alainna shifted her shoulder under his arm to offer her support as they walked out of the woods and made their way slowly toward the loch, Finan beside them. As they passed the great stone, Ruari urged her toward it.

"Swear by the Maiden," Ruari said. "Swear to me that no one else but Esa and Giric will learn that I am here."

"Will you not trust me?" she asked.

"I trust you," he said. "But I know you care so much for an old kinsman that you might try to help him too eagerly. Swear by the Maiden that you will keep my secret."

Alainna hesitated, unsure how she could hide this from her kinsfolk—or from the knight who would soon be her husband.

"Swear it, dear girl," he said kindly. "Or I will go back into the forest, and you will not see me again."

She sighed and placed her hand on the cold granite. "I will guard your secret, Ruari *Mór,* and do my best to keep you safe. By earth and sky, by stone and water, by the Maiden herself, I swear it."

"Done," Ruari said. They moved toward the shore, where a small boat rocked in the long reeds. "We shall make Giric and Esa swear the same. Though Esa will not like that at all, if I know my wife," he added wryly.

"Worry more about her temper after she learns you are alive and have not sent her word," she said. Ruari chuckled.

Once Ruari and Finan were crouched in the bottom of the round, hide-covered boat, Alainna took up the triangular oar and rowed cautiously toward the island, a dark, misted mass at the center of the loch.

While she rowed, and when they landed on the stony shore, she was grateful that they stayed hidden from view in the deep white folds of the fog.

Chapter Fourteen

"**B**astien, there you are," Hugo said as Sebastien entered the hall. "The Scots want us to hunt with them today. But they want us to wear blankets like they do," he added disdainfully. He pointed to the folded plaids that Una and Morag held in their arms. Una smiled, her small head trembling, and offered one of the plaids to Hugo, who shook his head.

"I will not go bare-assed and bare-legged like these savages," said Etienne de Barre, standing beside Hugo.

Sebastien frowned, looking around him as he removed his sword belt and sheathed weapon, which he had used during his dawn exercise, and laid them aside. He had expected to find his men just rising from their pallets and Una stirring a kettle of porridge over the fire.

Instead, he had entered a place filled with commotion. His men stood about with several elderly Highland men and women. Some of them, having no language in common, argued loudly, with wide gestures. Bright plaids were strewn across the floor. Niall and Lulach, along with their wives, Mairi and Beitris, tried to coax some of the knights, who shook their heads in refusal.

Sebastien looked at Robert, who stood nearby. "What is going on here?"

"Giric came in while you were gone and said the hunt would be today," Robert answered. "Then the elders came in, carrying these tartaned garments that the Scots wear."

"Those are blankets," Hugo said. "I will not dress like a barbarian. I am a Norman knight."

"Why should we give up good serge and fine linen for burlap and horse blankets?" Etienne grumbled beside him.

"Highlanders wear neither burlap nor horse blankets."

A smooth feminine voice spoke in English behind them. Sebastien turned to see Alainna approach. "My kinfolk wish your knights to wear our Highland dress," she told Sebastien. "It is Highland tradition for guests to wear the *breacan an fhéilidh,* the belted plaid, on a hunt."

"It is not a Norman tradition," Etienne said stubbornly.

"The plaid is an ancient and honorable garment among the Highland people," Alainna said. "Our men are proud to wear it."

"If it is the custom of our hosts," Sebastien said, "we do not wish to insult them."

"Then you put it on," Hugo said. He folded his arms.

"Oui," Etienne said. "You show us how the blanket is worn. You are soon to be one of them, after all, when this marriage is done." He grinned and elbowed Walter of Coldstream, the knight beside him.

"Ho, Bastien will wear it!" Walter hooted.

"Better him than us," William, another knight, remarked.

"The king's own honor guard will not go naked as a savage," Richard de Wicke said. "I wager he will not."

"I will wager against you," Eitenne said.

"I will, too. We back a brave man," Hugo boasted.

Sebastien glanced at his grinning men. He saw Alainna's eyes sparkle, too.

"We will be glad to show Sir Sebastien how the *breacan* is worn," she said. "You must remove your tunic, sirrah." Someone guffawed. Alainna's cheeks bloomed pink.

Sebastien slid them all a sour glance. He sat on a bench and pulled off his boots and hose while his men murmured and chuckled. Then he stood.

With a decisive motion, he stripped off his long brown tunic and shirt, pulling them over his head and dropping them on the floor. His linen *braies,* rolled at the waist over a drawstring and slung low on his flat abdomen, left most of his long legs bare. He felt a chill on his skin, still coated with sweat from his sword practice.

Some of his men hooted, and others grinned or laughed outright at the bold manner in which he approached their dare. Sebastien offered them all a little mocking bow, and his own grin grew wide. Next, he bowed to Alainna and her kinswomen. Una grinned, while Morag and Beitris giggled.

Alainna, he saw, no longer smiled, her eyes wide, her cheeks pink.

Sebastien turned to Niall and Lulach. "I would be proud to wear the plaid," he said in Gaelic, "if you will show me the proper way to put it on."

Niall gestured with his single hand toward a plaid spread on the floor. "The *breacan* is folded again and again," he explained, "and a belt is under it, see. Lie down on the floor, and we will show you what to do."

"Lie on the floor?" Sebastien repeated incredulously.

Lulach nodded and Sebastien settled into position. Niall crouched beside him.

"The *breacan* serves as a garment as well as a sleeping blanket when we are out in the hills," he said. "It is why we lay it out like this, to dress quickly if we are caught by an ambush, or need to leap up to chase after a herd of deer, or stolen cattle, eh? Here, wrap this side over the front of you, so. Now grab the ends of the belt, and fasten it around your waist. Like that, good."

Within moments, Sebastien stood, the plaid securely draped and belted around his waist, the excess billowed behind him. His legs were bare from the knees down. Lulach tucked some excess into the leather belt, then pulled the pouched section up the back to cross one part over the left shoulder and another part beneath his right arm, joining them at the left shoulder with a straight iron pin. He showed Sebastien the large, useful pocket formed by the drape, and stood back.

Sebastien strode in a slow circle, testing the fit. The knights grinned and applauded, some of them still hooting and laughing.

" 'Tis quite comfortable," he announced to his men. "And the wool is warm and lightweight. It is a good garment." He took a long step, then another, appreciating the freedom the shorter length and generous folds gave his legs. He was used to a long tunic that, unless split, could hinder a fast stride.

"It is more suited to climbing hills than our own tunics are," he said, circling. "And 'tis practical, for it can be used for a pallet and blanket, and yet one can be dressed within moments. I like it."

He inclined his head to Niall and Lulach, then to Alainna. "I like it well," he announced in Gaelic.

"You will be cold with no breeches!" Hugo said.

"So will you," Sebastien answered. "We will all wear the *breacan* for the hunt to honor our hosts' customs."

The knights, with some muttering, began to take off their tunics and surcoats, although each one retained shirt, boots, hose, and *braies*. The elderly men and women came forward to help them put on the plaids.

As Sebastien walked the length of the room, he saw Alainna walk toward him, carrying a garment over her arm. He waited for her in the shadows of a raftered side aisle.

"Sebastien *Bán*," she said. He liked the mellifluent sound of the affectionate name Una already used for him. "Thank you for your courtesy. My kin are well pleased."

" 'Twas naught, my lady," he murmured. He glanced at the Highlanders, who laughed, chatted, and gesticulated merrily when language failed while they helped the knights. "And you? Are you pleased?" he asked.

"I am." Her gaze strayed to his bare chest, and rose to his face. Her skin was so translucent that Sebastien could see the heat in her rise in a pink blush. "Here," she said, thrusting out her arm, draped with a garment. "I want to give you this. It is the *léine*, the linen shirt that our men wear with the belted plaid." She held it up.

Sebastien fingered the long, generously cut buff-colored shirt, its cloth sturdy but soft. "My thanks," he said. "I confess I was wary of hunting without a shirt in cold weather," he added wryly.

She chuckled, her fingers deft as she unpinned the upper part of his plaid and freed the billow. As she swept it behind him, her hands smoothed over his bare shoulder.

Sebastien pulled on the shirt, and Alainna leaned close to tuck it in at his waist. Her hair softly brushed his chest, wafting a trace of lavender scent. Her hands were warm and he closed his eyes briefly to savor the intimacy that enveloped them.

Alainna looked up, her cheeks blushed. "You must pull the shirt down," she said, pointing to the skirt of the plaid.

"Ah." He reached underneath to tug it into place.

She adjusted the neck of the shirt and repinned the plaid.

Her hands gentled over his shoulders and flattened on his chest. Sebastien watched her, entranced, feeling a languid tingle wherever she touched him. His heart pounded and his body deepened the innocent contact into desire.

The urge to touch her, to pull her close was strong. He wanted to kiss her deep and full, and wanted far more than that to satisfy the hard drumming of his heart and the warm, heavy surge in his groin.

He leaned closer. She glanced up at him, her indigo eyes limpid, her mouth partly open, soft and lush as a rose. She swallowed slowly, and he saw the delicate line of her throat.

He lifted his hand to brush away a silken lock of hair that had slipped over her cheek, and let his fingers trace over her head before he lowered his hand. "My thanks," he murmured.

She tipped her chin. "Now you look as fine as any Highland man, sirrah."

"Although I do not match your ideal of a Celtic warrior."

"More than you think," she murmured. "You could make any heart flutter, I think. Beitris and Morag are smiling over there, I see."

"And your heart?" He looked only at her.

Her cheeks and gaze burned bright. "Mine," she said, "does not flutter easily." She looked away.

Nor does mine, he wanted to say. But his implacable, steady heart beat fast a bird's wing in his chest.

"Giric," she said, turning as her foster brother crossed the room toward them, carrying boots and shirts in his arms. Sebastien had not noticed that the young Highlander had entered the hall.

"I see the Normans are nearly ready to hunt," Giric said.

"They are, and we must thank Sebastien *Bàn* for that."

"So I hear. Niall told me of your courage." He smiled.

Sebastien made a wry face. "Small courage."

Giric chuckled. "Where there is small courage, there is greater courage, eh?" He looked at Alainna. "Lorne and I brought some other things for the knights to wear." He handed her a pair of fur boots. "I think these might fit this one"—he indicated Sebastien—"if you do not mind giving him your father's belongings. I am sure Laren MacLaren would not mind."

She offered the boots to Sebastien. "My father wore these with pride, for they were made from a wolf he once killed. You killed two wolves the other day, and he would have been impressed by your deed. You are near my father's build, though he was heavier. It is his shirt you wear, too."

He accepted the gift. "I am honored."

She stared up at him silently, her eyes filled with something new, a flash of sudden wonder and warmth that sent a deep thrill into the core of his being. He returned her gaze and smiled a little, his heart thumping hard.

"Will you come out with us, Alainna?" Giric asked.

"I will leave this hunt to you," she replied. "The women will enjoy some peace at Kinlochan with the men gone for the day." She smiled at Giric, and he chuckled.

Sebastien's own smile faded. He had noticed the loving ease between them before. Though aware that their affection was like that of siblings or cousins, he still felt a stab of jealousy.

"We will leave soon," Giric said. "I hope you and your Normans have strong legs. We chase the deer here, in a race with the hounds, and our garrons carry the game we kill." He grinned in a good-natured challenge.

"We will keep up," Sebastien answered. He nodded to both and walked away, carrying her gift of the hide boots.

Anxious and elated, thinking about Ruari MacWilliam's return, Alainna could not settle her mood or her thoughts. She had not yet had a chance to tell Giric about Ruari, and could not share the news with anyone else but Esa. She went to her workshop after the men departed for the hunt, hoping to lose herself in carving. Focus, effort, and simply pounding with the mallet could often dissolve her worries and ease her mind when nothing else could.

She settled on a stool beside her workbench and picked up her mallet and tools to work on the finishing stages of one of the gray limestone pieces. She smiled to herself as she imagined how joyful Esa would be when she discovered that her husband was alive.

Her heart pounded hard as she realized that Ruari was hiding dangerously close to Kinlochan fortress and the king's men who sought him. She had rowed back and forth to the island twice the previous day under cover of the fog, a risk she had hardly considered, for her concern for Ruari was paramount. She had brought him food and plaids, had dressed his wounds and started a cozy hearth fire for him.

Trained in basic healing ways by Una and Morag, and by her own grim experience with injured and dying men at Kinlochan over the past several years, she knew how to treat him. Now that he was bandaged properly, and had taken herbs in an infusion of hot water to help cleanse his blood, she was certain that he would heal well, provided he took care to rest.

Ruari had promised to stay on the island inside the old ruined broch, an ancient stone tower broken by time and weather. He had asked for something to occupy his time while he recovered, offering to carve some bowls and spoons for the extra guests at Kinlochan. Alainna had brought him pine wood and a small, sharp blade for carving. She and Ruari agreed that he need only stay on the island until he regained enough strength to travel on.

Even though Alainna was accustomed to wielding the mallet, her arms and back ached from the rowing she had done. She flexed her stiff shoulders, feeling as if the knowledge she guarded weighed heavily on her.

Her thoughts strayed again and again to Sebastien. She had helped to hide the renegade that the Breton knight intended to capture, and she had sworn upon the Stone Maiden to keep Ruari's secret. She could never reveal it to Sebastien, although she knew that torn loyalties and desperate secrets had no place in a marriage.

Even a week ago, there would have been no question of where her loyalties belonged. Now, though, whenever she was with Sebastien, she seemed to see him with new clarity. He was far more than the land-hungry Norman she had once thought. A kind, thoughtful, lonely man existed within him, well protected by a barrier of strength and will.

And the memory of deep and glorious kisses in the shadow of the Stone Maiden made her knees go weak, made her heart drum faster, made her long for more, endlessly more, from him. She wondered if she could actually love the king's choice for her husband.

She wondered, then, if she had already begun to love him.

After a while, too distracted by her thoughts to work effectively, she put away her tools, wrapped her plaid about her, and went outside, whistling to Finan as she headed first for the kitchen and then for the gate, and for Ruari. She would bring him fresh oatcakes and keep him company. Once she fetched Esa from the hills, she knew that Ruari, whatever his injuries, would be fine.

The hunters returned to Kinlochan hours later, leading garrons that carried two red stags, a hind, and a brace of hares whose fur had wintered to white. In stride with Robert and Giric, Sebastien walked past the great stone pillar, which cast a long shadow over the brown grasses of the meadow. Niall and Lulach followed, drawing the reins of the horses. Hugo and the rest of the knights lagged behind on foot.

Giric glanced over his shoulder. "Good hunters all, your knights, but none of them hill-climbers."

"Highland slopes are hell in places," Robert said. "We know that now." He rubbed his flank as if it ached.

"Hah," Giric said. "Try one of the black mountain steeps to the north, and then tell me it is hard to climb the hills of Kinlochan." He grinned and clapped Robert on the shoulder. Robert stumbled slightly, limping on weary legs. He looked sheepishly at Sebastien.

"Bastien, you were right to urge us to dress like these barbarians, I will give you that," Robert said. "Plaids are far more practical here."

Giric made a scoffing sound. "Barbarians, we! And what fools thought Spanish horses could climb mountains, and argued to bring them along? Highland hunters must run and climb if they want meat, and let the garrons carry it back for them."

"Your Highland garrons are surefooted," Robert admitted, "but their owners are still the savages of the north." He grinned at Giric and slapped him in turn on the back.

Sebastien smiled, watching them. After chasing the

wolves the other day and taking down a stag on the hunt, Robert and Giric had become fast friends. Giric turned to murmur to Niall and Lulach in Gaelic, provoking laughter among the older men.

Robert slowed his step, and Sebastien kept pace. He glanced at the loch, calm and blue beneath the late afternoon sky, reflecting the heights of the white-capped mountains. "This is a proud and strong land, like its people. I can understand why so many Norman knights hunger to gain land grants from the king of Scots."

Robert nodded agreement. "I would not refuse a grant anywhere in Scotland."

"I will be sure to tell King William when next I see him."

Robert slid him a glance. "Thinking of leaving?"

"I cannot do that yet, but I am anxious to return to Brittany. The year draws to a close. I had hoped to be there for the Yuletide season, but 'tis not to be."

"Even if you left Kinlochan now and rode to Dunfermline to make your report to the king, no ship could sail to Brittany by Christmastide."

"There is still much that must be done here before I can think about leaving. Thankfully, we were fortunate in the hunt today. Kinlochan has many mouths to feed, and will for a while."

"Much to be done, aye," Robert said. "You will have a wedding soon, my friend." Robert grinned.

"Aye," Sebastien said. "We are to visit the priest tomorrow to discuss it, or so Una says."

"Then Christmas will bring wedding revelry with it." Robert raised a brow, and Sebastien shot him a dry look. "I suspect we may spend the winter here among the savages if the weather grows poor, as the Highlanders claim it will."

Sebastien sighed. "Christmas already, and I can only hope that my letter has reached the abbot. I have to trust that he has been able to keep watch over my son." He frowned. "Conan will look for me by Christmas Day, and I will not be there. I was not there for him when he was in danger, either."

"You will be there as quickly as you can, and the monks will care for their charges as best they can."

Sebastien nodded. "I thought it wise to install him in their care, rather than leave him with his grandparents after his mother died. I was wrong about that—mayhap wrong to come to Scotland altogether, at least where Conan is concerned."

"How were you to know what would happen at the monastery? And you could hardly leave him with his mother's family," Robert said. "Once those vultures had him in France, you would never see him again. They do not like you well, Sebastien, though you were wed to their precious daughter."

"True. I could not keep him with me, and I had no real home to offer him." He fisted his hand. "If I had only stayed there!"

"You did what was best, Bastien," Robert said quietly.

Sebastien nodded silently. He gazed at the fortress gleaming in the afternoon sun. It was a home and a haven for many, and had been for generations. But he had not intended to live there with Conan. A home in the Highlands of Scotland would not benefit his son.

Or would it? he wondered. Was he wrong to want to raise Conan in Brittany? He frowned, feeling as if his goals and his ambitions had begun to shift beneath him, as if he tread on quicksand and did not know in which direction lay sure ground.

The gates of Kinlochan swung open as the men climbed the rocky slope that led to the palisade. Donal appeared at the entrance to wave them inside.

Sebastien, with Robert and the others, gained the top of the slope and approached the gate. Alainna stood in the bailey, slim and pale in her gray gown. If not for the fiery color of her hair, Sebastien thought, she would be a small sister to the granite pillar by the loch.

Then she moved, a statue come to life. She ran toward them with slender grace, her face alight, and greeted her kinsmen. When Sebastien entered, she turned to him with the brightness still upon her like a lantern.

He felt his heart leap, but he kept his expression plain, nodding a greeting. Something in him bubbled like a spring at the sound of her laugh and the sight of her smile. The sensation was rare and precious, and he kept it close.

She turned and spoke to the others, asking questions about the day, obviously delighted by what they had gained on the hunt, and proud of their success.

Sebastien lifted the brace of hares from the garron's back. Alainna, laughing at something Giric had said, whirled suddenly and stumbled against Sebastien.

He took her elbow quickly, then loosed it and stepped back. "Pardon, I did not mean to touch you. I am grimy from the day."

"As am I," she said, holding up her palms to show him the stone dust that covered her hands. "If you carry those to the kitchen, Morag and Beitris will take them from you." She pointed toward the building. He nodded and began to walk away.

"Sebastien," she called. He turned. "It was a good hunt."

"It was." He watched her.

"We will have food for all, for a while at least. I . . . I was worried about that, I confess. But now I am pleased."

"Ah. Then I am pleased, if you are." He inclined his head.

She stood with her hands clasped in front of her. "Will you change out of the *breacan* now that the hunt is done?"

"I am a Breton knight, not a Highland man," he said. "I should wear what suits me best."

She tilted her head, watching him. "That suits you well." She smiled and turned, then glanced over her shoulder to send him a shy flash of a smile.

He stood in the bailey with the rope of hares dangling from his hand. The day had grown chilly, and the sun went behind a cloud. Sunshine lingered in the radiance of her smile, the color of her hair, the chime of her laughter.

He watched her, thoughtfully, wondering just what Alainna MacLaren was coming to mean in his life. He had not planned to linger here when he had reluctantly accepted the king's grant. But he had not thought to find her so enchanting, and he had not expected to like her kin and her home as much as he did.

Too much, he thought, for a man who had decided to settle where his roots, such as they were, existed. Heart beating like a drum, he turned and walked toward the kitchen.

Chapter Fifteen

"The church of Saint Brighid is just over there," Giric told Sebastien, pointing east. On the low rise of a hill, a stone building with a square tower shone pale against a snowy backdrop of high slopes.

"And that stone cross ahead on the path?" Sebastien asked. "What does it mark?" A tall cross soared up from the ridge they traveled, its stone arms stretched against the overcast sky. Pocked with age, the cross was carved in an intricate, overall pattern of interweaving vines and spirals.

"Long ago, these crosses marked meeting places for priests and their parishioners," Alainna replied. "Prayers and masses were said out in the open then, but now there are parish churches throughout the Highlands."

Sebastien walked toward the cross, drawing the reins of his horse behind him. At Kinlochan, as the Highlanders and the knights had gathered in the bailey to travel the two miles to the church, Sebastien had lifted Una onto his ivory-colored Arabian stallion, choosing to walk. Robert, Hugo, Etienne, and some of the other knights had followed his example and lent their horses to elderly clan members.

"Some still come here to pray, or to make vows of marriage." Alainna walked toward Sebastien. "Private vows of handfasting can be said at these isolated crosses, with or without witnesses."

She was lovely in the clear light, he thought, her cheeks pink with cold, her eyes a brilliant blue, her hair amber where it showed beneath the brown plaid pulled over the crown of her head. He felt a rich surge of desire, remembering the luxurious feel of her in his arms.

"Shall we do that, then?" he murmured.

She turned her cool, perfect profile to him, but the rosy

stain in her cheeks deepened. "I thought the king required a marriage of you and me, with contract and witnesses."

"He does," Sebastien said. "Still, it would be good to have this done, quickly and simply, without the fuss of a wedding." He tipped a brow and sent her a wry smile, deliberately charming, hoping to coax some levity into her. She gave him a reluctant smile.

"Father Padruig will be waiting the Mass for us if we do not hurry!" Una called impatiently behind them. Alainna moved ahead, as he did.

"Look west, there," Alainna said. "That is Turroch, which belongs to Cormac MacNechtan."

He noticed a wooden fortress a mile or more away, crowning a mound surrounded by a crescent of pine forest and backed by mountains. "I mean to visit him soon with the king's message," he said.

"Wait until after the marriage," Alainna said. Her pleading tone caught his attention, and he frowned at her.

"You will see Cormac sooner than that," Giric said. He and Niall ran to join them, their breaths frosting in the cold. "Look south—there comes Black Cormac and another, on foot."

"His brother Struan," Niall added.

Sebastien whirled to look, as did Alainna. Two men walked over the swell of a hill and came toward them. They were huge, unkempt, and fierce-looking, one black-haired, one redheaded. Both wore plaids of red and brown over coarse shirts and vests of fur, with fur leggings. Sebastien saw in them the sort of men who had given Highlanders their reputation as savages.

"By the look of those spears and bows, they are out for a hunt," Robert said, walking up to join Sebastien and the rest.

"Or worse," Giric drawled. "They will behave themselves. They are but two alone, while we are twenty and more strong, with armored knights among us."

"And women, on the Sabbath day," Alainna added.

"They will behave," Niall said, "unless they have a host of MacNechtans hiding in the hills to ambush us."

Hearing Alainna gasp, Sebastien caught her glance and shook his head to reassure her. "They are alone," he said.

"The view from here is widespread. There is no one else about. No cause to worry, my lady."

One of the men called out a greeting as they drew near. They were brawny men, armed with spears, bows, and targes. The redheaded man carried two limp hares strung on a cord.

"Cormac MacNechtan," Alainna said. "Struan."

"Alainna of Kinlochan," the black-haired man said. "We heard Normans had come to Kinlochan, and would greet them, too." He spit on the ground, an obvious insult.

"Be on your way," Alainna said. "It is the Sabbath."

"We mean no harm to you or yours," the redheaded man said.

"You are ready with bow and spear to battle some hares, I see," Giric said.

"Do you fear that you are those hares?" Cormac asked.

"We would be wolves," Giric snarled.

"Peace," Sebastien warned. His horse, sensing tension in the air, sidestepped restively. Sebastien handed the reins to Lulach nearby, and walked toward the Highlanders.

"You are no priest, to order peace between enemies," Cormac said, narrowing his gaze at Sebastien. "What does a Norman knight want in the Highlands? Did you come here to stir trouble and claim land that is not yours?"

"Are you Cormac MacNechtan of Turroch?" Sebastien asked in Gaelic. He glanced over his shoulder and saw that several clan members, including Alainna, now stood behind him.

"I am. Who are you?"

"Sebastien le Bret, sent here by order of the king. I bring a message from the king, which I must deliver to you, but later. Here is not the place for it."

"A reply to my petition at last," Cormac said. "I trust the answer will please me, and bring me a fine wife." He glanced at Alainna.

Sebastien shifted to block Cormac's view of her, as if that dark glance might sully her. "The king orders Clan Laren and Clan Nechtan to put their weapons and their anger aside. We will discuss the details later."

"We can only resolve this feud through marriage between our clans," Cormac said. "Our grudge is older than the king's own Celtic bloodline. He cannot simply order us to stop and expect it to be done, without suitable reward."

"The king wishes to establish your loyalty before he grants a reward. I am certain you will be eager to prove that to him."

"Tell the king we are loyal," Struan said. "The Mac-Williams are the rebellious ones. And those rebels who are not dead have fled to Ireland."

"We are neither dead nor in Ireland, as you see." Cormac grinned. "So how can we be rebels?"

Sebastien watched them steadily. "If you are trustworthy, it will go well for you. But those who support Celtic rebels risk all, land and life."

"Of course," Cormac said. "Lately I have heard that the rebel MacWilliams are returning to the Highlands to beg support. I have heard that Ruari *Mór* is among them, returned from the dead. If I see him, I will be sure to refuse him help." He looked hard at Alainna.

"Even if he were alive, Ruari would never ask support from you!" Alainna snapped.

"Would he not?" Cormac asked. "We have strength of men, where Clan Laren does not. If Ruari *Mór*'s ghost or any rebel comes to my gate, I will let the Normans have him. Would that please the king, Norman?"

"Nothing you do could please the king," Lulach growled, stepping forward. A murmur went through the gathering.

Sebastien moved to stand between the MacNechtans and the rest, determined to stem the rising tempers on both sides. "We will meet to discuss the king's orders," he told Cormac. "For now, be warned that the crown demands that you prove your loyalty, and that your clan cease to feud with Clan Laren. If you do not, you risk all. The king has the right to cast you out from your lands."

"And give them into Norman keeping?" Cormac snarled. "Why are you at Kinlochan? What is it that Clan Nechtan does not yet know?" He looked at Alainna. "Tell me what this is about."

"Sir Sebastien le Bret has been appointed baron of Kinlochan by king's order," she said.

"Laird of Kinlochan!" Cormac glared at Sebastien, breath heaving. Sebastien tensed his hand, ready to pull free his sword if Cormac touched a weapon. Cormac pivoted toward Struan. "I will kill that priest," he muttered. "I paid him to write a petition that would gain me Kinlochan, not lose it to Normans!"

"You cannot blame this on the priest," Struan said.

"Bah!" Cormac turned to Sebastien. "What of Alainna MacLaren? She had best be my bride. I am the closest and strongest neighbor to Kinlochan. If she is not to be mine, there will be strife."

Sebastien stood unyielding, his hand steady on his sword hilt, his gaze hard. "We are prepared for that."

"Ask the king for another reward," Cormac said. "Mac-Gregor land would suit you."

Giric lunged forward and Sebastien put out an arm to stop his advance. Robert and Hugo and two other knights stepped forward. Sebastien felt a base urge to shove his fist into Cormac's gloating face, but he forced himself to remain outwardly impassive.

"Who will marry her?" Cormac demanded. "The Norman who flattered the king for the lady's lands? Myself, who submitted a rightful petition? Or her foster brother, who lusts after her in secret?"

Giric leaned forward again, but Sebastien shot him a glare, arm outstretched. "Keep to the king's purpose here, not your own," he hissed. Giric narrowed his eyes in fury but stilled.

Alainna pushed past Giric and Sebastien then. They both reached for her, but she avoided their hands and glided over the brown grasses like a queen, her head high, her hair shining like a red gold crown. Sebastien took a long step to stand at her side like an honor guard, hand on weapon, gaze keen.

"Cormac MacNechtan," she said. "I will choose my husband myself. You will not tell me who to wed."

"Do you choose the Norman?" Cormac asked.

"The Norman is a great warrior, and I am in his debt. He killed a boar with one thrust of his spear, and saved my life. You are in his debt, too. This man saved Eoghan and Lileas from the wolves along with another man, who went into hiding. If that man was a rebel, you should not be so quick to turn him over to the king's men."

"Then we are in the Norman's debt, and the other man too," Struan said to Cormac.

Cormac frowned at his brother and at Sebastien. "Whoever helped my son," he said carefully, "if he be enemy, remains enemy. But he shall not die by my hand. I can promise no more than that."

Sebastien maintained a steady gaze at Cormac and said nothing.

"It is enough," Alainna said. "This knight has proven his strength and his willingness to help my people. If I choose to wed him, you will know it by the posting of the banns."

"Do not make the mistake of becoming his wife," Cormac said.

"It is my choice, for ill or good," Alainna said.

"Cormac MacNechtan," Sebastien said. "The king orders peace here, and sent us to see it accomplished. I will meet with you at Turroch to discuss the king's writ and his message to you. If you threaten this clan or these people, then prepare for battle with the king's own army."

Cormac flexed his thick fingers on the staff of his spear. "Come to Turroch, then," he said stiffly. "For now, I wish to speak with Alainna in private, as one chief to another. I have more to discuss with her."

"He has that right," Alainna said.

Sebastien flexed his hand and slithered the tip of his sword loose. "We will tolerate no trouble," he warned. He stepped backward so that Cormac and Alainna stood alone.

"The holding of Kinlochan is mine," Cormac said in a low voice that carried in the crisp air. "You should be mine. Your father wanted peace as much as anyone. He would have given you to me to gain it. He gave me his promise on the day he died."

"He would not promise that!"

"He would and did. You are meant to be mine."

"I will never be yours!"

He snatched her wrist. "Remember the Stone Maiden. Nothing can protect you once spring is here," he hissed. "Neither kinsmen nor Norman, nor the faeries themselves."

Sebastien strode toward them, sliding his sword free. Bright steel flashed in a falling arc to touch Cormac's forearm. "Take your hand from her or lose it to the blade," he said. Behind him, he heard the sound of steel slithering free from leather sheaths as the elderly clan members and his own knights grasped their weapons.

Cormac let Alainna go. Sebastien eased her behind him with an extended arm, and rested his sword tip on Cormac's chest. "Be on your way," he growled.

"Norman," Cormac said. "Now that you are laird of Kinlochan, you and I are enemies. I will spare your life because you helped my son, but I will never call you friend—unless you honor Laren MacLaren's promise to me and give me his daughter and a fair portion of her land."

"My father made no promise to you," Alainna countered.

"Giric knows!" Cormac said, turning. "Tell her about the day Laren MacLaren was wounded to his death!"

"I told her what she had to know," Giric said. "That he was ambushed by you and your men. What should she know, but that tale of treachery?"

Sebastien saw Alainna close her eyes in anguish, then look at her foster brother. "What does he mean, Giric? What more should I know?"

"No more," Giric said through tight lips, glaring at Cormac.

"Laren MacLaren gave me permission to wed his daughter," Cormac said. "He gave our marriage his blessing."

"You are a liar," Giric snarled.

"I should kill you where you stand," Cormac said. "Your life is only saved today because it is the Sabbath."

"Enough!" Sebastien cut in. "Be on your way."

"You and I will meet at Turroch, Norman," Cormac said. "Alainna MacLaren, ask Giric about that day. Do not forget that you are mine. If you value your clan—what is left of it—you will choose me for your husband, for I know your lands as well as my own, and I am a Highlander to my bones, unlike some." He glared at Sebastien and turned away from the pressing edge of the sword, striding away with his brother behind him.

Sebastien watched them vanish over a hill. Once he was sure that they had no other men with them and had gone, he sheathed his sword. He turned to discover Alainna and

Giric standing not far from him, talking earnestly. Beyond them, the others resumed their journey over the hills.

"It is not so," Alainna said as Sebastien came closer.

"It is," Giric said, and reached for her arm. She pushed his hand away. "I am sorry, girl. I hoped never to have to tell you. It is true. I heard them talking that day."

She glanced at Sebastien, and he saw longing and fear in her eyes. "My father promised me to Cormac?" she asked Giric. "How could he do that?"

"He was hurt badly, and he knew he would not survive. I saw it in his face, that awakening that comes into a man's eyes when he knows his death is upon him."

Alainna put her fist to her mouth and squeezed her eyes shut for a moment. "Go on."

"Cormac had not wounded Laren with his own hand, but he saw your father fall. I could not get to Laren myself, for I had a wounded leg, and Aodh the Red had fallen beside me. His weight trapped me with my back against a rock."

"Aodh," she said. "He was a good man. But tell me what came next, with my father."

Sebastien began to walk away to give them privacy, but Alainna held up a hand as if pleading for him to stay. He did, standing quietly, watching her with concern.

"I saw Cormac kneel beside your father. He could have given Laren the killing blow there and then, but he did not."

"My father spoke to him?"

"Cormac demanded that your father surrender the feud to Clan Nechtan. Laren refused. But he asked for peace and an end to the feud."

"Cormac asked for my hand, and my father agreed?"

"I do not know what was said between them. But Cormac nodded as if he were satisfied. He called to his men to leave when they could have killed us all, for they were five times our numbers and had taken us by surprise. And I know what your father told me when I finally crawled to his side."

"You told me he said nothing to you that day," Alainna said. "You did not tell me any of this before."

"How could I hurt you when you were already suffering?" Giric asked. "I kept it to myself. I knew what Laren wanted." He drew a long breath as if he fought a powerful emotion. "Laren told me that you would be chief in his place soon," he went on. "He asked me to watch over you. He begged me to make sure that you married, before spring arrived, the strongest warrior to be found, someone to defeat Cormac."

"He must have given Cormac permission to marry me once the spell over the Stone Maiden ends," Alainna said. "Then he asked you to see me wed to someone else before then, to thwart Cormac."

"I think so. Cormac is sure he will have you when spring comes. But your father wanted you to be safe, Alainna. Laren would approve of your marriage to Sebastien."

Alainna nodded, and looked at Sebastien, her gaze fastened to his. "My father would want this marriage for me," she echoed.

Sebastien watched her steadily, while the cold wind whipped at his cloak.

"He would want you to be happy," Giric said quietly. "As all of us want for you."

She looked at him. "Do the old ones know about my father's request?"

"Some of them," Giric said.

She nodded slowly, her eyes spilling over with tears.

Sebastien felt something tug inside his heart. He took a step toward her, compelled by the need in her expression. Her hand lifted toward him.

Dear God, he thought. He wanted to hold her so much that it was painful, a sudden physical ache inside him. He took another step forward.

Then Giric took her shoulder and turned her into his own embrace.

Sebastien paused. He saw the loving look that Giric gave her, saw her crumple against him. He clenched his hands against the yearning that swelled in him.

Giric belonged here in her world, he told himself. He did not, regardless of king's orders, regardless of the game destiny played with their lives. No matter if he longed to be part of such a kinship, such a legacy. No matter that he craved Alainna with every part of his being in that moment.

His was a wandering soul, as Alainna had termed it. He had never known a true home, and he wondered if he would ever belong anywhere, no matter how much he wanted it.

Giric smoothed his hand over Alainna's back, and Sebastien felt a stabbing sensation in his gut. He turned away in silence. Alainna regarded Giric as a brother only and needed her kinsman's comfort, he knew, but he did not like the sight of it.

He drew a sharp breath and walked away. He felt a strange hurt inside, as if a strand of his heart had been torn away, as if he left part of himself on the windy hilltop with Alainna.

Chapter Sixteen

Alainna waited while the others filed out of the church after Father Padruig gave the final blessing. Their voices echoed against the whitewashed walls, and soon the priest's booming laugh rose above the rest as he joined them outside. She heard Lorne introduce Sebastien to Father Padruig, and she saw Una and Giric glance toward her as they left. She motioned them ahead. They would understand, she knew, what she must do.

She crossed to the north side of the church and went through a narrow doorway. A candle flickered in a wall niche, and she lifted it, shielding the flame as she walked down a few steps into a dark crypt.

The underground chamber, with an earthen floor and a low, vaulted stone ceiling, contained several tombs. Alainna went to the farthest corner, where the tombs of her parents and brothers were placed, the space forming a small chapel. She set the candle on the floor, knelt on the cold earth, and bowed her head to pray for their souls.

Tears streamed down her cheeks as she thought of her father. Knowing his wound was fatal, harassed in his weakness by his mortal enemy, he had been forced to agree to something he did not believe was right. He had protected her by asking Giric to make certain she wed a warrior before Cormac could claim her.

She bent over her folded hands and cried out of sorrow and thankfulness. But the knowledge that her father would approve of her marriage to the Breton knight was a great relief and a true blessing. She wiped her tearstained face, feeling exhausted, washed clean. Sorrow would return again, she knew, unbidden as a storm, capable of overwhelming her. She weathered it a little more easily each time, though she knew she might never fully recover from the hurt of losing her family.

She could only find niches for the pain, the emptiness, the memories. And she felt as if she had grown stronger from the burdens she carried.

After a while she whispered a prayer for her sleeping family, rose to her feet, and went to the crypt stairs. From above, she heard the scrape of boots on stone.

Sebastien stood in the narrow doorway. She looked up at him, candle in her hand. Then, silently, she beckoned for him to come down into the crypt.

"Are they here?" he asked as he entered.

She knew what he meant, and nodded. "Come, I will show you." She spoke softly in English, the language they most often used with each other. She held the candle high and led him to the corner. "My parents are on that side, and my brothers are there," she said. "They too are buried side by side. Conall and Niall were soul-friends in life. We put them together in death, beneath one tombstone."

"Soul-friends?" he asked.

"Souls linked to one another through love and loyalty all their lives. They can be comrades, brothers and sisters, or lovers. Not everyone has a soul-friend, but those that do are blessed." She touched the sandstone slab that covered them; carved in raised relief, two warriors surrounded by an intertwining vine wrapped around two swords.

"My cousin Malcolm made this tomb for them," she said, brushing away the dust on its surface. "Malcolm is not buried here, for he died in Glasgow and was laid to rest there. He made my mother's stone, just there, when I was a small child. She never knew the sorrow that came to us later."

Sebastien nodded. Tall and broad-shouldered in his armor, his hair sheened gold in the candlelight, he seemed to fill the tiny space. Quiet power radiated from him, bringing a sense of comfort and security that Alainna had rarely experienced before.

That tangible steadfastness came from more than a muscled, skillful body, or the reassurance of few words. He emanated a reserve of inner strength. She wanted to draw from it as she might draw water from a well. She desperately wanted to give him something of herself, too, but she was not sure how to do that, and not sure what he would accept from her.

He seemed a private, guarded man, but she had glimpsed compassion, gentleness, and tenderness in him. His brief references to his childhood revealed vulnerability that contrasted the hard shield of his power.

Strange, she thought, glancing up at him in the shadows, to have such thoughts about a man she had once thought only to resent and resist. Strange to think, too, that soon she would be married to him. That thought stirred a subtle excitement that quickened her heartbeat like a drum.

He turned to the tomb beside her mother's. "And your father's stone? Who carved this, if your cousin was gone?"

"I did this." She traced her fingers along the interlaced border that framed a knight holding a sword, with a fortress carved beneath.

"You?" He sent her a keen glance. "My God, girl." His voice was hushed, awed. She blinked tears away again, and turned to stand beside him, her arm pressing his in the small space. He did not shift away, his solidity a comfort. She stroked the stone, so familiar to her fingers.

"Sandstone is easy to carve," she said. "It falls away from the chisel like dry clay, and does not take long to work. I do not generally carve it, for its dust is unpleasant and causes a bad cough. But Malcolm had cut the other slabs of the same stone, and we had several blocks of it. We have endured so many deaths, you see," she said softly. "We had many tombstones and crosses to carve in the years that Malcolm was with us. There are more stones here in the crypt, and several outside the church, for other members of my clan.

"But this one," she said, stroking her father's effigy, "this one I needed to do myself."

He covered her hand in his. The heat of his palm sank into her, flowed into her blood like wine. She curled her fingers around his thumb, and they stood, hands interlocked, in silence.

"It must be unbearable to have lost them all," he said.

"I still have the others," she said. *Will I have you?* she wanted to ask, but held it back.

He squeezed her hand lightly and let go. She wanted that

warmth back again, almost reached for it. But he turned away.

"Come," he said. "Your kin await you outside the church. I have met Father Padruig, and he is eager to talk to us about the marriage arrangements."

She picked up the candle and moved through the crypt with him. "We can only talk to him briefly. It is a full league to travel home again, out in the open with the old ones."

"You and your kin are safe among so many armored knights."

"I know. Cormac will not attack us on a Sabbath day. He respects the laws of the Church." She paused. "But your safety worries me. Yours, when you meet with Cormac."

"We will be battle ready in case he thinks of treachery."

"He will. What then?"

"Then we fight," he answered simply.

She heaved out a sigh. "Men fight," she said. "And women wait. And I am weary of it all. Am I to choose a husband, only to lose him so soon?"

"You will not lose me," he said. He stood an arm's length from her in the shadows, his voice deep and gentle. Something ached within her to hear those words. She had lost so many—father, brothers, kinsmen. She wanted desperately to believe him now.

Suddenly she yearned to reach out to him, to feel his strength surround her. But the space between them seemed a wide gap. She felt uncertain and turned away, the candle flickering in her trembling hand. "At least if you leave for Brittany, you might return here someday. If you leave for Turroch, you may never return."

"I will return from both places." His voice was calm.

"You may not," she insisted. Longing and fear sharpened. "And so it is, for the men in my family, to go out to battle with MacNechtans and not return! Do you think I want that for you, too? I do not!" She whirled to go to the stairs.

He grabbed her arm and turned her to face him, taking the candle from her hand and setting it aside. "Come here," he said gruffly, pulling her toward him.

He slid his hand along her jaw and tipped her face toward his. "Would I take a wife, and leave her so soon?" he asked as if half to himself. "Am I such a fool as that?"

"Are you?" she whispered.

"Never," he said, and touched his mouth to hers.

His lips were dry and warm, his kiss tender. She moaned soft and grabbed his forearms, swathed in chained steel. His hand cupped her head, and his fingers slipped into the thickness of her hair above the heavy braids that hung down.

She tilted her head to accept a deeper kiss, her heart pounding. A force rose from the kiss, swirling down into her body and shivering along her backbone like a torrent, like wind and flame and water all at once.

He drew back and rested his brow against hers, his hands still framing her face. "Jesu," he whispered hoarsely.

She tilted toward him, yearning for more of the incredible marvel she had discovered in his arms. He only kissed her cheek.

"If I am to be near you so much, I had better wed you, or risk dishonor."

"There are some kinds of dishonor," she murmured, "that I know naught about."

"Better you never learn," he whispered.

"I am curious," she answered, tilting her face toward his, closing her eyes. He kissed her again, harder than before, his mouth demanding and sure, his hand cradling the back of her head. He pulled her to him at the waist, curve to countercurve as he bent over her.

She rose on her toes, looping her arms around his waist, stunned by what she felt, how soothing, how perfect it was to kiss him and to be kissed, to be wrapped in his embrace. Chain mail bit into her through layered wool, and she felt the taut support of solid muscle beneath.

His mouth lifted away and she turned, seeking him again. He made a breathy groan and slanted his lips over hers once more, open and full. His hands slid around to cup her face. She grasped his bare, sinewed wrists as if they were the buttress that held her upright. She craved more, conveying that with her lips, all the while sinking into the thrill that whirled through her body.

"Ah," said a voice above them, "I see it is not too soon to talk about making a marriage."

Alainna gasped, tore away, looked up. Father Padruig grinned at them from the top of the steps.

"Come up, come up," he said. "Out of the darkness and into the light, if you will. That crypt can be cold enough to freeze the devil's own nose—though you two found a way to make some heat, eh?" He chortled and waved them upward.

"But Father Padruig," Alainna asked, her voice rising a little in anxious pitch, "a little while ago you agreed we should be wed. Now you say we should not?" She looked incredulously at the priest, and then at Sebastien.

The priest's announcement had puzzled him as much as it did Alainna, but Sebastien remained silent, merely lifting a brow.

"I know your reasons for wanting to be wed," Father Padruig said. His English was rapid and lilting. "And I am thinking it is unwise for me to witness your marriage now."

"Unwise?" Alainna said. "It is unwise to ignore what the king has ordered! My clan could lose Kinlochan altogether, and the king could grant the land to some other Norman knight. We need Sebastien and his men to help us resist Clan Nechtan. This marriage is imperative for us. Neither of us have a choice."

"Nevertheless, I believe you should wait a while. Unless you want to handfast. That might work."

"Work?" Alainna asked. "Do we need some scheme? What are you talking about?"

Sebastien frowned, his thoughts racing as Alainna continued her earnest argument with the priest. They stood clustered in the nave of the plain stone church. Daylight poured in from two unshuttered windows. Outside, he could hear faint conversation among the members of Clan Laren and the king's knights.

Raised by pious, quiet monks, Sebastien had never encountered a religious quite like Father Padruig. The priest looked more like a seasoned warrior with his broad, muscular build, his large hands, and his florid, weatherbeaten face. Although he wore his thick reddish hair in the ear-to-ear tonsure of the Celtic priests, he hardly seemed priestlike.

Sebastien found Padruig to be intelligent and book-learned, affectionate and even boisterous in character. He had embraced Alainna like a daughter, pounded Sebastien on the back like a drinking comrade, and punctuated his speech with a rippling, contagious laugh.

"Let me explain," Father Padruig said, lifting a thick forefinger in the air. "If I witness the marriage between you, as must be done on the porch step of the church while you speak your own vows, any and all will know you are wed."

Alainna nodded. "That is how it is done."

"If I agree to witness your union," Father Padruig went on, his finger lifted as if testing the wind, "before you stand on the porch step, I must post the banns for three Sundays. For some, that is a short time. In this case, it is too long."

"Do you think we are so lustful that we cannot wait . . . oh—" Alainna stopped, sounding embarrassed. Sebastien pinched back a smile, but Father Padruig snorted in amusement.

"I understand what the good father means," Sebastien said. "He thinks a public marriage is not safe."

Padruig nodded. "If I witness your marriage, word will get to Cormac. He is unpredictable, and you do not want to aggravate him further. Wait, and let Sebastien negotiate the king's orders with Cormac first. Cormac must give up this belief that he has first claim to Alainna's hand."

"The king requires a copy of our marriage contract," Sebastien said. "And I have promised to sail for Brittany in the spring. How long do you intend to wait before posting the banns?"

"A challenge for you two to wait, eh? But there is more to a marriage than carnal pleasures, you know. And I suspect that neither of you is at peace with this marriage. You both need time to think about this."

Sebastien saw Alainna turn away suddenly, as if the priest's remarks distressed her. "The king has made this decision for us, Father," he said. "According to the writ I hold"—he tapped his belt pouch—"the marriage contract must be in the king's hands or the charter to Kinlochan will not be final. Alainna and her kin could indeed lose much if the marriage is not made, and soon."

"You could handfast," Padruig said.

Sebastien looked at Alainna in surprise. She frowned.

"Make vows before witnesses to be together for a year

and a day," Father Padruig said. "If you cannot agree on the matters between you at the end of that time, then you can be done with each other. There will be no obligation between you unless there is a child. Sebastien must acknowledge the child, of course, but marriage does not have to take place even then."

"It would satisfy the king's order," Alainna said slowly. "We can make a marriage contract and sign it, as is done with betrothals."

"No banns need be posted for handfasting," Father Padruig said. "Cormac will not hear of it before you want him to know."

"A good plan," Sebastien said.

Alainna nodded, eyes downcast.

"I suggest that you handfast on Christmas, or the eve before," Father Padruig said. "That is excellent luck. A good future for you both. You will resolve your conflicts well with that sort of omen." He smiled.

Sebastien noticed that Alainna's cheeks bloomed a lovely pink. She turned away and hastened toward the door.

The wind was brisk and billowing as Alainna walked beside Sebastien in silence on the return to Kinlochan. Some of the others walked ahead, while more trailed behind, leaving a circle of privacy around them.

After a while she sighed. "So we will handfast, and neither one of us wanting to do it," she said. "I am sure you want a French or a Breton wife, and a home there."

"And you want a Celtic warrior." He glanced at her. "A paragon of myth, a strong man to ride out of the mists and defeat your enemy, and father a new branch of Clan Laren."

She lifted her face to the winds. "I do."

"I am not that man," he replied.

"You could be," she said on impulse, her heart pounding.

"I have planned another life," he said firmly.

"And I am not a French noblewoman, nor do I care to be."

He walked beside her without reply, his stride long and leisurely. He looked upward, his eyes gray and sad.

"Will you take my name, sir knight, and give it to your children?" she asked.

"Will you take mine," he countered quietly, "and give it to your children?"

"I cannot. An ancient clan will disappear if I do that."

"And I have fought my entire life to bring some worth to my name so that I could found a new legacy."

"You have brought worth to yourself," she said. "What name you use would not change that."

She heard him sigh as he gazed at the hills. She sighed too, walking beside him. "What are we to do, Sebastien?"

"Somehow we are to make a marriage out of this."

"And if we have children?" she asked.

"There are ways," he said, "to avoid that."

She looked at him, stunned. "That is not what I want in a marriage." Tears pricked her eyes. "I want children, and a husband who wants me and my kinfolk."

"Do you think this pleases me?" he asked bluntly. "I must choose between you or my son. The choice seemed easier when I first came here," he added softly, looking away. "It grows more difficult each day."

"If we do not turn the handfasting into a marriage," she said, "we can both be free in a year and a day."

He nodded slowly. "It may be the only path out of this tangle. Robert and some of the others can remain here after I leave, and supervise the building of the castle. Your people greatly need the crown's protection. The king may be willing to negotiate, and portion the land between us."

"Is it possible?" She felt a glimmer of hope.

"Much can happen in a year's time."

"You and I understand each other," she said, the idea taking better form in her mind. "We know what the other wants. We can give each other the company of a friend, and say no word to anyone of our plans to part at the end of the year."

He looked at her and lifted an eyebrow. The scar along his left eye gave him a tough, roguish appearance. His eyes were the somber color of the cloudy sky. "Is this an offering of peace, my lady?" he asked.

"It is," she said. "For a year and a day."

He walked beside her in silence, his stride strong and

agile. "So be it, then," he said finally. He smiled, slow and sad.

She returned an uncertain smile. For several moments, her steps were even with his. "I will visit Esa tomorrow if the weather allows," she said after a while. "I will ask her to come to Kinlochan."

"Ah, the mysterious Esa. I look forward to meeting her." He spoke in the cool tone that she knew he sometimes used to mask his thoughts. She wondered if he suspected that Ruari MacWilliam was alive, and if he would talk to Esa about it. If so, she was determined that he would discover nothing that could bring harm to any of her kinfolk.

Earlier, she had told Giric about Ruari. He had reacted as she had expected, with perfect calm. She knew that he would keep the secret.

"I must ask my kinsmen which one of them will come to see Esa with me," Alainna said. She looked behind her and paused while Niall, Lulach, and Giric came toward them.

She explained what she wanted to do. "Once we have deep snow, it will not be easy to fetch Esa to Kinlochan," she added.

"It will not be easy no matter when you go," Niall said.

"I want Esa to be here for our handfasting," Alainna said. "I hope one of you will go with me."

"Huh," Lulach said. "I would sooner rip an oak from the ground than fetch Esa out of her house. She is sweet but stubborn."

"*Ach,*" Alainna said. "I will get her to come with me. You just do not know how to do it." She smiled.

"We have tried three times of late," Lulach said. "She refuses, so calm and dear that we hardly know she's refusing. But that woman is like a piece of stone."

"I know how to work stone," Alainna said, still smiling. "Which of you will go with me? Niall? You enjoy seeing Esa."

"I will not come," Niall said. "She would make me do all her chores, and I would end up carrying that great loom of hers on my back down the mountain—if she would even leave her little house. Which she will not."

"Giric? You will come."

"Alainna, I promised the knights I would take them out deer hunting tomorrow. Can we go the next day?"

"I do not want to wait," she said. "The weather will worsen. Una says she is certain of that. And I want Esa here for the handfasting and for Christmas. Lulach?"

"Donal and I are going to clean the forge and make repairs over the next few days," he said. "Una and Morag want the fortress cleaned and made proper for the new year. There is much to be done to please them."

"You go," Niall said to Lulach. "You have been a fool for Esa since you were an infant."

"Me? You were the one in love with Esa!" Lulach barked.

"I think you both loved her," Giric interrupted. "I have heard it said that when Esa married Ruari she broke a hundred hearts."

"I must meet this woman," Sebastien said, sounding amused. "I will go with you, Alainna."

"You?" she squeaked, and looked quickly at Giric, who frowned. "Lorne might go with me," she said quickly.

"Lorne will be in his poet's bed," Giric said. "He told Una it was time for that again."

"Poet's bed?" Sebastien asked.

"Now and then he takes to his bed for a full day, from dawn to dawn," Alainna told him. "He lies in the darkness, with a cloth over his eyes and a stone on his belly. He remembers every line of all the poems and stories he has ever learned. It is part of his training as a bard to do that."

"Ah," Sebastien said, nodding as if fascinated. "I will go with you," he repeated firmly. "I have yet to find all the boundary stones. Some of them lie up that way. I must ride in that direction sooner or later."

She sighed. "Very well . . . But we must walk, for she lives in the high hills."

"That will be fine," he replied. "Whatever you wish, my lady."

"Aha!" Niall cried. "The man is to be handfasted! He does not want to leave the girl's side!"

Alainna felt herself grow hot under her kinsmen's grins, and under Sebastien's calm, unwavering gaze and slow smile.

Chapter Seventeen

"There is a boundary stone down there," Alainna called down to Sebastien. "Do you see it?" She stood on the shoulder of a steep hill far above him.

"I found it," Sebastien called, waving. He stood at the base of the hill, where a burn flowed fast. He dropped down to scoop a quick, cold drink with his hand, drying his fingers on his cloak. On the bank was a large rock painted white, the stone he sought. He stood again, narrowing his eyes to scan the hills and estimate how far he and Alainna had walked from the last boundary marker farther along the same winding burn.

For much of the morning, they had climbed ever higher into the hills, where the slopes were brown and barren and rocky, where the wind whipped past and thick white mist obscured the peaks.

He took his wax tablet and bone stylus from his belt pouch and wrote a few notes about the stone's location. Then he walked back up the hill, where Alainna waited beside a large boulder.

"May I see?" she asked, extending her hand. "Have you made a map of Kinlochan?"

He hesitated. "A simple one," he said, as he handed her the wax tablet. She studied the tiny drawing he had made showing the approximate shape of the property, with loch, fortress, and the long, wide burn marked there. Then she looked at the small, careful drawing in one corner.

"I did not know you had such a fine hand for drawing," she said. "This little castle is excellently made. Is it one that you have seen somewhere?"

He held his hand out, but she kept the tablet. "It is my own design."

"It is lovely. And I like the three towers in the walls. I imagine there is nothing like it in the Highlands. Is this what Kinlochan castle will look like when it is made?"

He shrugged. "Mayhap it will." He took the tablet from her hands, sliding it back into his leather pouch.

"So you understand mapmaking and building?"

He gave her a flat smile. "Did you think I am interested only in matters of war, or jousting, or standing guard for kings?"

"I have seen you practice for war and ride out to hunt. And of course I have seen you stand guard for the king. But that is all."

"I would design buildings," he said, "if I had not become a knight in the service of a liege lord. If I had been given the privilege of a university education, I would have studied the art of architecture."

He looked out over the sweep of the slope as he spoke, aware that he had rarely voiced that wish to anyone. The drawing of the castle might seem simple to someone else, but it represented something precious and private to him.

He had studied and sketched many structures over the years, fascinated since childhood by their design. He had learned much through observation, through reading whatever he could find in the libraries of the noble lords he served, and through his experiences in the service of an English baron who had allowed him direct involvement in the raising of three castles.

The little wax sketch was a culmination of observations and ideas, an expression of his cherished dream to design his own castle. King William's directive concerning Kinlochan had been more than welcome in that way, but frustrating as well. While he wanted to supervise the construction of a stone fortress, he did not intend Kinlochan to be his home.

The brightness in Alainna's deep blue eyes told him that she was intrigued. He wanted to tell her more. Sharing this with her felt safe, he realized suddenly. He wanted to hear her thoughts, to see her eyes sparkle with the passion she seemed to bring to all things.

"How did you come to know the art of architecture?"

she asked. "You did not attend university. How were you schooled?"

"So many questions," he said, smiling a little. "Shall we rest here for a bit? Una sent food with you in that bundle."

"She did. If you want to sit here . . . wait," she said, as he shifted to sit on the boulder. He stepped back. "Watch."

She touched her fingertip to the stone. The boulder was as long as a man, and nearly half that length wide, but it began to rock gently back and forth at her light touch.

Sebastien laughed in surprise. When the stone stilled, he touched it himself. The rocking began again. Curious, he dropped to his knees to peer underneath.

The curving underside of the slate boulder rested on a flat base of shale. Daylight leaked through at all points but the centermost juncture between the upper and lower stones. He stood, shaking his head in astonishment.

"It is a jury stone," Alainna said. "The ancient people used it to decide justice in cases of crimes and disputes. Lorne has told me all about this. The accused would stand there"—she indicated the end of the boulder that pointed downhill—"and a priest or a clan chief would stand at the other end, and speak the case aloud for the witnesses. Then the leader would give the stone a tap with a birch wand, and the stone would answer by rocking one way or another."

Sebastien gave the boulder a few experimental pushes while she spoke. "Sometimes it moves north to south, sometimes east to west," he observed, walking around it.

"North to south was regarded as a judgment of innocent, and east to west was seen as guilty. If it stood still, that meant undecided, which allowed the accused to go free of punishment. No one uses the stone now," she said, and sat. It shivered gently beneath her weight. "It is a curiosity only."

"Curious indeed." Sebastien sat on the stone too, bracing his feet on the ground until it stilled. Alainna rummaged in the tied cloth bundle that she had carried with her. She handed Sebastien an oatcake and a thick slab of cheese.

"Tell me how you were educated," she said as they began to eat. "And how you became interested in designing castles."

"The monks who raised me gave me excellent training in languages, in reading and writing skills, in mathematics and theology. The arts of architecture and geometry intrigued me, and I pursued those on my own. But I do not have a specialized education from a university. There was no one to pay the cost of it," he added.

"Have you no family, Sebastien?" she asked quietly.

"Only my son now." Plain words that did not reveal the loss and anguish of a few years before. He broke off a bit of cheese and chewed it slowly before he continued. "The monks are more my family than any other. Abbot Philippe has been like a father to me. I came to his monastery when I was but two years old, and he a young man and not yet abbot."

"No wonder you feel that you must return to Brittany."

His simple nod belied the intensity of his conviction. "I must find Conan and the monks, and do whatever I can to help them. It is . . . hard for me to stay in Scotland without knowing what has become of them." And hard to admit his feelings aloud, he thought, although he could do so with Alainna more readily than anyone.

"When I first met you," she said in a musing tone, watching him, "I thought that you and I could not be more different. But more and more, I think we are alike."

"In pride, most assuredly." He smiled a little.

"More than that. We both would do anything for those we love. You would leave this excellent holding"—she waved a hand around the hills—"just to be with them and know they are safe."

As he swept his gaze over the hills, he felt a twinge of regret. He had begun to love this country of slopes and lochs and open sky. Leaving here, he realized, would be far harder than he would have thought, for several reasons.

"I would give my soul to know they are safe," he murmured.

"As would I, for my kin," she said. "Although if I were separated from my kin and in a strange place, among strangers, I would not be as courteous to them as you have been with us. I would leave as quick as I could. And be thought a barbaric Scotswoman, I suppose."

He smiled. "I thought you were weary of my courtesy and chivalry, my lady."

She half laughed. "Not all of your chivalry, sirrah." She glanced down at his long legs and braced feet. "You are very kindly keeping this stone still so that we can eat."

He laughed and bit into the salty, chewy oatcake. She ate too, and after a while brushed the crumbs from her hands.

"You said once that you knew something of your parents. Have you no connection to their families?"

He broke up the last of his oatcake and tossed it into the snags of heather for the birds and animals to find. "I was a foundling," he said, "left at the gate of the monastery with a gold ring and a bit of salt to show that I was of noble birth and baptized. The monks did not know my name or where I came from, at least then. They named me for their patron saint, since I was found on his feast day. The monastery is Saint-Sebastien, near Rennes in Brittany."

"Ah. So you became Sebastien le Bret. It is a fine name." Her eyes showed only sincerity, no mockery.

"My name may lack the value of generations of warriors and worthy daughters behind it," he said. "It may lack the 'de' to show a noble, landowning family. But it is mine."

"And you will never give it up," she said slowly.

He leaned forward to rest his arms on his knees. He looked out over steep slopes frosted with snow and mist, over sweeping meadows and the meandering, white-frothed burn.

"My name is all I have," he said. "All that is mine alone."

She touched his arm. He did not look at her, but was aware of the pressure of her hand. Her slightest touch stirred him, quickened his heart and his body, warmed him to flame. Best, he told himself, that she not know that; best that he not think about that.

"Do you know anything of your parents?" she asked.

"Abbot Philippe made inquiries for years, and finally, when I was nine, a priest from a Breton village came to see him. A woman had begged the priest on her deathbed to go to the monastery with her story." He paused. "She claimed to have left a child there, not of her own womb.

She described the ring and the swaddling found with me. She said she was the wet nurse employed by the mother's family."

"She knew your parents?"

"The priest reported that my mother was the daughter of a Breton lord. I never learned her name or family, for the woman insisted that it be kept a secret. My father was the youngest son of an English baron, a family called de Lindfield."

"So you do know your name!" She smiled.

"It is not my name. I have no right to it."

"How can that be?"

"My father was a priest. The sons of priests have no legal claim to their father's surname. Only in Scotland," he added, "would I be legitimate and named, as the child of a priest."

She stared at him. "Who was your mother?"

"Her family had intended her for the convent," he said. "My father was an English priest at the Breton court. My mother's father hired him to teach his daughter to read. They fell in love . . . and so I was born. My mother died at my birth, and her brother sought out my father and killed him."

The silence grew as thick as the mist that wreathed the top of the slope. Alainna murmured a wordless sound of sympathy, and leaned against him, arm to arm. Her presence was a welcome comfort. The stone beneath them rocked gently. Sebastien did not stop its motion.

"The wet nurse left me with the monks after I was weaned, as my mother's family had paid her to do. They did not want a bastard child, a disgrace and a reminder of tragedy. She had other children and could not afford another mouth. She told the priest that her heart broke to give me up, and said that she worried about me, yet could not come forth."

"But she was a kindhearted woman," Alainna said.

"It would seem so. When I was young," he said, "I used to dream about a round little woman with brown eyes who sang to me and held me." He shrugged. "I wondered then who she could have been, since the only family I knew were the monks."

"I am sure you remembered her," Alainna said.

"Mayhap." He sighed. "The monks were good to all the boys in their care, but it was a strict upbringing. A little play, and a lot of prayer and study. Not the usual life for a child. Such a life makes a good monk, but I was not interested in that."

"You left to make your way in the secular world?"

"Abbot Philippe located my father's kin in England. A cousin came to the monastery, and took me into his household in England when I was eleven."

"You do have kin, then."

He shrugged. "I suppose. But none of them were eager to acknowledge me, and I soon learned to expect nothing of them. I was given a place in the stables, where I learned much about training horses. Eventually another knight took me into his household, where I became a squire and finally a knight. Sir Richard was a good man. He gave me many opportunities."

"You have come far from that Breton monastery."

"In some ways. I learned quite young to make my own way in the world. I wanted what other knights had—name, wealth, land, family. I determined to obtain that." He glanced at her. "In other ways, I have not come far from the monastery at all. I am still a solitary man. I live the *vita activa,* but I retain the *vita contemplativa* in my nature."

She sat quietly, her gaze earnest, her head tilted as she did so often when she looked at him. "So that is your tale," she said in a musing tone.

"Part of it. And you? What of your tale?"

She shrugged. "Mine is not so interesting, and you know much of it already. I have lived at Kinlochan all my life, with my family close about me. A sheltered life, made even closer and more guarded because of the feud and the losses and danger to my clan. But the gift of my family and my home has more than made up for the curse of that strife."

She stood to pack the rest of the food away as she spoke.

The stone undulated beneath him like the bobble of a boat on water. Sebastien stilled it again with his foot. "What an odd stone this is," he said pensively. He slid his hand over the cool, hard surface.

"Some people still come up here for predictions on the

first of May—lovers' questions—and for portents for the
new year."

"I can imagine," he said. He stood and leaned forward.
"Tell me, stone, will it snow?"

Alainna laughed, a silvery trill. "That is easy to answer."

He touched the stone gently. It slipped into an immediate
rhythm. "North to south," he announced, grinning at her.

"It will snow, sooner or later. We hardly needed the
stone to tell us that."

He put his foot on the stone to still it. "Will the mysterious Esa consent to return with us?"

Alainna laughed again. "I think I know the answer."

"Hush, you," he said, giving her a mock frown. She giggled, a sweet sound. He touched the stone, and the rocking began.

"North to south," he said. "Esa will come back with us."

"I could have told you that." She looked smug and
pleased.

"Who needs a judgment stone when they have Lady
Alainna?" He was glad to see her smile grow.

"Ask something you could not know," she suggested.

He tilted his head, pondering. "Will Alainna . . . find the
Celtic warrior she wants?" he asked, mildly teasing.

She grimaced at him. He smiled, leaned down, and
touched the stone. It moved north to south in the
affirmative.

He felt a frisson of disappointment. "Ah," he murmured.
"It seems that you will have your heart's desire."

She looked dismayed. "Let me try. Will Sebastien"—she
walked around the stone as she spoke—"find himself a fine
Breton lady?" The stone shifted when she touched it. "East
to west," she said. "Oh. You will not. I should have asked
if you would find a fine French lady," she amended.

"No doubt," he murmured.

"Will Sebastien . . . find a home for his wandering soul?"
Her voice was soft.

He felt himself go very still, spirit and flesh. Alainna
touched the stone. After a moment it undulated slowly.

"North to south," she murmured, and looked at him.
"You will find what you want."

"Will I?" He watched her for a long moment. Then he placed a foot on the stone to stop its motion.

"It is said the jury stone is never wrong."

"We have tested it well," he said. He walked around the stone toward her, bending to pick up her cloth pack. As he straightened, he heard Alainna gasp.

"Look!" she cried.

A few snowflakes fell gently from the sky. He put up a palm to catch them, and showed them to her.

"The stone was right," she said. He smiled, more pleased by her delight than by the stone's prediction or the delicate snowflakes in his hand.

She looked up at him, so fresh and beautiful that he felt as if his heart fell to his feet. He reached out to gently brush at the snow that dusted her hair, and swept his thumb over her cheekbone, where a few snowflakes sparkled.

"There is one more question I want to ask," he murmured.

"What is that?" she whispered.

"Will Alainna," he murmured, grazing his thumb along the line of her jaw, "kiss me?"

She closed her eyes in answer, and he glided toward her to rest his mouth on hers. The snow danced over his face and the air was cold, but her lips created a circle of warmth. He knew he should not have responded to her allure, but he had discovered a weakness within him where she was concerned. He found her more and more irresistible, although he was aware that answering that desire could open both of them to sorrow.

Just for now, he thought. Just once, to taste her again. He slipped his hand along the side of her face and kissed her more deeply, savoring the glow of spirit that he sensed in her.

A moment later, too soon, she pulled back. "You did not touch the stone for your answer," she said.

He grazed his fingers over her hair in a cherishing gesture. His heart thumped oddly. He settled her plaid over the crown of her head against the snowfall.

"I did not mean to ask the stone," he said. "I asked you."

He smiled at her and although he wanted to pull her

back into his arms, he shouldered her pack instead. "Where is your kinswoman's house? I long for a warm hearth."

"We do need to get out of this wind," she agreed.

"I would warm you," he said, "until you were like a fire." She stared at him without answer, but he saw longing flare in her eyes. It flared within him, too, sudden and hot and fierce. He looked away. "But that would not be wise. What we just did was not so wise, either."

"Must one only be wise?" she asked. "If that was foolish, fools are happier than sages."

"Fools," he said soberly, "have their own sort of wisdom." He turned. "Is it this way?"

"It is," she said, and walked ahead along the shoulder of the hill.

A little while later, the snow had thickened to a white haze. Sebastien saw, along the slope ahead of them, a stone house with a thatched roof, protected from the wind by the lee of the hill. A spiral of smoke curled out of the roof and an orange glow lightened one of the two windows to either side of the door.

A goat ambled toward them, stood staring with unblinking eyes, then wandered away. The door of the house opened, revealing the tall, slender silhouette of a woman.

"Alainna? Is it you?" The woman stepped out. The goat slipped past her through the open doorway.

"Esa!" Alainna ran forward. Sebastien hung back while they embraced. Then Esa turned and smiled at him, and he was, for an instant, struck dumb.

She had a startling beauty. Her smoothly knotted dark hair was threaded with silver, her frame tall and thin, clothed in a simple gown of russet wool and a blue plaid *arisaid*. She moved like a swan on water. Her face was exquisitely modeled, with rare, perfect symmetry, her smile was charming, and her thick-lashed brown eyes were warm and bright.

He saw all of that in an instant. He saw, too, kindness and sorrow in her magnificent eyes, tinted with shadows, fragility in the slender curve of her throat, and determination in her narrow, straight shoulders. He liked Esa immediately, and he understood why the men of Kinlochan seemed terrified of her and in love with her all at once.

He took her hand. "Dame Esa," he said, bending over her slim fingers. "I am honored to meet you."

She bowed her head graciously. "Sir, it is my pleasure to welcome you to my home." Her voice was low and mellow.

"Esa MacLaren, this is Sebastien le Bret," Alainna said.

He glanced at Alainna. Her vibrant coloring was cream and fire beside Esa's cool, dark elegance. A sudden, small shock thrilled through him. Esa was a stunning and perfect beauty, but Alainna was the flame in the center of his being.

He smiled then, his gaze only for her. The snow drifted down around them, but he hardly felt the cold.

"Come in," Esa said, opening the door. "I can offer you hot porridge and a warm hearth, and a sleeping pallet tonight, for the snow is getting thicker. But I hope you have not come all the way up here to ask me to go to Kinlochan with you."

Alainna went into the little house with Esa and stood in the dim interior. She urged the goat through the doorway and looked at Sebastien. "Will you lead her around to the side of the house? There is a turf block there for her to feed on. And take the sheep with you as well." She urged a fat sheep outside after the goat, and gave Sebastien a beautiful smile.

Sighing, he did his best to shoo the animals toward the other side of the house. A tiny hillock had been built against the stone wall, where grasses and heather grew, ragged and winter-brown. The sheep took to its meal immediately, but the goat trained its strange golden gaze on Sebastien and followed him in a circle.

He stepped around it and went back to the house. As he ducked his head to cross the threshold, he saw the women embracing each other. Alainna was whispering something to her kinswoman. He heard Esa gasp and clutch Alainna's arms.

Then Esa drew back, her eyes sheened with tears. "We will return to Kinlochan at first light," she said firmly.

Chapter Eighteen

The fire flared, and sparks floated like faery lanterns. Around it, the little room spun. Alainna blinked and watched as the earthen floor and low rafters seemed to tilt, along with the table, the benches, and the loom. She wished she had not finished the heather ale so quickly after supper.

Beyond the fire's glow, Esa and Sebastien stood beside the huge loom that dominated the center of the single chamber. The reds and deep greens in the weaving stretched there shone rich in the firelight. All the colors around her seemed saturated and luminous. Sebastien's hair, she thought, was like molten gold, his eyes like silver. Just like the golden warrior in her dream, she told herself . . . but he did not want to be that for her.

She sighed as she remembered the feel of his arms about her, the taste of his lips on hers. She watched as he spoke with Esa, but the room only tilted more. She put a steadying hand on the floor beside the pallet upon which she sat.

"It is just as well the snow storm kept us here," Sebastien said quietly, glancing at Esa. "Alainna looks ready to fall asleep. She would never have made it back to Kinlochan."

"I would," Alainna protested, curling up on the floor beside the hearth. The fire was so warm, and the pallet beneath her, two thick plaids layered over a dense mat of heather and straw, felt as comfortable as her own feather-stuffed mattress. She rested her head on her folded arms. "I could walk down those hills faster than you if I had to do it."

He chuckled. "I am sure you could." He came over and knelt beside her to pull another plaid over her, settling it about her shoulders. "Now rest."

"Do as he says," Esa told her. "Rest. The night will be

long and quiet, with the snow falling so thick out there. If
it is not too deep, we can go to Kinlochan tomorrow. We
will have to bring the goat and the ewe. I will not leave
them here."

Alainna yawned and snuggled down, and Sebastien
reached out to brush strands of hair away from her brow.
"Sleep," he said.

She closed her eyes under the caress of his fingers. His
hand rested on her shoulder briefly, then he stood. She
heard him murmuring with Esa again.

"I notice that you wear a plaid of my own weaving," Esa
said. "But you do not wear it as a *breacan*."

"I am not a Highland man," he murmured.

"You remind me of one. You are much like my own
Ruari *Mór*."

Alainna propped her head on her bent arm and watched,
knowing that Esa would never reveal Ruari's secret. In the
hours since Esa had learned about Ruari, her natural
beauty had deepened to radiant, and the shadows had left
her face.

"I have heard that your husband was a great warrior."

"A great man," Esa said. "Brave and kind. Handsome
and strong. You are fair, and he . . . was black-haired and
blue-eyed. But you make me think of him." She considered
Sebastien for a moment. "It is the quality of gentleness
beneath great strength, I think. Strength of heart as well as
of body. Not every man has that, and only the best have
it so strong in them that it shines like a vein of gold in
solid rock."

Sebastien inclined his head. "I thank you for such a fine
compliment. But if there is any vein of gold in me, it only
shines because of the reflected light of two such beautiful
women." He smiled, a sparkle dancing in his eyes as he
looked first at Alainna, then at Esa.

Esa laughed with delight. "Indeed, you are very much
like my Ruari," she said. "If you two knew each other, you
would be fast and loyal friends."

Sebastien said nothing, but his gaze slid toward Alainna.
She watched him steadily, and her heart fluttered to see
him look to her so naturally, so intimately.

She rested, listening as they talked, their laughter soft

and genuine, their friendship forming and strengthening. She felt a small pang of jealousy, knowing that Sebastien had fallen under Esa's spell, as did most men who gazed upon her beauty, and discovered her warm and wonderful soul.

Yet she could not envy the attention Sebastien gave to Esa. Her kinswoman had a fine, stubborn spirit, and was not afflicted by pride, which Alainna knew was her own shortcoming. Esa had given her heart to Ruari, and thinking him gone, had retreated into solitude. The love between them was rare and beautiful, and Alainna felt tears spring to her eyes as she thought of that joy restored to them.

"Look," she heard Esa say. "Alainna has fallen asleep by the fire. I meant to share my bed with her, and to give you that hearthside pallet. But we cannot wake her to move her now."

"I can lie down in any corner."

"Rest beside Alainna, close to the hearth," Esa said. Alainna opened her eyes quickly in surprise. "You two will be handfasted soon," Esa went on. "In our custom, promised couples often rest together, even share the same bed, when the girl is swaddled in blankets, as Alainna is now."

"It is not—" Sebastien began.

"It is good for you to be alone and to be close before you are joined in marriage," Esa said.

"That is not the way of it," Sebastien said.

"Is it not?" Esa asked gently. "I have seen the way you look at each other."

Alainna's heart thumped hard as she waited, eyes now closed. Sebastien's reply must have been wordless. Next she heard Esa's footsteps as she crossed the room.

"Good night to you, then," she said. Alainna heard the sliding sound of the iron rings on the curtain that closed off her bed from the room.

Alainna waited, motionless. She heard Sebastien stir, heard the thump of his boots as he took them off. Then he knelt beside her and stretched out as she lay on her side facing the hearth.

She kept still as he shifted and pulled a plaid over himself. His breathing was soft and steady, and his hand curled close to her back, bridging the narrow space between them.

The fire crackled, the wind whirled, their breaths fell into a rhythm. His quiet strength wrapped around her like a mantle, but she could not sleep. Her awareness of him was too keen. The handspan space between them felt so palpable that she could have dipped into it like a flowing stream.

After a while, his hand shifted. She felt his fingers glide up her backbone, down again. Her heart pounded hard, and small shivers cascaded through her. This was not the effect of the ale, she knew. Only his touch could stir her like this. She ached to turn into his arms, but lay still, uncertain.

His fingers glided over the mass of her hair, caught back with a thong tie. Then his gentle caress stopped, and his hand rested again at her back.

She tried to rest, but sleep eluded her. Growing uncomfortable on her side, she shifted to her back, turned her head, and opened her eyes.

He watched her, his face close to hers. Firelight illuminated the lean structure of his face, turned his eyes silver. She gazed at him, her breath quickening.

His fingertip touched her chin, and he leaned toward her. She tilted her face as he kissed her, quiet and slow. His unshaven beard felt rough, but his mouth was silken on hers.

The kiss seeped into her blood like heated wine, spilling throughout her body. She drank in his lingering kiss, and felt herself open like a flower, heart and body and soul.

His fingers brushed her cheek and trailed down her neck and shoulder to settle upon the upper swell of her breast. She lay still, though her heart beat like a storm. If she moved, if she shifted, she feared that this beautiful moment would end.

Tilting her head to accept his deepening kiss, she opened her mouth to his exploring, gentle tongue, felt his fingers drift over her breast. Delicate shivers slipped through her, and she arched eloquently into his palm, giving him her silent assent.

His hand soothed over her breast, shaping the pearl, finding the other, sending such exquisite sensations through her body that she gasped low. He kissed her harder, deeper now. His hand glided down her abdomen, moving over the curve of her hip to the top of her thigh. Her heart jumped, her breath caught.

She shifted, hungry for more, quickly aroused by the power of his languid but deliberate touches. Her body thundered for him.

She slid her fingers through his thick, silky hair and glided her hand downward. His body was hard and warm beneath his tunic. She traced over the firm curves of his back, his flat hip, the strong line of his muscled thigh.

He wrapped his arm around her and drew her closer until her abdomen pressed against his. The hard power of his arousal was evident, and she found herself neither surprised nor shocked. Moaning softly, moving against him as he kissed her again, she felt his own breathy groan slip into the recess of her mouth.

His hand spanned her hips and rolled her against him. She melted within when his lips trailed over her cheek to her ear. She craved deeper touches, deeper kisses, craved the merging of her body with his with a sudden, ravenous hunger. She gasped into his mouth and writhed against him, pleading, her hands sliding over his back.

He sighed, and separated his lips from hers, rolled his body away from hers. The heated layer of air between them seemed to pulsate. Alainna opened her eyes and met his gaze.

"Not now," he whispered. "God. Not now." He brushed his hand along her face, and she leaned her cheek into his palm.

"Why?" she breathed in protest, suddenly certain what she wanted, what she needed.

"Turn away," he whispered, his hand on her shoulder. He rolled onto his back, raising his forearm to rest it over his eyes.

She whirled and lay on her side. His words echoed, and she closed her eyes in anguish. She stiffened, hurt by his rejection, her heart and blood pounding.

After a while, he shifted, wrapping his arm around her as if in silent apology. She stayed rigid, but his embrace was comforting though chaste, his chest firm at her back. Relaxing in spite of herself, yearning for passion to simmer again between them, she soon succumbed to sleep.

* * *

The next day, Alainna was the quietest of the three as they journeyed back to Kinlochan. Their descent went far more quickly than the long climb upward, even with a thin blanket of snow on the ground. The sheep and the goat came along with them, guided by calls and firm pushes. Esa was filled with smiles and dazzling charm, and Alainna knew that it was the thought of Ruari that made her beauty so breathtaking and gave her mood such sparkle.

Sebastien spoke often enough with Esa, although he said little directly to Alainna. She did not join much in their chatter, although she saw the concern in his quick, sober glances. Her heart leaped whenever he touched her—a hand to her arm as they negotiated a rocky slope, a tug to settle her plaid when it slipped down.

When they at last sat in the warmth of Kinlochan's hall, Alainna watched her kinfolk lavish an affectionate welcome on Esa. They included Sebastien in their family circle for supper, and thanked him repeatedly for helping to bring their kinswoman back into their fold. Alainna smiled and shared their joy, but part of her felt distant and pensive.

The handfasting would be upon them the next day, she knew. The priest had been invited, venison had been hunted for the feast, Una and the women had worked hard all day to prepare the hall, and Lorne had kept to the isolation of his poet's bed during the day to hone his story skills for the celebration.

She felt as if she hurtled toward something unpredictable and breathtaking. Handfasting with Sebastien would veer her life in a new, thrilling, passionate direction—or it could lead them both to devastation. She did not know, and she could not express her fears or her hopes to anyone.

First, before any of that must be faced, there remained a task to accomplish in secrecy for Ruari and Esa.

"Aenghus mac Og, god of love and youthfulness," Lorne said, as he settled in his chair beside the hearth, "fell in love with a maiden one day. And when the god of love succumbs to the spell himself, it is a powerful weaving of souls indeed."

Alainna leaned forward to murmur a quiet translation as Lorne spoke, changing his words into English for the knights who had fallen into the habit of taking seats near her so that they, too, could listen to the evening stories. Robert and Hugo sat to either side of her, and several other knights were nearby.

Sebastien, she saw, had taken a seat in the shadows once again, a place he seemed to prefer. She glanced at him as she spoke, discovering that his gaze was already upon her, a gray and steady caress. Her cheeks burned in response.

"Aenghus saw this beautiful maiden in a dream," Lorne said, and Alainna echoed him. "She appeared to him again and again, kind and exquisite, sometimes playing for him a harp. Mad with love for her, unable to have her, his longing grew great. He searched for her endlessly. Finally he learned that she was Caer, the daughter of a king, and that she could be found at a certain loch with other maidens. Aenghus hurried there."

Pausing when Lorne did, Alainna glanced at Sebastien. She thought of her own dream of a magical warrior. That man now sat in the shadows, and her heartbeat quickened.

"When Aenghus arrived at the loch, he saw thrice fifty white swans swimming there. Caer was among them, and her father told Aenghus that she was enchanted. If Aenghus could recognize her, he could have her. He knew her, his love, immediately.

"Caer was the loveliest of the swans, the purest white, the most graceful. He called to her and she swam toward him. But she could not be his because he was in the shape of a man and she a bird. And so he took the shape of a swan for her.

"They rose into the air together, linked by a golden chain, and flew side by side to his fortress, where they lived forever in happiness. Every other year they became swans together."

As Alainna finished her translation, a certain line echoed in her mind.

And he took the shape of a swan for her.

She had asked Sebastien to take her form, to become a Celtic warrior with a Highland name. He had refused. Closing her eyes, she wished, wildly, fervently, that she and Sebastien could be like the swans in the story, sharing the same form, together forever.

She opened her eyes and found him gazing at her. And she knew that he understood the story of Aenghus and Caer as she did.

The choice was his, and the power was his, to stay or to go.

The hour was late, and the mist was thick and cold. Alainna was glad that Giric was there to row her and Esa out to the island after everyone else had gone to sleep.

Ruari waited for them on the shore, a tall, silent figure in the mist and the moonlight, his hair silvered. The boat touched the pebbled beach, and Giric stood, stepping out to pull the boat firmly ashore. He turned back, holding out his hand.

Esa rose from the boat and stepped out, gliding past Giric. Alainna watched from her seat.

Slim and graceful, Esa stood before the man on the beach. Ruari held out his hand. She took it in hers and lifted it to her face, looking up at him with wonder that was pure and clear in the moonlight. She kissed his hand.

She touched his cheek, his hair, his chest. He slipped his hand over her head and said something. Then she laughed, a sound like a silver chime, and threw her arms around him.

Alainna looked away, her eyes glazed with tears.

Giric sat down beside Alainna, and took up the oar. "I will return," he said, "before dawn, to fetch her to back to Kinlochan again. And every night, I will row her out here to him, so long as Ruari wishes to hide here." His voice sounded thick.

Alainna nodded, unable to answer for the tightness in her own throat. She dashed tears away and pulled her plaid closer about her head as the boat floated with the current of the loch.

The love that Ruari and Esa shared was deep and strong. She hungered for such passion in her life. Now she knew that she felt that for Sebastien, and she was sure that he felt something genuine for her.

What was there could grow and deepen, could last forever. But pride and honor separated them, and she did not know if that barrier could ever be breached.

She looked over her shoulder one last time. Ruari and Esa had vanished together into their private, misted world.

Chapter Nineteen

Snowflakes spiraled down in lazy paths as Sebastien walked through the bailey. He glanced up, wondering if the snow would grow heavy, for the wind had a bitter edge. He ducked his head against the cold, wishing he had not left his cloak in the hall as he crossed the yard toward Alainna's workshop.

In the few days since they had fetched Esa, he had glimpsed Alainna here and there as she walked toward the kitchen, or carried a bucket of water from the well, or exited the hall as he entered. He had exchanged only brief greetings with her, and she had not attended supper or storytelling. Una had told him, when he had asked, that she was busy with her stonecarvings.

In the evenings, the hall seemed cold and dim without her there. Even Lorne's tales sounded flat without Alainna's soft voice echoing translations. He and Giric had translated, neither of their efforts as lyrical as hers. For Sebastien she was the warm, bright heart of Kinlochan.

After his weapon practice that morning, he had returned determined to seek her out to discuss Kinlochan and its tenants, although in truth, he simply wanted to see her. They were to be handfasted in another day, on Christmas Eve, and he found himself thinking about that often.

Another reason he wanted seek her out was to clarify certain issues and questions before he could finally approach Cormac MacNechtan with the king's orders. He wanted to ride to Turroch soon, certainly before the new year.

Sebastien brushed snow from the sleeves of his dark tunic, the flakes so large and white that their patterns stood out against the wool. Long strides took him through the middle of the yard. Hearing his name called, he looked around.

Una stood in the doorway of the kitchen, beckoning to him. He changed his direction and strode toward her.

"Come in, Sebastien *Bàn*," she said. She tugged at his sleeve to urge him inside. "I want to speak with you. The snow is light, eh?"

"I wonder if it will thicken," Sebastien answered in Gaelic.

"It may." She walked to the wide hearth constructed of fieldstone and set against the back wall. Several oatcakes were baking on a large iron griddle just over the fire. She used a wooden spatula to turn a few of the cakes.

"I always watch the weather omens," she said as she worked. "Birds, shadows, wind, clouds all tell me what to expect. That, and my husband's aching bones."

"What did you want to tell me, Dame Una?" Sebastien asked. He inhaled the aromas of baking oatcakes and something savory that bubbled in a kettle over the fire. The kitchen was fragrant and dimly lit. Long and low-ceilinged, it was the only building in the fortress constructed of stone and roofed in slate to discourage fires. A thick oak table, knife-scarred and scrubbed clean, filled the central space. Herbs and onions hung in bunches from the ceiling; baskets of apples and carrots and sacks of grain lined one wall.

"I want to give you a gift," Una said. She slid the steaming oatcakes off the griddle to cool on the table surface. "A kitchen is not a place for a warrior, I know, but I thought you might be hungry. I saw you outside at the pillar not so long ago, like a fine warrior protecting our Maiden." She grinned, her delicate head trembling a little.

He chuckled. "I practice at swords in the mornings. Though I would gladly protect your Stone Maiden if she were real."

"She is," Una said matter-of-factly.

"You mean Alainna."

"Both of them. Here you, eat. These are made with honey and salt. Sweet and good. You need it."

Sebastien took one obediently and bit into it. The cake was thick, hot, and delicious. He swallowed, and accepted the cup of fresh, cool ale that Una handed him.

"How is the Stone Maiden real?" he asked.

"She is caught inside the pillar stone," Una said. "She waits there, watching over us. She is under a spell of magic cast by the faeries, but she will be free soon."

"Ah, the faery spell. Alainna told me."

"I want to thank you for going out each morning to protect our Stone Maiden," Una went on. "Her strength may be waning now, as the seven hundred years draw to a close. She is grateful that you guard her." She smiled. "Here, Sebastien *Bàn*, I want you to have this." She held up a folded plaid of a rich dark green, threaded with yarns of black and red.

"This is a fine gift," he said. "I cannot—"

"Tcha, you can," she answered, draping it in a swath over his left shoulder. "You have done much for us. And I am thinking you are cold in Norman cloth. This is good Highland wool, woven by our own Esa, from yarns that the women of Kinlochan have prepared from Kinlochan sheep. Such a garment will keep you as warm as if you sat at our hearth, eh?" She patted his chest and smiled at him.

Sebastien felt his heart wrench beneath her small mothering hand. "It will," he agreed, smiling fondly at her. "It is a good garment indeed, and a good gift."

"May it bring you joy and blessings, and may it keep you safe." She paused, her lips trembling. She handed him a long iron pin, twisted decoratively at one end, to fasten the plaid. "Wear it in the manner of a Highland man. You look fine in the *breacan*." She gave him a quick and impish smile.

"But I am not a Highland man."

"You are, in your heart, if you but allow yourself to be," she said cryptically. She pushed him toward the door. "Go, you, and find Alainna. She is working this morning."

"Working again?" He had not meant to say that.

"She does her carving every day, every night, even on the Sabbath. Go talk to her," she urged. "Tell her she works too hard and does not rest enough. Tell her you want to see her in the hall laughing and sharing stories with the rest of us."

He smiled ruefully. "I doubt she will listen to me."

"*Ach,* she will. After all, you were sent here to protect the Maiden."

"The Stone Maiden, or the Maiden of Kinlochan?" he asked as he opened the door.

"Both," Una said, and pushed him outside.

Sebastien smiled to himself as he crossed the bailey, and paused to adjust the dark green plaid around his shoulders like a cloak. He folded its long length, draped it over his shoulders, and wrapped the excess across the front, using the iron pin to fasten it closed. The thick wool blocked the wind admirably as he resumed his walk through the falling snow.

"Now that," a man said, "is not the way to wear a plaid."

He swiveled to see Lorne coming toward him. The old man's long hair seemed whiter than the snow itself, his beard a pale dusting on his gaunt cheeks, his eyes piercing blue. He carried a long sword in his hand, and Sebastien looked at it, puzzled, knowing the bard was not a warrior.

"Do I need to show you how to put on the *breacan* again?" Lorne asked.

Sebastien shook his head, smiling. "I remember," he said. "Una gave me this length of plaid just now," he explained. "I am honored by her gift. But I am not certain that I should wear the plaid in the Highland manner, being Breton by birth."

Lorne smiled. "That plaid belonged to our son."

Sebastien stared in astonishment. "Morag's husband? I did not know—"

"No matter. Wear it with courage and grace, as he did. It is no good to him now, and it is no good to hide it in a chest wrapped in bog myrtle to keep out the pests. Una is right to give it to you."

"You should give it to a Highlander."

"We have many plaids to share in this clan. We have so many, Sebastien *Bàn,* because we lost many men. The women have chests full of things stored away. You wear it, and may it bring you good fortune." Lorne clapped a hand on Sebastien's shoulder.

"I am grateful to you."

Lorne held the shining sword upright by the hilt. "And I was coming to find you today, to give you this." He offered it to him. "Take it. It is what we call a *claidheamh mór,* a great sword. A Highland sword."

Sebastien took it in two hands. "I have heard of these claymores, and I have seen them used," he said, looking at the long, heavy blade, the two-handed grip swathed in leather, the brasswork on the hilt. "This is a very fine weapon. I cannot accept such a—"

"We want you to have it," Lorne said brusquely. "My kinsmen and I. Lulach and Niall, Donal and Aenghus, we all talked about this. We have seen you at your swording nearly every morning, out there beside our Stone Maiden. You have excellent skills and great strength. You need one of these."

Sebastien hefted it experimentally. The claymore was far longer and heavier than his own blade, but beautifully balanced by the weight of the longer hilt and the downward-sloped guard. "I have used two-handed broadswords before, but this is even longer than those. It is taller than some men I know."

Lorne grinned. "You can use this well, for you are a tall man yourself." He reached out to take the hilt again, placing the sword tip against the ground. "The pommel should come just below your chin. Ah, a good fit." He handed it back to Sebastien.

"It will be a challenge to wield this, for it is much longer and larger than the blade I am accustomed to using," Sebastien said, as he admired its strong, simple design.

"You will practice, and you will master it. We will show you how—or my kinsmen will. For myself, I do not wield weapons of war, only for hunting. It is not seemly for a clan bard. But that is a good weapon, and it will keep you safe. It will help you to defend Kinlochan—and our Maiden."

Sebastien held it horizontally and smoothed his fingers along the fuller, the indented channel that gleamed along the length of the sword. "I am very grateful indeed. You are kind to share this, and the plaid, with me."

"These belonged to a strong warrior once, and now they do again." Lorne's voice thickened.

"Your son?" Sebastien asked quietly.

He nodded. "A thing is the bigger for being shared, they

say. If the leaves of the forest were gold, and the foam of the sea all silver, the great hero Fionn MacCumhaill would have given it all away—so who are we to withhold what we have?" Lorne smiled. "You were sent here to protect this clan, and you bring us help and hope. We wish to thank you for it."

Sebastien glanced away, uncertain how to respond to the faith this clan had placed in him. "I value these gifts, Lorne MacLaren, and I will try to do them justice," he replied. "Though I am a Norman knight and not a Celtic warrior."

"Be what your nature tells you to be," Lorne said easily. "Either way, you are welcome here."

Sebastien's throat tightened. "I would like to give you something as well, to mark the Christmastide and new year," he said.

"*Ach,* you will give us more than you can know when you wed our Alainna, when you defeat Clan Nechtan, when you father sons for Clan Laren and become our clan's leader." Lorne smiled.

Sebastien stared at him. "Lorne," he said. "I have not decided to settle here at Kinlochan. You know that."

The old man continued to smile, and Sebastien saw a deep gleam of wisdom in the pale blue eyes. "You will decide to do what is most honorable."

"Honor is a tender thing," Sebastien murmured, remembering what Una had told him once.

"It is," Lorne agreed. "We are thinking that you will bring good changes to Kinlochan, and many benefits for our clan."

"Alainna does not want anything to change here," Sebastien said wryly. "But change comes in spite of what she has wanted for the clan."

"Ah, that one feels it is her duty to protect our traditions. She was raised with war and danger all around her. And her father, on his deathbed, asked her to preserve the clan, our legacy, our lives, our future. She made a vow to him. Young she was for such a vow, but she has the strength to carry it through."

Sebastien nodded. "I know she does. And I understand now—any harm to the clan is a failure for her as a leader, and as a daughter. But she is not responsible for whatever fate befalls her clan."

"I have told her that, but she is stubborn, that one. You tell her, Sebastien *Bàn*." His gaze was direct and clear. "You can show her that change is not failure. She must learn that what is new, when it replaces the old, is not always undesirable."

"She wants no Norman influence to affect Kinlochan. I cannot even convince her that her tenants must gather grasses to make fodder for the horses and cattle next winter. Alainna sees it as a Norman custom. But it is simple common sense."

"Then make it a Highland custom." Lorne grinned. "A Kinlochan custom."

Sebastien smiled ruefully. They crossed the width of the bailey in companionable silence, with the wind whispering around them and the snow pale and delicate on their shoulders. Sebastien went to the door of Alainna's workshop and raised a hand to knock.

"Stop," Lorne said, holding up a palm. "Wait. We will not interrupt her just now."

Above the wind, Sebastien heard Alainna's voice in song, drifting through the half open window in a haunting melody.

> *Alas for those who are gone,*
> *Brave men,*
> *Fair women.*
> *Alas for those who are gone,*
> *Strong men,*
> *Kind women.*

Through the window, Sebastien could see Alainna bent over her stone, her back and arms moving in steady rhythm with the cadence of her song. She was lost in the weaving of work and melody. She did not realize that they watched. Sebastien looked at Lorne, and saw that the old man's eyes had misted.

Her voice softened and continued.

> *Peace there be, joy there be*
> *Courage there be, kindness there be*

Safe we are in the stream of life
Shield us and bring us home.

Her song faded. Sebastien heard the faint, steady scrape of iron upon stone. He blinked at the moisture in his eyes. "Why does she sing?" he asked Lorne.

"Women sing as they weave, shepherds sing, boatmen sing, mothers sing, lovers sing," Lorne said. "We are a race of poets and singers as well as warriors. This is a special chant, not to be disturbed until it is done. We could go in and listen, but not this time."

Her song began again, the same phrases, soft and low.

"She is singing back the soul," Lorne said then.

A chill went through Sebastien. "Whose? Her father's?"

"The soul of our clan," Lorne said.

He nodded thoughtfully, listening to the gentle cadence of her voice. He remembered what Alainna had told him when they stood together beside the Stone Maiden. No doubt she felt the pressure of the short span of time that remained until the faery spell of protection was gone.

"She sings back the soul of her clan, drawing it home as it begins to depart. She wants to summon it back before our clan vanishes into the mists of time. It is a kind of magic she does, very old." He smiled.

"Can that be done?" Sebastien asked.

"Think of her song as a prayer," Lorne said. "An appeal. What she does in there is as sacred as if she knelt in a church. She is asking God for help. She is pleading for her clan."

Sebastien nodded wordlessly and looked down at the slate doorstep, dusted with snow, at his feet.

"You," Lorne murmured, "are part of God's answer to her, I think." He patted Sebastien on the shoulder and left.

Sebastien stood by the door for a long moment, wishing he could go inside, wanting to talk to Alainna, to be with her.

He had so many questions now, some for king and crown, some for himself alone. Her song ended, and he lifted his hand to knock.

But he could not bring himself to disturb her. What she did seemed too precious to interrupt. He stood there, wrapped in a Highland plaid and a Norman tunic, and felt like an intruder.

He was an outsider here. The manner in which he wore a length of plaid would not change that. Neither would the weight of the great claymore in his hand.

He could listen to their stories, speak their tongue, drink their water of life, hunt in their hills; he could build a stone fortress to overlook their loch, and become a lord among them. He could marry their beautiful chief. He could stay here forever, and raise his children here, if he chose to do so.

But he wondered if he could ever truly share in the loyalty and caring, in the history and the sense of kinship that existed at Kinlochan.

He flattened his palm against the door. The longing he had felt since childhood welled fresh and painful in him. He stood on the threshold of all he had ever wanted: home, heritage, love, and welcome. Yet he was not part of this. The fine life he had always imagined for himself lay elsewhere, across a wide sea.

He closed his eyes and knew that he would do his utmost to protect these people, to preserve their lives and their way of life. He could not let them falter.

Alainna began her song again. Sebastien bowed his head and stepped back from the door. Her voice drifted out, as pure and beautiful as the snowflakes that swirled around him as he walked away.

Chapter Twenty

"Ach, Morag dear, did you scrub the stone dust from her hair?" Una said. She turned away from the glowing brazier with a length of warmed linen toweling draped in her hands. "Did you use that lavender soap, the fine soft stuff from the summer market, that came from France?"

"I did, and I did," Morag said efficiently, and dumped a bucket of warm water over Alainna's head. As the suds cascaded over her, Alainna ducked her face into her upraised knees.

Her kinswomen had hardly given her a moment to speak or even to bathe herself in the past hour. They had hastened her from her workshop, where she had been working since long before dawn, unable to sleep. Led to her bedchamber by her unlikely handmaidens, she had been all but tossed into a tub of hot water and vigorously scrubbed as if she were a child.

"Morag used all the soap," Beitris grumbled, picking up the empty clay pot. "And the last of the dried rose petals too."

"A bride deserves the best on the day of her marriage," Esa said from her seat on the edge of the bed, where she was busy with a needle, thread, and Alainna's dark blue woolen gown. "And a Christmas Eve wedding will bring great fortune." She smiled.

"Handfasted." Alainna sputtered as more water flowed over her head. "We are to be handfasted, not wed. I am not a bride."

"Oh, you are," Morag said. "You are. I have watched you and your Sebastien. There is more between you two than a king's order, I swear it."

"There is only a mutual need to obey," Alainna said. "Neither of us want this."

"If that man does not want you, then I am blind," Beitris said. "And if you do not want him, then you are blind."

"Indeed," Una agreed, and Esa laughed.

"And since the handfasting lasts a year and a day, we can have a full wedding next Christmas Day," Beitris said. "Oh! It will bring the best luck ever, for the entire clan!"

Alainna frowned as Morag squeezed the water from the length of her hair. "There," Morag said. "Why would you go without sleep the night before your wedding to carve those stones? Your hair was full of stone dust and chips. And you are so tired that you have purple shadows under your eyes."

"I have a lot of work to do."

"And a lot of dreaming about that fine husband you will marry today," Beitris said, smiling.

"It is only a handfasting," Alainna insisted.

"Whatever it is, we must hurry. There is so much to do," Una said. "Esa is repairing the tear in the embroidered hem of your beautiful gown. It would be bad luck to wear something worn or imperfect today. And our clan cannot afford any poor omens. Christmas brings extra blessings this year for all." Una beamed as she held up the linen sheet for her.

Alainna rose from the water and wrapped the sheet around herself. She stepped out and dried off, and rubbed her hair with another piece of linen.

"Handfasting is as good as a wedding in my opinion," Beitris said. "Lulach and I were handfasted for our first year. It was a fine start for us, and will be for you."

"Perhaps we do not want a fine start," Alainna said. She lifted her arms as Morag tugged a soft, lightweight linen chemise over her head. She dropped the damp toweling on the floor and kicked it aside, sitting on a low stool to pull on the woolen hose that Una handed her.

"Tcha!" Una shook her head, hands on her hips. "Just accept the marriage. Everyone else has."

"Sebastien tells me to accept it too," she answered, tying ribbons above her knees to keep the hose in place.

"He is wise as well as handsome and brave, and

you should listen to him," Esa said. "He will be a good husband."

"He may not be a husband at all," Alainna answered. "He means to leave me and go back to Brittany as soon as he can."

Una gasped. "He cannot leave you before the year and a day of the handfasting is over! Surely you told him that."

"I did not know it myself. What do you mean?" She stood, lifting her arms to slip into the brown woolen tunic that Una handed her. Morag turned her by the shoulders and began to work the tangles from her wet hair.

"Once handfasting vows are spoken, a man and woman cannot spend more than three nights away from each other, for the whole of a year and a day, or the union is annulled," Morag said.

Alainna looked at her in surprise. "Sooner than a year?"

"As soon as a long separation occurs," Morag said. "If he goes to Brittany and does not take you with him, the union is no longer valid. If he goes anywhere—even out hunting, or to visit the king at court—and is gone for more than three nights from your side, it is annulled. Any nuptial contract you sign with him is made null, too. Did Father Padruig not tell you this?"

Alainna shook her head. "He only said that if he witnessed the vows we said, that would make a marriage and not a handfasting. That is why he said he would come late in the day, for the feast only, and not the ceremony between us."

"If your Norman knight sails to Brittany, he must take you with him," Morag said, drawing the comb through the thick, damp length of Alainna's hair.

"I will not leave Kinlochan, and he will not stay here. He has a young son in Brittany living with . . . friends who have had troubles of late. Sebastien is concerned about all of them."

"A little son!" Una beamed. "See, the luck has already begun! There will be a child at Kinlochan soon!"

"Sebastien wants to keep the child in his own homeland," Alainna said. "Sebastien cannot stay in Scotland because of his son, and I will not leave here."

"*Ach,*" Una said, shaking her head. "So much pride."

"And so much loyalty each one has to their kin," Morag commented. "There must be some way to work this out."

"Tell your knight not to leave you behind," Una said. "You could certainly sail with him to Brittany."

"He will not be back for a long time," Alainna said.

"Beitris, take Alainna's tunic and shake it out at the window, if you will," Una directed. "It is full of stone dust. And we will have to shake her shoes clean of dust as well. Have we flowers for her hair? There is so much to do, and so little time, with the handfasting before the feast!"

"Be calm, Una," Morag said. "Mairi is working in the kitchen now, and Beitris and I will go help her soon. We have dried heather sprigs to weave into a wreath for Alainna's hair. We do need more juniper to decorate the hall, and to burn so that the smoke will banish ill luck. Alainna can go find some when her hair is dry."

Beitris went to the window, opened the shutter, and flapped the garment in the air like a banner. "Look!" she said, peering out. "Now surely that is a good omen for the wedding!"

"It is not a wedding. Ow," Alainna mumbled, as Morag pushed her head forward to pull through a stubborn tangle.

"Let me see," Una said, going to the window. "Ah, a good sign indeed, that!" Esa set down her stitching and followed her.

"What is it?" Morag rose to join the others at the narrow aperture that lit Alainna's small, timber-walled bedchamber. "He looks like Aenghus mac Og or some warrior hero from a story out there," Beitris said admiringly.

"Ah, he does," Morag agreed, and sighed.

Alainna tugged the comb through her hair. "What are you looking at?"

"Your man," Una said. "Come see."

Alainna crossed to the window to join them. She looked beyond the palisade wall and the loch to the meadow where the Stone Maiden stood, a serene giantess in the morning light.

A giantess with her own guard. Sebastien circled the base of the pillar, thrusting with the claymore, lunging, pulling back. He was intent on his practice, his hair gleaming golden, his blade a bright edge as it arced and swooped.

"It is a good portent to see the groom guarding our Maiden on the morn of his wedding. Handfasting," Beitris added hastily.

"He is circling *deiseil,* sunwise. That is definitely good luck," Una said. "Alainna, did I tell you to be sure to walk sunwise around him before you stand with him today?"

"You told me," she said as she watched Sebastien circle the Maiden as if he protected her. He raised his sword and held it high, facing the stone. Light sparked off steel, and he lowered the blade and turned away to picked up his cloak and his long shield, painted blue, its insigne scarcely visible.

Although from this distance she could not see it clearly, she knew the design well: a single white arrow on a blue field. She had seen it in his possession in reality, and in a dream, although then she had not known Sebastien le Bret.

The golden warrior of her dream did indeed exist, she thought. He walked toward Kinlochan even now, and toward a handfasting with her. A shiver traveled up her spine, and her heart quickened.

Suddenly she wished that he could stay with her forever, that he would take her name and accept her clan as his own family. In so many ways, he was the champion of her dream.

But he did not want to be that champion for her. He would be glad to learn that his journey to Brittany would annul the handfasted union between them.

She sighed in dismay and turned away from the window.

Sebastien waited alone in the center of the hall, the fire crackling behind him, its heat close on his back and legs. He wore his dark green surcoat trimmed in silver over his brown tunic, and had fastened the dark green plaid over his shoulders like a flowing mantle. He cleared his throat nervously.

The others formed a wide, firelit circle around him. As the door opened, all he heard, suddenly, was the pulse of his own blood rushing in his ears.

Alainna came forward alone, dressed as he had first seen her in the king's hall. The hem of her midnight blue gown, sparkling with red-and-gold stitchery, swept over the rushes as she walked toward him. Her loosened hair flowed to her waist like a sunset cloud, its dazzling color framing her pale face and upper torso. She wore no plaid, the elegant drape of the gown enhancing the taut curves of her body. A narrow wreath woven of dried heather sprigs crowned her head. Beneath that delicate ring, her eyes seemed brilliantly blue.

She came toward him, then around him in a circle, brushing behind him, circling in front, and again, twice more, until she stood before him.

He held out his hands, and she offered hers, joining with him left to left, right to right, so that their arms made a crossed loop like an interlaced design. They stood still, their gazes steady upon one another. Her hands were silken but strong in his. He tightened his grip for a moment, and she pressed back in reassuring answer, a silent agreement to proceed.

He closed his eyes briefly, recalling Lorne's earlier instructions. Lorne had patiently taught Sebastien lines of poetry to use, and had advised him on how to phrase his vow, which, he said, should come freely from his heart.

But when Sebastien looked at her, what he had planned to say slipped from his head like mist in the sun. She was radiant in the firelight, her eyes shining. He felt the fine tremble that ran through her like a drawn harp string.

She clung to his hands, drew a breath, and began.

> *A shade you are in summer*
> *A shelter you are in winter*
> *A rock you are*
> *A fortress you are*
> *A shield you are about me*
> *I cherish you*
> *I help you*
> *I enfold you*
> *I promise you.*

Alainna paused. "I will take you, Sebastien le Bret," she said softly, "for my handfasted spouse so long as we both agree, in peace, in joy, in grace of promise." She tightened her quavering fingers on his.

He sensed in that tremor the shimmer of her soul. She was strength honed by grace. What she offered him was precious and genuine. He drew in his breath, overcome by awe.

He knew what to say. But he had not known until this moment that he would say it with such conviction.

"I will take you, Alainna MacLaren," he murmured, "for my handfasted wife, in peace and in joy, in grace of promise." He tightened his fingers over hers and closed his eyes. The poem that sprang into his mind was not one that Lorne had taught him that morning, but one the bard had recited a few nights ago. Somehow it seemed perfect, and he began.

> *I found in the garden*
> *My jewel, my love*
> *Her eye like a star*
> *Her lip like a berry*
> *Her voice like a harp.*
> *I found in the meadow*
> *The bright-eyed maiden*
> *Her eye like a star*
> *Her cheek like a rose*
> *Her kiss like honey.*

Small tears sparkled in her eyes. He drew her toward him, hands clasped. "It is done," he whispered. "So be it."

"And so it begins," she murmured, and tilted her face toward him, her eyes half closed. He touched his lips to hers, a kiss of peace between them. Her lips yielded, warm and giving.

He felt his heart leap into a new pattern within his breast, and he knew then that he was securely caught in its infinite turning.

Chapter Twenty-one

The delicate jingle of silver bells echoed around the hall. Startled, Sebastien looked up from his quiet conversation with Robert and glanced around. He saw only the tops of heads and the shoulders and backs of those near him. He picked up his wooden cup and sipped at the potent water of life.

The handfasting supper was still on the tables in half-empty wooden bowls, flanked by horn spoons and eating knives. Platters and larger bowls still held generous portions of roast venison and mutton stew, carrots and onions, oatcakes and honey, cheeses and apples. Jugs of spiced wine, heather ale, and bladders of *uisge beatha* sat about, lifted now and again by those still thirsty.

Though most were sated, Sebastien had eaten little. He knew that Alainna, who sat beside him talking quietly with Giric, had hardly touched her food either. Some of the Highlanders and the knights still sat at the trestle tables, while others had moved to stools and benches or found places on the floor, anticipating the storytelling entertainment.

The chiming, rhythmic sound came again. The chatter in the hall stilled. Sebastien looked up again. This time he saw Lorne enter the doorway and walk through the room.

Lorne's hair drifted over his shoulders like snow as he raised one hand high. He held a curving branch of an apple tree, the twigs strung with colored threads, from which dangled small silver bells, sparkling crystals, acorns, and nuts. As he shook the branch in a distinct rhythm, it made a light, musical sound.

Alainna stood as Lorne entered the hall. She went to the hearth to pull a carved chair into position beside the fire,

then poured ale from a jug into a silver cup, which she left
on a low stool. She returned to the bench, slipping back
into her place between Giric and Sebastien, who looked
questioningly at her, his curiosity sparked.

"What is he doing?" he murmured.

Alainna leaned toward him, her arm snug against his. He
leaned down to hear her answer. "He carries the silver
branch, an honor allowed only to bards who have trained
for at least nine years," she whispered. "He is more than
a storyteller. Lorne is a trained *fili,* a master poet. He
learned his skill in a school of bards in the western Highlands, whose traditions trace back to ancient Ireland. He
studied for nine years as a youth and young man to earn
the right to be one of the *filidh.*"

Sebastien nodded, fascinated, enjoying the simple closeness between them, made so natural by the crowded bench
they sat upon.

Lorne circled the hearth, shaking the decorated branch
in a lively rhythm, bells and acorns and crystals vibrating.
The faery-like music filled the room. Lorne sat, laid the
branch on the stool beside him, and picked up the cup to
take a sip of ale. Then he settled in his chair and looked
around, his profile strong and commanding in the firelight.

Each movement he made, each glance he gave was slow
and deliberate. Sebastien felt anticipation mount in the air
like a tangible thing. One by one, the audience leaned forward, eager for the story to begin. The old man picked up
the branch again, and created an airy cadence this time,
lifting the branch and letting it sink, again and again, until
he finally stilled it. The silvery chime of the bells faded
to silence.

Alainna sat hip to hip and arm to arm with Sebastien,
crowded on her other side by Giric and the others who
occupied the bench. Sebastien shifted, turning his torso to
allow her more room. Her shoulder pressed against his
chest. Heat swirled between them. Aware of how easily he
could draw her into the circle of his arm, Sebastien kept
still and watched Lorne.

"Long and long ago," the bard said, "into the mists of
time, a warrior called Conall of the Victories traveled with
four of his comrades into the west. They saw a green and

beautiful isle sparkling on the water, and fetched themselves a boat, and sailed there to seek adventure, which is what they found.

"The king of the green isle had a beautiful daughter whom he had placed inside a high tower of silver, with a door of bronze and a roof thatched in white birds' wings. This tower rested on tall pillars. And the king told Conall that whoever could bring the princess out of that tower should have her for his wife, and have the green isle for his own when the old king died."

As he spoke, Robert, Hugo, and the others leaned closer to hear Alainna's quiet translation. Sebastien listened to both Alainna and Lorne, and felt the warmth of her body, so close to his, flow through him, a sensation like mellow wine. The vibration of her voice entered his chest, and he closed his eyes.

Peace enveloped him like mist in a forest. He savored the feeling, uncertain if it was created by the soothing echo of two beautiful voices; or the warm pressure of her body beside his; or perhaps it came out of the serene, listening mood in the room. He did not know. He only wanted to feel it envelop him, rare and warm.

". . . . And after all the warriors had tried and failed, finally Conall gave a mighty shove, and pulled down the pillars that held the tower," Lorne said. "The princess fell out and into his arms. When he held her and looked into her eyes, love turned within his breast like a living thing. . . ."

Sebastien opened his eyes. He knew that feeling well. He glanced at Alainna, and she looked at him, pausing in her translation, as if she shared his thoughts.

"But Conall knew that his companion Mac Morna loved the princess of the silver tower too," Lorne went on. "And Conall loved his friend, for he was the friend of his soul. Whoever wed the princess would stay on the green isle forever. Mac Morna was ready for such peace in his life, while Conall hungered for more adventures. His heart was torn.

"Then he turned and handed the girl into the arms of his friend. And Conall told the king that Mac Morna had taken down the pillars and won the princess. . . ."

Something intangible constricted in his chest. He knew what heaven it was to hold Alainna. He could not imagine giving her into another man's arms, to be another man's wife.

He knew now how much he wanted her; he knew he had been a fool to think he could leave her. Handfasted for the price of a contract and a charter, bonded by a king's order. But a deeper bond had somehow formed between them, when neither of them had wanted that to happen.

Pride, his and hers, could break that bond like an iron mallet on stone. He closed his eyes in anguish.

Hearing Lorne and then Alainna stop their narratives, hearing the delicate sounds of the silver branch again, he opened his eyes. Alainna smiled at him.

"That tale is one of my favorites," she said, still leaning into his side.

"A marvelous story," he murmured. He felt a smile rise from his heart to his eyes to his lips.

He was glad, just then, that the bench was crowded, so that Alainna had to press so closely against him. He was glad that he had not sought his customary place in a shadowed corner, as he had originally thought to do, even now.

And he was glad that he had taken the handfasting vow with her, if only for a little while. No matter what the future held for either of them, he would treasure what this day had wrought.

"The priest is drunk," Una said. Alainna peered around Sebastien's shoulder to look at Father Padruig, who sat at Sebastien's other side.

"What, already?" Niall said, sitting across the table. "He usually waits until the stories are done. Here, Padruig, give me that." He swiped the sheep's bladder out of the priest's uncertain grip and put it to his own mouth, swallowing lustily. He set it down and grinned at Una. "There, less for him, see."

Una eyed them both with disgust. "He has hardly been here for a few hours, since the handfasting ceremony ended, and already he is foolish with drink."

Father Padruig looked up. "I am not foolish," he said expansively, "and my friend Niall of the One Hand told me what was said at the ceremony. *Ach!* I am unhappy to have missed it! Niall says it brought a tear to his eye."

"It did that," Niall agreed. "And if you had witnessed it, we would be celebrating a marriage and not a handfasting." He and the priest snorted with laughter.

Una made an impatient sound. "This one is not drunk," she told Padruig, pointing to Sebastien as if he was exemplary. "And he has been sipping the water of life along with the rest of you. And you a priest!" She shook her head and walked away.

"I am a fine priest," Padruig said defensively to the air.

"You are," Niall agreed. He slanted a look at Sebastien. "How is it this knight is not drunk, if all he ever had before he came to Kinlochan was French wines and thin English ale?"

"I was raised on Breton wine, which should be sipped cautiously, and only while leaning against a wall." Sebastien smiled languidly and looked at Alainna, his gray eyes sparkling. She smiled, amused.

"When you go there, bring some back for us," Niall said.

"He cannot do that for a year," Padruig said. "He cannot go to Brittany or anywhere for a year and a day, unless he takes Alainna with him. And she will not go!" He tugged the bladder from Niall's single hand.

Sebastien looked at Alainna. "What is he talking about?"

She looked down, her heart thumping. "He means that if you leave me for more than three nights in a row, the handfasting is annulled."

"Annulled?" he asked.

"As if it never happened," she said.

He stared at her. Then he looked away suddenly, frowning as he, turned his half-empty cup in his fingers.

She glanced away. "I did not know it myself until earlier today. I thought you would be glad to hear about it," she murmured. "Since . . . you must go away."

Sebastien did not reply. Unable to read his silence, as she often could do, she did not know if he was pleased or displeased with the revelation.

"That nuptial contract that I wrote out for you is now signed and valid." Padruig leaned toward Sebastien. "But it needs a marriage to keep it so. Be careful that you do not go anywhere without her, eh!" He grinned sloppily.

"Alainna will not leave Kinlochan," Niall said. "She takes after her kinswoman Esa. The roots of home and hearth are deep in both of them."

"What more should I know about handfasting that I do not?" Sebastien asked, his tone grim. Alainna glanced sharply at him.

"If you bed her, you wed her," Padruig said. "That makes a marriage union in the eyes of God, if not the Church."

"That I know," Sebastien said in a low growl, a muscle flashing in his jaw.

"And as far as I am concerned, as a priest, a bedding is a marriage, no matter if you undo the vows or not," Padruig said sternly, summoning himself to stare hard at them both. "Handfasting is allowed by old Celtic law, you see," he said, wagging a thick finger in the air. "But Holy Mother Church in Rome does not recognize such unions." He shrugged. "Still, if you leave her, and do not return for three days or more, by custom, she is not your handfasted wife, and never was."

"And all your fine poetry will be wasted," Niall lamented, his eyes reddening. The priest handed him the bladder.

Sebastien sat wordlessly beside Alainna. He did not look at her, nor did he cease to turn his cup around as if its simple design fascinated him. Yet she felt the deep pull of his thoughts like a strong, unseen cord between them.

Bedding made a marriage, she told herself; regardless of vows spoken or cast aside, in the eyes of God they would be wed forever if they gave in to the delicious temptations that she had sampled already with him. She glanced at Sebastien, but he did not look at her. She sighed.

"So you had best think carefully," Father Padruig said, sober in tone. "Handfasting is never a step to take lightly."

"I know, Father." Sebastien gave Alainna a quicksilver glance. She felt it through to her toes, like a physical touch.

"But then you both obey royal orders," Niall said, grinning. "What is the problem? The thinking has been done, eh? And now you will find peace and happiness together, as the king wishes for you, and as we all wish for you." He smiled at them.

Sebastien angled his head, a slight frown puckering his brow. Alainna turned away, her cheeks heating, desire spinning in her belly just from looking at him, just from sitting beside him.

She glanced up as Giric and Lulach sat down at the table on either side of Niall. Not long ago, she had noticed them laughing with Robert and some of the Norman knights. Now the room quieted again, for Lorne leaned his harp against his thigh and began to play a soft melody. Alainna relaxed, resting an elbow on the table as she listened. She yawned.

"Bed soon, eh?" Lulach asked, and winked at her.

She blushed. "I did not sleep well last night. I worked late at my carvings."

"No more of that, eh, Sebastien?" Niall chuckled.

Sebastien did not reply, but folded his arms on the table and faced Giric. "Tomorrow or the next day, if weather permits, I will take some men and ride through the northwestern part of Kinlochan."

"To measure the boundary?" Giric asked.

"That, and to look for renegades. One of the tenant farmers that I met the other day told me that he saw a man hiding in one of the caves in those hills a few days ago. He thought it might be one of the rebel Celts. That fellow we saw fighting the wolves could be one of them, since you and Alainna did not recognize him. I will continue to search. The rebels will be seeking support from the Highlanders in this area."

Alainna cleared her throat. "Clan Laren does not support the MacWilliam cause. I speak as chief of my clan."

"As it should be, but the rumors of rebels are persistent," Sebastien said. "There is at least one of them around here. The tenant said that he has heard that the Mac-Williams are coming back from Ireland one by one."

"I, too, have heard that," Father Padruig said. "One by one, each preparing the way for the rest, going quietly about the Highlands to raise support for their cause. Later they mean to gather together in a strong force."

Alainna bit anxiously at her lower lip as she listened. She

thought of Ruari, safely hidden on the little island; she could guess what Sebastien would think of that, but she wondered what the rest of her kinsmen would do if they discovered the truth. Would they support Ruari, or turn him over to the crown?

"Ruari MacWilliam is gone," Giric said firmly, without looking at Alainna, "so the rebels have no leader in Scotland."

"If he were alive he would come here," Niall said. "I wonder if his kinsmen seek supporters in our region."

"They will not find it here," Lulach said. "We never followed Ruari in his clan's cause, though we would have watched his back because he was marriage kin to us."

"Hush, all of you," Alainna said, leaning forward. "Do not let Esa hear you speak of Ruari." She glanced at Esa, who sat with Una, Morag, Beitris, and Niall's quiet wife, Mairi. Esa smiled graciously at those around her, the glow of happiness so evident on her face that Alainna smiled to herself, glad to have had some part in that joy.

"Would you help him now, if he were here?" Sebastien asked.

Alainna clasped her hands beneath the shadow of the table, grateful that Sebastien had looked at the men and not at her.

"Ruari *Mór* was a great man," Lulach said. "A mighty warrior and a man who should have been a king, if kings were chosen for their worth and strength. I would not hesitate to help the man if I saw him here and now, and I would fight at his back to defend him. But I would not help his clan's cause."

"I, too, would watch Ruari's back, were he but a ghost," Niall said. "I loved the man well. He had a lion's heart and a lion's pride. But the rest of his clan are hot-tempered and overproud, and I do not care for them."

Alainna looked at Giric, and saw him watching her, somber and knowing. Beside her, Sebastien frowned thoughtfully.

"It would not surprise me if Clan Nechtan is involved with the MacWilliams," Lulach said then.

"Cormac claimed complete loyalty in his letter to the

crown," Sebastien said. He glanced at Padruig. "Did you write out his petition for him?"

"I did," Padruig answered. "He insists on his loyalty, and that much you know. As his priest, and as the grandfather of his little son, I cannot say more."

"We can see in your face what you think," Niall said grimly. "You would not go far out of your way to defend the man."

Padruig grabbed the bladder and took a drink, wiping his mouth and exhaling hard.

Alainna leaned forward, eager to change the subject. Her heart leaped nervously at every mention of Ruari and Cormac. She hated to think that Ruari might have come back to the region only to seek support from Cormac. If that was so, her own loyalty would be badly torn.

"Look there," Niall said. "Una and the rest of them are coming over here. They must be thinking it is time these two bound themselves further." He grinned at Sebastien.

Alainna heard Una and Beitris laughing, and looked up to see several of her kinfolk rising from their seats to come toward their table. Most of them wore broad smiles and most were chattering at once. Esa moved among them too, tall and and dignified.

"We have yet to have the bedding of the bride, and it grows late," Una said, walking in the lead. She carried two folded plaids in her arms. "Stand up now, the pair of you!"

Sebastien stood, stepping outside the bench, as Alainna did. She felt her stomach lurch, and her heartbeat grew fast and heavy.

"A bedding for a handfasting is done differently than for a marriage," Beitris told Sebastien. She lifted the plaids out of Una's arms and handed one to him and the other to Alainna. "We will not escort you to the bedchamber with songs and blessings, for that is reserved for weddings. You two are to go outside, and find yourselves a place to be alone in one of the other buildings."

"Or up the steps in Alainna's warm bedchamber, if you want to sneak past us," Morag added, smiling. "We will pretend not to see." She looked the other way pointedly, while laughter rippled around her.

"We will not follow you," Una promised. "You will have

your privacy to do what you will." She grinned, to more laughter.

For all their delight, Alainna could not smile. Her cheeks grew hot. She glanced at Sebastien, and saw with surprise that his cheeks were stained rosy. She had never seen him blush before, although he was a fair man. He looked awkward, standing with the plaid in his arms as if he was not sure what to do with it.

"We will not follow you," Lorne said. "But we will give you a *seun,* a charm of blessing. Come here, and stand with me." He beckoned to them.

Alainna went toward him, as did Sebastien, while the rest stood back, creating a wide circle around them.

Lorne lifted his hand. A length of red thread, knotted and strung with small, shining crystals, dangled from his fingers. He shook the string gently, so that it rang and sparkled.

Alainna stood beside Sebastien while Lorne walked around them sunwise, and shook the string in a sweet rhythm. He recited a blessing as he moved, and Alainna closed her eyes and listened.

> *Be the smooth path for the other*
> *Be the bright star for the other*
> *Be the kind eye for the other*
> *Be sun and moon for the other*
> *Be grace and peace for the other*
> *Be shield and strength for the other.*

He shook the string of crystals and circled them again.

> *Each day be joyous*
> *No day be grievous*
> *All days be blessed*
> *And well and seven times well*
> *May you spend your days.*

Lorne stood still and let the crystals fall silent. Alainna felt the warmth of Sebastien beside her, and sensed his presence like a rock, like the fortress of the vows she had taken.

Quiet lingered like a veil of peace. Alainna opened her eyes and saw her kinfolk watching her, smiling fondly, forming a wide circle around her and Sebastien. Lorne had stepped back too. Standing among the Highlanders, the knights watched, their expressions somber and respectful, aware that they watched something sacred.

She looked up at Sebastien. Shadows and firelight flickered across his sculpted profile. Then he turned his gaze upon her and tilted his head to indicate that it was time for them to leave the hall.

She turned toward the door. The crowd parted like a wave of the sea as she and Sebastien moved forward together.

Chapter Twenty-two

In the starlit bailey, their breaths formed pale frosted clouds. Alainna was silent as she walked beside Sebastien, hearing the light strains of Lorne's music wafting out behind them.

"We can go in here," she said as they neared her workshop. She opened the door and Sebastien entered behind her, ducking his head beneath the lintel.

The room was cold, dim, and eerily silent, the carvings mute, pale presences on benches and tables. A faint red glow emanated from the brazier in the center of the room. Alainna crossed over to it, her footsteps crunching on the layer of stone chips. She grasped an iron poker and bent to coax the live coals to better brightness. After adding a few peat chunks, she brushed off her hands and straightened.

She turned uncertainly. Sebastien crossed the room toward her, his boot soles loud on the crushed stone. He took a tallow candle from a shelf and hunkered down to light it at the brazier. Then, standing beside her, candle held high and folded plaid beneath his arm, he lifted his brow laconically.

"Shall we sleep here tonight?"

She hugged the plaid to her chest. "I spend many nights here. It is cold just now, but it will soon be warmer." She watched him scan the room with his gaze: floor littered with stone chips, benches and tables crowded with carved and raw-cut stones, shelves full of iron and wooden implements, and a coating of fine, pale dust on nearly everything.

"Cozy," he drawled.

She laughed a little, and went to the far corner of the room, where she laid her plaid out on a long slab of pinkish sandstone, which rested, tablelike, on three stout wooden trestles, one end inclined a little higher than the other. Sebastien joined her, tossing his plaid down beside hers and setting the candle on a corner of the stone.

"If you are tired and do not wish to go back into the hall to seek a bed, you can rest here." She patted the slab. "It is not an appealing bed, I know, but . . ." She let her voice trail off.

He brushed his fingers over the slightly grainy surface. A border of knotwork, composed of interwoven lines in endless circles, had been carved in low relief to form a frame. The interior section was flat and blank.

"Is this one of your projects?" he asked.

"Malcolm began this," she said, touching the stone. "It is the last of the pink sandstone slabs that he brought here several years ago. The other pieces were made into the tombstones that you saw in the church." She frowned. "I hope I will never have to finish this carving."

He nodded grimly. "The dog's pallet by the brazier will do fine for a bed."

She wrinkled her nose, and half laughed. "If you like the company of fleas."

He chuckled, the sound echoing among the stones in the room. "And if I went back to the hall, just where would I seek a bed?"

"You could hardly take a pallet beside the other knights and my kinsmen. Not now."

"True." He crossed his arms and leaned a hip against the stone. "Do you not expect us to live as man and wife now that we are handfasted? It part of the custom."

She crossed her arms too, a mirror of his pose, and leaned against the stone. "Couples who take handfasting vows also have the . . . privileges of marriage. But they are usually in love and eager to be married. They handfast until a priest can be summoned, and so the custom grew into a year and a day. We are fortunate to have a priest near Kinlochan, but it is not the case in much of the Highlands."

"Ah," he said, nodding his understanding. "But it can still be undone, even if it is a marriage made in the eyes of God."

"According to our custom, it can." Her heart thudded

hard. "My kinfolk think that we will . . . complete our union. They believe that we have handfasted to keep our marriage secret from Cormac for a while." She sighed. "They want us to stay wed, and they want you to agree to take our name for your own, and give it to our children."

"I cannot do that," he murmured.

She shrugged. "Still, they expect you will. They find it hard to believe that anyone can refuse our name, or leave Kinlochan."

"It is a beautiful place, and a proud name," he agreed. "But my ties are in Brittany, just as yours are here."

"You could bring your son back here with you, to your new home—if you wanted to live here," she added.

"Home," he said, as if he had never heard the word before. He rubbed the edge of the stone with his fingers.

"They believe that you will stay here to defeat Clan Nechtan and rebuild Clan Laren. My kinfolk want to accept you not only as the champion sent by the king, but as a leader."

"You are their leader, not I."

"Now they place their faith in you, too," she said. "They believe in you, their golden warrior." She had not meant to utter her own thoughts, and bit at her lower lip.

He frowned at her. "Their what?"

"Their hero. You have proven your worth to them." She turned to spread out the plaids. "It is not a comfortable bed, but you can rest here if you want."

"And you?"

"I am not tired," she said. "I have some work to do."

"I may not know you as well as a husband knows a wife, but I can see that you are exhausted. Your voice sounds hoarse and there are shadows under your eyes. You need rest."

She shook her head. "My work eases me. I am overwrought after such a day. I will rest later."

"Here?" He tapped the sandstone, then glanced at the rough floor. "There is no suitable bed in this place. What of tomorrow, and after that?"

She had given that some thought already. "I will share my bedchamber, but not my bed. Only you and I need know that."

He nodded slowly. "You will do nearly anything to please your kinfolk, I think."

She stilled her hands on the plaid. "How can I go against their wishes? They have had so much disappointment, so much loss. I cannot tell them that we do not want this."

"Some of them may be growing fragile with age, Alainna, but they are tough, and they are wise." His voice was quick and stern, almost a reprimand. "They are not so needy as you think. There is no reason to protect them from the truth."

She shook her head. "I cannot tell them. Our handfasting, and your arrival here, has brought them hope and joy. I did not know how much it meant to them until I saw their faces this evening, heard their laughter. I will not shatter that. Not yet." She stepped away.

He reached out to cup her shoulder. She halted, her back to him. "You love them so much," he murmured, "that you will even let them believe that we are living as man and wife. Is that respect for them, Alainna, or does it allow you to avoid the truth?"

"The truth is that we do this only to ensure help for Kinlochan . . . and to ensure the land grant for you."

"I did not come here just for the land."

"Why then?"

"For you," he said. "I came for you."

A chill ran through her. She looked at him, captured by the sincerity in his voice. Caught, too, by the memory of her dream.

"I watched you make your plea to the king," Sebastien said. "I saw your pride and your desperation. Clearly you cared about your people, and you greatly needed a champion. I came here to help you."

"I am grateful," she said quietly. "But we need far more than virtuous chivalry at Kinlochan."

"You have a low opinion of courtesy, I know. Yet courtesy and honor keep you safe, here and now."

"How so?" She stepped away from the pressure of his hand.

"Courtesy will keep you safe tonight in that unforgiving stone bed," he said, and indicated the slab with his thumb. "And in your own bed later, I assure you. If I had no courtesy in my nature"—he bowed in a mocking way—"I could not guarantee your virtue, my lady."

"I know how courteous you can be," she said. "And I will allow you into my bedchamber for now, but not my bed."

"So be it." His voice was smooth and cool, that polite veneer in place like opaque glass. She wanted desperately to see through that glass. She craved to know more of him, yearned for the fire, the passion, the sheer challenge she sensed in him. Yet her declaration had erected a barrier between them.

Wordlessly, she picked up the candle and carried it to a bench, which held a cloth-covered stone and several tools. She set the candle down so that its light poured over the covered stone. Lifting a plain, loose-cut tunic that lay nearby, she slipped it on to protect the fine-spun woolen gown from stone dust. Deftly and quickly, she drew the waving mass of her loose hair over her shoulder and plaited it into one long braid that she tossed back.

Sebastien looked at the stone on the bench as she removed the cloth and chose a chisel and mallet from an assortment of tools. She positioned a toothed chisel and gently tapped the mallet against the wooden handle of the chisel, moving the teeth over a section of the slab.

Aware that he came closer, she could not seem to calm the fast thud of her heart or the tremor in her hands. She continued to manipulate the chisel.

"What stone is this?" he asked. "I have not seen you working on it before. A beautiful color, like fresh cream," he said, tracing a finger along the edge. "And smooth to the touch, too. Is it limestone?"

"Caen limestone. Malcolm brought this from France, I think."

"Normandy. Caen is in Normandy. I have been there myself, and I have heard of its famous limestone."

"Justly famous, for it carves beautifully. The stone is soft enough to be easily worked, compliant to the slightest touch, but hard enough to take fine detail and polish like good marble." She chose another chisel as she spoke. "It does just what the tool wants, just what the hand and the mind want, yet only needs the lightest touch, the gentlest hand."

"The perfect stone for you, I think," he murmured.

She lowered her glance, but loved his quiet compliment. "I wish I had more of this limestone," she said, and tapped again with the mallet, focusing on her task for a few moments. "Since I have only this piece, I want to carve something unique."

He bent closer to look at the stone. "What is this scene?"

"Parts of it are only scabbled—roughed in—but there is a tower here, with a palisade around it, and a man and woman waiting inside the gate. . . ."

"And outside, trees, and water, and birds flying. I see. Is it meant to be Kinlochan?"

"It is a scene from a very ancient tale of a legendary place called *Tìr Tairngire,* the Land of Promise, or *Tìr na n'Og,* the Land of Endless Youth. A beautiful green island far to the west, where the sun sets like melted gold on a shining sea. On that isle, there is a tower whose walls are made of silver, its roof thatched with the wings of white birds, surrounded by a palisade of new bronze," she said in a dreamy voice.

"You are as much a poet and storyteller as your great-uncle, though you do not see it." He spoke in Gaelic, although they had been using English. His voice dropped to a tender, deeper level.

She felt herself blush, felt a shiver ripple through her. "The lord of that land is the bravest warrior among men, and his lady the most gracious and beautiful among women. Their land is full of plenty, fruit trees on the hills, salmon in the river, birds in every tree."

"Paradise," he murmured.

"Paradise," she repeated, running her fingers along the plaited design of the carved border. "A land full of joy and hope. A land where no one grows old or feels sorrow." Tears of sudden longing stung her eyes. "It is not Kinlochan."

He tilted his head. "Is this where you wish to be?"

"Who would not want to live in a land of peace and plenty?" she asked, and leaned forward to choose a different chisel.

"Indeed," he said. He stood beside her as she worked.

After a while she looked up. "I meant to tell you that Donal and Lulach went out to talk to the tenants on Kinlochan lands to request whatever oats and barley they could

spare to feed your horses. I think we can acquire enough
to last through the winter."

"Good. Next year, though, we will have to bring in
grasses for hay, or our livestock will suffer for it."

Our livestock. She looked away, putting down her chisel
to choose a sharp point. "If the horses are here next year,
certainly we will care for them well." Setting the tip of the
point against the stone, she angled it carefully, pounded it
once, and knocked away a chip, which fell to the floor.

"So long as we are talking about Kinlochan matters,
rather than our own marriage—whatever sort of marriage
it is," he added, while Alainna frowned quickly at him, "I
wanted to mention to you that I looked for you the other
day, when the fog was so heavy, to talk to you about provisions for the livestock. I thought you would be here at your
carving, or with Una and the other women, but no one had
seen you."

"Oh. That day," she said, heart leaping. She glanced up
at his unwavering gaze. He frowned, his eyes crystal gray
and somber. "I was . . . I went outside the walls."

"Poor weather to be out," he commented. "Or to row
a boat."

"B—boat?" She knocked the mallet into the point again.

"I walked out to the Stone Maiden to look for you, and
saw you far down the loch, in a small boat with Finan."

Her hand, around the iron tool, slipped, and the mallet
smacked into her hand. Wincing, she dropped the tools and
grabbed her throbbing thumb.

Sebastien reached for her hand. "Let me see."

"It is fine," she insisted, but his fingers were warm and
strong, and she allowed him to cradle her hand in the palm
of his own. "I am used to such," she said, with a rueful
laugh.

"It is a shame for you to be used to being hurt." His
fingers rubbed over hers, creating pleasant chills in her.

"It will ease quickly," she murmured, pulling away, but
he kept hold of her hand, smoothing his fingers over hers.

"You were out on the loch," he said, resuming the topic
she wanted to avoid. "I wondered why you went to that
island alone on such a day. I would have called for you, or
gone after you myself, but one of the squires had trouble

handling my horse in the stable during a shoeing and someone ran to get me. By the time I looked for you again,
Una said you had returned and were in your bedchamber."

"Oh. Oh," she said, searching for an answer. "I . . . when
I was a child, I used to think of that little isle as *Tìr na
n'Og*. In the summer especially, at sunset, it is a beautiful
place, green and lush on the shining waters. Sometimes I
go to the island to collect stones for carving. Most of my
small crosses are made from stones taken from there." That
was all true, she thought frantically.

"On a cold day, in fog, it can hardly be a paradise."

"The island is a . . . a quiet place, a haven for meditating
on God, which Father Padruig urges us to do often."

"You took your dog in a little boat and went to that
island there to meditate on God and holy matters?" He
looked incredulous, his fingers still over hers.

"To . . . ah, contemplate acts of charity." Close enough
to the truth, she told herself. "Fog and mist, and dawn and
sunset, are thought by the Celts to be mystical times. Good
for meditation, do you not agree?"

"Ah," he said. "And your dog meditates with you?"

She smiled angelically. "He is a remarkable hound."

"Indeed." He released her hand, and she flexed her
thumb and reached for her tools. He frowned down at her,
his fingers resting loosely on his hips. "As for charitable
acts, to my mind, you perform those daily around here. If
you wish to meditate upon holy matters too, you must be
near a saint."

She stopped, chisel poised on stone. "I am hardly that!"

"My lady, if you are compelled to contemplate heaven
in cold, mystical places, you would be happier in a convent
than wed to anyone," he said. "You did mention that when
I first came here."

"That was my temper, sirrah, which should prove that I
am no saint or martyr." She bent to her task once again
and gave the chisel a sharp whack. "What is it you wish to
say?" Her hands trembled and her heart paced rapidly, but
she had to know what he suspected, for Ruari's sake, for
the sake of her people. "I find the courteous Norman style
of speech confusing at times. Highlanders are so forthright

as to be blunt, and that is what I am accustomed to. Just say what you think."

He frowned, folding his arms over his chest. "I can be blunt, if that is what you want. What you did was dangerous and irresponsible. And it made me wonder if there is something you wish to keep secret on that island."

She stilled her tools and stood, thinking fast, wiping her dusty, trembling hands on her smock. "I often like to be alone, as I think you do, sirrah. What more reason could there be?"

His gray eyes seemed cool and wary. "It was odd behavior when there are men hiding in the hills, and who knows where else. I would not want you to be harmed."

"I am safe at Kinlochan."

"That is why I am here," he answered simply. "To see that you stay safe, and that your people are kept safe."

She nodded. "And that is why we are handfast, when neither of us wants to be. Now be blunt with me on another topic," she said, anxious to change the subject. "Do you still plan to leave Scotland as soon as you can?"

"I do. And I plan to return from time to time to ensure your welfare. Such is the case with many marriages between knights and their ladies."

She searched his face. "So you do intend to keep this marriage between us."

"It is the king's expectation and his order for us."

Her heart slammed in her chest. She waved an arm in impatient, passionate anger. "A marriage of chivalry, where the knight does as he pleases, taking his adventures here and there, gaining land and wealth and more and more worth, while his wife sits in a tower and waits for him, and fends for herself and her own kind, and raises their children alone, all the years that he is gone?" Her voice rose to a shout. "It would be better never to wed than to have that sort of protection and good company!"

He reached out and took her by the upper arms, his fingers like steel bands. She flattened her hands on his chest, where she felt the heavy pulse of his heart and a tension, as if he held back a wellspring of power.

"What sort of marriage do you want?" he demanded.

"The sort that are made in the Highlands. The sort that I see in my own family."

"Enlighten me."

"Honest and strong," she said. "Shared lives, filled with love."

"Do you think I do not want that?" he growled under his breath. He pulled her toward him, dipping his head, his mouth finding hers with a sureness that took her breath, sent her spinning deep into a thunderous kiss.

His arm slid behind her like a rod of iron, and his hand cradled the back of her head, fingers sliding into the wealth of her hair, loosening her thick braid. His mouth moved over hers with a power and a gentleness that stunned her, his body hard against hers.

The kiss lengthened, grew hot and exquisite, until she made a soft moan and felt her knees weaken. Sebastien pulled back, holding her tightly—if he had let go just then she would have stumbled, unsure of her legs. He looked into her eyes, his gaze a keen, clear pool.

"Is that what you want?" he asked hoarsely.

She closed her eyes, her body yielding to the strength in his arms, her thoughts muddled. She nodded fervently. "I asked," she breathed, "what you wanted."

"I want what you want. Paradise." His voice vibrated within her body, and his fingers brushed so gently over her hair that she felt the tenderness all the way to the soles of her feet. "But I do not think that exists for me anywhere."

He let go of her. She reached out to cold limestone for support, her heart pounding, flattening her other hand on her chest. He turned and went to the door. When she thought he would open it and go out, he paused.

"Alainna," he said, "I am a solitary man by nature. It is not easy for me to reveal what is most dear to me."

"What is that?" she asked, her near whisper carrying.

"My dreams," he said, his voice husky. "My son." He placed his hand on the iron latch. "You, now."

She moved to him, her spirit so full of longing that her body trembled. "Stay," she whispered. "Do not go."

"Stay for what purpose?" he asked huskily.

Her heart pounded hard. "For peace," she said. "For hope."

"Our pride will not allow us peace, or hope, or a marriage."

She touched his back. "Stay. Tell me your dreams."

"My dreams are my own. My own to meet, or to lose."

"And yours to share." She trailed her hand over his shoulder, feeling the hard strength in his arm, the tension there. "I have shared mine with you."

He turned, face partly angled, partly shadowed. "Your dreams? Ah. Your carvings."

"Especially my Land of Promise," she said. "I have never shown that stone to anyone. It is the dearest one among them all, to me. It holds . . . all my hopes. All my dreams."

He turned and gazed at her. "Then I suppose you expect to hear my dreams." He sounded wry, but gentle. She nodded. "A boy raised in a monastery learns to be silent and still," he said. "I kept my thoughts to myself. The habit endures."

"Tell me," she said. "Make another habit."

He chuckled, flat and dry. "I dreamed much, as a child, of what I wanted in life. I created ambitions and goals that grew stronger until I had to act on them."

"What was it you wanted?" she asked.

He looked past her, and she knew he looked at the cream limestone with her scene of the Land of Promise. "A noble title, land wealth, status as a knight, the worth of a name," he listed. "A home. Family," he added quietly.

Her heart wrenched for him, thinking of that young, lonely boy. "You achieved those."

"Nearly all. I lost . . . the most important part of the dream. My wife. My home . . . possibly now, my son."

She watched him, waiting.

He looked keenly at her. "There. I have told you."

"If you have more to say, I will wait," she said. "I think I would wait here forever . . . if you needed that of me."

He almost smiled. She saw it in his eyes. "For a high-tempered woman, you are exceeding patient."

"I have learned to be patient. Patience," she said, "wears out stone."

He laughed then, an airy huff, and pushed his fingers through his hair. "Sit, then," he said, touching her shoulder, turning her. "Sit, and I will tell you more of my dreams."

Chapter Twenty-three

While Alainna chose a fine-edged chisel and resumed carving, Sebastien pulled up another stool and set it beside hers. He watched her delineate the palisade surrounding the tower with careful, lightly driven strokes. He leaned forward, listening to the thudding rhythm of the mallet, impressed by her precise movements and the deftness with which she brought out the image.

"You never cease to work, even on your wedding night," he commented, "such as it is."

"Not even then," she said. The candlelight flowed over her, turning her smooth skin and gleaming hair to warm amber. "Tell me, Sebastien," she said, and blew at the fine dust that collected on the limestone.

He let out a long breath. "Very well."

She smiled and picked up a small piece of gritty stone to rub at a rough edge in the design.

"About six years ago, when I was twenty-five and as yet unwed, and in knight service to the duke of Brittany, I married the daughter of a French count. She was young, and a pious and studious girl, more suited to the contemplative life than most. Her parents would not permit her to dedicate her life to God. She would have been better off if she had," he added bitterly. "She died in childbed, after two years of marriage. She was just nineteen."

Alainna folded her brow in wordless sympathy, her silence encouraging. He wanted to tell her more. She set down the sandstone that she had used to smooth the limestone, and he picked it up, its mass still warm from her hand, and turned it idly in his hand.

"We lived in her dowry castle in the Loire valley, which

she was to inherit from her father. Now our son will inherit it."

"The castle belongs to you now, does it not?"

"Not to me. Her father had that specified in our nuptial contract. It was to go to her eldest child, to be held by her father. If there was no child, it was to return to her father. Her family did not approve of me. I was not worthy, in their eyes, to marry her."

"Then how did you come to marry her?"

"I won her in a tournament," he answered.

She blinked at him. "You won her?"

"Her father was drinking heavily one Twelfth Night, and announced to the company gathered at a feast hosted by the duke of Brittany that whoever won the joust the next day could have his youngest for a bride. I won. Her father was displeased by that, a bastard orphan, but he honored his word."

"Was she pleased?" Alainna asked.

He shrugged. "She seemed so."

"What was her name? Was she beautiful, and kind, and . . . deserving of you?"

He smiled at her eager questions, at her curiosity and the loyalty in her remark. He smiled, too, at the memories, poignant rather than hurtful as they once had been. "Her name was Heloise," he said. "She was lovely. Dark-haired and brown-eyed and a little plump, which she disliked— but it was part of her charm, part of her softness and warmth. She spent much of her time with books and in conversation with her priest, and she would have done well in a convent. But she was happier to wed me than her father's choice for her."

She held out her hand for the sandstone, and Sebastien leaned forward. "Where?" he asked. "Here?" He pointed to a rough edge, and she nodded. He rubbed at it with the stone, as she had done, and both leaned forward to blow the dust away.

"Did you love her?" she asked softly, and gave the chisel a few gentle taps with the mallet.

He hesitated. "I did. She was kind and pleasant. She brought me what I wanted most."

"A son."

"A son, and a home. I had never truly had a home before that, a family, a castle and estate. The years with her were the best of my life, in some ways."

She tapped the mallet again, a frown creasing her smooth, pale brow. "You were happy with her."

"I was happy, but she was not content. I was not a good husband to her."

Her eyes widened. "You would be the best of husbands," she said quickly, then lowered her eyelids. "No doubt you were content to be with her."

He looked away, still angry with himself, although years had passed. He had never spoken of the guilt he felt about Heloise's unhappiness. Somehow, though, admitting his feelings to Alainna seemed no more difficult than admitting them to himself.

"My ambition was very strong then," he told her. "I had a great hunger to win tournaments, to gain wealth and property, to have my name known and respected among lords and kings. And I did that. I achieved much in the few years before I married Heloise, and in the years afterward. But I did not know then what harm I did to her."

"I cannot believe that you would ever do her harm. You loved her." Her voice was subdued. She set down her tools and picked up a cloth to rub the surface of the stone, cleaning dust out of the carved crevices.

"I thought Heloise was content. We lived in a castle on a pretty bend of the river. She loved her garden, and her manuscripts—I brought her a new one each time I returned from a journey. Later she took great joy in little Conan. She had all that she could want." He looked away. "She told me, once, that she did not have me."

Alainna stilled her hands. "You were not there often, were you." He heard the understanding in her voice. "She was lonely. She loved you." Her whisper was passionate.

"I was away more than I was with her. I was not there when Conan was born, although I came as soon as I could. And I was not with her when she went to childbed again. Heloise and our daughter, born too soon, both died before I returned."

"Oh, Sebastien," Alainna murmured. She rested her fingers on his wrist, a feather-light touch that he felt to his soul. Silent, he turned his hand to cradle hers. Her fingers were coated with a fine, pale dust that left a powder on his skin.

"She was discontent," he said. "I did not realize it until it was too late. All that mattered to me was achieving my dreams." He paused. "I was wrong—prideful. And what I loved best, what I wanted most in my life, I lost."

Alainna sighed and turned to face him, leaning forward to take his other hand with hers. "Her discontent was not your doing," she said.

"I could have eased her loneliness, and I did not. And now I have done the same to my son without thinking. I left him in the care of others so that I could pursue what I thought he needed, and what I wanted. I was wrong. And I must return to Brittany." He closed his eyes briefly, desperation rising like a dark, heavy wave. "I must."

"I know." Her hands were quiet and smooth in his. "Your son needs you. He does not need a father with a noble title, or huge parcels of land wealth to his name, or even a name with great worth. He needs *you*."

He sighed, ran his thumbs over her hands idly as he thought. "When I was a boy," he finally said, "I wanted to be lord of a castle, proud of my name and my demesne, proud of my children and the legacy I would leave them. My dreams became my ambitions. The more I gained, the more I hurt those I loved. Now I must give my son a true home in Brittany, on one of my properties there. I see no other way."

"Can you not?" She reached up and touched the scar that ran through his left eyebrow. Her fingertip smoothed gently along that path and lifted away. "Can you be blind, when your way is so plain?"

He narrowed his eyes. "It is not so plain as you think."

"Here is a home for him, Sebastien," she said, low and certain. "Here is family, and a castle someday—the one you will design. Here is what you want for Conan. And for yourself."

He stood and turned his back to her, hands at his waist, head lowered. Longing overwhelmed him, threatened to sweep away cool reason. He summoned sheer will to resist its force.

"And what is the price, if I do?" he asked gruffly. "My name? All that I am?"

She stood, too, her gown rustling over the stone-littered floor. "Your pride. That is all."

"Pride helped me to achieve what I wanted. Without it, I was naught but a nameless orphan raised by monks. When I came to England, I could have stayed a servant in the stables, but I became a knight. My pride fueled my ambition, and that was founded on my dreams. I cannot stay here and let all of that go. Surely you see that."

"Such pride gives power to dreams," she said. "But it can hinder them as well."

"I do what I must for my son's sake, not mine. But I cannot give up . . . what is myself."

"I would never ask that of you."

"Then what do you want of me?"

She watched him evenly. "Stay with me."

He gave a bitter laugh. "Leave with me."

She looked away. He knew her answer. He felt the tug and pull of the strong will and the duty that lay in conflict between them. He felt a deeper pull, too, like an undertow, stronger by far than what swept on the surface. The thread of that bond had spun out between them from the first moment he had seen her, and had glimpsed the fire and the purity in her soul.

Those bonds had woven more securely this evening with poetic vows spoken with earnest respect. He knew it was not so easy to walk away from that. How could he have believed that he could? He turned his head, shaking it in dismay.

"Sebastien *Bàn*," she said, "we need you here. This can be your home. Our legacy can be the one you bring your son."

"What of your Celtic warrior?" he asked.

"My kinfolk welcome you. This is what they want, this between us."

"And you?" he asked softly.

She stood in shadows, the reddish flicker of light moving over her face. "I want you to stay," she said quietly. "I did not want that before. Now . . . now all seems changed."

Her voice and pose were calm, but he sensed the passion and the strength beneath the words.

He paused, frowning, wondering if indeed he could stay here, if there was some way. Then a host of reasons why it could not be crowded into his mind, casting the fragile thought away. "I cannot," he said. "And you cannot come with me. We both feel our duty to others."

"We are alike, we," she said softly.

He nodded. And he suddenly knew now that he wanted to be with her more than he had wanted any goal, any dream. He held himself still, so that he would not whirl and pull her into his arms.

"If we cannot be together, and cannot agree, it may be wisest for us to end this marriage before it has begun," he said finally. "I cannot hurt you, as I hurt Heloise and Conan."

"You would hurt me in another way," she whispered.

He stood stone still, but for his aching, beating heart.

She drew a breath. "I cannot expect you to live here—as a Highland man, in a Highland way. I will not ask you again."

"When I leave," he said, "you and your kin are welcome to stay at the fortress. I will order the castle to be constructed on another site within Kinlochan's boundaries. I will appoint Robert or another to oversee it, and ask the king to keep a garrison of knights here to protect you." His voice echoed in the stone-filled chamber. He felt wooden.

The goals and duties that once had seemed honor-bound and firm no longer seemed right. At some point, his world had shifted, and he felt like a falling man seeking a hold, seeking balance.

She stepped past him, her arm brushing his, and went to the corner, smoothing the plaids on the stone slab. "I am grateful that you will allow my clan to stay." Her voice was cool.

Something broke in him. He moved toward her swiftly, took her arms, and gazed down at her through candlelight and shadows. "Do not be grateful to me," he said vehemently. "I am not the champion you want. I am not the one you deserve, you and your kin. You will find the one you need—for you, for all of them."

"I have found him." Her eyes were dark and limpid in the shadows. "But he does not want me. Or us."

"He does," he growled. She was a lodestone, and he was iron, and he could not, for all his strength of will, keep from kissing her. He pulled her to him, his mouth over hers.

She slid her arms around his waist and pressed herself against him, curves cushioning the hard contours of his body. The feel of her was warm and sensual even through layers of wool and serge. Her lips were pliant and giving beneath his, her hands soothing on his back. He felt himself sinking, spinning.

He slipped his hands into her hair, and the thick braid loosened its hold, spilling in a wild mass. He took a handful to pull her head back gently, ending the kiss to look at her.

"For all my pride," he whispered, "for all my ambition, I have never wanted any dream as much as I want you."

She moaned, the sound deep. He took her mouth again, and felt her falter where she stood. Circling his hands around her slim waist, he lifted her to sit on the edge of the sandstone slab. She wrapped her arms around him, pressed her knees to his waist. He sought her mouth again, stirring a thirst that only grew greater and demanded to be slaked.

His blood simmered in his veins, his body throbbed. With his lips and hands, he explored her, cajoled her, while she bent and moaned like a willow in the wind. She was strength and grace and passion come to life, and she was finer to touch than any woman he had ever held.

He should cease, he thought; this would only lead them into a further entanglement, a plaiting of love and pride that would never come undone. But he could not cease, savoring her lushness and her bright spirit and wanting more. He wondered how he could ever leave her, wondered how he could exist without her.

When she twined her arms around him and her hair tumbled around her like a cloud, he surrendered the will of his pride to the wisdom of his heart. Just for now, he thought; just this, and no more. Yet each touch, each kiss brought more delight, another step deeper into a garden that fascinated him, lured him, nurtured and soothed him.

Smoothing his hands over the curves of her body, he

drank from her lips as if she were a fountain of all that he
needed to sustain him. The pulsing desire within him grew
so urgent that he could not think past it, so strong that it
buckled his own knees even as he stood and lent her his
strength to lean upon.

More of his resolve was lost to her seeking lips, her touch
strong and soothing on his shoulders. Though her gown was
bunched between them, she drew him closer, pressing her
leg to his, as she sat and he stood before her. He skimmed
his hands along her back, feeling the fine-boned planes, the
deep curve of her waist. He shaped her breasts, his fingers
forming a delicate cage.

She gasped softly into his mouth and twisted in his arms
as he trailed his fingers over the firmly pearled nipples
thrusting beneath the wool of her gown. He caressed there,
and her mouth met his, her hands fervent on his back, on
his waist.

The slightest touch, the whisper of her breath, drew him
deeper into the eddy of sensation, suspending thought. He
glided his lips over hers, over her jaw, her throat, the ridges
of her breastbone. His fingers sought the neckline of her
gown, found the placket, the loose chemise beneath, and
slipped inside.

He dipped his head to kiss the upper mound of a breast,
feeling the heat reflected within the fabric, sensing the beat
of her heart. Her breast filled his hand, and her nipple
tightened as he shaped and swept it. She leaned back
against the upper incline of the slab. He braced a knee
beside her, there, and within the space of kiss, a caress, he
lay beside her.

A turn of her head made a sweet arc of her throat. He
trailed his lips over the curve, his heart pounding. He wondered what sort of fool he was to pursue this temptation,
what sort of fool he was to lead her with him.

The tip of his tongue opened her lips, and the motion of
his hands over her body seemed to open her, shift her more
fully toward him. She was willing, warm, languid. He
groaned silently as her lips traced along his jaw and found
the lobe of his ear, sucking lightly. As his body grew hotter,
harder, he cupped her hips and pulled her toward him, the
draped cloth separating them.

With one hand he rucked the generous folds of the woolen gown and lighter chemise higher until he felt the warm silk of her lifted leg. He traced his fingers along her bare thigh, slipping deeper under her clothing to caress her taut abdomen, where her breath quickened.

Her hands trailed over him, tender and persuasive, the rhythm of her breath as urgent as his own. Strong, deliberate, quick, her hands plucked at his surcoat and the tunic beneath and pulled them higher, found the gathered waist of his *braies* and drew it down. When her fingers slid over the flat, warm plane of his lower belly, his heart bounded and flesh and spirit leaped.

He angled away from her touch, wanting to savor her, his mouth over hers, swirling his tongue within. Gliding his hand lower, he found the silken tuft and the cleft below, warm and damp. He slipped a gentle finger inside, and she sucked in a breath and tilted toward him, a moan low in her throat.

Stroking, caressing, he coaxed her with his fingers. Her body moved like waves from ocean to shore. She tensed and cried out, a small, tender sound that spun through his own aching body. He closed his eyes against a rush of ecstasy and anguish, took her in his arms, and held her.

He wanted her fiercely. His body strained, fevered and swollen, for release. Every element of his blood and flesh urged him to ease himself in her. But as he hesitated, he felt a pull, as if the strands of his soul grew taut.

She might have felt it too, for she groaned in protest as he paused, and tucked her head into the lee of his shoulder. He dipped to kiss the silken skin of her neck, his breath ragged.

"I promised courtesy," he murmured. It seemed ages ago, that promise, and he regretted it, yet it had been made.

"I do not want your courtesy," she breathed. "I want you." She turned to kiss his mouth, open and deep, wringing a low groan from him. He dragged his lips from hers.

"If we continue," he said, "we fix the vows forever."

"It can be undone if you need it." She kissed him. "It can be undone, by our custom."

He was not so sure; the custom was hers, not his own.

Her hand came up to cup his face. "It is the eve of

Christmas. Listen to your heart. We will find a way. We want this, you and I. We need this." She drew his head down toward hers to kiss him again. He groaned deep.

"Alainna—"

"What you feel, I feel." Her voice was low, soft, but he sensed the fire in it. "What you want—truly want, in your heart—I want. We are alike, we. I know that now."

He knew it, too, and could not have said why, but he surrendered to the truth the instant that she whispered it. She touched her mouth to his, and pressed her body against his, her hands pulling at his clothing, while he drew fabric away from her. The first full touch of his bare flesh to hers, warm and silken, was like a close flame. He sighed deeply, and went onward.

Thought left him, reason left him, and blood and breath took him over; he could not have stopped now. Not now, as he delved his tongue into her mouth, as he slipped his fingers over her legs and into the willing space that opened for him. He caressed her honeyed warmth again, and felt her languid moan in his mouth.

He lowered his head to kiss her breasts, warm and damp with sweat, carrying the fragrance of heather and lavender and woman, a scent that took him deeper. Cradling her hips in his hands, he drew her close. The soft plaids beneath them slid over cold stone as she moved, as she took him in her hand and guided.

In silent accord, he pressed forward and she opened, and he felt himself tremble at the cleft and sink inward, cautiously, firm and waiting for the catch of her breath, for the pain he did not want to cause her.

That passed quickly, and weaving his breath with hers, he felt a tremor run through her, felt a force stream through him. The current took him faster, harder, deeper into the whirlpool than he had ever gone, toward an exquisite fire of the spirit. He knew the spark passed through her, and then faded, and he sank into her, and felt her sink with him.

He lay wrapped in silence with her, aware that more than lust had swept him away. *Dear God,* he thought, as new clarity came into his mind. He loved her.

The realization took the breath from him.

He held her for so long, silent and rocking, thinking, that he was not aware at first that she had drifted into sleep. He smiled ruefully into her hair, knowing how exhausted she had been before the handfasting had even begun.

He slipped away from her and stepped back into the shadows. Stone crunched quietly beneath his boots as he took up the plaid he had worn for a cloak and went to the door. The wind was high and whipping, and he could still hear the strains of music and laughter from the tower in the bailey. Golden light leaked around the door frame and the small, square window. He turned and began to walk the perimeter of the yard.

A thick branch lay in his path, lost from one of the pine boughs that had been carried to the hall. He picked it up as he went, using it first as a walking stick. Then he swiped it at the wind. He turned, stopped, and whipped it again.

He stripped off the thinner branches, releasing the piney tang from the wood. Setting his feet square in the yard, he balanced his weight from one foot to the other. Holding it with two hands, like the claymore that he had recently included in his practices, he cut through the air with the stout branch, sheered into the wind, turned, lunged, whirled.

And then he flung the stick high and far, watched it sail out over the palisade wall. He stood, heart beating, like a pillar while the wind beat at him.

He had surrendered to his heart and his blood, had ignored reason and caution and ambition. Love had swept through his life, fast and powerful, from a direction he had never anticipated. And all of his goals would have to change.

He himself had changed. The knowledge of that spun him, staggered him. He was not sure what to do, how to proceed. He was not the man he had been, and he was not yet sure who he was.

He looked up at the sky, midnight deep and dusted with diamonds. The eve of Christmas had stirred a miracle, and he was not sure what to do with it.

He was not a man who welcomed change easily. He breathed out, hard and fast, a pale, frosted cloud, and looked at the workshop. A thin golden light edged the shut-

tered window. The candle was still burning. He walked forward and eased open the door.

She lay on the sandstone slab, curled like a child. He
looked down at her while she slept, and brushed back her
hair. Then he took off his plaid and folded it into a pillow,
sliding it under her head.

She lay inside a carved framework of endless knots, the
braiding that determined the path of the soul through life.
The thread of his soul had been drawn into the weave of
hers now. Only cutting, only the destruction of the chain,
would free them from the design, if either wanted to be
free of the other.

He circled to the other side of the slab and stretched out
beside her on the cold, hard bed. He drew her plaid-bun-
dled, softly breathing form into his arms, set his cheek upon
her head, and let himself drift to sleep.

Chapter Twenty-four

Smoke and flames rose from the bonfire at the head of the loch, swirling into a gray column that obscured the pale sky. Sebastien stepped back, feeling the intense heat of the blaze despite the icy wind. He looked at those who stood in a ring around the fire, their bright faces smiling at one another, smiling at him.

Christmas Day had dawned silvery and cold. Father Padruig had left the fortress that morning, accompanied by several of the Highlanders and the knights, including Alainna and Sebastien, who had then attended Padruig's early Christmas Mass at the church of Saint Brighid. Those who had not walked the distance had ridden tough, sure-footed garrons out over the hills, for the thin coating of snow had frozen overnight.

Upon their return, the clan members had set the bonfire, the branches and logs having been piled high the day before. Now they gathered around the huge, hot fire to sing traditional Gaelic songs and charms, and to burn the Yule log. Highland Yuletide customs were few and simple, Sebastien had learned; the holy day was celebrated on a more subdued note than he had seen in England and France, while the new year, he had been told, was welcomed with rousing good cheer.

Heat wavered over the joyful, familiar faces. Of them all, Sebastien thought, Alainna shone like a star, clear and beautiful in his eyes. Her head remained bare, for she had refused to wear the white kerchief common to married women, insisting to her kinswomen that she was not, as yet, officially married.

But she was, and they both knew it. Her kinfolk had guessed, judging by their pleased glances, that the handfasting had been consummated. He had the impression that the elders also assumed that he would stay with them at Kinlochan—he could see the hope of it in each smiling face, in every light step and heartfelt laugh.

He frowned, standing apart from the rest, conscious of the burden of their joy. He knew Alainna felt it too. He saw traces of the strain in her pale face, in her shadowed blue eyes, in the lush, somber curve of her mouth. She forced a smile, he saw—he had forced many himself that day—and came around the bonfire's perimeter with Lorne.

He sighed, for he had woken from the most wondrous night of his life confused. He did not think he could leave her now.

In the center of the fire lay the enormous Yule log. One section had been carved with a wizened face, an image Alainna had cut into it a few days earlier. Crackling flames shot up, and the curious countenance stood out clearly as the log burned.

"That face in the Yule log is the *Cailleach Nollaich*," Esa said. Sebastien turned to see her standing beside him, her plaid wrapped snugly around her head and draped over her body. Her face was serene and perfect inside that frame. "She is the old woman of Yule. The *Cailleach* is also said to be the old woman of winter, soon to be gone. We burn her image to bring good luck to all for the coming year."

Sebastien nodded, watching Esa, captivated by her stunning beauty. A light seemed to shine deep in her lovely dark eyes, and the finely etched lines and shadows around them had somehow lessened in the last few days.

"You look well," he said. "Are you content here at Kinlochan?"

Her smile seemed almost secretive, and held a certain quiet joy. "I am very content here," she said.

Esa took his right hand then, and Alainna moved toward him to take his left. Wreathing the bonfire, Highlanders and Normans linked hands, and the Highlanders began to sing.

Unfamiliar with the words, Sebastien listened to the charming cadence. The rhythm seemed to vibrate in his chest, unexpectedly stirring his heart.

The song rang clear and sweet, rising with the bright flames into the pearly sky. Sebastien tightened his fingers on Alainna's hand, and felt the slender strength there, felt her fingers caress his, although she kept her gaze ahead as she sang.

They sang another verse and began again. This time Sebastien lifted his voice with the rest, forming a low, mellow foundation for the harmony around him.

Alainna glanced at him, her cheeks pink with cold, her eyes dazzling, her heart shining within them. For a moment, Sebastien forgot his dilemma. He pressed her fingers with his and sang on, his gaze still touching hers, his own heart brimming.

"Warriors we have about us now, warriors to fight at our backs, and it is good," Lorne said that night, after they had finished supper, another modest feast of the same foods offered at the handfasting. "And long and long ago, beside another fireside on another winter's night, the three warrior sons of Uisneach sat with the beautiful Deirdre, who came to be called Deirdre of the Sorrows. And the finest of the handsome sons of Uisneach was Naoise, with raven black hair and skin pale as snow, with cheeks red as blood. Deirdre loved him more than her life.

"Naoise sat that night and played a game of chess with Deirdre, she of the golden curls and gray eyes, her beauty enough to make men wild, her spirit sweet as a dove. She would forsake the love of a king and forsake her own land to be with the son of Uisneach. And listen, and I will tell you how Deirdre and the sons of Uisneach came to be in exile in Scotland together, and I will tell you of the end they came to. . . ."

Sebastien listened, leaning his shoulders against the wall. He had taken his seat on the shadowed bench again, where he could sit in solitude after the revelry and camaraderie of the day before, with the handfasting, and this day, Christmas.

He watched the others and sipped from his cup of spiced wine, resting his back against the timber wall. The tale Lorne told was poignant and beautiful, full of love and loyalty, longing and sorrow. When Lorne recited Deirdre's stirring and poetic remembrance of Scotland, a description of the glens and hills that she had come to love during her stay there with the sons of Uisneach, he felt a tightness gather in his throat.

He, too, loved this land, with its white-swept mountains, deep glens, and silver lochs; its proud crags and stately trees; and its women like pearls. Alainna shone among them all, and he could not keep his gaze from her while Lorne spoke and she echoed a sultry-voiced translation.

"And when the sons of Uisneach were dead," Lorne said, low and sonorous, "and when they were laid in a grave, Deirdre looked down upon their still and beautiful faces, and saw Naoise lying between his brothers, and her heart turned within her for sorrow, and for love.

" 'Do not break this day, O my heart,' said Deirdre, and she threw herself down, and lay dead among Naoise and his brothers, the thread of her soul braided to the thread of his, and theirs, for eternity. . . .' "

Sebastien swallowed hard, and sipped at his wine. Alainna finished her translation and rose. She glided through the crowded room toward Sebastien's bench beneath the rafters.

Finan stood, where he had been curled at her feet by the fire, and followed her. Sebastien roughed his fingers over the dog's head and patted his shoulders. Finan circled and then lay at Sebastien's feet, his tail thumping on the toe of his boot.

Alainna sat beside Sebastien. The reddish light in her hair was muted by the shadows in the raftered aisle, and he could not see her face as clearly as he had when she had sat near the fire.

She took his hand in silence, and he was glad. The sadness of Lorne's tale rested upon him like a mantle. He wrapped his fingers about hers, hands cradled between them.

Lorne picked up his harp and began a song with a quiet, steady rhythm and melody that was exquisite and heartbreaking. Alainna leaned toward Sebastien to be heard above the music.

"They say that there are three kinds of music from a *clarsach,* a Celtic harp," she said. "There is the strain for weeping, the strain for sleeping, and the strain for joy. All harp music, they say, is one or another of those, and all harp music has the power to stir the soul."

"This one must be the strain for weeping." He felt it pull as he had never felt music stir him before. Just the blend of Lorne's story and the wine, he thought, and the sadness he bore in his own heart at the thought of leaving Alainna, this place, these people.

"Lorne ends his tale of Deirdre of the Sorrows this way, but he will lift our hearts again with a strain for joy, and then give us a more relaxing tune for sleeping."

He nodded, listening to the the harp strings, her hand warm in his own. After a while, Lorne began another song, light and quick. Alainna glanced at Sebastien.

"I want you to stay," she whispered.

He sighed and looked away. Then he lifted her hand, clasped in his, to his lips. He kissed the smooth mound of her knuckles. Even that small contact between them swirled like luscious fire through his body. He said nothing, but his silence was an eloquent refusal.

She slipped her hand from his.

After a while he leaned toward her. "Alainna, I must seek out Cormac MacNechtan soon. I must speak with him about the king's orders, and make some determination of his loyalty. The king awaits word from me."

"Must you ride out to Turroch so soon? Christmas is scarcely past."

"The weather is unpredictable, and this cannot wait much longer. We have accomplished what we wanted, my lady," he said. "We are handfasted without Cormac hearing of it, and the marriage contract has been written out and signed. Father Padruig has promised me a copy so that I can send it to the king by messenger. I must also send a report explaining what I have found at Kinlochan, and what I know of Cormac MacNechtan's loyalties."

"Who will go with you?" she asked.

"My men," he said. "Giric has agreed, and Lulach as well. The rest of your kinsmen will stay here. In two or three days I will seek him out."

"He will want only battle."

"We will be prepared to fight."

She opened her mouth to speak, then subsided. He saw

the glint of tears in her eyes. She stood, murmured a quick good night, and walked away.

Finan lifted his head, looking curious, and stood to follow her. Instead of going to her workshop, as she so often did late in the evening, she climbed the slatted wooden steps to her bedchamber above the hall. The dog went with her, padding silently upward where they both disappeared.

Sebastien watched the empty steps for a long while. The temptation to take her now, tonight, rushed so strong over him that he tensed with the urge. As desperately as he wanted to be with her, he knew he must distance himself for now.

He tightened his hand on his thigh and swallowed the rest of his wine in one long gulp. He sat unmoving.

Lorne played a soothing harp melody, and began another. Sebastien felt his tension gradually mellow. The elders began to seek their beds, one by one, and some of the knights had gone to the other end of the long chamber to set out their pallets; the three young squires had long since retired, their tousled heads peeking above their blankets.

He sat alone on the bench while Lorne played. Finally he stood and nodded to those who watched him, and climbed the stairs to the upper floor.

He eased open the door to her bedchamber. Her steady breathing emanated from the shelter of the bed that was hung with curtains of dark plaid. The small room was over the main part of the hall, so it was warm and close, and the harp was muted but clear. In one corner, the iron brazier gave off enough reddish light to reveal the pallet of plaids that she had left for him.

Her own comment, he saw; her thoughts agreed with his. A distancing was better.

Finan slept curled close to the brazier on a straw pallet. He lifted his head with scant interest when Sebastien walked past, and settled back to sleep with a lazy thump of his tail.

Sebastien went to the bed and parted the curtain silently. She was a cluster of shadows in the darkness, her breathing a susurration. He could smell the lavender-sweet, womanly warmth of her. His body surged like a fire. He reached out to touch the cloud of her loosened hair, drifted his fingers down to her shoulder beneath the fur coverlet.

She turned and the fur slid, and his fingertips grazed the bare skin of her upper chest. She writhed in sleep and made a kittenish sound. He felt his groin contract, fill, ache.

He drew his hand back, flared his nostrils, and cursed his pride and every goal he had ever had. He shut the curtain abruptly and turned away.

Removing only his boots and his woolen hose, he lay down on the wooden floor, scarcely cushioned by plaids. When he gave out a resounding sigh, he heard its gentle echo from the bed. Turning on his side, he went to sleep listening to the harp.

She waited by the Maiden while snowflakes whirled, light and fast, around her. Finan stood beside her, every so often circling her impatiently, his long face and wide brown eyes questioning and begging. He clearly did not want to be outside on such a day.

The gates of Kinlochan had been opened early, and when she had run out, with the dog in tow, few had taken notice of her. The men in the yard were busy with necessary tasks as the knights prepared to ride out, while the women were in the hall and the kitchen, no doubt sure that Alainna was busy in her workshop.

She saw them gather inside the gate, Sebastien on his creamy stallion, the others mounted on their own steeds, Giric and Lulach on dark garrons. Chain mail and weaponry gleamed gray in the pale light.

Alainna glanced up. The sky was powdery white with a snowfall that might thicken or vanish. When she looked toward Kinlochan again, she saw the riders moving out through the open gate, a host of horses and armed men, a grim vision of might.

She spared a glance for the island. Ruari still hid there, though in the few days since Christmas he spent less time in the broch, where he had managed to keep snug despite the weather. His arm had strengthened quickly, and she knew he now rowed himself to and from the shore, sometimes going out before dawn, or returning after dark, when

Giric rowed Esa out secretly to stay the night with her husband.

The loch had not iced as yet, but when it did, he would have to find another hiding place. She suspected, although Esa had not said, that he and Esa would return soon to their house in the hills. Likely Esa would announce to her kinfolk that she was done with company and ready for solitude no matter the weather.

Now Alainna fully understood the depth and passion of the devotion between Esa and Ruari. She sighed, and watched the knights canter around the end of the loch, Sebastien and Giric in the lead.

Through the veil of falling snow she saw the faery warrior of her dream riding toward her once again. Her heart surged within her, and she closed her eyes briefly, savoring the memory of the passion that had flared between them like a need-fire. If he left her, she would have that memory of him always. If he left her, she prayed she would have his child within her, too, to carry on the blood of her clan. And to give her a part of him.

She stepped away from the shelter of the Stone Maiden and stood, draped in her long plaid, a small twin to the stone. Sebastien reined in his horse. When Giric and the others slowed, he waved them on and walked his mount toward her.

She reached up to hold the horse's bridle while she looked at Sebastien. "I wanted to talk to you before you left," she said.

"If the weather concerns you, do not worry," he said. "We will be back shortly."

"It is not that. There is something I must say to you."

"The ride to Turroch is not far. We will discuss the king's terms there and return before the snow decides what sort of storm it wants to bring today." He smiled, his eyes as gray as the sky. "Go inside. It is not safe for you to be out here without a guard."

"Finan *Mór* is with me, and besides, I am always safe beside the Maiden," she said. He gave her a doubtful glance. "Get down from your horse," she said. "There is something I must do."

"What you can do is go back to the fortress as fast as

you can. Finan, home," he ordered, pointing. "Take your mistress home."

"Finan, stay," she said. The dog whimpered and circled. "Do not torment him, sirrah," she told Sebastien. "He gives you his loyalty now as well as me. He wants to please us both. Get down from your horse. I need but a moment with you."

Sebastien lifted a brow laconically, then sighed and dismounted with a creak and jingle of mail and leather. He seemed to tower over her, and for a moment she remembered the first day she had spent time with him in the abbey church at Dunfermline, when he had stood like a guard of honor for her, patient and strong and beautiful.

"What?" he asked. She took his hand and drew him away from the horse, positioning him so that he faced the Stone Maiden.

"If you insist on meeting with Cormac, I must give you a charm of protection," she said.

"Alainna, all will be well, I need no—"

"Hush," she said. "This I must do, for myself as much as for you. I cannot watch you go to meet the MacNechtans without a *seun* to protect you." She squared his shoulders so that he faced the Maiden, then walked around him in a circle, sunwise, while she spoke.

> *A shield of mist I put on you*
> *From heather and mountain*
> *From sea and stone*
> *From man and maiden*
> *Till you return to me.*

She placed her hand on his chest, the steel mesh cold beneath her palm. "No blade shall cut you, no arrow shall strike you, no fire shall burn you. Shield of angels around you, shield of faery. May you come back to me as you go out from me."

She closed her eyes and bowed her head, her hand flattened over his heart, and stood for a long moment in silence, with the cold wind soughing, damp with snow, around them.

When she opened her eyes, Sebastien was staring at her,

his silvery gaze keen and deep. He framed her face in his fingers.

Silent, swift, he took her mouth in a deep, hungry kiss. She arched her head back and felt her knees sway beneath her. He released her and stepped back, his gaze steady on hers.

"That," he said, "is my blessing for you." He turned and strode through the feathery snowfall, mounted his horse, and cantered away.

Alainna touched her fingers to her lips, watching him. By the time he reached his companions, the snow had blurred her view.

She could still feel the bond between them, like a silvery thread spinning out. And she felt the subtle strain upon it, and she grew suddenly, deeply afraid.

Chapter Twenty-five

Sebastien tossed the document down on the broad, scarred table surface. "Cormac. There is the king's message to you."

Cormac slid a glance around the dim hall, his own at Turroch, a longer and more spacious hall than that at Kinlochan. In the few minutes he and his companions had been here, Sebastien had already noted the dingy, neglected feel to the place, with filthy rushes, bowls of food still on the tables, several napping dogs, and a cat or two stalking mice in the shadowy corners.

The place definitely lacked a female presence and influence. Sebastien told himself that he would be damned before he would allow Cormac to take Alainna into a household like this.

Yet he knew that his own actions were all that stood in the way of Cormac marrying Alainna.

Frowning, he observed the others in the room who watched Cormac. Struan stood a few feet from his brother. Giric, Robert, and Lulach gathered behind Sebastien. Out in the bailey, he knew, fifteen knights waited inside the gate, armored and carrying weapons, with orders to attack should anything unwelcome happen.

A few of Cormac's kinsmen sat or stood on the other side of the stone hearth, a mean and motley guard, silent and rough-hewn in plaids and hide boots. Their weapons, at Sebastien's earlier suggestion, had been grudgingly laid aside on a table.

He hoped that he could rely on Highland hospitality, the strict tradition that dictated no harm could come even to an enemy inside another's walls. Struan had assured them of this upon their arrival, although Sebastien and the rest wanted to deliver the message, discuss what was necessary, and depart. He doubted Cormac would be so foolish as to attack the king's men as they delivered the king's message inside his own hall.

The edgy silence lingered. Cormac picked up the parchment, broke the seal, looked inside, and tossed it on the table. "I spent my boyhood days with weapons, not books. Read it."

Sebastien read its curt message aloud, then folded it. "The king commands Clan Laren and Clan Nechtan to put weapons and anger aside," he summarized. "Cease your aggression against these people or be cast out of your lands and put to fire and sword. In addition, I am to report to the crown any suspected ties between Celtic lords in this vicinity and Celtic rebels."

"What of Clan Laren?" Cormac asked. "They are kin to one of the rebels, which we are not. Surely you suspect them, and will cast them out of their lands."

"Clan Laren has cooperated with the king's wishes," Sebastien answered. "As for the rest, the king awaits my word and my report. One of the questions that needs a clear answer is which Celtic lords in this region are loyal to the crown and which are not. Clan Laren has established its loyalty. Prove the fealty of your clan and you will benefit."

"We can prove that," Struan said. "We have never supported the rebellion, though we know men who do."

"True," Cormac said. "In fact, we know them so well that I can give you the heart of the rebellion itself, if you wish."

Sebastien narrowed his eyes. "What do you mean?"

"Ruari *Mór* MacWilliam," Cormac said. "I know where he is."

"He is dead," Lulach growled.

"He is hardly dead." Cormac smiled slowly. "I have seen the man myself and spoken with him recently."

"You have seen him?" Sebastien demanded. "Where?"

"He has been here at Turroch a few times in the past weeks. I gave him a sleeping pallet by my hearth. He came from Ireland to muster support for his clan's cause against the king."

Sebastien shot a quick glance at Giric, who glared stonily

at Cormac from an otherwise impassive face. "When was he here last?" Sebastien asked Cormac.

"Two days ago," Struan said. "You have seen him yourself. He fought those wolves to save Eoghan and Lileas."

Sebastien turned to Giric. "You knew," he hissed in a low voice. "Alainna knew."

Giric looked away, but Sebastien understood the unspoken affirmative. He realized that Alainna had deliberately kept the truth from him to protect Ruari. Esa knew, too, and Giric. He wondered how many of them knew, and had kept silent.

He felt betrayed, like a blade to the heart.

Certes, he thought. Alainna had said there was a ruin there, and he had seen her rowing a boat on the loch. Anger and dismay rolled through him. They had not trusted him. They had kept him out of their secrets—with reason, he admitted to himself. They respected and loved Ruari, and Sebastien had been sent to find him, even to kill him.

He could not help but wonder what else they hid from him. If Clan Laren supported the Celtic rebellion against the king, he must report them, even arrest their chief, as ludicrous as the idea seemed.

Cormac smiled. "Ruari saved Eoghan, so I gave him shelter here. He went to Kinlochan to see his wife, did you know that? He hinted that they meet secretly there."

Sebastien felt trust and hope fall away from him like a collapsed scaffold, taking the buttress of their friendship and the sense of family that he had felt from Alainna's people. He looked at Giric again and scowled.

Giric shook his head. "Only we two knew," he murmured. "It was only to help Ruari. For no other reason. I swear to you that she is loyal. We are all loyal to the crown."

Sebastien looked away, wanting to believe that, but unsure.

Cormac's dark eyes glittered. "I see you did not know. Well enough, now you do. And I can deliver Ruari to you, as the king requires."

"What guarantee do I have that you are not a traitor as well?" Sebastien asked.

"I am not so foolish as to follow Guthred MacWilliam. He claims a right to the throne, but he is a hotheaded young fool. He does not deserve the fine ancient blood that

courses through his veins. Ruari follows his lead like a dog
to a master, no matter that the master is worthless."

"Ruari *Mór* is no follower," Lulach said. "If he is alive,
and in the Highlands, he works for his own purpose, and
not that of a pup."

"Your kinsman's heroic deeds have blinded you to his
treacheries," Cormac said abruptly. He turned to Sebastien.
"Ruari believes that he has my support and the strength of
my clan behind the MacWilliams. Of course," he said
smoothly, "I would not commit treason."

Giric laughed outright, a bitter and skeptical sound.

"Where is Ruari now?" Sebastien asked.

"I do not know. But he will be here in a day or so, and
then, if you wish, you may have him."

Sebastien tensed. Behind him, his companions were like
tightly drawn bows, even Robert, who understood little of
the Gaelic conversation and relied on Giric's hurried
whispers.

"We will speak alone," Sebastien said, motioning for the
others to retreat to the door. They cast him dark looks and
shuffled back only a step. He moved closer to Cormac,
trying not to inhale the man's unwashed, meaty odor.

"What price for this?" Sebastien asked, although he
knew the answer he would hear.

"You want Ruari MacWilliam. I want Alainna of Kinlochan. Promise me that Alainna will be my wife, as her
father once agreed. Gain for me the king's word—I know
you can get it—that Kinlochan will be mine."

"And then?"

"Then I will give you Ruari MacWilliam, and in so doing,
give the king the entire rebellion. Ruari is the key," Cormac said. "He is Guthred's most trusted kinsman. Ruari
knows all their plans."

Sebastien's gaze trained hard and unwavering on Cormac.

"Do this, Sebastien le Bret, and you will be the most
powerful Norman knight in all of Scotland. The king will
reward you—and me." He smiled, his teeth, at close view,
gray and broken. "Think what the king will give you in
return for this. Kinlochan is nothing compared to what he
will grant you. One of the Celtic earldoms, perhaps. Whatever you desire."

Sebastien stared at him. Like the proverbial demon crouched on a dying man's bedpost, Cormac had found the pulse of his ambition, the hub of what he wanted, and laid before him the devil's own temptation.

"The king's sister is the duchess of Brittany, I hear," Cormac said. "King William need say but a word to her, and you will receive honors in Brittany for saving her homeland. Land wealth, a bride—a duchess, perhaps even a princess. With the king of Scotland and the duchess of Brittany in your debt, you will have all you could ever want."

Sebastien narrowed his eyes. He expected ambition to swell within him and drown his reasoning. He waited for the hard, swift current of material desire that had carried him forward for years to sweep through him.

He felt nothing. He did not want the promised boons that Cormac dangled before him.

He wanted Alainna. He wanted to be part of her clan. Yet he felt as if they had shut him out and betrayed him by protecting Ruari.

Sebastien fisted a hand at his side, stared once again at Cormac. "And all this when you betray Ruari MacWilliam to me?"

"All this," Cormac said.

"And what, then, for yourself? Surely you want more than Kinlochan and a bride."

"I will have all the reward I need," Cormac said. "The favor of my king, the land my clan has claimed and fought for generations. Our enemies in the palm of our hand." He smiled. "The bride my father and grandfather meant for me to have."

"All you could ever want," Sebastien said mockingly.

"Indeed. It is a simple choice. What will you do?"

Sebastien glanced at his friends. They were silent as stones, as wolves. He was part of their solidarity, no matter what they had withheld from him. He could never take part in the ignoble plot Cormac suggested. No prize, no ambition, was worth betraying a man, or worth losing the respect of the people whom Sebastien cared for deeply.

No ambition was worth losing Alainna.

If he did nothing to stop Cormac, the man would betray Ruari MacWilliam himself and earn royal favor. If Sebastien returned to Brittany, Cormac could eventually gain not only Kinlochan, but Alainna's hand in marriage.

"All you could want, I am sure," Cormac repeated.

He knew what he wanted, knew it with such clarity that he sucked in a fast, hard breath.

"What shall it be?" Cormac said. "Shall you meet me here in a few days to collect Ruari MacWilliam, or shall I bring him to Kinlochan's gates for his kin to see? Surely they would like to see him before he is taken away to the king's dungeon, and hanged by the heels and quartered apart in a traitor's death. What shall it be?"

"Send word to the king yourself," Sebastien said brusquely. "I am not interested in treachery."

While Cormac gaped at him, he pivoted. Giric, Robert, and Lulach turned with grim precision and strode out of the room in his wake.

"Prepare yourselves, my friends," Sebastien said as they crossed the bailey through spitting, whirling snow. "There will be a storm before long. And we have a renegade to rescue." He heard Giric laugh in relief and agreement.

All he wanted, as he mounted the Arabian and rode through the gate, was to get home to Alainna before either storm, the one that swirled in the sky or the one that brewed among men, hit.

They rode east over broad, rock-studded meadows and low hills covered in a new mantle of snow. The flakes slanted out of a bleak sky, and the wind gusts were bitter. Sebastien became aware of an unease that had nothing to do with the threatening weather.

"Snowstorms turn dangerous quickly in the Highlands," Giric said. "See there, in the distance, that strange cloud. 'Tis a snow squall over the mountains, heading this way. We must go quickly to Kinlochan, for we cannot turn back and seek shelter at Turroch if we are caught by a squall. No matter the rule of Highland hospitality, they will not take us in," he added grimly.

Sebastien scanned the leaden sky and looked westward, where a large, gauzy formation obscured the mountaintops. "I am not as concerned about the weather as I am about the trustworthiness of the MacNechtans."

"I agree," Robert said. "But we are armed and mounted on warhorses. We are skilled fighters. They are wild savages."

"Lulach and I," Giric reminded them wryly, "are savages too."

"Made civil by good friends," Robert retorted. Giric chuckled and Lulach grinned.

"In this weather, Cormac will keep to his warm hearth. No one will come out here now," Hugo said, riding behind them.

Lulach laughed harshly. "Do not trust what you see out here. Those hills are not empty. Even poor weather does not deter a Highlander with a purpose or a grievance. Though heavy snow might discourage a smarter man than Cormac MacNechtan."

The back of Sebastien's neck prickled. "This way, back to Kinlochan quick as we can," he said, urging his horse ahead.

"There is a faster way," Giric said. "To the left. A track between those hills will take us back directly."

"We must take the longer route," Sebastien said. "We can keep an open view of the countryside the rest of the way."

"Why? There is no one out here," Robert said.

"Sebastien *Bàn* is right," Lulach told Giric. "We should take the longer track."

"The horses will tire faster carrying armored men over these hills in such cold," Giric said. "Your horses are not as nimble as Highland garrons on slopes, and the snow on the hills can be treacherous."

Sebastien sighed, realizing there was little choice. "We will follow the pass between the hills. Keep alert for danger."

He felt it coming now, with every fiber of his body. He watched through the thickening snow, his logic telling him that Cormac was behind them at Turroch, sitting by his warm hearth and cursing them, making plans for later. But his gut told him otherwise.

The hills were craggy, powdered white, cold and empty. He rode on, listening to the creak of leather, the jingle of steel, the strike and thud of horse hooves on stone and ground.

Giric guided his garron ahead to lead the way, setting a walking pace. The horses filed in pairs along the narrow track, which snaked between the sloped bases of two steep, rocky hills.

Starry flakes dusted the Arabian's mane. The wind whistled softly, like a faint, eerie song from the faery world. Sebastien heard the distant croak of a raven. He glanced up slopes so steep that he could scarcely see the tops through the falling snow and gathering mist.

The raven sounded again. Sebastien felt the prickle strongly. He turned to say something to Lulach.

A shriek, long and unearthly, tore from the bowels of the hill. Sebastien reined in his startled horse and looked up one slope, then another, seeing nothing but rock. The sound repeated, short and horrifying in its echo.

He drew his sword, the one-handed Norman blade that fit in his palm like an extention of his strength. The heavier Highland blade was sheathed in a loop on his saddle. Ahead of him, Giric turned, pulling free his own claymore, which he carried sheathed across his back. Behind him, Sebastien heard other swords slither free, and crossbow bolts clicked into place.

Then a roar and a crash, and a boulder shifted and hurtled down the right-hand slope. Sebastien backed up his horse, its flank bumping into the garron behind it. All around him, men shouted and tried to turn their horses.

The boulder slammed into the earth a few feet in front of Sebastien's horse, causing the Arabian to rear and twist. While he hung on and tried desperately to control the horse, another boulder bounded and crashed down the other slope, closing off the rear exit of the pass.

The hillsides erupted as men leaped from behind the crags and rocks on both slopes. Cries and unearthly howls made the air vibrate. Stones and small rocks hurtled down, striking some of the knights. They pulled out their long shields and crouched beneath them, still on horseback, angling the shields to protect the horses' heads as well as their own.

The knights returned a vicious hail of arrows shot from

crossbows. Sebastien pulled his own loaded crossbow from the side of his saddle and aimed toward one of the slopes. He could not see clearly through the curtain of snow and missiles, and his scarred left eye hindered his vision.

Giric turned his garron and waded through a tangle of horses and men who had fallen or dismounted. Beside and behind him, the knights drew their weapons, hoisted their shields, and circled their horses around in a protective flank, but some of their comrades had already fallen.

Highlanders swarmed down the slopes toward them, a filthy, bare-legged, bare-headed, plaided host, emitting unnerving shrieks, their faces distorted, their hair flying wild in greased braids. Some held dirks, some hoisted long, huge swords. Others carried spears, slingshots, or rocks.

Fearlessness gleamed in their eyes. A deep chill ran down Sebastien's backbone when he saw it. At the upper part of one hill, he saw Cormac and Struan MacNechtan. He realized that somehow they had arranged the ambush, probably long before the Normans had left Turroch.

He and his men were penned in the narrow pass, unable to go forward, backward, or up the slopes. Impeded by heavy armor and weaponry, and by warhorses unaccustomed to such terrain, they were not only trapped, but at a staggering disadvantage.

He raised his shield against thunking rocks, against the arrowheads and spears that slammed past him. He lashed out with his sword and cut a man down. An arrow sliced into his thigh, catching his armor, tearing it and zinging past. His arms and back ached from the force of the blows he withstood and the blows he gave.

Around him, he glimpsed his friends and comrades struggling with their attackers. He saw some of them fall from their mounts. Highlanders slipped between the jostling horses, bringing down some of the fine-blooded, bold animals with fast, cruel blades, while their riders fell, lost to two-handed swords.

Sebastien leaned low under his shield and slung his leg over the saddle to dismount and gain the ground. He stood and whipped his broadsword in a wide arc to bring down an approaching Highlander. He strived to keep to his feet, to protect his back, and to watch the back of whatever knight was closest to him. He heard his men's screams swell the haunting cacophony that echoed between the hills. His blood went cold in his veins, while he fought on and on.

A lightning-fast scan of the pass and the hills revealed the snow-frosted bodies of the fallen, lending them a strange pristine beauty. The wind muffled the cries of terror and rage and agony.

Sebastien felt an anguished cry of rage build within him. He felt will surge within him like fire. He shouted, loud and raw, a bellow from his depths, summoning the power and the pride innate in him, drawing strength and anger from his soul. He swung the sword and lunged, turned, thrust, swiped, and cleared his way out of a corner.

Unaware if he killed or hurt or merely pushed back the savages that swarmed and smothered the knights, he knew only that he was trapped, that he must free himself, that he must defend his comrades. He turned again, lunging, slicing. He saw a Highlander drag Hugo from his saddle. Leaping sideways, he locked blades with the man, deflecting his spear.

Robert turned from another direction and stood over Hugo's fallen form, swinging his sword to knock the Highlander to the ground. Sebastien glanced anxiously at Hugo and saw him stir, saw his rise to his knees and fall again. Robert dropped to a knee to pull at him.

Sebastien spun away again when he heard another terrifying savage shriek. He saw another Highlander charge at him, spear brandished, face wild. He balanced his sword, swayed his weight, ready to thrust, swinging his sword as the man lunged at him.

Each movement, each thought took on terrible clarity. Sebastien felt wrapped in fog, yet his core was crystalline. He saw what he must do at each moment to ensure survival for himself and for whatever comrade was near him, each way that he turned.

Every moment of the struggle showed him that victory was not possible here. Yet he had never lost, and would not allow the thought to enter his mind now.

Thrust, swing, lunge, turn, thrust: a chant formed in his head like a litany, until the words became one with the blows and the thrusts. He was fed by pure wrath.

He turned again, and saw Giric jerk backward, struck by a hurtled rock, then fall from his saddle.

Giric struggled to his feet, swaying, face bloodied, and swung his own great sword around his head to take down a man who lunged at him. Sebastien turned away as another Highlander advanced toward him, yelling. He could not look back to see if Giric had survived the moment.

Everywhere men twisted, shrieked, and fell among the graceful, whirling veils of snow. Sebastien fought fiercely, aware only of the instant, following instinct, abandoning slower thought.

The snow thickened and the wind grew wild, and the storm became a bitter fury, a stinging, unforgiving new foe for all, enemy and attacked alike. Sebastien spun and shouted and strived, constantly searching for a channel of escape that could take them all to safety. But none was evident.

Two Highlanders surged toward him, and he turned to take them both on. A third came from behind, and a fourth. He felt the heavy strike of a blow to his side. Slowly, in sharp and eerie focus, he glanced down and saw the torn surcoat, the ragged edges of mail, the red sheen of his own blood on the steel tip that withdrew. Yet he felt no pain.

He struck out in defense, and took the man down, then whirled. A fifth Highlander appeared beside him, wielding a claymore, as did many of the Gaels. As Sebastien turned to strike at him, he realized that this particular Highlander was fighting the men who surrounded Sebastien.

The man cut down one MacNechtan, then another, with vicious, powerful blows of his sword while Sebastien fought the others, who dropped away, wounded.

Breathing hard, Sebastien paused, turned, and looked into keen blue eyes beneath dark, arched brows. He recognized the man who had once struggled with a wolf.

Ruari nodded to Sebastien abruptly and turned away, raising his sword again to aid Giric, who had risen and fought off two MacNechtans.

Stunned, deeply grateful, Sebastien lifted his shield and his sword and fought on through the whirling, bitter, engulfing whiteness.

Chapter Twenty-six

Alainna bent over the stone propped on her workbench, frowning in concentration. She maneuvered the chisel with a delicate hand, driving it with light taps of the mallet, as she carefully edged the tip around the elaborate twists and turns in an interlaced border. The chisel's path was a detailed design, drawn with chalk on the stone, which required caution and focus to follow.

Finan, lying in the warmth near the iron brazier, lifted his head and barked softly, then stood. Over the thunk of the mallet and scrape of the chisel edge, Alainna heard shouts in the bailey, and looked up.

She set aside her tools and went to the door to pull it open. The snow had thickened, and the light had a lavender sheen. The floor of the bailey was white and drifts had gathered at the base of the palisade. She wrapped her plaid over her head and shoulders against the wind, and stepped outside. The dog went out with her, and they moved side by side through a pale, stinging haze of snowflakes.

She saw Lorne, Niall, and some of the others running toward the gate, and she quickened her step while Finan ran ahead, barking furiously. "What is it?" she called to her kinsmen. "What has happened?"

Niall turned, gesturing with his single hand toward the entrance. "Giric and the knights are back! Aenghus saw them coming through the snow. Something has happened. Some of the men are wounded."

"Who is hurt?" she called, feeling the chill of true fear as she thought of Sebastien and her kinsmen wounded—or worse.

Niall ran past to join Lorne and Aenghus as they lifted the wooden beam that secured the palisade gate. After they swung the gate wide, horses and riders began to straggle into the bailey. Giric rode in the lead, and Lulach followed behind.

Alainna sighed out with relief to see them safe. She scanned past him to see who followed, recognizing Robert, Etienne, Richard, and several other knights. Blood smeared their faces and darkened their armor and weapons. Lulach looked haggard but unhurt, while Giric's face was bloody. Alainna scanned them all frantically. Nineteen men had left that morning, but only thirteen came through the gate.

Sebastien was not with them. Her heart plummeted.

While her kinfolk helped the knights dismount, she ran toward Giric. He looked at her, his brow bruised and bleeding.

"Ach Dhia," she cried, reaching up to him. "Oh God, what happened? Where . . . where are the rest of them?" She looked toward the empty gate, then again at Giric.

She saw shock and sadness and devastation in his eyes, a look she had seen too often before in other kinsmen returning from battle. Sobs tore at her throat.

"Giric, what happened?" She reached for his hand.

"Ambush," he said hoarsely. His fingers did not grip hers. "Cormac betrayed our trust."

"He gave you no chance to speak with him?"

"We spoke. We met with him at Turroch," Giric answered. He wiped a hand over his face, streaking blood across his brow from a wound beneath his hair. "Sebastien gave them the king's message. We left for home." He sighed out, shoulders bowing. "They attacked us and trapped us in a pass between two hills. Cormac and Struan must have planned it well ahead of time, to be so many waiting for us. They must have taken a quick route to get there when we left Turroch. The Normans were trapped in their heavy armor, with their horses—not suited to—"

"Get down," she said, seeing him lean forward, weakening. "Let Morag or Una tend to your head quickly. Save the tale for later." She reached up to help him as he dismounted.

Around her, her elderly kinfolk assisted those who had returned, helping them to dismount and walk toward the hall, while the three squires came out and led the horses to the stable. Niall and Donal half carried Robert, who seemed unable to walk on his own. Lorne led Etienne, whose arm was saturated in blood. Una approached with bandages and stanched the bleeding as they stood in the whirling snow.

Alainna gazed at the gate, but no others came through. Sebastien had not returned. She felt stunned, as if the breath had been knocked from her. She swallowed another sob as she supported Giric standing beside her.

"Giric . . . where is Sebastien?" she asked, dreading, hoping.

"He . . . I do not know,"—he gasped and shook his head—"I do not know where he is. I did not see him when we made our escape. Alainna, he fought like Fionn himself."

Her heart froze. Just then, Giric lurched and she instinctively slid her arm around his waist. He leaned his weight on her. Blood seeped down his face.

"Ach," she said. "Wait. You should not try to walk."

"It is nothing," he said. "I gave worse than this." More blood darkened his brow. He lifted his hand to cover the wound and stepped forward, Alainna under the weight of his arm.

"Una! Lorne!" she called. They left the knights they were with to Morag and Donal's care and hurried toward them. Alainna handed Giric over to Lorne's sinewy embrace, and Una pressed Giric's brow with a cloth. He nearly collapsed against Lorne, and roused himself to look at Alainna. "I must tell you—" he began.

"Later," Alainna pleaded. "Not now. Go inside."

"You must know. Ruari was there," Giric rasped out.

Alainna stared at him. "Ruari?" She heard Lorne echo her.

"Poor lad, he's having visions of those who have gone before," Una said.

"He *was* there," Giric insisted. "He helped us, Alainna. When Sebastien was put upon by five men at once, Ruari fought at his back. And then he came to my aid, and saved Robert's life too. I saw that with my own eyes. We all did."

"Giric—" Lorne began.

"Where is Ruari now?" Alainna asked quickly.

Giric shook his head. "I do not know."

Lorne, frowning thoughtfully, nodded. "If Ruari is out there," he said, "we will find him. I will ask Donal and Aenghus to search for him."

Alainna looked at Giric, who nodded. She knew he felt the same tremendous relief that she felt. "Send them to the island on the loch," she said.

Lorne agreed, while Una stared at all of them in disbelief, but neither of them asked questions. They guided Giric toward the tower, while Alainna turned away.

She lingered, watching the open, empty gate, where the snow blew in gusts. She felt as if a hole had formed in the center of her being, as cold and desolate as the deserted entrance.

A few men still stood in the bailey, though most had been helped into the tower. Two Norman squires soothed a restless horse and pulled him toward the stable. She saw nothing else. No one else.

She walked toward the gate and looked out. A gauzy white veil diminished the world beyond the fortress. She could barely make out the loch, and could see neither the Stone Maiden nor the forest and mountains.

The snow stung her cheeks, and the cold wind whistled around her, tugging at her plaid. She should go inside, she knew, and help those who had returned.

Yet she could not leave the gate. She stood like a pillar, alone in the whipping wind and snow, and wanted to plunge into the freezing haze to find him. Hugging her arms about herself, she stamped her feet against the cold, and waited.

She walked back and forth or stood prancing from one foot to the other for so long that darkness began to gather, lit eerily by the constantly falling snow. Numb and exhausted, Alainna paced, or stopped to scan the endless curtain of flakes. She was aware that she was watched now and then from the firelit doorway of the tower. But she could not go inside where it was warm, and where she was undoubtedly needed. She was needed here, too, to stand like a beacon at the gate.

To leave her sentry position would be to give up hope. She could not do that, for she was sure that she sensed Sebastien's presence like a heartfelt pull between them. She could only pray fervently that it was his living spirit she sensed, homing toward her through the increasing blizzard.

At long last, when she thought she could stand upright no longer, she saw a blur of figures emerging through the whiteness. A man on horseback slowly mounted the hill toward the palisade, leading other horses behind him. Riderless horses. Alainna gasped and ran forward as he cleared the top of the rocky slope and came toward the clearing that fronted the gate.

Sebastien swayed in a weary rhythm with the horse, a dirge of movement that tore at Alainna's heart to watch. In one hand he gripped the reins of three horses, which bore the bodies of five fallen knights. She nearly cried out, hands covering her mouth.

He rode through the frozen veil of snow, his face still and fierce. His mail coif sagged on his shoulders, his surcoat was torn and bloody, and his hair was matted and darkened. But he was alive. He was here, and her relief felt like golden sunlight.

She ran to him, skirts flying, feet wading through the powdered snow. "Sebastien!" she called, her voice catching on a rising sob. "Sebastien!"

He halted his horse. Alainna stopped an arm's length from the Arabian, whose creamy coat seemed eerily pale in the lavender light. The horse snorted, blew out, hung his head with weariness, and pawed at the snow that collected around his hooves.

Alainna looked up at Sebastien as the snow danced and deepened around them. He watched her, mouth hard, cheeks drawn, his silvery eyes vivid with sorrow, deep with a need that she had not seen in him before, as if she saw clear through to his soul.

She reached out. He grasped her hand fiercely, his fingers cold on hers, and let go. She sensed the devastation he felt, and tears filled her eyes.

She glanced past him at the bodies arched over the backs of the three horses he led. "So many," she said.

"Too many." The mellow voice that she craved to hear was wooden, flat. "Hugo is gone, Alainna. Hugo."

A sob wrenched her, but she stifled it, pressing a hand to her chest, looking at the sad burden of lost friends on the horses behind him. She knew Hugo had been like a brother to him.

With stiff, careful movements, he dismounted and stood beside her. She gasped as she saw how much blood covered the front of his surcoat, and she prayed it was not his. He held his left hand over his stomach, the arm tight against his side.

Wordlessly, with the reins bunched in his hand, he turned and led the horses toward the open gate. Alainna walked beside him, extending her palm in a silent plea for some of the leads.

He gripped them hard and did not look at her. She understood, and waited as he entered the enclosure alone, leading the horses in a slow walk.

Inside the bailey, he halted the horses, patting the Arabian's broad neck. Alainna saw him lean against his horse's side for a moment, then move around the horse, staggering slightly. She ran to him just as he took his hand away from his side. His fingers were red with blood.

Fear struck through her like lightning, but she strived to remain calm. "Come inside," she said quietly, touching his arm. "Someone will take the horses, and . . . see to the men."

He shook his head. "I cannot leave them like that. There are prayers that must be said over them. We cannot send for the priest in this blizzard, but we can—"

"Later," she said firmly. She touched his hand, fisted over the reins. His fingers, long and cold, opened at her touch. "First we will tend to the living."

She put her arm around his back, and he circled his arm around her shoulders. His partial weight and the pressure of his body beside hers felt solid and good amid chill and hurt and death. She held back her tears and her questions and gave him her support, moving forward in patient tandem with him.

Lorne emerged from the falling snow like a ghost, his face gray. Donal was behind him. Alainna handed the clutch of reins to Donal, who nodded to Sebastien. "I will see to this," he said. "Do not worry. See to yourself."

"Come," Lorne said. He tossed a plaid about Sebastien's shoulders. "You are weary, my son, and in need of a hearth." His subdued voice was warm and reassuring. He put an arm around Sebastien's shoulders and turned with him.

Alainna saw the growing pallor in Sebastien's cheeks, but he walked forward without faltering. He did not lean on either of them, but she kept her arm around his waist. Whether he needed it of her or not, she needed to help him.

As they approached the tower, the door opened at the top of the steps, and torchlight flared there.

He slept, and woke, and slept again, wrapped in mist, floating in a river of shadows. The warmth of her touch soothed him, her voice caressed him. He felt strength in her hands, and gentleness, and surrendered to both.

While he lay in Alainna's warm, dim chamber, in Alainna's own bed, drifting in and out of a soporific state, he heard voices other than hers, quiet, concerned, and kind: Lorne, Una, Esa, Niall, Giric, others. Una was there often, quick and nervous as a bird. He was vaguely aware that she had stitched his wound closed, the deep sword cut in his side that he had held closed all the way home from the ambush to keep his life from flowing out.

Home. He caught himself in his thoughts. *Home.* Kinlochan seemed like that to him now, and those who hovered at his bedside seemed like family. But that could not be. He could not think why, for his mind was muddled. For some reason, he could not stay here. But he wanted to, very much.

He heard them say that he had lost much blood, that he had nearly died. No wonder he felt so weak, he thought. Then the shadows descended again, and he let their conversation pass over his awareness like clouds. Only Alainna's voice remained, sustaining him, a light in the shadows.

He dreamed of a place where Alainna waited for him inside an open gate set in a wall of gleaming bronze. Behind her rose a tower with walls of silver, brilliant in the sun, the roof thatched with doves' feathers.

This was her Land of Promise, he knew. He was glad that she had found it at last. She called to him, holding out her hands to invite him inside. He wanted desperately to go to her, but when he tried to move forward he was rooted to the ground. He looked down to see his feet deep in a hole, entwined by vines.

He woke again, turning his head with effort. Alainna was there, bending over him, her hand cool on his brow.

"Sleep, Sebastien *Bàn,*" she whispered. "Sleep, and do not die. Too many men have died in my life, and I am weary of it. I cannot lose you too. Not you." He felt her lips on his cheek, and soft on his mouth, and he thought he tasted her tears.

He reached for her hand, though it took effort, and he held it, slim and cool and strong, while he slid into another dream of contentment, another dream where he was with her.

He willed himself to open his eyes and keep them open. What day it was, he did not know; the third day in this bed, the fourth, or more. Alainna sat beside him, her hair glorious, her eyes like a deep sea. He reached out to her.

"Am I awake or dreaming?" he asked in a gruff voice. His fingers grazed her arm. He realized, with a sense of surprise, that he had spoken in Gaelic without thinking.

She smiled and took his hand, squeezing it. "Awake," she said. "I was about to bathe you again. You have been fevered." She touched his brow with her cool palm. "Ah, it is nearly gone. Good. Una will be pleased."

He smiled a little. "And are you pleased?"

"I am." She drew down the linen sheet that covered his nude torso, settling it a little below his waist. His side was bandaged, and his muscles felt stiff and painful when he shifted. She dipped a cloth in water and wrung it, then slid it over his chest, her hands infinitely gentle.

"Mm." He cocked a brow and looked at her. "That is not the touch of a stonemason, but the touch of an angel. Ah, now I remember. You are both." He gave her a teasing smile.

She laughed. "I think you are dreaming after all."

He could not seem to stop smiling. "I might be. You have been in all of my dreams." She smiled as she turned away to dip the cloth fresh and wring it again. "How long since . . ."

"Four days," she answered. "We have worried about you, Sebastien *Bàn*. You missed the new year. We welcomed it without you." She smiled, but he saw traces of fatigue in the purple shadows under her eyes and the pallor on her face.

"My men? Robert, the rest? Giric? How are they?"

She stroked the cloth over his chest and up over one shoulder, frowning. "Better. Giric scared us, too, with a bad head wound, but he is stronger now, and up and about. Robert had a spear wound on his leg that needed closing, but he is already walking. Etienne's arm was cut, and is mending too. The rest are well enough."

"And the . . . others?" he asked. "Have you sent for the priest, and buried them?"

She shook her head. "The snow is too deep. We have not been able to send someone for Father Padruig. Lorne said prayers over their bodies, and we held a wake and watched over them the first night. Una and Morag tended them and shrouded them. We will do what must be done as soon as we can."

He nodded, then turned his face away. "We were betrayed and trapped, Alainna. We were attacked without honor."

"I know," she said. "Giric and Robert told me what happened. I am sorry, Sebastien. I am sorry, too, about Hugo. I know he was your friend."

He closed his eyes briefly against an intangible pain that cut far deeper than the wound in his side. "He was like a brother," he murmured. "If I were a Highland man, that death alone would make this feud my own," he added in a fierce voice.

"It would." She slipped the cloth back into the basin and twisted it to dampness. "But you are not a Highland man. I do not want you to make this feud your own."

He sighed in frustration. "Alainna—"

"Hush. Do not speak of this now. You must rest and relax, and think only of pleasant things. That is the way to recover."

He sighed again, his mind still muddled. Thoughts took effort; the sadness and anger he felt took effort too. But whenever he looked at her, quiet joy flowed through him like water.

"The rest are well?" he asked.

She tipped her head quizzically. "They are. I told you."

"Ruari?" he asked softly, deliberately. "Is he here?"

The cloth, gliding along his shoulder, stopped. Alainna kept her profile to him, her hair like plaited fire in the reddish light. "He is here," she said quietly and apprehensively.

"He came to our aid and fought the MacNechtans."

"Giric told us. Ruari is here now, where he belongs, with his wife and her kin." He heard the defiance in her voice.

"I will need to talk to him. I want to talk to you too," he added somberly. "You knew he was back, Alainna."

"There is time for that later," she said calmly, avoiding his steady gaze. "What is most important is that we are all safe. That you are safe," she murmured.

He sighed, watching her, and kept silent. She slicked the cloth down his midsection, and he flinched, highly aware of her touch. Her gentle strokes took the wet cloth over his abdomen, though she avoided the bandaging, wadded on the left, tied at the right.

"You spoke a charm of protection over me before I left," he began. "But I did get cut, after all." He smiled teasingly.

"Sometimes the protection works in different ways than we would like," she answered lightly. "But you did come back to me as you went away from me—alive."

He nodded, watching her. "True. I might have died there."

"Too easily, Sebastien *Bàn*," she murmured. "You lost a lot of blood. But the cut was in the muscle, and no deeper. Una is skilled at closing sword wounds. You will heal quickly now that the fever is gone."

While they spoke, she stroked the warm, wet cloth over his skin, up and down his torso. The water glistened in firelit beads on the golden brown hair that covered his chest and midline. She slipped the cloth over his arms, over his hands. He felt like a babe under her careful ministrations, and he lay back in and let her soothe him, body and spirit.

Wounded and weak, stripped clean of everything, even his pride, he gave himself wholly into her care. He savored the compassion, and the sensual pleasure inherent in her touch, in her presence.

He watched her as she worked, and felt the warm slick of the cloth over his body, and thought how much he would like to try that warm cloth on her in turn. He imagined delights that he lacked the strength to pursue then, although his body responded.

Responded well enough that when she rubbed the wet cloth down his abdomen again, he took her wrist. "Alainna," he murmured, his gaze steady on hers and his grip strong, "unless you wish to join me in this bed and risk taking the rest of my strength, let the washing be."

She blushed and set the cloth aside, then picked up a piece of thick linen to rub his chest and arms dry. "Well enough," she agreed. "Your fever has broken, and there is not the need that there was earlier."

"Ah," he said. "You have bathed me before, and me unable to enjoy it?" He rested his head back on pillows that were soft and fragrant with heather and lavender, the two scents that he most associated with her. He raised his arms to fold them behind his head. The room was warm, with an extra brazier on the floor, he noticed. He felt no chill, even with dampened skin.

"I bathed every part of you. Una and the others left the room and left the task to me, as your handfasted wife."

"Every part? I am sorry I missed that," he said wryly.

She rubbed his arm and hand dry. "It needed to be done to bring down the fever, though perhaps a proper lady would not have done such a thing for a knight."

Her cheeks burned hot as a fire, he thought. He longed to touch her, wanted to know if the heat in her was as strong as the heat that swelled and burned, healthfully now, in his own body.

He reached out and drew his forefinger down the sweet curve of her cheek and lifted her chin. "A lady might not do that for a knight," he said, "but a wife would for a husband."

She tipped her head in the cup of his hand and watched him solemnly. "She would," she answered.

She stood so quickly that his uplifted fingers closed on

air. She picked up the bowl and the cloths and went to the door, opening it and shutting it behind her without a word.

He made a soft fist and covered his eyes with his forearm, sighing heavily.

Sebastien scratched his side where the healing wound itched, and he scratched his head, longing for a bath. Una had denied him one steadily for days; in the morning, he decided, he would set aside his dignity and beg. Alainna would have relented by now, he thought, but in the last few days he had seen her for no more than moments at a time. Una said she stayed a great deal in her workshop now that Sebastien was healing so well.

He missed her. He knew she had not slept in her own bed since he had been wounded, and he suspected she slept on a hard, flat bed of sandstone while he recovered in a cozy nest of heather-stuffed pillows and warm furs and blankets.

He tried once more to rest, turned over a few times, scratched again, and swore. The hour was late, but he was not especially tired after spending over a week doing little else than sleeping. The sounds of music and laughter, and Lorne's voice raised in rhythmic poetry, reverberated through the floor of the bedchamber. He sat up in the bed.

He looked at the companion who had spent more time with him in the last few days than anyone else. Finan sat on the floor by the brazier and lifted a hind leg to scratch himself. He set his head on his front paws and looked at Sebastien, tail thumping.

"Ah," Sebastien said. "So it was you gave me this itching, was it?" He shoved the furs and blankets aside and stood cautiously, straightening to his full height with care, for the muscles of his side and abdomen were still tender. Flexing his back and shoulders, he unwrapped the bulky bandage from around his middle and laid it aside. The neatly stitched wound was less bruised, he saw, and healing well. He felt far more comfortable with the bandage off, although he was sure Una would not approve.

He walked nude across the room, his feet compressing the rushes, toward the corner, where a bench held a pile of his folded clothing, cleaned and mended. He dressed carefully in shirt, *braies,* and brown tunic, pulling on hose and boots. The green surcoat had been washed and mended, but he laid it aside.

Opening the door, he stood back while Finan slipped out ahead of him. Then he slowly descended the steps into the hall, standing in a raftered bay and watching for a few moments.

One by one, they noticed him. Faces turned toward him, smiling, and friendly voices called out welcome and blessings. Lorne halted his song on the harp, though Sebastien gestured for him to continue. The old man smiled and changed the song he was playing to a joyful strain.

Una rushed forward, clucking like a little hen. "Back to the bed you are going!" she said, pulling at his arm.

"I am fine," he assured her. "Far better than I was, thanks to you—and to your clan chief." His gaze scanned the room behind her, looking for Alainna. "Though I would like a bath. I think Finan shared his fleas with me," he added.

She looked at Beitris, who stood behind her. "We must put more bog myrtle in the mattress and pillows," she said.

He walked past them, pausing to greet clan members and knights as he went, his gaze scanning the room until he saw her.

She sat on a bench at one of the tables, surrounded by Giric, Robert, Etienne, and Lulach. She glowed in his eyes more than the hearth fire itself. He went to her.

Near her sat another he wanted to see, a tall man, wide-shouldered and handsome, his face craggy, his dark hair streaked with silver. Esa leaned against him. Quiet descended upon the room as Sebastien came forward, silence with a note of tension. He knew they waited to see what he would do.

He went to Alainna first and held out his hand. When she placed her hand in his, he lifted it to his lips and kissed the smooth knuckles. His gaze was only for her, and he smiled.

"Welcome back to the hall," she said softly. "My kin are glad to see you well at last."

"And are *you* glad?" he murmured.

"You know I am," she said.

He lowered her hand and let it go, and turned to the man who sat across from her. Ruari stood slowly and faced Sebastien across the width of the table.

Wordlessly, Sebastien leaned forward and picked up a wooden goblet and a jug of ale that sat on the table. He slowly poured a cupful, and handed it to Ruari.

"I owe you thanks," he said. "We all do here."

Ruari accepted the cup with a nod and a wry smile. As he sipped and raised his cup in turn to salute Sebastien, a cheer rose in the room.

Chapter Twenty-seven

The bronze bell in the church tower echoed a lament over the hills. Alainna listened, standing in the open doorway of her workshop beside Finan, her hand stilled on his head. Every strike of the distant bell rendered a mark upon her heart, as if grief were a chisel. Father Padruig had promised to toll the bell every hour in a dirge for the fallen knights until they had all been buried.

Snow flurried down again, but the snowfall of the previous week had melted enough for a solemn procession to leave Kinlochan to carry the slain knights, and to attend a mass. Giric, Lorne, and some of the others were still at the church, digging graves in the almost frozen ground, but Alainna, Sebastien, and others had returned a little while earlier.

Blinking back tears, she saw that the bailey was silent, cold, pristine with snow. Beyond the palisade, the rugged blue mountains wore a crown of pale clouds.

She saw Sebastien walking through the yard, his long, agile stride filled with natural masculine grace, although she knew he was still weary from injury and illness. The wind whipped at his golden hair and billowed the plaid that he wore wrapped about his shoulders, draped like a mantle.

Her heart seemed to reel in her breast, as she often felt when she saw him. "May God make smooth the path before you," she said in Gaelic as he came near.

"And may you be safe from every harm," he answered. Finan nosed under his hand, and he scratched the dog's head, then leaned a shoulder against the door frame. "The world sleeps beneath a white coverlet lately," he mused. "We will have even more snow by the look of those clouds."

"The queen of winter rules now, while Aenghus mac Og, the golden one, sleeps. Soon he will awaken, and he and Brighid will bring the springtime back, and we will have sunshine and greenness once again."

"Ah, is that what we wait for," he murmured. "Spring."

She looked out over the whiteness the snowfall that lazily filled the air. "I always think of snow as one of the time-between-times," she said. "There is magic in such times, the stories tell us. Mist, fog, dawn, twilight . . . when the world is neither one, nor the other. Snow and ice seem that way to me, the world gone white and still and beautiful, conjured out of crystals and clouds."

He tipped his head to look down at her. "It is a magical time, in a way. Life is frozen. Time can seem frozen too."

She nodded. The distant bell pealed again, and Sebastien lifted his head to listen, his profile strong and handsome.

"I am sorry about your men," she said.

"I know," he said. "I should be there, helping the others."

"You were there this morning," she said. "And I asked you to ride back with me and my kinswomen, which you kindly did."

He smiled ruefully. "You and Una sought an excuse to bring the invalid back home."

Home. The word echoed between them silently.

"We did," she agreed. "You should not be doing the work of digging now, and risk opening your stitches."

He nodded. "Lorne told me that you have been making stones for the graves. Thank you."

She nodded. "I am glad to be able to do something for your friends. Our friends," she added quietly. "Come, I will show you." She stepped into the workshop, and he entered too. Finan rushed past them to claim the warmest spot by the brazier, and Alainna shut the door and turned.

He went to the workbench and she followed. "I used some small slabs of sandstone." She pointed toward one of the stones. "I incised the lines rather than carved them in relief. It is a faster method, and can make a handsome image."

Sebastien nodded as she spoke. The outlined crosses were filled with a pattern of interlaced lines. "These require careful effort, I am sure, yet you have done four of the five already."

"Sandstone is soft enough to carve rapidly, but it does not take fine detail well, so I used a simpler zigzagged key design. I usually do not like to work with sandstone."

He lifted a brow. "Because you make tomb sculptures in it?"

"That," she admitted, "and because it is soft and gritty and raises a choking dust that makes me cough. And it wears my tools out too quickly. Lulach grumbles when he has to sharpen them too often."

"You made these quickly. You have been working hard."

She sat on the stool and picked up a v-shaped chisel and a wooden mallet. "It needed to be done." She moved the tools in a rhythm, making channels in the stone, which fell away like clay beneath her tools. The light tapping sound filled the air for several moments.

"That blue hound of yours sleeps deeper than any hound I have ever seen," Sebastien commented, lifting a brow to glance at Finan, who nestled, eyes closed, beside the brazier. "The noise does not disturb him at all."

"He is used to it, and nothing can stir him awake if he wants to sleep," she said. "He is getting older, too. He seems to sleep more often and more deeply lately." She sighed, thinking that he was yet another one of those she loved who was growing older.

Sebastien watched her. "You look tired. You are thinner."

She gazed at the shadows in his face, at the new gauntness that revealed the classic balance of the bones beneath his skin. "So are you."

He reached out to brush at her cheek with a thumb, taking away some stone dust. "There are dark circles under your eyes."

She half smiled. "You sound like Una. Next you will want to know when last I ate, when last I slept, and for how long."

"Well," he said. "Tell me." She grimaced, and he smiled. "One of the monks at the monastery of Saint-Sebastien would peer into our faces and comment on our pale cheeks or red noses, and tell us to eat more or to get more sleep.

He meant well, and cared about us. I suppose I learned it from him. I mean well. I care about you," he added softly.

She ducked her head over her work. A sneeze began high in her nose. She released it into her hand. "The stone is making too much dust." She picked up a damp cloth and rubbed down the powdered surface of the stone.

"Alainna, I think you should rest for a bit," he said.

"I want to finish this today." She picked up her tools again. "It is the last of the knights' crosses."

"I can see the strain of the work in your face and your voice. You have been up too many nights with only a bed of stone for your head." He lifted the silken tail of one of her long braids, shaking a few tiny stone chips from it.

"When I cannot sleep, the work soothes me," she said.

"The work does not let you sleep. There is no need to hurry so to finish these stones."

"They are nearly done. It is not difficult carving. If I am in a hurry at all, it is to return to my own work."

Sebastien went to the table beneath the window, where her gray limestone pieces lined the table top. He looked at them, pausing at each one. "You have done much in the last weeks. Three more are finished. And the scene of the Stone Maiden is done." He bent to examine it. "This is truly beautiful work. You are an artist."

"I am a craftswoman," she said, and tapped the mallet as she spoke. "An artisan. A preserver of my clan's heritage. I am a woman who works hard, who does not give up once she sets her mind to something. I fear that I only have until spring."

"You have your entire life." He turned. "The work you do is outstanding, yet you do not see that. You see only the need to work, the need to finish another stone and move on. Stop, Alainna," he said. "Stop for a moment and come here."

He beckoned, and she shook her head. "I cannot stop," she said, and tapped her mallet on the chisel, blew away the dust. "There is so little time left."

He crossed the room and took both of her arms in his, nearly lifting her from her stool, turning her, urging her ahead of him with his hands on her shoulders. "Here," he said, halting with her in front of the table. "Look."

"At what?"

He touched a finger under her chin and turned her face a little. "Look at your stones," he said gently. He pressed her hand to the limestone, her fingers caught between the cool, hard stone and his warm, strong touch.

"Feel the texture," he said. "Smooth and polished, neatly carved. Look at the designs. There, Labhrainn and the mermaid he loved. That one, Mairead the Brave fighting a wolf to save her child. Here, under your hand, the Stone Maiden—Alainna, the beautiful one, who watches over her clan forever." His voice softened. "Look at the stones, Alainna *mo càran*," he urged. "Tell me what you see."

She looked at him, her heart beating fast and sweet. *Mo càran*, he had called her—my beloved.

"Tell me," he murmured again.

Alainna turned her head, and looked. "I see . . . oh," she said, tracing her fingertips over the intricate plaiting in one border, the knotwork in another. "It is lovely. The carving is . . . so carefully done."

"It is," he said. "What else?"

"I see pictures of . . . courage, and of love for the clan. Oh," she murmured again, suddenly surprised by the artistry in the stones, a balance of graceful curvilinear design combined with intricate detail. She had intended them to capture the stories, but she had not dared to hope that they could be beautiful, too. Her breath caught on a sob that bubbled up from deep within her. Tears sprang to her eyes. "They are wonderful," she said.

"They are." He took her hand in his, and kissed it. "We all know it. But you need to see it for yourself."

She nodded, and gazed at him through a glaze of tears, grateful for his kindness. He gathered her into his arms and she rested her cheek against his wool-covered chest, hearing the thud of his heart, sensing his vigorous strength, glad he was healing so quickly.

Most of all, she was grateful that he was here, and alive. Seeing him so close to death had frightened her to the depth of her soul. She had not told him how deeply her vigil by his bedside those many days and nights had affected her.

He lowered his head and kissed her, his mouth hot and

gentle. Her head arched back, long-throated, and her knees shook beneath her. No matter what her thoughts were, his touch always seemed to open the gates of her soul.

Parting his mouth from hers, he slid his hands along her back, holding her close, resting his cheek against her head. Finan slept at their feet, his tail swiping an idle rhythm. Outside, the wind swept past in a cold, whistling sound.

She sighed against him, sadly, the burden of her thoughts heavy on her mind and her heart, and she knew that she must speak, that she could no longer hold back what must be said.

What she wanted most could not be. The agony she had endured watching him slide so close to death made her choice clear. She feared for his life if he stayed at Kinlochan.

"Sebastien *Bàn*," she began. "I have done much thinking in the days since you were injured and ill. I have come to a decision." She looked at him, her heart pounding. "Do you still plan to go back to Brittany when the weather clears?"

"I have been thinking too," he said. "And I have talked to your men and to mine. We are all in agreement. As soon as the snow clears, we will move against Cormac, and repay him for the betrayal he showed us."

She sucked in a quick breath. That was not what she wanted to hear. She stepped away from him, frowning, thinking, and went to another stool beside a second workbench, where she kept the piece of cream limestone. Whipping the cloth from its surface, she picked up a fine-edged chisel and a wooden mallet and began to furrow into its surface.

Working with the Caen limestone was always comforting to her. The stone cut easily, willing as butter, never crumbling, never in need of force. It was almost fluid under the touch of her tools, as if the stone knew the shape she wanted it to take.

Not so her dreams. She heard Sebastien walk toward her.

"Alainna?" he asked. "What is it?"

"You cannot stay at Kinlochan," she said bluntly.

"I told you that I would go, I know. And I must find my son. But I will not leave here until I have returned the hospitality Cormac showed to us on his land," he said grimly.

Her hands trembled. "Do not change your plans," she said. "Go to Brittany and find your son. That is most important to you, and that is what you must do."

"Surely you can see that I must meet Cormac first," he said.

"I do not want you to fight this endless feud," she answered stubbornly. "You have other goals, other matters to attend to. You have fulfilled the king's orders here." Her fingers shook so on the chisel that she put it down. But she was too anxious, and could not sit idle.

Picking up the mallet and an iron punch, a pointed tool, she began to clear excess stone away from the left side of the design, where the background needed deeper cutting. She set the point in place and smacked its handle.

"Why this change of heart?" he asked. "Not so long ago, you wanted me to stay."

She smacked again, freeing a chunk of creamy white limestone. A new ridge was exposed in the stone. She brushed her fingers over it and drove the punch with the mallet again.

"Alainna," he said sternly, "stop that and talk to me."

"You cannot stay here," she insisted. "Your son awaits you. He must be raised in Brittany, and you must be with him." She hit the point handle hard.

"All I know now is that I will face Cormac MacNechtan and seek payment for the lives of my comrades."

"Do not change your plans. Go back to Brittany." Again she struck, and a wedge of stone flew to the floor. The lumpy ridge seemed larger now, an imperfection in the stone. She had not suspected the flaw earlier.

"I cannot as yet."

"We do not need you here. We can fight our own feud, as we have always done. When you leave, our handfasting will be voided, and . . . my kinsmen will choose another to help us, as we planned to do all along—before the king sent his champion."

Heart pounding, she regretted the words as soon as they were said, for she knew they would hurt him; she had wounded herself by uttering them. But she followed an almost desperate need to convince him to leave Kinlochan.

"I see. You have decided that you would rather have your Celtic warrior after all, than settle for a foreign knight."

"It is not that at all." She shook her head in misery. "If you stay, Cormac will attack again. He may kill you next time." She angled the point to cut away the flaw in the stone. "He will never give up until he sees you dead." She hit the chisel.

"So that is what troubles you," he said softly.

"Go to Brittany," she said. "Go to France, or even back to Dunfermline. Find your goals and be content."

"My goals have changed," he said. "Even as we speak, they are changing still." His voice was grim, hard, hurt.

"What will you do?" she asked in a flat tone. She scraped the stubborn fault in the stone with the chisel.

"Whether you want me here or not, I now have my own dispute with Cormac MacNechtan, and a matter to be settled."

"Cormac and his kinsmen will never settle with us!" She raised her voice frantically. "I have lived with this feud all my life. Too many of the men I have loved have died fighting the MacNechtans." She choked back a sob. "I cannot bear for that to happen to you, too!"

"I will be fine," he said calmly.

She shook her head. "Do you think I want to carve your . . . tombstone out of that piece of sandstone, where we . . . where we . . ." She gasped, remembering the incandescent passion of the night they had laid upon that stone. She turned away and smacked the stone again, hard. "I want you to leave. I cannot endure this."

"The risk of my death, fighting this feud for you and yours, did not seem to bother you before now."

"I had not seen you near death then," she said. "I did not love you so much then."

He lifted his hand toward her. "Alainna . . ."

If he touched her, she would crumble, she thought. She struck the punch forcefully with the mallet. Another piece broke away, exposing more of the obstruction.

Ach Dhia, she said to herself, wiping the back of her

hand over her eyes. She felt brittle, near tears. "It is a shell."

"A shell?" he asked. He came closer.

"Limestone sometimes has seashells in it," she said. She sighed wearily. "When they appear, it is difficult to tell how deep they are in the stone." She chipped at the rippled edge of the shell. "I can remove it, I think," she muttered. Placing the point, she stood to angle the chisel.

The obstruction to her own happiness could not be cleared away so easily, she knew. She tapped, freeing more of the shell. Carefully she positioned the point, using the sharp tip as a wedge.

"Alainna, wait." He reached out his hand.

She struck iron into stone, and heard a cracking sound. A gap appeared along the edge of the shell. The left side of the surface crumbled.

Then the stone split, and part of it collapsed to the floor.

Chapter Twenty-eight

Alainna stared in disbelief at the shattered, defaced stone. Then she dropped down to snatch at the creamy, splintered chunks, tears blinding her, slivers piercing her fingers as she frantically collected the pieces.

Sebastien hunkered beside her. "Let me do that," he said. She batted at his hands and he pushed hers away. "Let me!" he snapped.

He gathered the bits in his hands. Alainna stood, tears streaming down her face. When Sebastien tumbled the pieces onto the workbench, Alainna felt as if her heart broke within her.

"It is ruined," she whispered.

He brushed a hand over the intact part of the stone, where the relief was partially destroyed. "You can recut it. Here, and here. It can be redone."

She shook her head. Parts of the tower and palisade were gone. "It cannot be reclaimed." She stifled a sob with the back of her hand, hardly believing what had happened, what damage her impulsive temper and her relentlessness had done.

"We will fix this one, or we will find another stone." He touched her shoulder, turned her. "Alainna—"

She felt herself crumble. She slid into the opening circle of his arms with a dry, defeated sob. "The breaking of the stone is a sign," she said. "An omen. You must go and never come back. If you stay here, and give up all that you hold dear—"

"Not all," he murmured, his lips against her hair.

"—you could die fighting this feud."

"Nevertheless," he said calmly, "I will stay and fight. There is no other choice, Alainna. None at all. Not now."

She closed her eyes in misery as he held her. He feathered back the wisps of hair loosened along her brow. Grief welled up within like a fountain and spilled over.

She cried for all of them, then—for Sebastien, who had nearly died, for his five fallen knights, for her father and her brothers and the kinsmen beyond them, all lost to this feud. She wept for her mother, for all the kinswomen, and for a maiden, long ago, who had died beside the loch.

In the depth of her heart, she mourned the diminished clan that she could not save alone. Her carvings could not preserve them. Ultimately, only sons and daughters to bear the spirit and the blood of Clan Laren would do that.

She could not ask Sebastien to stay with her at Kinlochan, yet she wanted to be with him, as his wife, as his lover and soul-friend. She wanted to bear their children inside her body, and live side by side with him in their own Land of Promise.

But that place was a legend, and this place was fraught with danger. And the stone that had held her dream was destroyed.

He braced her patiently until her sobs quieted. "Sebastien," she snuffled into his chest.

"What is it, *mo càran?*" he murmured. His lips touched her brow, traced softly over her wet cheek.

"I love you." Her heart bounded to say the words, to know how deeply she meant them. "And it is why I want you to leave. I cannot lose you to this feud, too."

He pulled back to look at her. "Alainna, listen to me," he said. "I am here with you, and I am safe, and I will keep you and yours safe. I swear it. If you wish it, go out with me now, down to the loch, and I will swear it with my hand upon the Stone Maiden, and you may say all the charms you like around me."

She closed her eyes and rested her cheek against his chest, his voice sliding over her, comforting her. She wrapped her fingers in the plaid draped over his shoulders. "Wait a little to do that," she said. "It is snowing again. Stay here for now, with me. Just for now. Later we will talk of you leaving."

"For now," he said, and dipped his head to kiss her again. "After that, we will talk about my staying."

She placed a finger on his lips. "No more. Let us have some time without talk of what must be done. I am weary of it."

"Well enough." He gathered her close. "We will call it a truce between us. The time-between-times," he said. "For so long as the world is white and sleeping, for so long as winter holds us here, we will not talk about, or worry about, what may come later. Does that please you?"

"It does. Very much." She reached up to circle her arms around his neck. "No mention of names or legacies, duty or vengeance. We will go nowhere in this weather, and no one will come here. We will have peace at Kinlochan."

"If that peace could only last until spring." His hands caressed her back. "Until the day you mark the Stone Maiden." He lowered his face toward hers.

"Spring is closer than you think," she murmured. "By our custom, we mark the stone on the feast day of Saint Brighid. That is not so long from now—"

"Hush," he said, and covered her mouth with his own. She took in a quick breath, and felt her sorrow begin to dissolve, her body melt as the kiss deepened, lengthened. His hands grazed over the contours of her body, tender and knowing. She sank in his arms, willing, content to lose her awareness of the world, of all that troubled her, wanting only to be with him.

He pulled her close, his hand at the small of her back, so that her hips pressed into his and she swayed against him. A warm, exciting pulse stirred within her. She tilted her mouth under his and skimmed her hands up his back, beneath the plaid mantle, to his wide shoulders and the firmly muscled arms that held her.

He bent and slipped his arm beneath her, lifting her in a swirl of wool. He carried her to the sandstone slab in the corner of the room, setting her down in the shadows. Pulling the plaid from his shoulders, he swept it over the stone. She helped him arrange a padding, and she glanced up at him.

"I will never," she said, "carve this stone for you."

"Good," he said, bending over her. "We can put it to far better use." His hand was broad and strong on her back as he laid her down upon the stone. "If you would have it so."

"I would," she said, drawing him down beside her.

He kissed her deeply then, his lips caressing, his tongue seeking. She opened willingly to him and rolled more fully into his embrace. His hands skimmed, warm and sure, along her body, finding the curve of her hip, the swell of her breast. She sighed out with pleasure and arched her head back to rest it against the stone.

As his lips traced along her throat, she furrowed her fingers through his hair and leaned forward to kiss the shell of his ear. He flipped the single loop that closed the placket of her gray gown, while she pulled at his own clothing.

His breath misted between her breasts, a warm and wonderful sensation, and she sighed and shifted to welcome the sweet pressure of his mouth. She moaned softly as his hands cupped her breasts; she shivered as a deep throb stirred in her lower belly that she could not ease. Writhing, pressing against him, she kissed his shoulder and traced his ear with her tongue until he sought her lips again.

When she pulled insistently at his tunic, he stripped it off and rolled it to pillow her head. As he sank back down into her arms, she stroked her hands over his smooth, firm skin, the taut, muscular range of his back, the wide rib cage.

Her fingers gentled past the healing area on his side to touch the warm, hard contours of his belly, softened by the wedge of hair that arrowed under the waist of his *braies*. She pulled at the drawstring, and he groaned softly when she cupped him, when she stroked the hot, silken length she found there, discovering him as he explored her.

He traced his tongue over her breasts while he slowly slid her tunic up her legs. When she writhed and moaned, pulling at him, pressing against him, he hushed her and slowed her with long, luscious kisses, his hands firm and easy over her skin.

The night of their handfasting, she knew that they had fallen into each other's arms too fast, too impulsively. Now he loved her with languid heat, not gently, but surely, stripping her of her gown and chemise, wrapping her in the plaid with him.

He held her on the stone bed and cushioned her with

his taut body, warmed her with his breath. He kissed her bared shoulders, her arms, each finger coated in stone dust, smoothed back her hair from her brow, and hushed her again and again when she tried to urge him onward. Her yearning deepened with every caress, every kiss, until she was damp for him, until she shivered and pulled at him and cried out softly.

Wrapped in his embrace, surrounded by silence and peace, she lay back and let him love her, and felt time dissolve. The wind shushed against the window shutter, and the daylight that leaked through was silvery and cold. Beside the crackling brazier, Finan slept deeply, an oblivious and faithful guard.

Beneath Sebastien's lips and his fingers, she blossomed like a rose, turned and opened sweetly for him. When he knelt over her in a straddle and lifted her hips to meet his, she pushed upward, hungry for his thrusting strength, gasping when he filled her at last. Her fingers were tight on the edge of the stone, and she let go of her anchor and cried out in joy as a sensation streamed through her like a pure, bright flame. For a moment, for the space of a breath, she felt as if her spirit and his plaited together in an endless, beautiful pattern.

"I think," he whispered much later, his hand slow and sweet over her belly, "that we should try this in a bed."

"Tonight," she whispered, turning in his arms to seek his lips again, "after the stories, I would like to do that."

"If we can wait that long," he answered, and took her mouth with his once again.

She thought of those weeks as the time-between-times, and she did not want them to end. Neither she nor Sebastien talked about the feud, or of battles that might come, although she knew that he spoke of those matters with her kinsmen and with his own men. He spent long hours sitting with them in discussion. But he never mentioned what was said among them, and she did not ask.

When they were together, neither of them brought up the subject of battle, nor did they speak of plans to leave or to stay. Alone in her workshop, or walking beside the cold gray loch, or at night in each others' arms, they asked about each other, listening and telling stories about their adventures and incidents in childhood or as adults, but neither spoke of the future.

Here and now was all that existed, Alainna knew. Each moment moved into the next like beads sliding on a string.

During the days, they quickly found a routine. Each morning Alainna went to her workshop, for she wanted to make as much progress as she could on the stone carvings. Sebastien practiced his swordwork out in the bailey, or inside the hall when the weather was bitterly cold; she knew that he went slowly at that, for his muscles were still stiff and sore, but he soon gained his proficiency again with broadsword and claymore.

Later, every day, he spent time with her kinsmen, and with his own men and the three squires who were there like constant, quiet shadows. The men talked, practiced weapon skills, repaired equipment, and exercised the horses near the loch or in the bailey, for the weather did not permit them to ride out often to patrol the property.

Nearly every day, Sebastien joined Alainna in the workshop for a while, where he became a willing and capable apprentice. She taught him how to rough out her chalked designs, using an iron punch or a claw-toothed chisel and a mallet; she showed him how to use the various chisels to define areas of the relief carving, how to sand away roughness, how to polish, how to move the stones easily using wooden rollers for leverage so little lifting was needed.

His natural talent for drawing and design gave him an interest in the interlace patterns, and she taught him how to construct them using grids of squares and circles. Often, when she became absorbed in her own work, she would look up to see him drawing castle designs in chalk on cloth or on stone, while Finan snored happily at his feet.

Alainna cherished such moments of warmth and peace. She discovered that her interests and opinions were often similar to his, and found that they worked well together, sharing preferences for quiet and solitude, both capable of the discipline necessary to accomplish the tedious work of carving the stones. Harmony, respect, and quiet joy existed between them now.

Having given her word to him, she tried not to think about the spring, and the inevitable end of their time-be-tween-times. She thought only about now, each day like another golden link in a chain, each as beautiful, as pre-cious, as the rest.

When the days were done, the nights were filled with stories and music and laughter in the hall. Afterward, in the dark haven of her curtained bed, there were sweet, thunderous kisses and coming together like glove to hand, again and again, until she rocked with him in fervent, silent, hungry joy.

And each day, she looked out a window or over the palisade, glad to see the snow float down, glad to see a jewel coating of ice, or to hear the wind moan. Eventually she noticed that the snow had melted a little more, disap-pearing into the ground; the sun shone brighter and longer, and the first green shoots stirred through the bracken.

Even though the snow was still on the ground in cold pools, she felt her heart twist within her, and she turned away.

"There is an island far away that rises through the mist and shines in the sun," Lorne said. "And there are trees dropping heavy with fruit and blossoms, and there the berry-branches bow down. Rivers flow with honey and wine, and plains are wide and green. Mountains are high-crested with snow, fair and round as a woman's breasts."

Alainna slid a glance at Sebastien, who eased his hand over her back as she sat beside him on the bench. She stretched her back languidly beneath his soothing hand, and went on with her translation.

"And the ridges of the moors are purple and lovely, and the streams that flow through them sweet and mild. Weep-ing and treachery are unknown, and aging and illness are never seen. Music is ever light as it falls upon the ear, and the songs of birds and the golden strike of the harp string fill the silence in this many-colored land. This is the Land of Endless Youth, the Land of Promise. . . ."

Alainna paused when Lorne did, and closed her eyes with pleasure as she felt Sebastien slip his hand over hers, felt his thumb caress her hand, his touch warm and promising.

Too soon, she knew, they would leave the little island of time that they had created for themselves. Too soon, the snows would be gone, and spring would come.

"Tell me about the island out on the loch," Sebastien asked Ruari one day, as they walked together through the bailey.

"Out there?" Ruari looked at him in surprise. "It is a fine place, that isle. An old ruin is there, not much but a piling of ancient stones, though a few small rooms within its walls can still be made safe and warm." He smiled, his blue eyes crinkling.

"Safe enough to hide out, I know," Sebastien said, with a rueful chuckle. "Tell me about the isle itself. Is it large enough, solid enough, to support a stone castle?"

Sebastien walked beside Ruari to the earthen walk that ringed the inner palisade. They climbed up and stood looking over the speared timbers. The narrow loch seemed gray and dull as lead beneath the overcast sky, and the wind was high and damp. On the opposite shore, the Stone Maiden rose strong and solid against the sky.

The island in the middle of the loch was dark with bare trees, bracken, and rocks; at its center the strong, coarse outline of the old tower thrust up through a tangle of trees.

"It is a good isle, Sebastien *Bàn,*" Ruari said. "Quite large enough for a stone castle, I think."

"When the weather improves, I will row out and take a look at it. If it is a solid enough place, with no boggy ground and enough rock for a strong foundation, I may well build a castle there."

"Then you mean to stay here at Kinlochan," Ruari said.

Sebastien shrugged noncommittally. "I have orders from the king to plan a castle and organize its construction. I do not wish to tear this wooden fortress down, or to move a garrison in here while this place is remade into a stone castle. Another site must be chosen. The king awaits my report on that, and other matters."

"When you prepare your message to the king, will you take it to him yourself?"

"I do not intend to leave here just yet," he said. "I have a dispute to settle with Cormac first. I will ask Robert to take some knights with him and ride to Dunfermline to deliver my letter to the king. That report cannot wait longer."

"When you write to the king," Ruari asked slowly, "what will you tell him about the renegade and outlaw Ruari MacWilliam?"

Sebastien gazed out over the palisade, the wind whistling past his brow. "That man is dead, have you not heard? Dead, or in Ireland," he added.

"I did hear that rumor."

Sebastien glanced at him. "Why did you come back, knowing the danger? Knowing you would be hunted?"

Ruari stared out over the loch. "For Esa."

Sebastien fully understood the passion and need and love expressed in those two words. "What of the MacWilliam cause?"

"The rumors are only partly right," Ruari said. "I did not come back to the Highlands to gather support for my clan's cause. I have my own purpose." He glanced at Sebastien. "My son Iain, who is about Alainna's age, has been missing since the battle last year. That sadness sits heavy on my heart, and upon Esa. I have been making inquiries. I must learn if he is in fact dead, as they said, or if he is unable to send us word as I was."

Sebastien nodded, his throat constricting. "I understand."

"As for the rest, my cousin Guthred is young and high-tempered, skilled at fighting and at stirring others to fight, and many wish to support him for his heroics. But not I."

"You do not support him?"

"I do not encourage him. He would not be the best of kings, were he even able to gain the throne. I doubt that he can. The Celtic earls are against him, and always have been. He has little real influence, no personal wealth or education, no skills at negotiating with Normans and English and the clergy, as King William has. All he really has is a direct blood claim through Pictish descent. That is not enough."

"Many would disagree with you, thinking blood is all."

"Far more than old, proud blood is needed to make a good king or a good man."

Sebastien frowned, thinking how keenly that reflected upon his own background, his own heart. "Then you are loyal to the king."

"I am, and I always have been. But I am also loyal to my kinsmen and my clan, and so I have joined in this fight when necessary. What I want to do is bring my cousin Guthred around to a sensible position. But I think he will pursue this madness until he dies."

"Why then did you come back here, if not to gather support for your clan? If only for Esa, why did you talk to Cormac?" Sebastien looked at him sharply. "I know you saw him."

"I met with him, true," Ruari said. "He is loyal to the king, you know. He will not fight with Guthred when my kinsmen return here from Ireland. I do not know their plans for that, if you mean to ask me," he said quickly.

"Then what was your business with Cormac?" Sebastien asked.

"Inquiries about my son, first of all. And Cormac's father and I were comrades once," Ruari said. "I am not of Clan Laren, although my wife is. In the past, I was often the only link between these two feuding clans. I knew the desperate condition of Clan Laren, and the depth of the feud. I thought to forge a friendship with Cormac again, and to try to turn some good will toward my wife's kin."

Sebastien nodded. "Cormac seems grateful to you for saving his son's life."

Ruari shrugged. "Cormac can be grateful, and he can be loyal, but he is never to be trusted. Cormac serves his own needs first, before those of his clan. Keep that thought and you will do well with him."

"I will not forget it," Sebastien assured him. "I have already put in my report that while the man appears to be loyal to the crown, he will continue to disrupt this area if he is left unchecked."

Ruari nodded and looked up. "This weather will turn soon. Even now the snow is melting in the passes. Your riders can reach Dunfermline in a few days' time."

"I know," Sebastien answered. "Before they go, I must add one further note in my letter to the king."

"About Ruari MacWilliam?"

"It is possible the man is gone, as the rumors say. But I intend to emphasize to the king that Ruari *Mòr* was never a threat to the crown. Even if he is found, I will say, there is no need to pursue him or to arrest him."

Ruari stared out over the loch, and after a moment, nodded.

Chapter Twenty-nine

Sebastien stood in the bailey, the wind gentle upon his face. The feast day of Saint Brighid had dawned rosy and mild, brightening further as the morning progressed. He stood with the others in a circle, all of them wearing their finest garments. He wore chain mail beneath his green surcoat, with the dark green plaid wrapped over his shoulders for a mantle, and the wolfskin boots Alainna had given him wrapped tight with leather thongs. Standing quietly, he watched as Alainna entered the circle.

She looked like the blessing of spring itself, and he knew in that moment that he had never loved her more. As she strolled the inside of the ring, she stopped to murmur to each person in turn. Dressed simply in her gray tunic over a pale linen chemise, she wore a crown of white snowdrops and delicate violets on her unbound hair, which fell in a mass of rippled, coppery silk; her eyes were like bluebells, and her cheeks were flushed pink.

Sebastien knew that the day before the women had gone out to search for flowers newly budded in sunny, rocky crevices. Even though snow still coated much of the ground, the long grasses had begun to green again, and the women had returned with the snowdrops and violets.

They had spent the evening wrapping the blossoms into a wreath for Alainna to wear the following day, and then they had made small dolls from dried rushes, meant to be figures of Saint Brighid, the reeds woven in patterns that would bring good fortune. Sebastien smiled as he remembered their laughter as they decorated the dolls.

Alainna walked sunwise around the inner side of the circle and bowed her head before each person, murmuring a question and holding out her hands for the gifts they gave her.

"We each give something to the Maiden, you see," Una whispered to Sebastien, standing beside him. "Alainna accepts as Brighid, and as the Maiden. Later she will lay the offerings at the foot of the pillar stone."

Sebastien nodded. Alainna had told him about the gifting the evening before, and he had thought about what to contribute, knowing that it should be simple and meaningful. He watched as Alainna accepted each offering graciously: an apple from Beitris, a handful of nuts from Aenghus, a horseshoe from Lulach, a birch wand from Niall, and one of rowan from Ruari.

One of the young squires followed her with a basket to hold the things: a red thread, knotted and charmed, from Morag, a few carrots from Donal, a folded plaid from Esa, a white, polished stone from Giric.

Even the knights, a few of whom had remained after Robert and others had departed three days earlier, seemed to know what to do, Sebastien noticed. Richard gave her a silver coin and Etienne a handful of snowdrops to match those in her hair, and the other two, Walter and William, offered her pretty stones.

Then Alainna stood in front of Sebastien. She smiled up at him. "What will you give the Maiden?" she asked, as she had asked each one before him.

He reached out and took her chin in his hand, tipping her face toward him, and leaned down. He kissed her, gentle and lingering, on the lips. "My heart," he whispered, "to keep forever."

She looked at him in silence, her eyes blue and deep and filled with love. A pleased murmur ran through the circle of those who watched. Alainna smiled and moved past him. Una gave her a handful of oats tied in a cloth, and Lorne handed her a shining smoky crystal.

When she had circuited the group, she led the way toward the gate, which stood open. They followed in a procession, with the women behind her and the men after them, Sebastien, Lorne, and Giric falling naturally into the lead.

Light glistened on the surface of the loch, and the waves

drifted to shore in a slow cadence. They walked past the end of the loch and approached its opposite bank.

The gray granite pillar of the Stone Maiden stood tall and silvery in the early sunlight, as if polished for this day. Alainna approached the pillar, and the rest of them formed a wide ring around it. Sebastien watched as Alainna went, with the slender young squire behind her, to lay the offerings at the foot of the pillar. Then the squire ran back to join his comrades, and Alainna faced the great stone, chisel and mallet in her hand.

She circled sunwise around the stone, and Sebastien heard her voice lift in a softly chanted list of names.

"She recites the genealogy of Saint Brighid," Una told Sebastien as he leaned down toward the old woman. "Then she will say the genealogy of Alainna of Kinlochan, the maiden caught within the stone. Now, hear, she offers a charm to Brighid, and to the Maiden who protects this clan."

Alainna stepped around to face the stone, head lifted. "Brighid of the mantles, Mary mild, and Alainna the Maiden, the nine pure graces are yours, gifts of the angels who shield us always." She bowed her head as if waiting, then continued.

> *Be the bright flame before us*
> *Be the guiding star above us*
> *Be the smooth path beneath us*
> *Today, tonight, and forever.*

She knelt and smoothed her hand over the row of lines engraved in the stone like the embroidered hem of a gown. Angling the chisel at the end of the row, she struck the tool with the mallet, and struck again, until another mark appeared in the face of the stone. Once more she swept her hand over the granite, as if to soothe the wound. Then she rose to her feet and turned, bathed in a stream of thin sunlight.

"We thank the faeries who protected our Maiden, and we thank Alainna the Maiden for watching over her people. The spell is ended," she said. "The Maiden is free."

The circle of people stood quietly, as if waiting. Alainna

stood like a slim, beautiful pillar herself, while the breeze sifted through the bright strands of her hair.

Sebastien could not take his gaze from her. He caught his breath inwardly as a subtle, powerful force moved through him. He felt as if the last stone in the wall surrounding his heart shifted and fell away. Alainna turned her head and her gaze touched his, and he held it gently, knowing that she was part of him, and he of her.

He knew, too, that he must leave her soon, as they had implicitly agreed he would do. Spring had come, and the time-between-times was ended, and decisions must be made.

He had a young son, alone and small, who needed him more than this strong, beautiful woman needed him, more than these proud, loving people needed him. His going would break the bond of their handfasting, and break his heart and hers, he knew, but he had to leave.

He desperately wanted to return to her, but one decision remained. Although he told himself that the issue of the name did not matter, he was not able to abandon his name and his identity so easily. His pride was still strong in what he had gained for himself, in who he was.

Loving Alainna had challenged every part of him, down to the bedrock of his soul. But carving a new identity for himself was not so easily done.

He saw a haunting sadness in her eyes as she looked at him. Then she walked away from the stone and through the circle, and the people turned to follow her. Sebastien fell into step with Lorne and Ruari, and glanced up at the hills surrounding the loch.

He halted and held up a hand to the men closest to him. Ruari, Lorne, and Giric stopped. "We are not the only ones who have come to see the last mark made in the Stone Maiden," he said. "Look."

At the top of a long hill that overlooked the loch, a host of men stood, plaids and braids blowing in the breeze. Cormac, his brother, Struan, and nearly forty MacNechtans watched them, still and menacing. Then they began to walk down the hill.

The MacNechtans had no women among them, as Clan Laren did, Sebastien noted; they had not come to watch the ceremony. Armed, grim, and glaring, they were prepared for battle.

Near Sebastien, the others turned, and gasps rippled among them. The small gathering parted as Alainna walked past them to meet the MacNechtans.

Reaching out, Sebastien took Alainna's arm. "Be wary," he said. "They do not come here seeking peace."

"They might," she said. "The chief of Clan Laren and the chief of Clan Nechtan have always met on the day of the marking of the Maiden. It is part of the tradition. Truces have been declared then, and our clans have had periods of peace in the past. This is the day the old spell ends. It is the right time to begin a new era for our clans."

"That may be the tradition, but you cannot trust this man," he said. "Alainna, stay back. It is not safe for you to do this. Let me negotiate with him."

"You," she said, "have no interest in negotiating with him."

He frowned. She turned, and he strode beside her as she went toward the MacNechtans, who halted at the foot of the hill. Alainna paused, facing Cormac in the open middle area.

Sebastien stood with his hand on the hilt of his sword, a silent and alert guard. Cormac glowered at him. Sebastien returned a flat, even stare.

"Cormac MacNechtan," Alainna said. "I ask you formally, before all, as is custom on the day of the marking of the stone, if you will agree to peace between us. The deaths of the Maiden and of the first Nechtan have been avenged over and over, to ten times a thousand. You and I can end this long and bitter and pointless feud, and put forth forgiveness."

"I do not ask your forgiveness," Cormac said brusquely. "I do not offer you mine. I came here to talk of more important matters than forgiveness."

"What, then?" Alainna asked.

"The power of the Stone Maiden has ended. I have long waited for this day. Your protection is at an end."

"Her protection continues," Sebastien said curtly.

Cormac laughed harshly. "A few knights sent by the king?"

"A husband," Sebastien drawled. He knew, with a powerful and certain conviction, that the vows he had taken with Alainna had bound him to her, and her to him. Nothing could undo that. His heart pounded hard as he faced Cormac, and as he felt Alainna's gaze, soft and wondering, upon him.

"Husband!" Cormac barked. "You!"

"I told you that I would choose," Alainna said quickly. "It is done. You cannot claim Kinlochan, or me."

Cormac's face flushed dark and his eyes glittered. "A husband is only a barrier so long as he is alive."

Sebastien tensed, ready to pull his weapon, but he stared calmly at Cormac. "You have no more dispute with these people. Take your men and go, or stay and fight me alone. Either way, you will never gain what you want here."

Cormac grinned slowly. "I have forty strong men at my back, and you have a handful of knights, with old men and old women."

"Would you fight elders?" Alainna asked, her cheeks flushed with anger. "Your father would never have done that, or his father and kinsmen before him."

"Tell the old ones to go home," Cormac said curtly. "I will not fight them. My dispute is with the Norman, doubly so now that he has taken my rightful place as your husband." He looked at Sebastien with narrowed eyes. "And I see you found Ruari MacWilliam. I came here to escort him to the crown myself, since you neglected to do it."

"MacWilliam is no threat to the crown," Sebastien said.

Cormac looked at Alainna. "You are the chief here, not this one. Your kinsman Ruari is a traitor. Will you witness a battle now, in front of your Stone Maiden, or will you order MacWilliam to come with me and face king's justice?"

"Ruari is no traitor," Alainna said. "He will stay here."

"Fine," Cormac bit out. "I will see all of your kinsmen killed this day, and your husband, too. This can only gain me what I want. Else give me the traitor, and avoid the bloodshed. Decide, girl!" he ordered. He grabbed the handle of his dirk. Behind him, his men stepped forward.

Sebastien slithered his sword free with the swift whooshing sound of steel drawn from leather. "Tell your men to stand down. This is between you and me, and no one else. Alainna, get back," he warned.

She turned. Sebastien watched with a sense of slowed time as she whirled, and her hair spun out behind her.

Quick as a snake's strike, Cormac leaned forward and snatched a handful of her abundant hair. He yanked her toward him so fast that she cried out and stumbled backward. In that flashing instant, Sebastien had no chance to grab her or to use his sword before Cormac swooped his long dirk blade under her chin.

She was within arm's grasp, but the steel edge at her throat changed all. Sebastien could not pull her back at the risk of her life. Cormac held her in a fierce grip and glared at him over the top of her head.

"Now," he said, "I will have what I want."

"Let her go," Sebastien rasped, waving his sword lightly, menacingly, in the air. "Your dispute is with me, not her."

"Tell the elders to get back," Cormac hissed.

Behind Sebastien, every man had stepped forward, Lorne, Ruari, and Giric in the lead. Sebastien held up a hand in command, and they halted.

Alainna pulled at Cormac's arm. "Let me go," she gasped.

"First I will get what I want of this," Cormac said. "Mac-William! Put yourself into the custody of my brother, Struan. We will ride to Dunfermline today."

Sebastien put up a hand toward Ruari. "Do not," he growled.

"Ruari, do not," Alainna echoed. She dragged on Cormac's arm, tight around her throat.

Lorne came toward Cormac and faced him. "Let the girl go."

"She is my hostage and my prize," Cormac said.

"Listen, now," Lorne said. "What Alainna said is right. The whole of your kinsmen, from your father to his father, to the great Aodh son of Conn, and back to Nechtan of the Battles, not one of them, fine men all, would do what you do today. Make them proud, and let her go."

"Be gone from here, bard," Cormac said. "You are no warrior to interfere in this. She is chief of her clan, and my hostage, and I want payment. Stand back."

"Cormac," Lorne said. "Remember what happened on the banks of this loch seven hundred years ago this day, so the legend goes. A man of Clan Nechtan harmed a woman of Clan Laren. Would you begin the feud again?"

Cormac gaped, then frowned. "There are no faeries here to curse us," he said, but Sebastien heard the doubt in his voice.

"There are," Lorne said. He moved closer, his voice deep and resonant. "They are always about, though we cannot see them. They watch us even now. Let the woman of Clan Laren go, and they will thank you. Hold her, and you will anger them, and endanger your clan for another seven hundred years."

Cormac stepped back, pulling Alainna with him. "The spell is ended for the Stone Maiden and for my clan!"

"Then why invite the curse again?" Lorne moved forward, still reaching out. "The magic is powerful, Cormac MacNechtan, and well you know it. Let her go now, and spare generations of your kin the sorrow of more feuding."

Cormac stared at him. Calmly, surely, Lorne took Alainna's hand. Sebastien tensed, ready to strike, and watched in amazement as Cormac loosened his grip. Alainna moved toward Lorne, hands outstretched.

Then Cormac bellowed a protest, as if realizing what he had done. He lunged to reclaim Alainna. She screamed and fell upon Lorne when Cormac leaped at her. Lorne turned with her, and Sebastien whirled, grabbing Alainna's arm to pull her out of the way. He stepped between her and Cormac.

In that instant, he saw Lorne crumple to his knees, his chest bright with blood, saw the glistening red tip of Cormac's dirk. Lorne fell forward, and Alainna cried out and dropped to her knees beside him.

Sebastien felt a deep, sudden wrench of anguish. He lunged toward Cormac, who stumbled backward.

"*You!*" Sebastien roared, pointing at Cormac with the tip of his extended sword. "You and I have a dispute, and no one else! Your men stay back, and my men stay back! We will settle this here and now!"

He strode in a sunwise circle around Cormac as he shouted. Anger surged through him like fire, like some dark magic, giving him a power and purpose and fury unlike anything he had ever felt before.

He tipped the blade to the earth and stood, feet planted apart, glowering at Cormac. "Here and now! A fair combat, without treachery, with no other lives put at risk!"

Chapter Thirty

"Here and now, then," Cormac answered, breath heaving. He glanced back at his kinsmen. Struan came forward with a claymore, which Cormac snatched by the great hilt. "Remove your armor, Norman. I have no such protection. A Highland man needs nothing but his *claidheamh mòr* and his will."

With fast, furious movements, Sebastien unlatched the thongs that tied his chain mail hood to the hauberk, stripped off his plaid mantle, sword belt, and green surcoat, and flung them aside. Etienne and Giric came over to help him tug free of the heavy, long-sleeved chain mail hauberk and the padded gambeson beneath it. He rebuckled the sword belt over his brown serge tunic, feeling lighter, stronger, more capable.

As he turned to face Cormac, he saw Alainna kneeling beside Lorne. Una bent over her husband as Esa and Morag quickly bandaged Lorne's chest.

Sebastien did not know if Lorne was alive or dead, but the wide, dark stain on the old man's shirt and the limp sag of his noble head alarmed him. His own heart nearly stopped then.

Alainna stared up at him, her face pale, her eyes filled with fear. He held her gaze steadily, then turned away.

Without a word, he led Cormac to the level, grassy turf that spread between the Stone Maiden and the stony beach. A crowd gathered in a wide circle around them, the pillar towering over all like a calm giantess.

Alainna remained with Lorne and the women. Once the ring of onlookers closed up, Sebastien could no longer see her.

Cormac circled him, dragging the point of the claymore

on the ground, his gaze dark and angry. Sebastien spun warily, his heartbeat strong in his own ears, his balance shifting from one foot to the other.

With a sudden roar, Cormac rushed toward him, lifting the huge sword over his head, slashing it downward. Easily sidestepping him, Sebastien turned while Cormac regained his balance and whirled to strike again. He could see from those wide, wild blows that Cormac's skill was less than the man's strength and his rage, which were considerable.

Sebastien caught the blade with his own steel edge, the impact jarring him. He shoved, then dipped low and skimmed sideways as Cormac brought the blade around to lash at him again.

Circling slowly, Sebastien noted that the Highlander was like a bull or a boar; large, fierce, determined, armed with a mighty weapon, he lacked finesse and cleverness. For all that, Cormac was not a fool. Sebastien saw the calculating look in his dark eyes.

The claymore had a longer reach than his own blade, and its heavier blows could do more damage to flesh and bone. Cormac wielded it with hacking strength, striking relentlessly. The one-handed, shorter broadsword gave Sebastien the advantage of a weapon that was easier to handle. He was leaner and more agile, better able to turn and dance away, continually avoiding the savage bite of the larger blade. That only made Cormac angrier, and increased the force and frequency of his blows.

The sound of steel ringing hard on steel was deafening, the slamming tremors along his arm and hand numbing, and the breath burned in his throat and lungs. Sebastien fought on, advancing, circling, lunging, blocking, as he had done so many times here.

He knew the ground around the Stone Maiden, knew its dips and runnels and rises. On more than one pass, he scarcely had to look to avoid a small tufted hollow in the earth that could have caught his foot. By instinct he kept his back to the sun where the morning light angled across the loch. Cormac repeatedly squinted as the light flared on the water, and Sebastien led him into that position again and again.

Every move he made had an eerie familiarity, as if he

had practiced for this very challenge many times. A strange sense of calm and confidence filled him. He let go of thought, let his ability and his cool, hard rage take over the task of fighting.

He saw an opening and made a lightning strike that caught Cormac's arm and sent a spray of blood over both of them. Cormac faltered, and Sebastien's downward stroke sliced into his opponent's iron-hewn thigh. Cormac, chillingly undisturbed by the injuries, raised his sword and brought it down in a move that, had Sebastien not shuffled aside, would have broken his skull.

Cormac wheeled and brought the claymore in a wide arc. As Sebastien parried on a downward swing, the tip of his blade touched earth. Cormac struck into the blade, snapping it neatly.

Lifting his broken weapon, Sebastien stepped backward, breath heaving, watching Cormac's grinning advance. He ducked to avoid the swing of the claymore, rolled over the ground and lay on his back, knees raised, about to spring up as Cormac lunged at him with a roar.

Someone shouted his name, and a sharp and shining edge appeared near his foot. He scooped up the long hilt of the claymore that slid toward him, and straightened to his feet. Now he held a blade the equal of the other, with a skill that was far superior. He hoped that would be enough, for Cormac was a relentless opponent; he never even saw him pause to breathe.

Accustomed by his practices to the weight and length of the claymore, Sebastien wrapped two hands around the cold leather hilt and felt a surge of power and assurance. He spared no thought for Lorne or Alainna, but he felt their presences nearby, and he felt his own anger flare brighter on their behalf. He advanced with cool control, his gaze steady as a rock, his fury a torch. Cormac retreated, weapon waving.

Sebastien created a wicked pattern of forceful, rapid looping strokes, punctuated with blow after blow against steel. Cormac backed away, slashing repeatedly as he went, his blows falling short, his thrusts weakening.

Sebastien blocked every strike, every arc, his muscles burning, aching, his inner core white hot with purpose. The

healing wound in his side pulled and ached, but did not
deter him. Neither did he feel any hindrance from the scar
along his left eyelid, for fighting with claymores required
brute strength and wide, sweeping blows, honest and bold,
without subtlety.

They neared the granite pillar, and the crowd moved
back. Cormac howled and lunged, and Sebastien skipped
away, bringing the flat of his sword smacking against Cormac's uplifted blade.

The angle was awkward, and Sebastien could not hold
Cormac's blade at bay for long before it began to force his
downward. He stumbled back, and his heel struck the stone
pillar. Arms uplifting, body straining to keep the opposing
blade from severing a limb, he leaned his shoulders against
cold, massive granite.

Cormac's claymore pressed down on his own, until he
could smell cold steel inches from his face, and felt the
smooth skin of the stone along his back. He strained, still
resisting, and drew a breath, determined not to surrender.
Then, on the next inhale, a sense of new strength surged
through him, as if the Maiden herself breathed her power
into him.

He pushed outward almost easily, forcing Cormac back,
and stepped sideways, skimming his shoulders along the
stone to slide out from under Cormac's pressing advance.

The Highlander overbalanced and stumbled against the
face of the stone, pushing off in an effort to whirl. Sebastien
waited, ready, blade upright, feet widely planted.

Cormac lunged like a roaring, raging boar, head down,
blade outstretched. Sebastien took the brunt on the flat of
the sword and threw Cormac backward again. The other
man fell back, his foot catching in the same hollow that
Sebastien had avoided before, and went down.

His head slammed into the pillar stone with such staggering force that Sebastien knew, even before Cormac
slumped to the ground, that he was dead.

Breath heaving painfully in his chest, he leaned on the
sword planted upright in the earth. No one moved, and he
did not look at them. The silence was as deafening as the
ringing of steel had been just moments before.

He swiped his forearm across his sweat-coated face and

wrenched the great sword out of the ground, then turned to walk away. The crowd parted at his approach, some of them drifting toward Cormac. He saw Struan and the other MacNechtans go to their fallen kinsman, but he did not stop to speak to them, nor did they stop him, though their expressions were dark and troubled.

He looked up. Alainna stood alone, straight as a pillar, head high, watching him. He did not know when she had left her post beside Lorne, but he knew, from the deep, haunted blue of her eyes, that she had seen much of the struggle.

Then she ran to him, crying out. He lifted an arm and gathered her in, her body firm and warm against his, her hair like a cloud beneath his cheek. A soft kiss on his mouth and the brush of her hands were a balm for every ache and sorrow he had ever had. He held her close and squeezed his eyes shut as they stood, motionless and silent.

He pulled back. "Lorne?" he asked apprehensively.

"He is alive, but *ach,* I do not know how much longer he will survive. We are afraid to move him—"

He let go of her and strode toward the figures huddled on the ground. Dropping to one knee beside the old man, he laid his sword flat on the earth. Alainna knelt beside him. He looked at Una, with her worried eyes and small, trembling head, and at Morag and Esa, flanking her like two angels wrapped in plaids.

Lorne opened his eyes. Relief rushed through Sebastien to see that keen blue gaze turn toward him.

"Is he gone?" Lorne rasped.

Sebastien nodded. "Gone. Dead."

"Good." Lorne closed his eyes. "And I will follow him."

"You will not, old man," Una said.

"Make my bed, woman, and sing my dirge," Lorne said. Una shook her head and grasped his hand.

Sebastien glanced at Alainna. Her gaze met his, wide and needing, and he wanted to wrap his arms around her. Instead, he put out a hand, and she took it quickly, fervently.

Lorne plucked Sebastien's sleeve. "I heard the ring of steel," he said. "It was a good sound."

"It was a good fight," Lulach said, dropping to his knees beside Lorne. Niall was with him, and leaned forward too.

"Sebastien *Bàn* has defeated our enemy's leader, as we wanted him to do when he came here," Niall said.

"I knew he would," Lorne said. More people gathered around, their bare calves and skirt hems wreathing him where he lay, with Sebastien and a few others closest beside him. "I knew he was the warrior we needed most. The one Alainna needed most."

"Hush," Alainna said. "Save your breath."

"Sebastien will not stay with us, now that our enemy is defeated," Niall said. "He has duties elsewhere."

"But this is his home," Lorne said.

Sebastien rested his hand over Lorne's, unable to speak for the tightness in his throat. When Lorne pulled on his sleeve, Sebastien leaned toward him.

"Sebastien *Bàn*," he said, "you remind me of my son—golden and strong, brave."

Sebastien squeezed his eyes shut for a moment. "My thanks."

"A good Highland man," Lorne said.

He swallowed hard, began to shake his head in denial, then smiled ruefully. "One day, perhaps."

"A good day for Clan Laren, that will be." Lorne smiled a little, and a pale light glimmered in his eyes.

Such love swelled in Sebastien in that moment that he felt as if he would do anything for this man, sacrifice anything—his pride, his name, his life itself, to save him. Nothing was too precious to give up, if the bard could live on.

"We must take him inside," Una said, looking at Sebastien.

He nodded and fetched his plaid, discarded on the ground, which he folded to form a hammock. Many hands joined to lift Lorne gently to the plaid, and several men prepared to hoist it. As Sebastien took a fistful of the cloth himself, Alainna stopped him.

"They want to speak with you," she said, and pointed at Struan MacNechtan and his kinsmen.

He nodded grimly. He bent to grab the claymore from the ground and straightened. Giric, Ruari, Etienne and a few others followed him.

Struan waited, his brown eyes stormy beneath russet

brows. He crossed his arms over his chest. "My brother is dead."

"I am sorry for it." Sebastien planted the sword upright in the earth and gripped the hilt. "The combat was fair."

"It was." Struan glanced at his kinsmen. "Hostaging a woman and attacking an old bard was a great dishonor for Cormac, and for the whole of our clan. That should not have happened, but it did. My brother was ever filled with anger that not all of us shared. What he brought upon himself was only justice."

Sebastien watched him steadily, his hand on the hilt of his sword. "This day ended the ancient spell that has threatened your clan for generations. It is a day that should end the feud, not begin a new one."

Struan glanced again at his kinsmen, then turned back to Sebastien. "That may be," he said. "For now, we will not fight you. There has been one death already, and there may yet be another. We will bury my brother, and decide among ourselves what shall be done."

"Will you lead your clan now?" Sebastien asked.

"Until Cormac's son, Eoghan, is old enough, I will."

Sebastien nodded. "I have hope for the future of Clan Nechtan. I sense in you a fair man, Struan."

"And I see one in you. Know this," he said sternly. "My brother invited his own death with every action he took, over many years, against Clan Laren. As that clan grew weaker, he thought himself stronger. We cautioned him against this, but he was our chief, and so we followed him. It was fitting, his death." He looked intently at Sebastien. "Your hand did not take his life," he added. "I saw it. The Maiden took his life. Her power is still strong. We are not so foolish as to dismiss that."

"Then heed it well," Sebastien said.

Struan frowned, then pivoted abruptly and gestured to his men. They went to the stone pillar to collect Cormac's body.

Sebastien turned. The others had gathered round Lorne in the hammocked plaid, and he hurried to join them.

Alainna took the claymore from him, hoisting its weight in her hands. The men had left a place for Sebastien at a front corner of the litter. He lifted in tandem with his comrades, feeling how light the burden, how easily they moved together. He was proud to walk among them.

Alainna fell into step beside him. They moved past the tall and silent presence of the Stone Maiden, through the long shadow cast over the meadow that edged the loch. As they headed toward the rocky slope that led to the fortress of Kinlochan, the entire clan began a low, melodious chant.

> *I am weary, and I a stranger,*
> *Lead me to the land of angels.*
> *Be my eyes in time of darkness,*
> *Be my shield against hosts of faery,*
> *Be my wings till I find my home.*

Listening, Sebastien felt his heart wrench. He had been a stranger here once, but he was a stranger no longer. This was home to him. He knew that now with the fullness of his heart.

He loved these people, loved the old man carried on his own plaid as if the man were the father he had never known. Tears stung his eyes, and he blinked them away.

He glanced at Alainna. She walked beside him, carrying his sword, her hair spilling around her like a hearth fire, her eyes bright like a summer sky. What welled in him then had the solidity of rock, the purity of fire. He loved her more than he had ever loved anyone, more than he loved his own life.

More than he valued his own pride, his own name.

The love he felt for her calmed him, stirred him, made him a finer man than he had ever been. A thousand strands tied him to her, to her kin, to this place.

Yet the pattern was not complete. He felt a longing still in his heart, a deep aching. If he could find the last missing strand and enter it into the weave, he would be a part of this place forever.

Chapter Thirty-one

The rain began in the night while they kept a vigil for Lorne with prayers and healing chants. Alainna sat with Una and the others in a bedchamber on the uppermost floor of the tower, which Una and Lorne shared.

Sebastien was there, too, a golden strength, his voice calm, his hand kind as he offered help to Alainna or Una, as he sat with the old bard, talking, or watching him sleep.

Alainna had little chance to speak to Sebastien alone, but she cherished their casual words, the smiles, and gentle brushing touches. Despite the tension of those hours, she felt a peacefulness when he was there, and a yearning when he was not.

She saw his concern for Lorne in his gray eyes, saw the downturn of his mouth and the creased brow. Wanting to smooth them away, kiss them away, she left him alone. She sensed a distancing within him, a need for solitude that she understood, for she was the same way.

Later, as dawn approached and the rain drummed hard on the roof and the outside walls, she went down to the hall to sit with the others. Giric and Ruari played chess while Niall and Lulach watched. Beitris sat winding thread on a spindle. Donal, Aenghus, the knights and squires had gone to rest on their pallets.

Sebastien stood by the doorway, looking out at the rain, his brow furrowed in thought. Finan stood beside him, his head lifted beneath the man's hand.

Alainna watched Beitris cut three strands of red yarn and weave them into a pattern of nine knots, chanting prayers of healing as her fingers flew in a rhythm. Alainna knew that Beitris, like each of them in their way, was calling back Lorne's soul. None of them would let him go.

Dawn came, silvery through the rain, and Una descended the steps. Alainna looked up. Her great-aunt appeared old and frail, her hair white as down, the tremor in her head like the shaking of a flower.

Una smiled and sat beside Alainna. "He is well enough, at last," she said. "And he will heal, I think." And she put her head in her hands and began to cry.

Alainna reached out and embraced her. Then she looked up toward Sebastien, who had turned by the door. She saw the gleam of great emotion in his eyes, and his gaze held hers for a long moment.

She wanted so desperately to go to him, to feel his arms surround her, to sink into the love she felt for him. But Una sobbed, and she bowed her head to comfort her.

And when she lifted her head again, he was gone.

She felt that loss, and felt a weariness. She longed to go after him, but Una needed her, and she was not certain that Sebastien did.

A hand touched her shoulder, and she looked up to see Esa.

"Go to him," Esa said. "I saw from the window. He has taken his horse and gone to the gate. Go to him. Do not let him leave. He is the friend of your soul, and you of his. That bond must not be broken."

Alainna rose and ran to the door. She pulled the door open and flew down the wooden steps to the bailey. Finan went with her as she crossed the rain-soaked yard.

The gate was open, and he was not there. Rain poured down in a steady patter. She sped through the gate, with raindrops streaming over her face, and saw the deserted slope, the loch roughened in the rain, the Stone Maiden, solitary and mysterious on the opposite shore, with the grass beginning to green around the base.

She stood in the gate and waited. But he was gone, and he had not said farewell. She thought of another time when she stood in the open gate waiting for him in freezing veils of snow. Now she stood enveloped and soaked by fine sheets of rain. And he did not appear, as she hoped he would.

She stood there with the dog, both drenched. After a while, she pulled the upper part of her *arisaid* over her head, a futile gesture, for the wool was just as wet as she was.

Finally, she sobbed heavily and covered her wet face. The deerhound pressed his shoulder against her hip as if to offer her his comfort and his simple strength.

He rode the Arabian through the rain across the wet meadow, hoofbeats thumping on wet ground. The plaid he wore tossed over his tunic protected him surprisingly well from the downpour, and he pulled part of it over his head like a hood. Ahead of him was the small group of horsemen that he had sighted from the tower. Even from a distance he could tell that they wore armor and carried the banner of the king. He had ridden out here to meet them and to learn their business.

As he drew nearer, he recognized Robert, and waved, calling out. His friend waved in turn and rode forward.

"Robert!" Sebastien cried, reining in his horse when Robert did, facing him across a torrent of rain, raising his voice to be heard above the patter. "What brings you back here so soon? I thought you would stay in Dunfermline! Is there word back from King William?"

"Word from William, aye," Robert answered. "And more. When we reached Dunfermline, there was word already there for you from the duke of Brittany."

"The duke!" Sebastien said. Alarm went through him. "Does he summon us back into his service?"

"He is content to let us stay in the service of King William," Robert said. "Duke Conan sent a reply to the king's letter regarding the welfare and whereabouts of your son."

"Word of my son!" Sebastien leaned forward, easing the restless Arabian in a slight turn. "Where is the letter?" He extended his hand through the rain.

Robert smiled and pointed. "There," he said. "A small package sent to you from the duke. His own namesake."

Sebastien turned. Three other riders came toward him. One of them, a monk, supported a child in front of him, wrapped in a fur-lined mantle.

He stared, heart pounding. Then he leaped down from his horse and ran forward. The monk stopped his horse and waited, opening the cloak so that Sebastien could see the small, oval face shadowed within, the wide brown eyes, the glossy silk of pale golden hair.

"Conan," he breathed, reaching up. "Conan."

"Papa," his son said, and went easily into Sebastien's arms.

The rain drummed on the earth, soaking her shoes, splashing mud on the hem of her skirt. Alainna shivered and touched Finan's head, his wet coat darkened to iron gray, his eyes mournful beneath the tufted brow as he looked at her.

She turned away from the gate. She had known that Sebastien had to go, but she had never imagined he would go so soon, without a farewell. Once he had learned that Lorne would recover, he had left quietly. Perhaps he had not wanted to break her heart.

But he had done just that.

She walked away, and the dog barked. "Come, Finan *Mòr,*" she said. "I am sorry to keep you out here. Come, now." She beckoned to him and walked ahead.

Finan barked again, then whined. He nosed at her arm. She grabbed his collar and pulled. He set his feet into the mud and refused to go, barking again.

Then she heard the thunder of horses' hooves, and looked up. Four riders came through the gate, one of them leading a creamy, riderless Arabian. She ran forward, alarmed, knowing Sebastien's horse, and knowing the leader. "Robert!" she called.

He dismounted and turned. "My lady," he said, smiling. "We are back from Dunfermline." Behind him, she noted three cloaked men, one of them holding a large bundle. She nodded toward them, and hardly looked further. Sebastien was not among them.

"Sebastien," she said to Robert. "You have his horse! Where is he?"

"He will be here," he said simply. "May we go into the stables, and then to the hall?" He smiled as he spoke, and she looked at him, puzzled.

"Please," she said wearily, "go inside and get warm and dry. I will wait for Sebastien." She turned toward the gate, and stopped in surprise.

A man stood in the rain outside the gate. A Highland man, dressed in a *breacan,* without a horse. The rain soaked his hair from gold to dark brown, drenched the wrapped and belted plaid and the shirt beneath it, soaked the hide of the wolfskin boots.

She stared at him, speechless.

"A thousand blessings on you," he said in Gaelic in formal greeting. "May God make smooth the path before you."

"A . . . a thousand blessings on you," she said in return, taking a step closer. "May you be safe from every harm."

Sebastien took a step closer, too, but did not cross the threshold of the open gate. "Long ago," he said, "a beautiful woman once came to a king's court. And the lady asked a favor of the king."

Alainna tilted her head, listening, her heart beating hard within her breast. "And what did she ask?"

"She asked the king to send her a warrior," he answered. "A fine Celtic warrior, she wanted. A man whose lineage was as ancient as her own, a man of compassion and courage, a man to defeat her clan's enemy."

"Ah," she said. "She wanted an exemplary warrior."

"She did," he agreed. "She asked that the king find a warrior who could speak the Gaelic, and who could travel to her home from his own lands within a day's time."

She fisted her hands against her hips. "And what happened, then, to this woman? Did she find her warrior?"

"He came to her," he said. "Dressed in fine Highland style . . . though he was wet as a pup in a bath," he added, "for the spring rains arrived with him. He walked to her fortress from his own lands within a moment's time, for his lands encompassed her own. And he spoke the Gaelic to her as best he could—which was rather well, actually." He smiled, while the rain ran down his cheeks, dripped from his chin, soaked his hair.

She pressed back her own smile. "And was he a man with heart and courage?" she asked, stepping closer. Finan went with her, panting and whining, longing in his way for the man's love and devotion, as she yearned in hers.

"He was," he said, "although the woman, who was finer

than the moon and brighter than the sun to him, challenged
him to be a better man than he had been before."

She choked back a sob. "And what of his lineage, which
the woman so foolishly asked, though it did not matter?"

"He was from a land of ancient Celts himself, though it
was far from her own land," he said. "It was the best lineage he could offer her, and he hoped she would accept it."

"I am sure she thought it an excellent heritage."

"He defeated her enemy," he went on. "Though his
heart nearly burst within him, he did that for her. And for
her kin as well, whom he loved like his own family."

Alainna felt tears well and overflow as she watched him,
adoring him. Tears mixed with the rain that poured over
her, over him, and over Finan, who circled between them
now, confused but happy.

"There was one other condition she gave," he said. "And
that was the hardest one of all."

Her heart surged within her. "What was that?" she
asked, breathless.

"A name. She wanted to gift her warrior with her name.
But he refused out of great pride, for he liked his own
name well."

"Ah," she answered. "And what happened then?"

"He came to her—in the rain," he added. "And he offered a trade. He would take her name, and carry it into
the future as she wanted him to, through their sons and
daughters. But she must take something of his in return."

The rain streamed down, and the thin light bloomed
brighter as they faced each other across the threshold of
the gate.

"What was that?" she asked.

"His heart."

Her own heart leaped within her, and she smiled, stepping closer. He took a long stride, and she stood face-to-
face with him, breast to chest, a delicate layer of rain between them.

"A name," she said, "is not so valuable as a heart. She
got the better part of the bargain."

He bent his head, and she tipped her face to him. Drops
of rain jeweled his eyelashes, and funneled from his hair

to fall onto her cheeks. "The bargain could be made more equal," he said. "She could give him her heart in return."

"She could." Alainna smiled up into his eyes, gray and soft as the rain. "A heart for a heart. What then, for the name?"

"Ah, well. He could give her a child to carry the name."

She threw her arms around his neck and clung to him, her lips under his. He took her into his embrace, his hands firm and strong at her back, his mouth wet and cool, warm within.

He pulled back to look at her, smiling. "Well? Do you want a husband, lady, as well as a warrior?"

"I do," she said, laughing, her arms looped around him, her body pressed to him. "Do you want a Highland wife?"

"I do," he said, and kissed her again, deep and full and endless. The dog circled them, barking. Sebastien chuckled against her mouth and drew back again.

"Alainna, *mo càran,* will you let a man in out of the rain?"

She laughed again and pulled him inside the gate. His arm was strong and warm about her as they walked toward the tower, where the light of torches showed within, and the sound of laughter drifted through the open door.

At the foot of the steps, when she would have climbed up, he stopped her. "There is something more the warrior brought to the woman," he said. He reached out and brushed the wet tendrils of her hair away from her brow.

"What was that?" she asked.

"A son," he said. "His own."

"Conan?" she breathed.

He nodded, then looked up the steps and smiled, and she saw the silver flash of deep love in his eyes. But it was not for her this time.

She followed his gaze. Just inside the open door, Una and Giric stood with a small boy standing between them, his hands in theirs. His eyes were dark and beautiful, his hair fine spun gold.

She gasped, and Sebastien tightened his arm around her. "Robert brought him back," he murmured. "Come up, *mo càran,* for the rain is cold. Come inside where the hearth is warm, and meet the youngest member of Clan Laren."

She placed her foot upon the step beside his, and they moved upward together.

Epilogue

"Is it time to go across the loch yet?" Conan asked in Gaelic, looking up at his father. Sebastien smiled, thankful that his son had a gift for language, for Conan had learned almost as much Gaelic in a few months at Kinlochan as Sebastien had learned in three years at the king's court. "I want to walk on the new path that the men made to the island!"

"Causeway," Sebastien said. "Not yet, though I know you are eager. We are waiting for the others, for we will all walk across today and see what the stonemasons have done. Have patience."

Conan jumped up and down on the stony beach of the loch beside his friend Eoghan, a year younger. The boys, dressed in wrapped plaids and shirts, ran toward the white-foamed waves that swirled around their small bare feet. They giggled and splashed, their glossy hair floating around their heads like dark and pale silk.

"When, Sebastien *Bàn*?" Eoghan asked. "When can we go?"

"Patience, my lads," Sebastien said again, but neither listened. He looked up when he heard a silvery laugh, and saw Alainna. She moved with the same grace he had always seen in her, though more slowly now, with their child increasing within her. As it grew, so did her lush beauty, and his endless love for her. He smiled, watching her.

"Patience, you say to them, and they but small boys," she said, smiling, teasing.

"Ah," he said. "They say that patience will wear out stone. It is a good virtue to have."

She tucked her hand inside the crook of his arm. "We will all need patience for your project at Kinlochan."

"Two years," he said. "Perhaps three, until our island castle is finished." He lifted a brow as he looked down at her. "Speaking of patience, you could hardly wait for the first cartloads of stone to come over the hills."

She laughed, lifting her face to the warm summer wind, which played with the tails of her long braids. "I confess," she said. "I was eager to see the stone. You chose well. The honey-colored sandstone quarried in the hills to the south will be beautiful on our island. It will shine like a tower of gold."

"John, the master mason, told me that they expect another load of stone today," he said. "And more loads over several days, until the stone for the foundation and first level is here. Then stone will be quarried and sent as it is needed."

She nodded. "And the limestone for the chapel?"

"That will arrive this week, I think."

"Master John finally seems to have accepted that a woman is going to carve the decorative reliefs for the chapel," she said. "He did not think that was possible."

"Until you showed him the work that you have done, and charmed him as well," Sebastien said.

"And assured him that I would wait until my child was born to begin," she added.

"That reassures me, too," he said. "About the stone that is to arrive today or tomorrow—Master John is certain that the Caen limestone will be with it."

She gasped with joy. "The cream stone! Here, already, from Normandy?" She threw her arms around his neck and kissed him. "You are indeed a wonderful husband, to ask the Breton monks to have that sent to me!"

"I could hardly go myself—if I left you, our handfasting vows would be annulled." He smiled. "When is our wedding to be? Can I not convince you to hold it before Christmas?"

"My kinfolk want us to wait the year and a day, so that they can have a Christmas wedding and benefit from all the luck that such an event would bring. And our child will be born by then, so I would prefer to wait as well."

He frowned, and stood silently, watching his golden-haired son chattering with Eoghan as they stacked stones on the beach.

Susan King

"What is it? Does the idea of handfasting still concern you? We are married, in God's eyes, and in the eyes of every Highlander."

He nodded. "I know."

"You are worried about the birth," she said gently.

He shrugged, unwilling to admit to her how concerned he was, how fearful he sometimes felt when he thought of what Alainna would face with the birth of a child, and how his first wife had not survived her second travail. He could not bear to lose Alainna. He took her hand in silence.

"We will be fine," she said, wrapping her arms around his waist. "This I know. Our future is bright and long before us."

He slipped his arm around her shoulders and hugged her close as they looked out over the loch. He kissed the top of her head.

"It is indeed," he said. "And we will live together in that castle on the green isle."

He pointed across the loch toward the island. The base of the tower, partly constructed of sandstone blocks, was golden in the sunlight. From the shore to the pebbled island beach a wide new causeway, built of stone and rubble, formed a walkway. The sound of mallets and chisels wielded by the masons echoed over the loch.

Alainna turned and looked over her shoulder. "Ah," she said, "here they come. Now the children need not wait much longer to see your castle."

"Our castle," he murmured. He heard a dog bark and looked up to see Finan dashing across the green meadow that skirted the loch, with the members of Clan Laren following him. Conan and Eoghan scampered to meet them, calling and waving. The dog barked ecstatically and ran up to lick their faces. Giric lunged forward to keep the dog from knocking the boys over with his enthusiasm.

Lorne and Una walked in the lead, with Ruari and Esa behind them. Niall, Lulach, Beitris, Donal, Aenghus, and the rest came behind them. Lorne laughed and bent down as the two small boys greeted him and showed him the stones they had collected. Giric picked Conan up and hoisted him to his shoulders, and Ruari swooped Eoghan onto his own shoulders.

Sebastien chuckled, watching them. "I sent word to Struan that I would be happy to foster Eoghan here at Kinlochan when he reaches that age," he said.

"I am glad. Lileas is not yet ready to give him up, but I have good news—she told me that she and Struan expect a child of their own by next spring."

Sebastien lifted a brow. "That wedding was a surprise to me, I will admit."

"Not to me. Cormac was never as good to her as his own brother was. And there is an old custom in ancient Celtic tradition that encourages a man to wed a widowed sister-in-law to take care of her and his brother's children. Struan saw fit to follow that old tradition. I think he has always cared for Lileas, and Father Padruig was certainly pleased. Clan Nechtan will be a different clan now, with Struan as their leader until Eoghan reaches manhood."

Sebastien gazed over his shoulder, where the Stone Maiden rose, silver gray and gleaming in the sun, overlooking the loch. "The Maiden must be greatly pleased by these changes, by the peace that has finally come to her land, and to her people."

"It is what she wants for us," Alainna said. Her smile was soft and beautiful, and he leaned down to kiss her lips, unable to resist that sweetness.

"Did I show you the newest design for the castle?" he asked.

"You show me a new one nearly every week, adding this feature, improving that, as the work goes along," she said. "You and the master mason have become fast friends, and you are on the island so much these days that I think I have lost you to your stone castle."

"You will never lose me," he said. "And besides, you have your own stones to keep you happy. Whenever you want me for any reason—"

"Any reason?" she asked, eyes glittering, smile delightfully wicked.

He kissed her then, hard and deep and fast, so that she moaned beneath his mouth, and he felt her begin to melt in his arms. "Any reason," he emphasized, as he drew back. "Just send someone across that new causeway, and I will run back to you." He smiled at her. "Master John and I have designed the walls of the great hall with niches all around the room, to allow for other stones to be inserted later."

She looked up. "My stones?" she asked.

He nodded. "Each one, as you finish it, will be set into place in the great hall, where the story of Clan Laren will be seen by generations of this clan, long into the future."

She hugged him, her head on his shoulder. "Thank you," she said, her voice muffled against his chest. "A thousand blessings on you for thinking of that."

"A thousand blessings, *mo càran*," he murmured, "are already mine."

"We are ready to see this island castle of yours, Sebastien *Bàn*," Lorne called as he and the others drew near. "And a fine day it is to see such a place." He smiled, his white hair blowing in the soft breeze.

"Then we shall go," Sebastien said, and took Alainna's hand to lead her down to the stony beach, the others falling into line behind them.

The causeway, built of a variety of limestone, sandstone, shale, and rubble, stretched in a bridge of stone from the beach below the Maiden toward the island, wide enough for three horses to ride abreast, high enough that the water, even in spring flux, would not cover the stones. Men sent by the king had worked for months to construct it, and although it was not yet done, it was ready to be used.

"What will you call this place?" Niall asked, as they stood together on the pebbled beach and looked across the water.

"We have not yet decided," Sebastien said.

"Castle MacLaren," Lulach said, and others nodded agreement.

"Kinlochan," Donal said. "Castle Kinlochan."

"Maiden Castle," Esa suggested.

Sebastien smiled as he listened to each one. He lifted his head to the winds that swept across the loch, and looked up at the stone pillar, and then smiled down at Alainna.

"What do you think we should call our castle, my love?" he murmured.

She tilted her head, considering. "Castle Promise," she said. "For the island that it rests on is the Land of Promise."

He smiled, and felt his soul fill to the brim with love for her, and for these people—his own—and for this place, his home. He reached down and took Conan's hand in one of his, and Alainna's in the other, and he stepped forward with them to cross over to the Land of Promise.

Alainna left an offering at the foot of the pillar stone at dawn, a handful of flowers and a small stone carved by her own hand, a relief of an endless knot inside a circle. She looked up at the Stone Maiden and whispered a chant of gratitude.

Then she stepped back, the green of summer all around her, the sun gentle and warm, a scattering of bright flowers in the grass at her feet. She began to walk away, while the waves of the loch shushed peacefully and birds sang in the trees.

She felt her skin prickle gently, and she turned back.

In front of the pillar, where the rising sun should have cast the stone's first shadow, a young girl stood gazing toward the loch. Newborn sunlight lent a soft glow to her form.

She was slim and delicate, with hair like pale gold spilling down her back. Her plain gown was the same dove gray as the stone. Alainna noticed that the long, trailing hem of the gown touched the granite and seemed to disappear within it, as if the girl were the stone's shadow come to life.

As Alainna stared, the girl turned and looked at her. Her eyes were kind, their color the soft silver of the light before dawn. Her lovely young face looked familiar, somehow.

"Alainna," the girl said, smiling. Her voice was like a breath of wind. "Peace and grace be to you, and to yours."

"Peace and grace to you, Maiden," Alainna whispered, awed.

The maiden smiled. "When all seemed lost for us, you were our only hope. The legends and the people of Clan Laren were placed in your safekeeping. You honored them, you and your golden warrior, and saved them. Now our clan will live on."

"And you?" Alainna asked. "Will you live on, now that you are free of the stone?"

"I am free," she said, her voice soft as the summer air. "And I will be with my clan once more. You will see me again."

"When?" Alainna asked. "Here?"

"Soon," the maiden said. As the sun rose higher, she became translucent, like a delicate slice of rose quartz.

"Maiden—"

"You will know me," the girl whispered. She vanished with the growing light, only the shadow of the stone remaining where she had stood.

"Hush," she heard a voice say. "Your mother sleeps."

Alainna opened her eyes. She sat in the summer grass with her back against the pillar stone, the granite warm in the sun. Fresh wildflowers lay pooled in her lap.

She looked up to see Sebastien and Conan sitting in the grass nearby, plucking flowers. Sebastien smiled at her, and tossed another flower into her lap. Finan watched Conan pull flowers and throw them, his ears pricking.

"You slept so peacefully," Sebastien said. "We did not want to disturb you. But the others have gone back up to the fortress, after seeing the castle on the green isle." He stood over her. "Our little adventure on the island this morning tired you out, *mo càran*. Almost as soon as you sat there to rest, you fell asleep."

She smiled up at him, and at Conan who laughed and stood to run in circles with Finan. She smoothed her hand over the sweet curve of her belly.

"Sebastien," she said, "would you mind if our first child is not a son, but a girl?"

He reached down and took her hand and helped her to her feet. "I would not mind at all," he said. "I would be pleased."

She smiled as she felt his arm settle on her shoulders. The child tumbled within her, a joyful turn. "I think our child will be a girl. A beautiful girl, with pale gold hair and silver-gray eyes."

"I think you must have had a dream," he said as they walked away, with Conan and Finan loping around them in circles.

"I am living a dream," she said, and smiled at him.

Author's Note

While many clan names originate from Normans who settled in Scotland, a few medieval documents exist to prove
that some Norman knights adopted the Celtic names of
their Scottish brides, particularly where the bride's inheritance was considerable. Although surnames were not in
consistent use in the twelfth century, a prestigious surname
symbolized honor, status, and lineage in Norman culture.
Highland clan names, which also indicated honorable, ancient heritages, appear in the documents with more frequency, especially as Normans filtered into Scotland.

The fact that Normans sometimes took Scottish names
became part of the inspiration for *The Stone Maiden*. I
wondered what might happen if the Norman sense of honor
and pride, so essential to twelfth-century knighthood, met
its equal in Highland pride and stubbornness.

Generally I am careful not to alter historical fact, but I
confess to some creativity regarding the origins of Clan
MacLaren. Although the clan traces its roots to a
thirteenth-century abbot, I have taken the liberty to provide a more ancient origin, complete with Irish roots. I did
take care to preserve their legendary mermaid.

Other aspects of the research for this book led me into
the fascinating web of Celtic culture. By the twelfth century, the art of bards and storytellers was already ancient
in Scotland. Certain practices described in this novel, such
as the "poet's bed" and the use of the silver branch, were
used by early Celtic bards, and were still taught to Highland
storytellers during the Middle Ages through at least the
eighteenth century.

Chants, charms, and invocations of heavenly and elemen-
tal powers have been common in the Highlands since an-

cient days. Many of these beautiful verses were collected by Alexander Carmichael, whose *Carmina Gadelica* ("Charms of the Gaels") was first published in 1899; a reprint edition was published in 1992 by Floris Books. The verses in *The Stone Maiden* are based on Carmichael's translations, but are a compilation of some original material with phrases and cadences common to Gaelic songs and chants.

Scotland has an abundance of native stone, and stone carving was an active art in medieval Scotland. Sculptures and carvings, produced in the Lowlands as well as the Highlands, combined Romanesque and Gothic features with Celtic elements in works of extraordinary beauty. Since medieval women played integral roles in the arts in Britain and Europe, it is possible that a woman could have wielded mallet and chisel upon stone in Scotland.

I am particularly grateful to Walter S. Arnold for sharing his expertise with me and for patiently explaining techniques and working methods. As one of the stone carvers chosen to work on the National Cathedral in Washington, D.C., he helped to preserve and continue the honored traditions of medieval sculpture. For more information about stone carving, and to see some examples of Mr. Arnold's own work, visit his website at *www.stonecarver.com.*

Thank you so much for reading *The Stone Maiden.* My next release will be *The Swan Maiden,* a tale of the fourteenth century and a sequel to *Laird of the Wind.* I love to hear from readers. Write to me at P.O. Box 356, Damascus, Maryland, 20872 (please include a self-addressed, stamped envelope for a reply), or contact me by e-mail through my website at *www.susanking.net.*